The Poker Game

ART BURTON

Library and Archives Canada Cataloguing in Publication
 Burton, Art, author
        The poker game / Art Burton.
Issued in print and electronic formats.
ISBN 978-0-9939632-1-6 (paperback).--ISBN 978-0-9939632-2-3
(pdf)
        I. Title.
 PS8603.U766P65 2016   C813'.6   C2016-
903339-2

                                                       C2016-
903340-6

Art Burton Publishing
7160 Hwy 236
Latties Brook, NS B0N 2L0
www.artburton.ca

Publisher's Note: This is a work of fiction. Names, characters, places, and incidents are a product of the author's imagination. Locales and public names are sometimes used for atmospheric purposes. Any resemblance to actual people, living or dead, or to businesses, companies, events, institutions, or locales is completely coincidental.

ISBN: 09939632-1-8
ISBN-13:978-0-9939632-1-6

For Aubrey, Paul and Gary

There are men, and probably women, everywhere who get together on a regular basis and play poorhouse poker where the bets are not worth enough to cover the cost of their beer. It's never about the money; for some it is about winning; for most it is a night out with the boys. This book is for you.

ACKNOWLEDGMENTS

Once again I have to thank my editor, Bev Dauphinee, for her dedication and persistence in making this the best book possible.

Thank you, the reader, for your kind words and encouragement.

I must acknowledge the group of guys I played poker with for over 20 years. We were never as dedicated as the players in this book, but we did stay pretty consistent. Our rules for betting were cast in stone and were exactly as the ones in this book. Our ending time was always the first hand finished after 2:00 a.m. This too was cast in stone. If ever you want to take up the game on a fun basis, I recommend these two things because they help keep things friendly when they are religiously adhered to. Try it; it's fun—as long as no one dies.

As always, I acknowledge my wife Flame for being my rock, pushing when I needed to be pushed, understanding when I disappeared into this other world of fiction where only I could travel and putting up with my tirades when I complained about the dropping value of the Canadian dollar as publication day approached.

The love of money is the root of all evil.

—1 Timothy 6:10

1

BANG, BANG, BANG. The heavy knocking reverberated throughout the cottage. George and Craig leaned over the kitchen sink to peer through the window.

"There's a police car out there," George said. Who tips them off, I wonder.

"They seem to have a sixth sense," Craig said. He turned and walked to the door, stopped, pulled back the curtain and smirked at the uniformed officers on the opposite side of the glass.

"Police. Open the door. This is a raid," came the commanding voice from the other side.

In the living room of the large, well-appointed cottage, Keith Grant and Shane Martin exchanged glances before putting down their beer steins and easing out of their luxurious leather recliners.

"I hope that's who I think it is," said Shane as he headed towards the kitchen.

"Fish night. You know it is," said Craig. "Someone must tip them off. He reached down and released the deadbolt lock on the door. Two smiling Mounties stood on the steps when he opened the door.

"This is a raid," the older one repeated. This time the bluster in his voice had been replaced by laughter.

"You're too early," said Craig. "We're just cooking the fish now." He stepped back from the door. "Come on in and wait."

"Oh jeez, too early? How long before it's ready?" The cop looked at his watch. It read two minutes before six. He looked around Craig towards the stove. The smell of the frying fish filled the kitchen. The sound of the french fries sizzling in the hot fat indicated the near completion of the preparations. George gave the metal strainer a shake and poured the crisp pieces of fish onto the rack beside the stove.

"Actually, your timing is uncannily perfect," George said. "Everything is just about ready. Grab a couple of plates and find a spot at the table."

Tom Dunford appeared from the hallway leading to a small office. He had been playing computer games on Craig's desktop PC.

"If the cops are here, it must be time to eat," he said. The older Mountie, Scott Bowen, smiled at him.

"You've got that right," he said. "Finding good food is one of the courses we take during training in Regina.

"I don't think you've met my new partner, Brenda Davis. She's learning about all the important places in the area." He smiled at the suggestion that Craig's cottage made the list. All five men reached forward, shook her hand and offered their own names along with a few words of welcome.

Scott put a hand on George's shoulder and turned to Brenda. "George prepares fish and chips better than anyone in the country. Believe me I know, I've eaten in every part of it. There is no way we would want to miss fish-and-chips night."

George Phillips, an accountant by profession, used his own secret recipe for the batter on his fried fish. Its taste was unsurpassed. Beer was part of the secret, added at the last minute, but most of the preparation took place privately at his home before leaving for the game.

Twice a year at the monthly poker game, George prepared his special fish and chips. Twice a year, the Mounties "raided" their poker game. No one knew for sure how they knew when to show up, but they never missed out. George always allowed for their presence when setting the amount of fish to buy.

During the other ten monthly games, they barbecued steak. Everyone brought their own meat—competitive-steaking it was called. The cuts were the best the local butchers had to offer. There was no police presence at these meals as there was no extra food. Each person brought only what he would eat. Truth be told, most of the steaks could easily be cut in half and serve two people but poker night was about rivalry, rivalry in all things.

Craig Flint hosted the games at his so-called "cottage." In reality, the outside appearance defied the features found inside. It contained all the latest appliances and gizmos found in the larger estates in the area.

Craig owned a charter airline company. He had three small jets in his fleet with ambitions of expanding it even larger. He lived at the cottage full-time when he was in the area. More often than not, he was somewhere else in the world. Once a month, his schedule was arranged to make sure he was present for the poker game.

The poker game. The four men—Craig, Shane, Keith and George—had met faithfully for over 15 years. The stakes were five cents, ten cents and a quarter. There was a three-bump limit on each round of betting. That meant the highest bet on each round was a dollar. To round out the rules, the game was $20 poorhouse.

There had never been an adjustment for inflation. It had always been this way. Obviously the poker wasn't the important part of the evening. It was the companionship.

The fifth and sometimes sixth player would vary from game to game.

Today, the extra player was Tom Dunford, a semi-regular who worked for Sky Jet Charter Services. He played as often as he could but still had to wait for the sought-after invitation on a month-to-month basis. On other occasions, rival charter company owners or frequent customers were invited to play. Craig assumed the task of filling the extra seats.

Steaming fish and crisp fries filled all the plates around the table. Exclamations of pleasure accompanied each mouthful of flavour. White wine flowed freely. Suddenly a discordant note interrupted proceedings. The walkie-talkie on Scott Bowen's collar gave a shrill beep.

"Domestic violence at 7893 Willow Road. Bravo five, please respond."

Scott reached up and touched his mike. In a reluctant voice he said. "Bravo five enroute." He looked at his partner and slid back his chair. "Let's go, Brenda. This son of a bitch had better not give us a hard time." He picked up a piece of fish and headed for the door. Brenda stuffed a forkful of fish into her mouth, snatched up another piece and followed.

"Remember, to protect and serve, that's your calling," Craig called out to the disappearing backs of the uniforms. He and Scott Bowen had known each other since high school. Good-natured kidding was part of their relationship.

The Mountie looked back and scowled. "Right," he said. "Save me some of that fish. I'll be back." He delivered the last line with a passable Arnold Schwarzenegger imitation. The flashing blue and red lights scrolled across the room as the big V-8 engine roared out of the yard and down the narrow driveway.

TRADITIONALLY, TOASTS AND after-dinner drinks followed the meal. An exotic menu of drinks filled Craig's liquor cabinet, made possible by his international travel. Some were scrutinized by Customs officials; others, well, he wasn't selling them on the black market. They were strictly for entertaining purposes. He didn't drink himself. He had to always be ready to fly.

His was a cut-throat, highly-competitive business and he was determined to be the leader by serving his clients better than anyone else. If they wanted to fly out at six in the morning, he was ready. If they wanted to fly out at 2 a.m. with an hour's notice, he was there, except on poker night.

Keith took his last sip of Cointreau and set his glass down on the table.

"Let's clear us these dishes and get on with the serious work of playing poker," he said.

"Now that Craig has an electric dishwasher, you guys get off pretty easy," George said. He and Craig did the cooking; Keith and Shane cleared the table. Craig filled the dishwasher himself.

Craig was a perfectionist. He had his own way of doing everything including filling the dishwasher. Less kind people might accuse him of having OCD, but it was his house they were using and his booze they were drinking; he could have his own way.

"I'd like to help," Tom said, "But Mary told me to stay out of the kitchen. She thinks I'm a klutz in domestic situations. I don't think she realizes what I do for a living." He shrugged. "Anyway, she says stay out, I'll stay out. Sorry guys."

The others, except for Craig, smiled and nodded. Mary controlled Tom like a warden dominates his prison.

"Mary's right," said Craig. "Stay out of my kitchen. I don't want anything broken." His voice contained no humour.

He picked up an envelope from the side table and pulled out some glossy advertising brochures. "I have a new soap product. I found it in my mailbox this morning. It's supposed to not only clean dishes but remove all soap spots without the need of an additive." He held up a package containing a blue and white cube. "I paid a bloody fortune for that washer and still sometimes I have to wash the glasses by hand to get rid of the spots."

"Yeah, man," said Shane. "What good is a glass if it doesn't sparkle?"

Craig gave him a dirty look before continuing. "I use it right away, go online and fill out a survey before Monday and get $5 worth of product coupons from the company."

Craig put the cube in the dishwasher and turned it on. The others retired to the living room ready to start the game. Craig stayed in the kitchen listening to the machine fill. He wanted to make sure the cycle started at the proper spot. George stood looking over his shoulder, listening to the various sounds of the machine.

"Sounds like you've hit the spot perfectly," George said and turned and opened the refrigerator door to retrieve a cold beer.

"Come on, Craig," Keith called from the other room. "The cards are getting cold. George, grab me one of those beers. The last one seems to have evaporated."

"I need a refill as well," Shane called out.

Craig came in and sat down at the head of the table. He picked up a big bottle of change from the floor. George followed right behind, three beers in hand.

"Everyone got enough change?" Craig asked. Tom handed him a 20-dollar bill and received an assortment of nickels, dimes and quarters in return.

"I'm good," said Keith.

"I only need enough for the first hand," said Shane. "I'll play with your coins for the rest of the night."

"Not bloody likely," said Craig. "Let's see your $20."

Shane plopped a plastic bag full of change on the table.

"My winnings from last month," he said. "Actually, I'll start off playing with your money."

George meticulously stacked a pile of nickels, a pile of dimes and several piles of quarters in front of him. "I've got mine," he said.

Craig picked up the deck of cards. "Dealer's choice," he said. "First jack deals." He started turning the cards up one by one in front of each player. On the second round, Tom had the jack of hearts presented to him.

"Oh damn," he said. As the only non-regular, he had hoped someone else would start things off. He hesitated. "Draw poker, deuces wild."

After two betting intervals, Keith hauled in the mediocre pot and dumped it into his dish. "Thank you, gentlemen, for the first contribution of what I'm sure will be a generous flow coming my way as the night progresses."

"Deal the cards," said Craig.

George picked them up, squared them in his hands and awkwardly shuffled. "Seven card stud, low Chicago," he said. "Best hand takes half the pot. Low spade in the hole takes the other half." He dealt the cards and he and Craig split the much larger pot. There had been five betting intervals instead of only two.

The deal passed to Craig and he smiled widely. "Seven-27," he said. The others groaned.

Tom looked down at the table. In a low voice, he said: "I'm not sure I remember how that game is played. It's pretty complicated as I recall."

"Not complicated at all," said Craig. "Everyone gets one card down. We bet. The cards are then dealt face-up one at a time to anyone who wants one, with a betting interval after each round until no one takes a card. Number cards are worth their pip value, face cards are worth half a point, aces are one or 11. Closest to seven and 27 without going over split the pot. Each person has three refusals at taking a card. Simple." He smiled at Tom. The others had played the game so often that it was simple to them. Tom was reluctant.

"Don't worry, dude. It's easier than it sounds," Shane said. "Besides, you might get a seven right off the bat and then you just sit there and bump a quarter every time it comes around to you. You'd be guaranteed a cut of the pot. The gravy will just roll in. If not, well, you can fold anytime you want." He looked across the table at Craig, challenging him to disagree with that statement. They were here for fun.

Tom anted up his dime. "I'll give it a try. I'm sure it will come back to me."

A smile lit up Craig's face. "Good. Let's play." This was his favorite game. The others endured it every time he dealt.

After three rounds, both George and Shane were still sitting on their down card. Three sevens had been exposed. One of them had to be bluffing. Shane caved and started the long climb to 27.

Keith stopped drawing cards after adding two to his hand, an ace and a five.

Craig's hand stopped building at four cards leaving a seven, three and eight face-up.

Tom folded after going over 27 with five cards and Shane ended up drawing seven cards altogether. That had produced 10 betting intervals with George and Craig driving the pot to the limit on every card. The pot built to over $40 in a $20-poorhouse game, a phenomenal amount.

Before opening the betting on the last round, Craig summed up his estimate of the hands as he frequently did.

"Keith, you're sitting there with six and half. You think George is bluffing." He moved on to Shane. "You've finally reached 27 but it took you seven cards." He made a dismissive gesture at Tom's discards and turned to the smug expression on George's face as he sat there with his hands folded over his one down card. "You, or course, have the seven. You don't bluff, and as you can see, I have four cards."

He opened the betting with a quarter, followed by a bump from George, a raise by Craig and the final bump from George. This meant George was being called and was the first to show his hand. He flipped over his seven.

"Half that is mine," he said, a smile lighting up his face. "I never bluff. I don't know how." He looked across the table at Keith as he made this last statement. "Too bad, buddy."

Keith returned the smile, but said nothing.

Craig flipped over a nine in the hole to add to his exposed cards. "Twenty-seven in four cards," he said.

"The other half is mine. Sorry Shane, you worked so hard to build your hand." He reached for the pile of money to start dividing.

Keith reached out and placed his left hand over the top of the pot. "Not so fast, my high-flying friend," he said. "I have way more sense than to bet against George. We all know he doesn't bluff." With his right hand he flipped over a second ace. "Twenty-seven in three cards," he said. There was a momentary silence in the room.

"No," Craig said. His face turned a brilliant red. "You were going low. You can't change at the last minute." Anger crept into his voice.

"Bad assumption on your part," Keith said. "Add them up, 11, five and 11. Twenty-seven. As you said, we all know George never bluffs. Why would I ever bet against him?"

"No. That's not true. You were going low. You didn't even do anything to build the pot. George and I did all the betting."

Keith gave him a wicked smile. "We reached the max each time. That's all that mattered."

The phone in the kitchen rang. "Don't touch those cards," Craig said as he got up. "This isn't settled yet." He disappeared through the kitchen door, closing it behind him. The phone rang once more, then stopped. A chair could be heard scraping across the floor. The others waited. No other sound came from the kitchen. It must have been a confidential call.

CORPORAL SCOTT BOWEN and Constable Brenda Davis pulled onto Willow Road. Ahead of them lights flashed on the top of another patrol car. Brenda picked up the microphone.

"Bravo five on location at 7893 Willow Road."

They pulled in behind the first patrol car.

"Bravo four on location at 7893 Willow Road," crackled across the air.

"Affirmative Bravo four and five. Your location is 7893 Willow Road, scene of a domestic violence call. Be advised that there are two rifles registered at this location: a lever-action .303 Savage and a bolt-action 22-calibre repeater." This information came from a database check of the federal gun registry.

All four Mounties stepped out of their cars and huddled in the area between them. Neighbours were standing in the street or staring from verandas. Shouts could be heard coming from the house but the words were muffled by the walls. Two women approached the police officers.

"I'm the one who called," said the older of the two. She wore a flowered housedress, brown leather shoes and a no-nonsense look on her face. "This has been going on for nearly an hour. I tried knocking on the door but they ignored me. That's when I called you.

There are two young kids in there and I'm worried about their safety."

"Has there been any talk of guns or any gunfire?" Scott Bowen asked. As senior man present, he took charge of the scene.

"No, just yelling, swearing and screaming," the lady replied. "I think there's a boyfriend in there with them. This has been brewing for a while." Her voice lowered at the end, embarrassed to be interfering in someone's personal business.

Even though the blue and red lights of the police cars strobed across the house windows and had to be visible inside, the yelling continued unabated.

Scott looked at the two constables, one male and one female, from the first car. "You take the front door." He indicated the front of the split-entry bungalow with the doorway in the middle of the house. "We'll take the side door." His view shifted up the side stairs to the upper level. This is where the shouting was coming from. "I'll knock, announce we're the police and we'll all go in at once." He looked around at his three fellow officers to see if there were any questions. It was a procedure they had all taken part in before. There were no questions. "Be careful."

All four officers took up their positions and pulled black leather gloves over their hands. Corporal Bowen pounded on the screen door with the side of his closed fist. The sound echoed off the surrounding houses.

"RCMP," he said in a booming voice. "Can we come in?" Without waiting for a reply, all four officers opened the doors and entered the house at the same time. As was expected in this quiet neighbourhood, none of the doors were locked. It wasn't necessary to do anything overly dramatic such as kicking the doors open. Immediate silence followed.

Two children, a boy of six and a girl of five. stood in the hallway dressed in their pyjamas. As soon as the police entered, they scooted down the front steps and out the door past the two officers just entering. Outside, the neighbour who had made the initial call captured the kids and took them safely into her house.

In the kitchen, the eyes of the three combatants turned to the entering cops, surprise registered on their faces.

"What's going on?" the woman asked. "Why are you in my house?"

"Are you all right, ma'am?" Scott Bowen asked. "We had calls about loud shouting and possible violence at this location." The smell of alcohol was evident on all three people.

"Can't people mind their own fucking business?" the shorter of the two men responded. "First, I come home and find my wife with this cocksucker and now some nosy bitch from across the street has called the fucking cops."

Scott looked from one to the other trying to assess the level of violence that had taken place. The second man had a slight swelling around his eye. There was one overturned chair on the floor but other than that, things appeared to be in order. The language was something he was used to hearing in these situations. The woman appeared to be unhurt.

"Is this what your children have been putting up with for the last half-hour?" Constable Linda Fraser asked from the top of the stairs.

The three turned at the sound of her voice.

"Holy shit, they sent out the entire force," the short man said.

Scott gave her a piercing look. Their job was not to further agitate the situation. Linda's face turned red. She was a mother as well as a cop. Most of the time she kept the two separate. When kids were involved and adults were acting stupid, that separation became a little more difficult.

"That would indicate how loud you were yelling," Scott said to the man. "We've had a number of calls. Would anyone care to explain what is going on?"

They all looked at each other before the woman spoke.

"My friend here agreed to drive me home from the local tavern and my husband came home and got all worked up. Nothing was happening."

"Nothing was happening," the husband said. "How come the buttons on your blouse were all undone? Don't tell me nothing was happening." Again the volume of his voice started to rise.

"Calm down, sir," Scott said. He looked at the "friend". "What happened to your eye?"

The man unconsciously reached up to touch the swelling. "I bumped it on a door," he said. "Honestly."

"He bumped it on my fist when I hauled the cocksucker off my wife," the husband shouted. He took a threatening step towards the other man. "I'd better not catch you in my house again or you'll get a lot worse than a punch in the eye."

Scott could see the problems in this marriage ran a lot deeper than anything he was going to be able to solve at this time of night. The best he could do was diffuse the situation and let them work it out when calmer heads and less alcohol prevailed. He took the husband by the arm.

"We're going to take you with us," he said. "You've confessed to committing an assault. I would suggest you go home." This latter comment was directed at the visitor. "Tomorrow, I would advise you to get professional help to work out your problems before someone gets seriously hurt."

"We don't need any professional advice," the woman said. "If he didn't spend so many nights working and spent more time at home, there'd be no problems."

"Someone has to work to pay all the bills you run up," the husband said.

The argument was cranking up again.

"Now is not the time," Scott said in a firm voice. "Get some help."

"Your kids are next door," Constable Fraser said. "I'd wait until after we put your husband in the police car to pick them up."

"The kids?" A worried look crossed the woman's face as the circumstances of the evening finally registered in her mind for the first time. "Jesus, what must they think?" She looked at the two men in her life. What had she been thinking? "Both of you get out. I've got to go get my babies." With that she ran out the door to the neighbouring house.

Scott was escorting the husband to his car when another call came across the radio waves.

"Respond an ambulance to 5 Mill Lake Road. Man down, possible stroke."

"That's Craig's address," Scott said. He turned to Linda. "Can you take this guy in? All he needs is a night to cool down and think about his life. There will be no charges." He turned to Brenda. "Let's go," he said, "lights and siren."

Not far away, standing at a pay phone outside a convenience store, Robert Crosley watched as the fire trucks and ambulance wound their way along the road to cottage country. Their presence confirmed his success. He had just made a call, let the phone ring four times, then hung up and waited. His work here was complete. Getting paid would put an end to this episode. He looked around. The surroundings looked vaguely familiar, but one small village looked like every other small village in the country. In his line of work, he got to see a lot of small villages, small towns and big cities. There were no geographical restrictions to his calling. It was in demand everywhere there were people in contact with each other. He climbed into his rental car and headed for the city.

4

WHILE CORPORAL BOWEN and his fellow officers were trying to return domestic bliss to the household on Willow Road and Robert Crosley stood waiting for the result of his phone call to take fruit, George, Shane and Keith sat fidgeting in the dining room of Craig's cottage. The cards lay untouched on the table. They all knew Craig was wrong, but they also knew it was best to let him come to that conclusion on his own.

"Twenty-seven in three cards," George said. "I've never seen that in all the years we've played."

Keith nodded. "If you hadn't had a seven, there could have been a real argument. I would have claimed both high and low pots. It also adds up to seven. I'd have raked it all in."

"We had better get a ruling from Craig on that before it ever happens," Shane said. "Unless it's him that gets it, there will be a royal argument, especially if he has one of the other winning hands." The others nodded in agreement. As far as they knew, Craig had invented this game. They had never seen it played anywhere else.

Tom returned from the front lawn where he had watched the ducks while finishing his cigarette.

"There's been a change in the air. I think it's about to start raining." He was surprised to see the game was not in progress. "What's the holdup?" he asked.

Shane looked at his watch. The time was ticking away. "It's not like Craig to spend this much time on the phone on poker night. He usually cuts any calls short."

"I think it's a new client," George said. "He was on the phone setting up some kind of deal when I first got here with the cooking supplies. He was expecting a return call." He looked at his own watch. "Still, it's been a long time."

"I could go out to the kitchen and get a round of beers," Keith said. "He wouldn't object to that and it will serve as a reminder that we're still here. Who all wants one?"

"Me," said Shane.

"I'll stick to the whiskey," said Tom.

"No, I'm good," said George. He seldom had more than one or two drinks for the entire evening. He had already had two strong after-dinner drinks of Baileys and cream and had been nursing a beer, now getting warm, since the game began.

Keith got up and approached the door. Before opening it, he stopped to listen. No sound could be heard. He looked back at the others for confirmation of his actions. Shane gave him a go-ahead nod. He grasped the doorknob and turned it, pushing the door open at the same time.

"Sorry to interrupt, I just wanted—" He stopped for a heartbeat. Sprawled on the floor of the kitchen lay Craig's unmoving body. His face was contorted into an unrecognizable mask denoting a stroke. A small gash on his forehead trickled blood onto the linoleum. The cut suggested that he had fallen to the floor without his arms shooting out to break the fall. One arm was under the body, the other twisted behind his back. His left leg lay straight out behind him, the right was bent at the knee causing Craig to lie slightly on one side.

Keith processed all this information before rushing into the kitchen. "Craig, Craig, can you hear me?"

Suddenly, he too sunk to his knees. His face started to contort, creating the same stroke-like features exhibited on Craig's face. Shane acted instantly. Taking a deep breath, he plunged into the kitchen, grabbed Keith's shoulders and hauled him back into the living room, shutting the kitchen door behind him with a kick of his foot. He was in and out before Tom could finish his sentence advising him to stay out, the air was poisoned.

"CPR, quick," Shane said. George dropped to his knees beside Keith's inert body. He blew two quick puffs of air into his lungs before starting to pump on his chest. Shane headed for the front doors of the house and opened them wide, allowing a rush of fresh air to fill the room. "Tom, call 9-1-1."

Shane rushed back to assist George but Keith was already coughing and choking. He pushed George's hands away. "For Christ's sake man, you're going to break my ribs." He rolled onto his side and took in several deep breaths of the air flooding in from outside. George rubbed his back, trying to assist the diaphragm to force the bad air out of Keith's lungs and good air in.

"Shit, that was close," Keith said when his breathing started to resemble normalcy. "Stay out of the kitchen. It's not safe out there."

"You figure?" Shane said. "Man, I thought you were a goner. We've got to check on Craig somehow, just in case."

"The fire department and paramedics will be here in no time," Tom said. "For now we can only assume the kitchen air is contaminated. I know it's hard, but we have to stay out. In fact we should get out of the house as well. That door won't stop seepage."

The other three men nodded reluctant agreement and headed for the front door. In the distance they could hear the first of the sirens. They walked around the house to the driveway. Keith sat in an Adirondack chair on the edge of the lawn overlooking the lake. Tom stared down the tree-lined drive to watch for the coming rescue vehicles. Shane went up to the kitchen door and peered in. Craig looked exactly as he had when Shane had rushed in to haul Keith from the kitchen. He tried the door. It was locked.

George joined him on the door step. "We need to break a window and get some fresh air in there." He looked around for something to use. Shane ran his hand along the top of the door frame. George shook his head. "Craig was too security conscious. You won't find a spare key anywhere." Shane rolled a heavy concrete flower urn to one side. Nothing. He looked around for other possible sites and spotted the barbecue. He knelt down and looked under the firebox.

"Bingo," he said. He pulled out a black magnetic container and slid it open. "Everyone has a spare key hidden somewhere." He withdrew the key and inserted it into the lock. He tried to rotate the key but nothing happened. He tried harder. Still nothing.

"He must have changed the locks," George said.

"No, man. This is the front-door key. I'll bet you anything."

"That's Craig all right. Do you suppose he has the kitchen door key hidden around the front door?" Before Shane could come up with an answer, George shook his head. "No, if he's going to walk around the house, he may just as well grab this key on the way and go in the front door. His only intention was to get in if he misplaced his own keys. Sneaky, but a good plan."

"Here comes the fire department," Tom said. He pointed across the small jut of lake to the parking lot. Two red trucks lumbered into and out of sight again, their strobing red lights flashing through the trees lining the driveway.

A man in his mid-forties jumped from the passenger door of the first truck. "Where's Craig?" His eyes scanned the four men in the yard. "Oh shit, Craig's not the man down is he?" He started for the kitchen door at a slow trot.

"Wait." Shane held up his hand. "The air in there is contaminated with something." He pointed to Keith still sitting in the big wooden chair. "When he tried to go in, it chopped the legs right out from underneath him."

The chief looked back at his assembling crew. "Air packs. Quick. He might still be alive. Jeremy, check out that man. Make sure he's all right."

Keith slowly got up from his chair. "No, I'm fine. Concentrate on Craig." He sat back down again. The fireman pulled a blood pressure machine from the side compartment of the truck.

"Let's check you out, just to be sure," he said. He wrapped the blood pressure cuff around Keith's upper arm and pushed a button and waited. The machine beeped a few times and stopped. "Do you have high blood pressure as a rule, sir?" he asked.

Keith looked down at the reading on the machine: 160 over 98, not good. The heart rate was 110 beats per minute. "No, usually it's in the normal range but I am a little stressed here. A good friend is lying on the kitchen floor in there, possibly dead."

"True, but I think you should have a doctor look at you, anyway. There will be an ambulance here any minute now."

As if on cue, the lights of the ambulance appeared passing through the parking lot at the head of the lake.

Meanwhile, Shane led the two firemen, wearing full rubber face masks with bright, yellow air tanks strapped on their backs, around to the open front door. They indicated to Shane to go back outside before they opened the door to the kitchen. Slowly, one of them stepped inside. His partner watched closely to make sure there were no signs of distress before following. The first man knelt beside Craig while the second opened the kitchen door and the window over the sink, creating a cross flow of fresh air.

A third masked fireman appeared at the open kitchen door carrying a backboard. Craig was loaded onto it and then taken outside where the paramedics were waiting with a defibrillator unit and a cylinder of oxygen. The first fireman lifted his mask. "Go ahead and try your luck but—" His voice trailed off.

The paramedic placed his stethoscope on Craig's chest, listened, tried another spot, listened again and shook his head. It was too late. Craig was beyond any help.

The chief indicated Keith still sitting in the chair on the lawn. "You should have a look at him. He was exposed, too."

Keith heard the comment. "I'm all right," he said. "I just need to catch my breath."

The paramedics ignored the comment and examined him anyway. "There's a little rattle in the upper part of your lungs, sir. You should go in and have a doctor check this out. Take a shot of oxygen. It will help you breathe."

Before Keith could answer, another siren could be heard. A white RCMP patrol car shot across the parking lot and appeared in Craig's driveway, adding flashing blue lights to the cacophony of red. Scott

Bowen jumped from the car before it was completely stopped. He looked over at Keith and the paramedics. Relief appeared on his face. He started towards them and Craig's lifeless body came into view. Bowen's face contorted as if he had been kicked in the groin. His shoulders slumped and his whole countenance went slack.

"Oh no. Not Craig. What happened?" He looked around at all the professionals for an answer. None was forthcoming. "George, what the hell is going on? We were just here."

George shook his head. "He went into the kitchen and collapsed. The air appears to be poisonous. Keith rushed out to help him and next thing he was down too. It's all so surreal. I don't know what to tell you."

Scott looked towards the house and the open kitchen door. "Is it safe to go in there now?"

"There is a Hazmat team on its way," said the chief. "It's better to be safe and let the experts decide for us. They won't be too long."

At that moment, two men appeared from a small path leading to the cabin next door. Both were casually dressed and flushed from either the exertion, alcohol consumption or both. The older of the two quickly assessed the scene and knelt beside Craig. "Oh my God, what happened?" He looked around at all the faces staring at him. "I'm Craig's doctor. I live next door."

The chief walked over. "Hi, Doc. We're not sure yet. May have been a stroke; looks like one or it may have been poisoning. The air in the kitchen is bad."

"It's not a stroke," the doctor said. "Craig just had a physical three days ago. He's in perfect health. I examined him myself."

Despite the circumstances, Shane couldn't resist a smile. "Perfect health, except for one small thing. He's dead." A few of the others involuntarily smiled. Not the doctor.

"He was in perfect health," he said.

Suddenly the wind picked up and a wave of rain swept in from across the lake. In the distance, a rumble of thunder could be heard. People jumped into their vehicles to keep from being drenched.

"Quick. Back inside," George yelled. "Give me a hand with Craig." The two Mounties each grabbed an end of the stretcher and headed around the cottage to the open front door. Shane took Keith by the elbow and slowly followed, assisted by the paramedics who were still holding the oxygen tank, all getting soaked in the process. The doctor brought up the rear of the little group.

Keith pulled the oxygen mask from his face. "That rain feels refreshing. It cleared the air and I feel a lot better."

"Yeah, right man. Cured by the rain," Shane said. "I'll write it up in the New England Journal of Medicine." He led Keith to one of the reclining chairs facing the windows. Outside the rain continued to fall.

Two more figures dashed across in front of the windows and up the three steps leading to the door. One was the fire chief, the other carried a big suitcase-shaped box.

"Hazmat," the chief said, as if that explained everything. He pointed to the closed kitchen door. "Through there is the area in question."

The newcomer set down his case and released two big clasps. He withdrew a full head gas mask, an air tank and a full body suit. He slipped into the suit, donned the mask and hooked up his own supply of air and took a big breath. The sound of sucking air filled the room. He grabbed several vials from the bottom of the case and slipped through the barely opened kitchen door. A couple of minutes later, he re-emerged.

"Nothing," he said. "The air is perfectly safe in there." He looked over at the chief. "Perhaps you were wrong about the contamination."

"The air was contaminated." Everyone looked at Keith. The statement left no room for argument. A combination of his authoritative voice and pasty, pale skin answered both sides of the question.

"Yeah man. There was something out there," Shane said. "Are you sure your readings are correct?"

"Errors in my line of work can be fatal. My readings are right." He looked over at Keith, studied him for a second or two before adding: "Perhaps you fainted, sir. It must have been distressing seeing your buddy lying on the floor like that."

"I did not faint. I'm sure of that." Keith's words stressed his belief but his voice lacked conviction. He looked around at the others. "It was more than fainting."

Combined with the Hazmat finding, or lack of findings, an element of doubt was introduced to the thinking of the others. Their only indication of contamination was seeing Craig on the floor and Keith go down. A stroke and a faint could just as easily be the answer.

"Contaminated air, what could cause something like that?" Scott Bowen asked, taking a notebook from his uniform pocket. "Are the causes natural or is foul play involved?"

"Accidental releases—carbon monoxide, radon, sewer gases—are common enough, but they usually leave some sort of residue behind and don't act that fast. I found nothing. I'll have to take a harder look."

"Well, there has to be something because it wasn't a stroke." The doctor was not backing down on his position on Craig's health. "Craig didn't drink, didn't smoke and exercised regularly. Strokes are caused by pre-existing conditions. They don't just happen to healthy people."

"Everyone stay out of the kitchen. I'll call in the crime-scene people." Scott looked around the room. "Is there a land line I can use? I don't want to broadcast this message to every police junky with a scanner. This is a homicide investigation now."

Silence fell over the room. All eyes looked at the resolve on the policeman's face. He was suggesting, no declaring, murder. From the kitchen, the silence was broken by the gurgling of the dishwasher as it went through its final rinse cycle and drained the water. There was a click and it too shut off. The silence was complete.

DETECTIVE SERGEANT JAMES Mcdonald, Jim to his friends, exited Highway 103 at Exit 6. Mindful of the wet pavement and falling rain, he eased to a stop at the stop sign and glanced left towards Route 3. A feeling of déjà vu passed over him. He recalled this as the location of a former case, one that was only partially resolved in his mind. He shrugged off the feeling and turned right towards Mill Lake.

The call from Corporal Scott Bowen had an ominous ring to it. Jim had been in the office cleaning up a few details from a recent drug case when the phone rang in the detective division. He had glanced at his watch before answering, debating whether to let it go to the main switchboard or not. All the night shift detectives were out working on cases of their own. He recognized Scott Bowen's voice and after listening to the details decided to respond himself instead of passing it on.

He and Scott had a history together. Scott patrolled the highways and byways of rural Nova Scotia, an area that saw little demand for someone from Major Crimes such as Jim. Like all Mounties in the smaller offices, Scott handled crimes of every description. There was little room for specialization, but he could count the homicides he was involved in on the fingers of one hand. Jim, on the other hand, usually had at least one open murder investigation on his desk.

The two men had had the opportunity to pool their resources on occasion—Scott's local knowledge of the area, Jim's specialized knowledge in solving homicides. They made a formidable team. Scott turned down any suggestion that he park his patrol cruiser and join the detective branch. He was happy serving in his area of police work.

Jim detected an urgency in Scott's voice that compelled him to forget it was the weekend, to forget it was his day off, to forget that he already had enough on his plate without taking on a new case. Stella, his girlfriend, was working an unusual weekend shift at the hospital leaving Jim at odds to fill this time off. He could at least go out and have a look.

The yard outside the cottage was a carnival of flashing red and blue lights from the fire trucks, a police car and an ambulance. He reached down and turned his grill lights off. There was no need to add his to the mix. Parking in the yard was at a premium, Jim noticed. Along with all the emergency vehicles were a Hazmat truck, a van, a black Durango SUV, a British racing green foreign sports car and two North American sedans, one white, one dark blue. He pulled over to the side of the road so as not to block anyone in and walked up to the house. His car would be here a lot longer than the other emergency units. Their work was finished. His was just beginning.

Scott Bowen met him in the doorway and stepped out onto the veranda under the overhanging roof. Scott pulled the door shut to block out the noise and to keep their conversation confidential. Quickly, he brought Jim up to speed with what little Scott knew. Looked like a stroke, but circumstances insinuated it was something else. An autopsy would be needed to determine the exact cause of death.

"I was here less than an hour ago," Scott said. "Craig was in perfect health at that time."

Jim noticed the familiar use of the first name of the victim. "Craig?" he asked.

"We go back a long way," Scott said. "I wasn't here in an official capacity." Dropping in at a friend's house for supper while on duty would not look good on any report. But his friend was lying on the floor dead. This was no time to be coy. "They played a friendly game of poker here once a month preceded by a meal. Often I dropped in when fish and chips were on the menu. The fish was to die for."

A blush lit up the corporal's face. "A poor choice of words," he said.

"Maybe," Jim said. "Did anyone check for a fish bone in the throat? Could this be a simple case of choking? You said he was in the kitchen alone for a while before the body was discovered."

"I doubt it. He was looked at by firemen, paramedics and a doctor. Also, that would mean Keith Grant just fainted from seeing Craig lying on the floor. A possibility, I guess. He certainly looks OK now. In a way, I hope that is the case. The alternative is we start investigating his friends. People I've come to know over the years. I'm sure none of them murdered him."

"How well do you know them?"

The Mountie thought for a while before answering. "George went to the same school as Craig and me but he was older. The others, I just know them from the card games. I guess I don't know them at all. Strange how we assume we know people from a few chance meetings when in reality we know next to nothing about them."

"All that is about to change. We are soon going to know more about these men than their own wives," Jim said. "Let's go inside and meet the starting lineup of suspects."

Scott cringed at the statement. He still thought of these men as his friends.

Once inside, Jim took in the scene. The kitchen was empty of people. The crime scene was badly violated. The body moved, firemen tracking through, the Hazmat guy taking samples, touching surfaces. It would make the investigation a little more challenging.

In the living room, three poker players were back sitting at the card table talking in low voices. They were not playing. The cards and money had been pushed to one end in a jumbled pile. The paramedics were packing up their gear getting ready to leave. Keith refused to go to the hospital with them. The doctor had examined him and advised him that it wouldn't hurt to be checked but left the decision up to Keith. His condition wasn't critical and by now the colour had returned to his face. His breathing was normal again and there were no apparent ill effects.

Tom appeared from the hallway. "I just phoned my wife to let her know what happened," he said. "She wasn't home. Out at some committee meeting, no doubt. She's president or chairman of so many organizations, I can't keep track anymore.

"I didn't leave a message." A tear ran down his ashen cheeks. "Jesus, I don't look forward to telling her Craig is dead."

The others nodded, agreeing with his decision. Tom's wife was Craig's sister.

Tom felt the need to continue. "She's not a person to sit around and do nothing. If she's not involved in something, she becomes moody, irritable and depressed. Last month she came up with an idea to start a new business and approached Craig about a loan. He turned her down flat."

Again the others nodded.

"This is when all the new officers are getting elected. She gets pissed if she's not one of them, really pissed if some less-qualified man gets put in a position above her."

Tom was babbling.

"When she finds out Craig died at one of his poker games, I don't know if she will break down in tears or break out in laughter. She hated Craig's commitment and dedication to, as she put it, these silly, juvenile card nights. She'd even get upset when I came to play."

"You're not keeping her satisfied, man," Shane said with a smirk on his face. "That's why she's irritable and moody."

Tom glared down at Shane. "I most certainly am," he said before flopping down into his own seat. Then he stared out the large picture window pointedly ignoring Shane.

Keith studied the two men. He had only met Tom's wife on a couple of occasions. She had shown up one afternoon with Tom and wanted to play poker with them.

Craig had gone ballistic. "Poker and women don't mix. This is our last bastion of male solitude," Craig had ranted. Keith remembered they had all felt embarrassed, but not one of us had the guts to stand up to Craig. Mary went home, mad, dragging Tom along with his tail between his legs. That's why he never became a regular member. He had the nerve to bring a woman, uninvited, to play. That's why he always had to grovel for an invite from Craig before he could attend.

Mary had never forgiven any of them. The next time they met, she was cold and distant.

Keith looked up as the three Mounties returned from the kitchen. Sergeant Mcdonald knelt and closely studied the distorted look on Craig's face. It certainly presented as a stroke. Keith knew the policeman would be wondering if a crime had even been committed or if he had been dragged out here to the country for a natural death. An investigation would answer that question.

The doctor got up from his chair and leaned down beside Jim.

"We'll have to do an autopsy to determine the cause of death," he said. "Craig was perfectly healthy. I examined him earlier this week and gave him a clean bill of health. Something suspicious must have taken place."

Scott and Jim exchanged looks. The statements seemed more defensive than positive. "This is Doctor Gordon Dow," Scott said by way of an introduction. He looked around the table. "George Phillips, Shane Martin, Keith Grant." He consulted his notebook. "And Tom Dunford. This is Detective Sergeant Jim Mcdonald. He's from major crimes, robbery and homicide. He will have a few questions for you folks if you don't mind."

The four men at the table looked around at each other before giving a communal shrug.

"Anything that will shed some light on this," said Keith. "I feel like I'm the one who killed him."

The sergeant looked up, surprised. "Oh, how's that?"

"The last hand of cards we played." Keith looked at the discarded pile of cards and then at the other players. "Well, you had to be here but Craig didn't take losing that hand too well. He was pretty upset."

Jim tried not to register disappointment on his face. He had been hoping for something more substantial. He wasn't sure what, but in all his years as a homicide detective, he had never seen a death by losing a hand of poker. At least not without the intervention of a gun, knife or some other weapon and some sort of cheating involved.

George nodded in agreement. "I've never seen him so upset at losing. He definitely thought the hand was his."

"It wasn't just losing," Shane said' "although he was never good at that. Craig prided himself in knowing what everyone else had. He liked to openly analyze the value of everyone's hand as he dealt out the cards. He could be quite accurate. Keith's hand caught him completely offguard."

"It was not a stroke." The loud words from the doctor brought the room to silence. His face was flushed. In a lower voice, he repeated the statement. "It was not a stroke."

"OK," said the detective, "the autopsy will resolve that. In the meantime, I would like to talk to each of you while everything is still fresh in your minds." He looked around the big room that took up half the cottage. "Is there a place where we could talk in private?"

"Craig has an office at the end of the hall," George said. "It is usually off limits to everyone, but," he shrugged, "I guess you guys will be all over it if Dr. Dow is right."

The two policemen went down the hall to check out the location. The others looked into the kitchen as a new wave of people arrived. These were the crime-scene investigators. The firemen and paramedics manoeuvred their vehicles out of the crowded yard. There was nothing more they could do except spread the story around the community about their friend and neighbour. Corporal Bowen's riding partner, Brenda Davis, joined the doctor and the poker players in the living room. She sat at the table in Craig's chair. Although it was unsaid, her job would be to keep the others from collaborating their stories.

Corporal Bowen poked his head out into the hall. "Doctor, could we talk to you first?"

The doctor disappeared down the hall and into the office. The door closed behind him. Less than five minutes later, he reappeared and indicated to Keith that he was next before disappearing out the door and heading home. "You'll see that I was right," he said as he exited the room. "It was not a stroke."

"Here we go," Keith said. He pulled back his chair and walked thoughtfully down the hall. Being innocent didn't make an interrogation by the police any more pleasant. The doubt over whether or not he had fainted didn't help. He went into the small office and sat down. Scott Bowen had a notepad in front of him with a pen poised over it.

"You realize you're not a suspect," Sergeant Mcdonald started. "We're just trying to piece together what took place here tonight. Hell, we don't even know if a crime has been committed." He was doing his best to put the man in front of him at ease and to encourage a flow of words that might bring some light to what had happened. Keith just nodded.

"How are you feeling now? Are there any lingering effects from what happened?"

"No, I'm fine. Shane got me out of there in time. Too bad we hadn't done the same for Craig. I don't think I fainted. There was something in the air."

"Could you smell it, taste it, see it?"

"No, none of those things. I rushed in to help Craig and the next thing I was on my knees."

The two cops exchanged glances. Fainting could not be ruled out.

"In your own words, what did you observe?"

Keith cleared his throat. "Well, we had just finished a hand of cards, 7-27, Craig's favourite game. He thought for sure he had won half the pot but it turned out I was the winner. George and I actually. It was a split-the-pot type of game. Craig was quite upset, even more than usual for him. He would bluster sometimes when he wasn't getting his own way, but this was more extreme.

"Then the phone rang and he told us to wait and went to the kitchen to answer it, closing the door behind him. George pointed out he was waiting for a business call."

"A business call?" the sergeant interrupted. "Was it strange that he took it in the kitchen and not here in his office?"

"It was strange he even accepted the call at all. He took his poker night pretty seriously. He must have been looking for a yes or no answer and didn't expect any discussion."

"The phone. When you went into the kitchen, was it on the floor beside him or still on the hook?"

Keith thought a bit before answering. "I don't remember. It all happened so fast. You realize an investigation was the last thing on our mind at the time?"

The sergeant nodded.

"I think it was still on the hook."

"Had it continued to ring after Craig went into the kitchen or might he have answered it, had his conversation, hung up and then whatever happened, happened?"

"No, Craig disappeared into the kitchen and the phone stopped ringing. I can't say if he answered it or not. We just sat there for a while waiting for him. After several minutes, we decided to remind him in a subtle way we were still here. I was going to the kitchen for more beer."

"What about the doctor's claim that it can't be a stroke? That Craig was healthy?"

Keith rubbed his chin looking for the right words. "Craig was a pilot. Every year he had to pass this stringent medical. He wasn't getting any younger and the good Doctor Dow was a friend. Doctor Dow may be in CYA mode."

Both policemen looked at Keith. "CYA mode?"

"Cover your ass," Keith said. "He just signed off on Craig's health. Declared him fit to fly. A stroke three days later doesn't look good."

"Are you familiar with the doctor?" Scott Bowen asked. The question seemed to carry some undertones of asking more than just a straightforward question.

"We've golfed together," Keith said. "Let's say he enjoys the 19th hole more than the other 18." Scott nodded in agreement.

The sergeant looked from one to the other. "We'll check that medical examination report. It will be on file with the aviation board.

"What were your ties with Craig other than playing poker?"

Keith hesitated before answering. "We have some business dealings in common." He offered no further explanation.

The cop waited before asking: "Would you care to elaborate on that?"

"No, I wouldn't. Frankly, it's none of your business."

The answer surprised Jim with its brusqueness. The statement was true. It was none of his business at this early juncture of the investigation. He let it slide.

"The others? Did any of them have any reason to harm Craig?"

Keith shook his head as if he found the whole concept repulsive. "No, they didn't. We've been doing this for over 15 years. We're all friends. Something happened to Craig in that kitchen; that is true. But we were all in the living room when it happened. Well, except for Tom. He was outside having a smoke." He thought about his statement for a second. "Tom had no reason to want to kill Craig, I feel sure of that." He slid back his chair, indicating he was through answering questions. "Who's next?"

The sergeant produced a digital camera from his pocket. "Do you mind if I take a quick picture just so I can remember who is who?"

Keith gave his shoulders a shrug. "Cheese."

The remaining three poker players answered the same questions with pretty much the same answers, shedding no new light on the evening's events. All agreed Craig was a little more upset than usual. The doctor's information was of little help. Jim had to agree with Keith's assessment. The doctor was in full CYA mode.

"I'd like a copy of your notes," Jim said to the corporal. Let's have a closer look at all these guys, especially Tom Dunford. His alibi is the weakest." He got up and went out to talk to the crime lab boys. He hoped they could offer something definite about the cause of death.

6

TUESDAY MORNING, JIM sat at his desk at police headquarters. In his hands was an advance copy of the autopsy report from the Craig Flint case. The results were inconclusive. The doctor had been right, Craig appeared to be in good health. However, he was dead and the results leaned towards a severe asthma attack. His throat had suddenly closed, causing him to suffocate. This accounted for the distorted look of his face and the appearance of a stroke. There was no apparent reason for this happening.

A close examination of the body showed only one three-day-old needle mark where the doctor had drawn blood during his examination. Craig had not been injected with anything on Saturday night. Nevertheless, more blood and urine tests had been ordered. Toxicology would take a week or two to come back to see if there was anything out of the ordinary in his system. In a week or two, the path could become pretty cold and the description of the witnesses called for a deeper look into the events. He decided to check out the principals just in case.

The autopsy had vindicated the doctor but he insisted Craig was not asthmatic. He could not rule out the possibility of late-onset asthma but it seemed to hit too suddenly to be unaided, especially in the familiar surroundings of his own home. Jim would check to see if this was a typical smoke-filled poker game. He couldn't recall anyone smoking at the time. He flipped through the photos of the players. Only Tom had a cigarette package showing. One smoker hardly made for a smoke-filled room. More than likely in this day and age, Tom didn't even get to smoke inside. He consulted his notebook. It was right there. Tom was outside having a cigarette at the time of death, the only one out of sight of everyone else.

Jim reached for a second folder on his desk. This was the early report from the crime lab, lots of numbers and charts. He went straight to the last page for the section titled conclusions.

"Nothing out of the ordinary that would not be in a normal, working kitchen. All fingerprints accounted for by those present. All surfaces swabbed, awaiting toxicology reports."

Jim had checked the telephone before leaving. It had call display. The last call came from an Aliant pay phone. Further investigation showed it had gone unanswered. Everyone present put the number of rings between three and five but with four being most probable. Was this suspicious or just an impatient caller? The previous call, which George had said was a business call, came from the same pay phone. It had been almost 10 minutes in duration. Perhaps someone else was waiting to use the phone during the second call, causing the caller to give up quickly. Like everything else about the case, this was inconclusive. That seemed to be the most prominent word in the investigation to date: inconclusive.

He would talk to the forensic guys and the pathologist to get a better feel for what in the reports. The clock on his wall read 7:38. He would give them a chance to get their days started before bothering them.

Jim added the new file to three active ones under his care and went searching for a fresh cup of coffee. None was to be found. This was the transition between night shift and day shift. He made a fresh pot and stood watching the black-brown liquid drip through while he planned his attack on the weekend case.

People were killed for two reasons, in Jim's mind. Love, maybe lust, or money. His first task would be to figure out which one it was in this case. He leaned towards the money.

Preliminary inquiries showed Craig to be the owner of a small charter airline company. The company ran three jets on unscheduled flights, had a staff of six pilots including Craig, a secretary, a three-man maintenance crew, a cabin steward and a number of casual employees who were hired as they were needed. Jim noted that Tom Dunford was the steward in charge of this aspect of the company. Most of the other required services were contracted out.

Clients of this company believed time had a value. They didn't arrive at the airport two hours early to check in and didn't travel on someone else's timetable. Instead the plane left when they arrived, not before and not long after. Also, if their destination was other than a major city, they didn't change planes. This kind of service cost money. The clients were willing to pay. Craig was more than willing to accept. In return, he supplied a top-of-the-line product.

On the other hand, his cottage looked like it had the potential to be quite the love nest. Jim would not jump to any preliminary conclusions until he had a few facts to go on.

When Jim got back to his desk with a full cup of fresh coffee in his hand, Scott Bowen was waiting for him.

"Good morning, Jim," he said. "Just thought I'd drop in for a breath of the rarefied air of the detective bureau." Scott smiled. He preferred to work on highway patrol. A moving desk was more his speed. The detectives could have the glory and the long tedious hours of knocking on doors, hoping for a lead, and the endless paperwork that went with it.

"Morning, Scott. You're up early." Jim knew the patrolman was on nightshift.

"Yeah, I am. There was a complaint about how we handled a domestic call the night Craig was killed. We were accused of just barging into a private residence unannounced and uninvited. The complaint was groundless but while I was reviewing the video tape from the car to prove it, I came across something that might be of interest to you."

Jim's interest stepped up a notch. Complaints about police procedure were old hat to him and he was only sort-of listening. "Great, I'll take all the help you can throw my way."

"You know there are a number of private cottages on the lake that can only be accessed by water?"

Jim shook his head no.

"Well, there are. The big parking lot at the head of the lake is where these people park their vehicles before taking their boats up the lake. We keep an eye on it as part of our patrol work. The cars are pretty easy targets for vandals."

Jim nodded.

Scott produced a digital smart card from his briefcase. "There was a rental car parked in the lot when we left Craig's on a domestic call. The licence plate isn't visible but you can see the Hertz sticker. The driver is just sitting there behind the wheel. The sun was just dropping below the horizon and there is a reflection on the windshield. All you can make out is that there is a person in the car but no details. It was a bright sunny day before you arrived. A short time later the heavens opened up. We could have used a couple of those clouds." He paused, glanced down at the smart card and continued. "It may be nothing but it's a strange place to be parked. Under different circumstances, we'd have stopped and talked to him. The car wasn't there when we first arrived and he's not in the video when we came back."

Jim reached out and took the camera card from his fellow officer. This could be an early break in the case. "There's a video technician down the hall. Let's have a look."

The three men watched the five seconds of video over and over until they all agreed that no amount of enhancing would bring the driver into view. His image just wasn't there. If the image wasn't there to start with, they couldn't make it appear.

"Sorry," the tech finally said. "The angle of the light obliterated anything that was behind that windshield. Ten or 15 seconds either way and we might have gotten lucky. I can work on it alone and try some things. It may take a while. No promises." He made a copy of the important five seconds.

Jim and Scott left the room. "I was hoping it might be a break for you," Scott said. The disappointment was evident in his voice. He may have preferred to be a patrolman but everyone likes to be the person to come up with the big clue that cracks a case.

"Don't be crazy," said Jim. "This is a break. We know there was a rental car in the area. We know it came from Hertz. A few phone calls and we should know who rented it. This is our first real lead. You know the phone calls came from a pay phone at the marina?"

Scott brightened a little. "No, I didn't. Then, the man in the car easily could have been the one to make the calls. Why didn't he drive up to the house?"

Jim nodded in agreement. "I'm wondering that as well. There could be an innocent explanation. He might have been meeting a boat to take him further up the lake. It's early. We'll keep our options open."

"That's why most of the cars park there," Scott said. "I hear the autopsy was inconclusive."

"We're waiting for toxicology," Jim said, "but healthy people don't often drop dead for no apparent reason. I'll talk to them today and see if we should start investigating right away or not. They can tell us things they don't put in writing. Reports that end up in court are no place for hunches. They can come back and bite your ass."

"Don't I know that," said Scott. "Defence lawyers. They're not looking for the truth. They are looking for loopholes. I don't know how they sleep at night."

"In big comfortable beds with very expensive mattresses on them," Jim said. Both men laughed. Putting up with the courts and the justice system was just part of their job. It made them work all that much harder at crossing their Ts and dotting their Is. That wasn't necessarily a bad thing.

Jim turned serious again. "Before you arrived I was trying to decide a) if this was a case of murder and b) if it was, was the cause love or money. In my experience, it is usually one or the other. Any thoughts?"

Scott smiled. "In Craig's case, you would want to change the 'or' to an 'of'."

Jim looked at Scott with a confused look on his face. "The or to an of?"

"Yeah," Scott said, "love of money."

Jim nodded. "I was leaning that way. Thanks for the confirmation. You could do something else for me."

Scott raised his eyebrows and waited.

"Could I get you and Brenda to make some routine inquiries among Craig's employees?" Jim asked. "See if there was any animosity or trouble brewing that they were aware of. Disgruntled customers, upset competitors, money problems, the usual bag of tricks."

"Sure thing," Scott said. "Anything to get this thing resolved." Secretly he was pleased to be asked to help. His friendship with Craig went back a long way. As a patrolman, the investigation was outside his jurisdiction unless the officer in charge requested his help. Now he had.

"I'll clear it with Inspector Holland. Our detective squad is swamped. We appreciate your help."

They shook hands at the door. Jim returned to his office with a new place to start. Scott, with his video evidence in hand, went to the offices of his superiors to vindicate himself and his fellow policemen. Him pounding on the door was clearly visible from the car camera and it was loud enough that even the audio picked it up. At least the technology was on his side, even if the people he was trying to help were not.

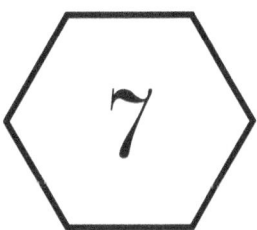

KEITH GRANT STUDIED his computer screen. Craig Flint's sudden death was causing him no end of problems. Keith was Craig's silent partner. He owned 30 per cent of Sky Jet Charter Service and was the principal owner of all three planes. These he leased back exclusively to Sky Jet. It was a tax-dodging arrangement that worked well for both of them.

As a silent partner, he took no part in the day-to-day operation of Sky Jet. This was strictly Craig's baby and he was good at it. That was the problem. Craig was too good. He micro-managed right down to the placement of serviettes on the bar in the passenger cabin. No one else made any decisions. No one else was even involved in the decision-making process. No one else was trained to step in and take Craig's place. Keith was now co-owner of a headless corporation.

The problem went even deeper than that, however. A large, important contract was to have been awarded to them this very day for shipping lobsters overseas three days a week. Three companies had made the short list with the winner being announced formally in the press today. It was common knowledge among all three companies that Sky Jet had won the contract. There was now a notice on the fish company's website saying that due to unforeseen circumstances, that announcement had been delayed.

Those circumstances would have been the death of the principal bidder. Keith did not blame the fish company. He would not have awarded the contract to Sky Jet without Craig at the helm. He especially wouldn't award the contract to Sky Jet with no one at the helm.

The third and most recently purchased jet had been procured with this contract in mind. It had been the clincher in the deal. With three planes, Sky Jet could guarantee no interruption in service. With a commodity as delicate as lobsters, there was no room for the product to be sitting around on a loading dock while a plane was getting last-minute service for an unexpected problem.

Keith had to come up with a new company CEO in a hurry or make an offer to one of the competitors to lease his jets to them. The latter move would make Sky Jet a nonentity, a tactic which left a bad taste in his mouth. Craig had come to him with this dream seven years ago and together they had nurtured it to a successful operation. Keith had no desire to just abandon it. This left the question: who could take over and win back this contract? The first thing to find out was who now owned the other 70% of the company. Keith could speculate but would have to wait for the reading of the will to be sure. When he found out, he wanted to have some concrete recommendations in mind.

While he mulled this over, his phone rang. He glanced down at the base unit. It was his executive assistant.

"Yes, Judy," he said.

"Sorry to interrupt but there is a police officer here to see you. A Detective Sergeant Jim Mcdonald."

This visit was inevitable but the timing was the pits. "Show him in."

Keith sat behind a large walnut desk in a high-back, maroon leather chair. The computer stood on one side of the desk, an empty in-out tray on the other and a marble desk set held the place of honour in the middle. The windows gave a view of the entrance to Halifax Harbour from 14 storeys up. He was also part owner of this building.

Jim came into the office and his view swept around the room to take in the art work on the walls, some modern, some traditional. There were a couple of degrees mixed in among them, business administration and political science, Jim noted. In one corner stood an electric organ keyboard, as out of place as a cat at a dog show. Keith indicated a leather chair to the left of the desk with his upturned palm.

"Please, have a seat," he said. "Have you learned anything new about Craig's death?" Keith did not waste time with small talk.

Jim sat in the indicated chair. "No, we are still gathering information. What about yourself? Any long-term effects from your own adventure?"

Keith shook his head. "No. Throat was a little sore but that could have been from walking around in the rain. Who knows? My own doctor had a look and gave me a clean bill of health. What can I do for you?"

Jim took his notebook from his pocket. "Financial adviser," he said as he gave a meaningful look at the expensive surroundings of the office. "That's what my notes tell me you said was your occupation when we interviewed you at the cottage."

"Exactly," Keith said, "that's what I am." He smiled at the policeman. "I'd be only too happy to look over your portfolio if that's why you're here."

Jim returned the smile. "Maybe some other time. We Googled your name on the Internet. It turns out you are a part owner of Sky Jet Charter Service or at least a company you own is a part owner."

Good work on your part, Keith thought. He didn't think the link would come to the surface this fast. "That's true," he said. He offered no additional information and wondered what site contained that bit of information and if anyone but the police could access it.

When Jim realized the acknowledgment of the truth was the extent of the answer he was going to get, he continued.

"You made the list of top 100 richest men in the country. Blue Bird Holding, that's you, right?"

"Did I?" His surprise seemed genuine. He ignored the question tagged on to the end of the information.

"Why didn't you mention you and Craig were partners the other night?" Jim asked.

"I didn't then and don't now see the relevance of me owning shares in Craig's company and his death. I own shares in a lot of companies, as I'm sure you know, and I don't get a visit from the law every time one of the principals die. The connection is irrelevant. I don't actively work at the company and I would hate to see you wasting your time on it."

"Well, that's what police work is all about," Jim said. "Sometimes these irrelevancies lead to a solution of a crime. How did you get along with your partner?" Jim recalled that Craig was upset at Keith over a hand of cards. These were millionaires playing for nickels and dimes. The money could not have been the cause of the dispute.

"We get along perfectly well. I am only a shareholder. I keep my nose out of the company and he makes sure the dividends keep flowing in." He paused as if rethinking that last statement. "I guess that sentence is in the wrong tense. All of that is in the past. In fact I was just sitting here contemplating the dilemma Craig's death caused the company. Let me assure you, his dying was the worst thing that could happen to Sky Jet at this time. We were on the verge of landing a multimillion-dollar contract, a contract that would have guaranteed the future of the company, not that the future was in any jeopardy. The announcement was to have been made today. Now everything is on hold."

Jim flipped his notebook to a clean page. "Tell me more," he said. "If you stand to lose, who stands to gain?" Follow the money. That was his strategy.

Keith's fingers danced across the keyboard of his computer. "There were three companies on the short list for this contract. Craig and Sky Jet had it wrapped up. Now it's up for grabs again so either of the other companies could stand to gain from this." He glanced back at the computer screen and hit Control P, enter. A printer in the corner of the room opposite to the organ keyboard started to chatter. "Here is the information on the other two companies. This is a cutthroat business but murder, that's a stretch."

Keith got up from his chair and walked over to the printer to retrieve the documents. "I'm not really familiar with Rapid Air Jet Delivery Service. They are new players in the field. They do own a jet, though which fills at least one of the criteria for the contract. I understand most people refer to them simply as Rapid Air."

He flipped through a couple of more pages before passing them over to the policeman. "My money would be on Lively Charters if Sky Jet doesn't hold the contract. The closing date for tenders has been extended by two weeks. They want to see what Sky Jet can bring to the table without Craig."

"Who takes over his shares?"

Keith shook his head. "I don't know. The will is being read tomorrow, I believe. I'm not in it so I haven't been invited to the reading. I did send some financial information to the lawyer yesterday."

"The company didn't make any contingency plans for something like this?"

Keith laughed. "If you suggested anything like that to Craig, his stock reply was: 'I'm going to live forever.' I'd ask 'How's it going?' and he would reply 'So far so good.' That was before Saturday. Day-to-day business is continuing as before. Craig's executive-assistant is keeping things on track. She appears to be the power behind the throne. I was looking at various options for the future when you interrupted."

The emphasis was on interrupted. Jim shifted in his chair. He was conducting a murder investigation even though murder had yet to be proven. When it was a clear-cut case of a crime having been committed, it gave him a little more leeway to force himself into the lives of people who may or may not be involved. He was treading carefully with this probe trying to gather facts before the trail became cold, if a trail even existed.

His body shuddered involuntarily. A bad thought came to mind. He recalled the last time he was unsure whether a crime had been committed or not. That turned out to be the work of a professional hit man, a damn good hit man. One who had never been caught. That man's weapon of choice involved car accidents. Was he at work again? Had he expanded his arsenal? Jim certainly hoped not.

"For someone not involved in running the company, you seem to be..." he paused for a second looking for the right word, "... quite active."

"Not by choice. Craig and I were the sole owners. Until the will is read, that just leaves me. My interest is forced. Being prepared is something I learned as a kid in Scouts."

"Sole owners? So your claim to be only a shareholder means that you are one of only two. The company is not public?"

"No need to be. We didn't need outside financing."

Jim got up from his chair. "I understand. Thanks for the information." He held up the papers to indicate what he was referring to and turned towards the door. Again the keyboard came into his view.

"I see you play the organ," he said.

Keith glanced into the corner of the room as if he were looking at some long forgotten artifact. "Not well and not often," he said.

Jim walked towards the machine. It was a Yamaha. He flicked on the power switch and picked out the beginning of *Mary Had a Little Lamb*. "I've always wanted to learn to play one of these things," he said.

"Me too," Keith said. "Maybe someday."

"Was there anyone in the poker group who might have a reason to hurt Craig?" Jim was back on topic again.

Keith didn't even pause to think about an answer. "You're barking up the wrong tree, Sergeant. We were all friends."

"Was there anyone alone in the kitchen before Craig went out there?"

This time Keith did think before answering. "Craig started the dishwasher and came into the game table. George was still packing up some of his cooking stuff— herbs, spices, stuff like that. Then he brought in three beers for himself, Shane and me." He thought a little more. "Tom went out for a smoke but he used the front door. The game had just barely started when it came to its sudden ending. We were only on the third hand. I've told you all this stuff before."

"You weren't out there alone?"

"No, sorry. I'm not a kitchen kind of guy. I usually order in."

Jim entered this information in his notebook and looked thoughtful for a minute longer.

"So, Tom had gone outside before Craig went out to the kitchen for the last time?"

"Right. That's my recollection. The outside kitchen door turned out to be locked. George and Shane tried to open it to provide some ventilation. Tom couldn't have been in the kitchen."

"And he appeared to be all right when he came back in? Didn't seem distracted or anything?"

"As all right as one could be after sticking a cancer stick in your mouth and sucking on it. That couldn't have been too good for him."

Jim contemplated this. "He often went out for a smoke?"

"Usually three or four times a night. Depended on how badly he was losing."

Jim plunked out another chorus of *Mary Had a Little Lamb.*

"Surely you can afford to take a few lessons." He glanced back at Keith who still sat at his desk studying something on the computer screen. Keith looked as if he had more important things to be doing but was giving the policeman all the time he wanted to take. Keith looked up from his computer and realized Jim was expecting an answer to his question.

"If only money could buy us everything we wanted," he said. "Unfortunately there are at least two aspects in reaching that goal. Money is one of them, for sure. The other is time, and you, my friend, have as much of that as I do. How much do you have to spare?"

Jim was surprised by the answer. "Time," he said. "You're right there. There is never enough of it to go around. But if music is your passion, perhaps you should invest some of your time in learning how to play. You're going to have even less of it in the future."

Keith nodded. "Perhaps you're right. The older we get the faster it seems to fly. But for now, Sky Jet is unexpectedly taking up a lot more of my time than I had planned to devote to it this week. I'm willing to bet it wasn't penciled in on your daily schedule either."

Jim grunted and thought about the other active cases he could be working on, should be working on. Ones where crimes had definitely been committed.

"You've got that right. If you think of anything that might be of help, no matter how obscure, give me a call." He took a business card from his inside pocket and passed it to Keith on his way to the door.

"Of course," Keith said. He opened his top drawer and placed the card in a file containing nothing but business cards. He flicked through the cards and placed it in the proper spot. "I still think it was natural causes—stress, lifestyle, losing at poker, something like that—but if I think of anything, I've got your number." He turned back to his computer. "Call me if you want me to look over your portfolio." The meeting was over. Jim let himself out.

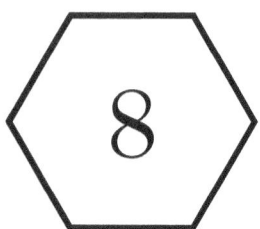

8

A VIBRATION TINGLED the skin of Jim's chest as his cellphone came to life in his jacket's inner pocket. He was waiting for the express elevator outside Keith's office to take him down the 14 floors to ground level. The display read Brenda Davis. Jim was momentarily confused by the name before remembering Brenda was Scott Bowen's patrol partner. Jim walked over to the windows overlooking Halifax Harbour and pressed the talk button.

"Mcdonald," he said.

Brenda sounded excited on the other end. "Sergeant, Brenda Davis here. I may have a lead in the Craig Flint case."

"Great. Go ahead."

"Scott and I are checking out the employees of Sky Jet as you requested. Scott's talking to the pilots and maintenance people and I have the office staff.

"Craig's secretary, strike that, Craig's executive assistant, saw Craig and a woman embracing in the hallway the day before he was killed."

Jim nodded to himself. Money was Jim's first choice for a motive. Romance was a close second. "Do we know who this lady was?"

"That's the point of the call," Brenda said. "The secretary claims it was Tom Dunford's wife. The embrace ended with a kiss." She paused to let this information sink in.

"I couldn't locate Scott but I thought you might want this information as soon as possible. Scott must have his phone turned off or is in a dead zone." Brenda was trying to justify why she had bypassed her superior with the call. She didn't want to appear to be advancing her own career at the expense of her partner's. Unlike her partner who was happy in a patrol car, Brenda had ambitions to someday carry a detective's gold shield.

"I'm glad you called," Jim said. "Tom Dunford is on my list of people to talk to this morning. I'll spring this information on him and see how he reacts."

Below him a huge container ship slowly wended its way up the harbour under the close supervision of two tiny harbour tugs. He recognized the red hat shape on one of them. It would be Theodore Tugboat. He had never seen the kid's show on TV but everyone in Halifax knew about Theodore. The bridge of the ship floated five storeys above the water's surface and had several containers stacked on its deck, cargo from all over the world destined for various parts of North America.

Jim continued watching as the ship approached one of the harbour bridges. From this angle, it looked as if the top rigging would hit the bridge as it tried to go under. Jim waited. The ship cleared with a generous margin. Coming back empty and riding higher in the water would be a lot closer.

Jim pulled himself away from the view and went back to the elevator bank. Already he was planning his interview with Tom Dunford. He wondered if Tom knew about his wife and Craig. Perhaps it was best that Brenda couldn't get in touch with Scott. Scott might want to protect his friend's reputation. Police work couldn't allow for feelings of friendship when murder was involved.

Jim pulled up to the address Tom had given him when the appointment was arranged. It was an older middle-class subdivision but the houses were still well-maintained. Jim looked around the neighbourhood. Playing 20-dollar poorhouse made more sense to people in this locality than it did to the millionaire class he had just left. Losing $20 would not take the food off of Tom's table but winning $20 could get him an extra case of beer for the weekend. No doubt all the players had their roots in these surroundings and the traditional cost of poker hadn't changed with their changing circumstances. It gave Jim a different view of the game.

Several cars were parked in the driveway of the two-storey white house, forcing Jim to park on the street. He got out of the car and started up the driveway when Tom came out the front door.

"Could we talk somewhere else?" Tom asked. "As you can see, there are several people here at the house. I wasn't thinking when I agreed to meet with you this morning. This isn't going to take long, is it?"

Jim shrugged his shoulders. "We could talk downtown."

"Downtown?" Tom visibly blanched. "No. No, I don't want to go downtown." He looked back at the crowded house searching for an alternative. "I have a small office in my basement. We can talk there."

The two men went around to the back of the house and into the cluttered basement through an outside entrance. Tom led the policeman past the furnace to a rough, paint-scarred door and opened it. Beyond the door was a small eight-by-eight-foot room. A small desk took up part of one wall. Beside it was an older model computer with the blue Windows-95 screen displayed. There were two reject easy chairs with their springs showing and a 13-inch TV. A sign on the end wall mounted above several shelves of books read "Tom's Hideaway." High on the other wall was a narrow rectangular basement window. It was below ground level and looked out into a water well.

Tom indicated the better of the two chairs to the policeman. "Welcome to my little piece of solitude," he said.

"Not fancy," Jim acknowledged, "but better than some men have." He thought of his own two-bedroom apartment with a small kitchen and combined living-dining room. His home computer sat crowded in one corner of the spare bedroom. He lost access to it when he had guests staying over.

"What have you learned about Craig's death?" Tom asked before Jim could initiate the interview process. "They've released the body and the funeral will be held tomorrow."

Jim was surprised by this bit of information. He didn't think a definite cause of death had been established. Tom's interest in the subject also surprised Jim, considering how indifferent Keith Grant had been to the whole process and he was Craig's business partner in some round-about way. Tom was just an employee.

"You were close friends beyond the poker games?" he asked.

"On several levels," Tom answered. "I worked for Sky Jet, as you know. I was in charge of detailing the aircraft between flights. And of course, we're related by marriage. There's no connection between the two. I got the job strictly on merit. I worked at Air Canada servicing their cabins for 10 years before going to Sky Jet." Tom sounded defensive about how he got his job.

Too many people for too many years assumed it was just because he was a family member.

Jim missed that point. He was still concentrating on Tom's relationship to Craig by marriage. "Exactly how are you related by marriage?"

"I'm his brother-in-law. Craig is my wife's brother. But I got the job because I'm good at it and for no other reason."

"Your wife and the victim are brother and sister?"

Tom studied the lawman for a minute before answering. "Yes, that's why all the people are here. For the funeral tomorrow. Is there a problem?"

Jim looked at his open notebook at the notation he had made early that morning. "I had a report that your wife was seen embracing Craig outside the office the day before he was killed. Kissing as well."

"Damn it. Why does she have to keep interfering?" Tom said.

"You said she was interfering. What do you mean by that?"

"Nothing. Every so often Craig and I get in a dispute about how to clean the cabins. I know I'm doing it right and refuse to back down. He fires me and then later in the day apologizes and things go back to normal. Last Thursday, he was going crazy about the upcoming contract he was bidding on and was particularly irritable. He fired me again and then rehired me Friday morning. This time I made him pay. I insisted on a raise. We argued but he needed me. He paid. He was still pissed Saturday night at the poker game.

"Mary must have heard about me being fired and stuck her nose in where it doesn't belong. She must have talked to him later Friday morning. By then, he had rehired me anyway. I didn't need her interference."

Jim nodded and took some notes. He wondered how often the sister got the job back for her husband. This would bear some additional checking.

"Is it possible Craig was embracing some other woman in the office? Someone who resembles your wife?"

Tom gave a short, barking laugh. "Possible, but unlikely. Craig didn't have much time for romantic endeavours with women. It wasn't part of his makeup."

"Oh? You mean men were?"

"No, no, I don't mean that at all. Craig was totally focused on two things: flying and making money. He always said he would be a millionaire before he was 30. He didn't quite make it but he was before he turned 40. He lived alone and had no interest in serious relationships with anyone else, except his family of course. He was always there for them even before he had made his money. Lately, he kind of lorded it over Mary that he's such a success. That annoys her sometimes, but that was just Craig."

"Making money can also make enemies. Do you know of any Craig made along the way?"

Tom shook his head. "He could be irritable and demanding at times but he got along with most people most of the time. I don't know of anyone who would be irritated enough to try and kill him. It doesn't make sense. Are you sure he was murdered or are you just going on the word of that drunken doctor?"

Jim looked up. This was the third reference to Dr. Dow in a less than favourable light.

"You don't think he was qualified to practice?"

"Maybe at one time but lately his practice consisted of a few rich patients and a lot of time at the country club bar. I wouldn't want my life to depend on his abilities."

Jim noted the concern and remembered he was going to check the medical report filed with the aviation board. He wanted to see how complete Dr. Dow's examination had been.

"When Keith Grant collapsed, you were reported as saying: 'Keep out, the air is poisonous.'" Jim was reading from his notebook. "Have you changed your mind?"

"No, that was my WHMIS training kicking in. In the workplace, if people start dropping like flies, you assume there are hazardous materials in the air and vacate the area. It appeared to be the proper thing to do. That was before we realized Grant had fainted."

"That's still only a possibility. It hasn't been confirmed."

"Well, it makes more sense than Craig being murdered." Tom gave an abrupt single nod of his head to punctuate his sentence.

"Who takes over the company now that Craig is dead?" Jim asked looking for another possible suspect.

"The reading of the will is tomorrow after the funeral. Mary, my wife, is the only living member of his immediate family but with Craig, you never know. It could all go to his cats. I'm surprised he even had a will. I guess we can be thankful for that regardless of what it says."

"How much has Keith Grant got to do with running the company?"

"Keith Grant? Why would he have anything to do with it? He's just a poker buddy."

Jim struggled to hide his surprise at that remark. Either Grant truly was a deep, silent partner or Tom had little knowledge of the operation of the company. Again, more stuff to look into.

"George Phillips was the company accountant. Shane Martin did a lot of the electrical service work but Keith, he just showed up once a month and played poker. I think he was a friend of Shane's not Craig's. Sky Jet didn't even exist when the poker games started. Craig flew for some other company back then. He only started the company seven years ago. I've been with it from the start."

Tom was silent for a minute and then asked: "Who saw my wife embracing Craig and told you about it?"

"I got the information from another investigator, but just like everything you tell me will be held in confidence, so is this. You can tell me anything and not worry about me revealing where the information came from," he paused, "unless of course it ends up in court and you may be called as a witness."

Tom ignored all the PR bullshit. "It was that secretary, wasn't it? That gold-digging bitch has it in for me. She had a thing for Craig but he didn't even give her the time of day. I think he was totally oblivious to her advances. I warned Craig about her but he just laughed it off. I try to look out for his interests. He can be so naive when it comes to women. In business, he's a man to be reckoned with but at other times, he was just a child.

"To make things worse between that bitch and me, Craig approached her about it. He told her he wanted to be sure her main concentration was on her job and not on personal relationships in the office. She's still pissed at me for bringing it up. She'd do anything to get me in trouble."

"Didn't she know your wife was Craig's sister? That seems kind of stupid to tell us they were involved with each other."

"Stupid. Yeah, that describes her quite well. But no, she didn't know. I keep my home life and my work life separate. Most people at the company don't know Craig and I are related. I got that job on my own merits, not because I'm the boss's brother-in-law, was the boss's brother-in-law, I guess now."

Jim nodded. "So you've said. Did you hold any resentment toward Craig? Did you feel he treated you like less of an employee and more of a person whose job was based on nepotism?"

"Family and job were separate. He approached me in the beginning. I had a good job. I didn't need him. I went on board to help him get his company rolling. But, yeah, sometimes he talked down to me in ways he wouldn't talk to any other employee."

"And you resented him for that?"

"No. I returned the favour. I talked back to him. That's why he fired me so often. He always hired me back. As I said, he needed me more than I needed him. I could always get a job at any other airline."

"So what happens now?"

"The company is still viable. We wait for the reading of the will and continue on from there. Nobody is irreplaceable. When JFK was assassinated, it took less than an hour to replace him and everybody thought he was the best thing to come along since sliced bread. The company will survive."

Jim thought about this before asking: "Was there anyone at the game who had a grudge against Craig?" This was a routine he would go over with all the poker players. Someone might offer some useful information.

"Not likely," Tom said. "We played poker all night for 20 bucks. That's hardly a motive for murder."

"Was anyone in the kitchen alone before Craig went out there?"

Tom considered this. "No, I think Craig was the last one in the kitchen before the game started."

Jim waited to see if there was more to the answer. When nothing more followed, he asked: "Where were you when Craig went out to answer the phone?"

"I was outside having a smoke. I'm the only smoker in the group and can't do it in the house, another of Craig's rules."

"You didn't see anyone else while you were out there? A car in the driveway perhaps?"

"No, just a few ducks in the lake. Dusk was settling over the yard."

Jim reached into his pocket and pulled out a business card. He handed it to Tom with the usual "if you think of anything else, call me," line. He let himself out while Tom returned to his guests.

Once outside, Jim sat in his car going over the interview. He would have to talk to the secretary himself. If she felt slighted, maybe revenge was a motive. Then there was Tom. How much did he stand to gain from this death? His wife was no doubt going to be a benefactor in the will. That could only help Tom. Perhaps Craig had fired him once too often and Tom was tired of his wife going to bat for him. Jim would have to get access to the will to see where the money was going. Follow the money, always a good idea in a murder investigation.

He flipped open his appointment book to see who was next and where. George Phillips, the accountant. That could also be part of the money trail. Jim glanced at his watch. This would be a good time to check in on the pathologist and see if she had come up with a definite cause of death. Since she released the body, something must have been decided. He put the car in gear and pulled away.

The white lace curtain in the living-room window of the house fluttered closed. Tom turned to join the crowd of mourners. The policeman had broached some subjects that he hadn't given much thought to. Who would take over the company now that Craig was dead? He pulled down his cuffs, threw back his shoulders and tried to look more like the CEO type. He could do it. He could manage Sky Jet. He would have to wait until tomorrow afternoon to see what exactly was in the will. Then he would know exactly how beneficial this death might be to him. It was only one day. He could wait.

In an Internet cafe in Winnipeg, Robert Crosley logged into the Halifax paper's website again. He ran through the articles, finding no follow-up to yesterday's brief filler story.

Monday's paper carried a story under an 18-point headline, buried in the Metro section, reading: *"Man dies suddenly at home."* The two-paragraph item reported that police, ambulance and fire members responded to a call in the Mill Lake area. Cause of the death was unknown and the name was being withheld pending notification of the next-of-kin. Strange, Crosley thought. Who in hell had called the police? It should have been a routine stroke with no additional investigation necessary. People Flint's age were in that high-risk group, especially those in stressful jobs such as pilots and small business owners.

He opened the obituary section of the site and scanned the names to see if the next-of-kin had been located. There it was: Craig Flint, age 47, died suddenly at home, blah, blah, blah. Funeral services to be held on Wednesday morning at 10 o'clock, etc. etc.

Crosley sat back in his chair. Died Saturday, buried Wednesday. Four days between the two events. It seemed everything was working out fine despite the police presence.

He logged off that website and logged in to the *USA Today* site, went directly to the classifieds and checked the personals. There were no new messages for him. After finishing his assignment here in Winnipeg, he might have a few days to himself. He had had a busy year. Settling differences of opinion with "extreme prejudice" seemed to be becoming a new way of doing business. He wondered if the Sopranos, the TV show about the Mafia, had any bearing on this change in attitude. To him, the why was a minor detail. It just gave him the option of being more selective in which clients he took on. Winter was coming. The weather would be a factor in his future decisions. He logged off the machine, finished his hazelnut-amaretto flavoured coffee and left the cafe.

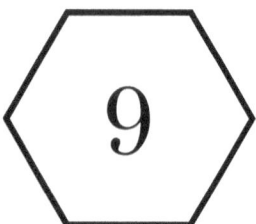

D R. JANE MELNICK looked up from a report she was filling out as Jim entered her office through the open door. She smiled at the detective and then shook her head.

"Sorry, nothing definite yet. Still waiting for toxicology," she said before Jim could even ask the question.

Jim slid into a chair at the side of the desk.

"I hear the body has been released. Isn't that a little premature considering we don't know how he died?"

"The family wanted to get on with the funeral. There was no reason to hold them up any longer. Besides, only the shell of the body was released. We still have all the vital organs—the heart, the brain, the liver, the lungs, the kidneys and all the rest that goes with that. We'll be able to do any follow-up that is required."

"You can do that? Keep all that stuff?"

"All the time. Once we take 'em out, there's no sense in putting them back."

Jim thought about this for a second or two. "I guess not. Nothing new on the cause?"

"Right now, it looks like a death of unknown origin. There seems to be some indication of metabolic asphyxiation possibly caused by hyperpnoea. This is caused by the stimulation of chemoreceptor of the carotid and aortic bodies."

Jim shook his head and held both hands in front of him in a stopping motion. "In English, please. I'm only a simple policeman."

The doctor laughed right up to her eyes. Policemen were often dropping in on her for the inside track, not wanting to wait for the official autopsy results. She liked to lay on the technical jargon as thick as possible. "It was an unusual deep and rapid breathing brought on by the actions of his own heart which served to suffocate him. Hydrogen cyanide in high concentrations has been known to cause this but none was found on the scene. We're checking for a hybrid of the chemical, a designer version of it. Synthetic drugs are much more difficult to determine.

"I'm hoping toxicology can shed some light on this. Sorry. All we know for sure is that something closed his throat off completely and he suffocated. None of the known toxins that would produce that effect appear to be present. We're searching for something more exotic but without much luck.

"These drugs tend to be of a dual-component nature. Two items, that of themselves are safe, merge to form a killer combination. You seldom see them outside of a laboratory. The problem with this family of drugs is they have an extremely short half-life, minutes. The initial blast would kill your vic in seconds. A few minute later, it would only be half as potent, still lethal, but less so. A few more minutes later, a quarter as potent, give or take. Then one-eighth, one-sixteenth, and so on. If your second subject was five or ten minutes after the first, he would have gotten a lower dose. I'd say you're looking at a homicide. This stuff doesn't just appear out of the ether but it tends to disappear into it. For now that's just a personal opinion. We're still looking for the hard evidence."

"What do you mean by a few minutes?"

"Sorry, I can't be more precise until we know the drug."

"The drug may disappear but whatever transported it should still be there. Either that or the person who transported it. What would it look like? A liquid? A powder?"

"Probably airborne. Can't say until we isolate what the components were. We're still looking." She shrugged. "How's your day going otherwise?"

Jim realized the final statement was to put a stop to any further discussion on a case which had no definitive answers yet. Dr. Melnick was not one for beating a dead horse. She might cut it up and examine it, but she wasn't going to put anything in writing about the cause of death until she had all the facts. Any more questions would be a waste of time.

"Thanks. Keep me informed," he said. Jim had too much to do to sit around and chat. By the looks of the pathologist's desk, she was in the same boat.

He returned to his car and headed to his next appointment.

The offices of Phillips Accounting shared the same building as Sky Jet Charter Service, although several floors lower. George Phillips did not have a room with a view, unless of course you counted the brick wall face of the building across the street. To call the decorating spartan would be doing a disservice to the ancient Greeks. Two diplomas hung by themselves on the wall behind George's desk. A small lap-top computer was slid to one side with the cover closed. A 20-inch monitor was hooked to the large Dell computer sitting on the floor beside the desk. One for home, one for away, Jim thought. A wide-paper printer sat on a table of its own. A large box of fan-fold paper fed from the box through the bottom of the table and into the printer.

George took a stack of blue presentation folders from a chair and offered it to Jim. Obviously he visited his clients' offices instead of inviting them to his.

George returned to his chair behind the desk and moved a stack of papers to one side. He folded his hands on the desk pad in front of him and waited for the policeman to begin the interview. Jim noticed the ragged edges of George's fingernails. George was a biter. The nails were chewed down to well below the tops of the fingers and into the quick. Biters were usually worriers. Jim wondered what George had to worry about. Were the concerns his own or those of his clients?

"Tell me again about the night of the card game," Jim began. "Was there anyone besides Craig who spent time in the kitchen alone?"

George opened the top drawer of his desk and pulled out a letter-sized folder. From this he withdrew two sheets of paper and spread them out on his desk.

"I took some notes when I got home Saturday night while everything was still fresh in my mind," he said. He scanned the notes before answering. Jim observed that not only were the notes typed but there was also a time line for the events. George ran his finger down the page until he came to the proper starting point.

"Let's see. Craig and I were the last ones in the kitchen after the meal. Craig was starting the dishwasher and I was putting some of my stuff back in my duffle bag so it would be ready when it came time to leave.

"We both went into the living room for the card game. I carried in some beer for myself, Keith and Shane. We started playing. Tom dealt the first hand, straight poker. I dealt the second hand, Low Chicago and Craig dealt the third hand, 7-27.

"During that hand Tom folded. He went outside for a smoke. We finished the hand. I won half. The other half was in dispute, although it belonged to Keith. Craig went into the kitchen alone and he died."

He looked up at the policeman. "To answer your question: Once the game started, no one was in the kitchen."

"Tom was not with the rest of you when Craig went out there?"

Another quick glance at the notes. "That's correct."

"Do you mind if I look at your notes?"

George hesitated. "I'd rather you didn't. I made them as a refresher for my mind. There are a few personal comments included that are private thoughts. Just some things to help me set the mood of what was taking place at the time."

Jim leaned back in his chair. He had been reaching forward with no thought of his request being rejected. He was surprised by George's reaction.

"When you got the beer, who else was in the kitchen with you?"

"Craig. Well, sort of. He went into the living room and I followed along right behind him with the beer. I might have been in the kitchen alone for maybe five or ten seconds while I got the stuff from the fridge."

"So, you were in the kitchen alone?"

George studied the man across from him. "Yes, I was in the kitchen alone." The tone of the interview was going downhill.

"You're the bookkeeper for Sky Jet Charter Services."

"I'm the accountant. There is a difference."

"You had access to the company's money?"

"I kept track of the company's money and made recommendations to Craig about the spending of it. I made sure proper records were maintained. He had a policy: nobody signs the cheques but himself. He was the only one who had access to it." George's voice still had an edge on it.

Jim nodded. "A good policy." He sat staring at George, smiling, but saying nothing further.

Finally George could stand it no longer. "What?" he asked.

"Welcome to the present," Jim said. "Of course, I know there is a great deal of difference between a bookkeeper and an accountant. I was just trying to get your head out of the notes you took Saturday night and into what things might have occurred to you since you took them. Get you thinking independently. Don't get me wrong, the notes are helpful, but we've learned a lot since Saturday night. Hell, Saturday we weren't even sure Craig hadn't had a stroke. Now we're pretty sure he was murdered."

George's face showed his surprise. "Are we? I didn't know that."

"We're just waiting for confirmation from toxicology but there is little doubt. So tell me, has anything else occurred to you since Saturday night?"

George glanced down at the two sheets of paper. He squared them up and set them to one side of his desk. "What is it you want to know?"

"You're the accountant. Who stands to win and who stands to lose from Craig's death?"

George shook his head. "I can think of no winners. Craig wasn't out to harm anyone. Whether or not there are losers depends on who fills Craig's shoes. They're big and it won't be easy."

"There's this contract for flying lobsters overseas that I keep hearing about. How devastating a blow will that be to the company if they don't get it?"

"Not a blow at all. I advised Craig against going for it. The company had more business than it could handle without it. It would just be an increased burden on the limited resources."

Jim didn't hide his surprise at this bit of information. "That's the first time I've heard that opinion expressed. I thought he acquired a third plane just for the purpose of getting this account."

"That was the original purpose of the acquisition. He got the plane before he put in the bid. He wanted to make it seem as if it was just a part of an ongoing company and not something that would disappear as soon as the contract was signed.

"But the funny thing was, he had enough business to justify having the plane without getting the additional contract. All three planes are in the air as much as their maintenance schedule allows. He didn't need the new contract. It would overtax his resources. He would have to turn away current business to handle the additional flights the lobster contract would require."

George stopped to think about how to phrase the next part of his statement without appearing disloyal to his former friend and associate.

"It was an ego thing with him. He got himself into a pissing contest with Bob Lively, the owner of Lively Charters. He didn't need the work so much as he wanted to prove that he could get the contract. He and Bob flew together before they started their own companies. Both had discussed their plans with each other. Bob was the first to get his company off the ground, so to speak. Craig resented that. He was always out to prove Sky Jet was the better of the two."

Jim was rapidly writing notes on this new information. "What about Rapid Air? How did he feel about them?"

"They are the new kids on the block. I don't know much about them except that Craig said they didn't have a hope in hell of landing this contract. According to Craig, Rapid Air only made the short list because the fish company wanted three names on it. It gave the speculators a little more to think about it. Anyone on the inside knew they were just window dressing."

This was new information to Jim, something he hadn't even considered.

"What about Rapid Air? Did they know they weren't contenders?" Jim was still writing.

"I doubt it. They were too new to even know they were in over their heads."

"How many shares of Sky Jet do you own?" Jim smoothly slipped in the personal question while George was in a talkative mood.

"None," George answered. "It is not a public company. There are no shares to be had."

"You're the accountant. You know that's not true."

"It is true. The company was owned by Craig who had 70 per cent and the leasing company that owned the planes which owned 30 per cent. Craig was a 30 per cent owner of the leasing company, as well. There were no shares open to the public to grab."

"Do you know who the other owner of the leasing company was?"

George hesitated before answering.

"Yes. Sky Jet Leasing and Sky Jet Charter were essentially one company. The leasing company had no other clients. The whole thing was a tax dodge,." George noticed the policeman perk up at that remark. He quickly added "All perfectly legal. Everyone is entitled to minimize their tax burden as much as they can as long as they keep within the rules. That's why there are chartered accountants." A smile flickered across his face and disappeared again.

"The owner of the leasing company?"

George got up from his desk and walked over to one of the filing cabinets and withdrew a folder. "Blue Jay Holding Company."

Jim wondered what these guys talked about at their poker games. They were playing for peanuts so they must have spent a great deal of time just talking, but no one seemed to know anything about the others. Except for Craig, that is, he had a tie to everyone. Of course, there was another possibility. Everyone knew everything about each other and they just weren't giving up anything to the police. If that was true, the question it raised was why.

Jim studied the man in front of him. No, he thought. George couldn't lie to save his soul. These were a bunch of strangers getting together for a little recreational poker once a month. They just didn't realize how much they had in common with each other. It would all come out as the case developed. Jim would choose when to let each of them in on the secrets of the others.

"You know that Tom Dunford is Craig's brother-in-law?"

"Of course. I went to school with them. I've known them for years."

"Craig was upset at Tom for some reason during the card game. Why was that?"

George reached over for his notes again and quickly scanned the second page. "This attitude was unusual for Craig. He played poker for enjoyment. It was so out of character that I made a note of it. Tom worked for Craig. There may have been something bubbling over from that angle. They were brothers-in-law. Families have the occasional spat. Tom didn't kill Craig though. The bickering wasn't anywhere near that serious and the only reason anyone mentioned it was because everyone at the card games got along so well together. People who took the game too seriously didn't get invited back. You're wasting your time working on that angle."

Wasted time. This was the second occasion one of the players had advised him on how to use his resources. They played for nickels and dimes, but the big thing each of them put into the game was time from busy schedules. Money was not a major factor in their lives. They all seemed to have enough of it. None of them believed in wasting a moment of their precious time. Spending part of an afternoon and an entire evening on an endeavour with almost no monetary return seemed out-of-character for these men. They did all have a connection to Sky Jet Charter Services. Jim would have to dig deeper.

"Who are some of the people who were not invited back?"

"I don't remember most of them. Customers of Craig's, competitors. The owner of Rapid Air played a couple of times when Keith Grant was out of town. He seemed to have been dropped from the list of invitees. I think it was Tom's idea to invite him."

"What did he do to get ejected, so to speak?"

"I don't know. He asked a lot of personal questions. We're just there for a little fun and relaxation. No one wants to be grilled."

Jim nodded involuntarily. That was for sure. What these guys didn't know about each other would fill a set of encyclopedias; what they knew wouldn't fill a page in his notebook.

"How much does your company stand to lose if Sky Jet folds?"

George let out a snort. "Sky Jet is not going to fold. Craig was good but not irreplaceable."

"That's not the impression I get. He was the company."

George laughed. "Take a bucket of water and insert your hand up to the wrist. Then withdraw your hand and look at the hole left behind. That's how irreplaceable anyone is, even Craig."

That's a pragmatic view, Jim thought, but it was what you could expect from an accountant. Their world consisted of taking the practical point of view. However, it didn't answer his question.

"Worst-case scenario. What would it do to your accounting firm?"

"Sky Jet took up one-fifth of my time. There's computer software that does most of the mundane tasks. Craig and I met once a week and went over the financials. I made recommendations. He did whatever he wanted. The lost business could be replaced with one phone call. I have a waiting list for clients.

"Unlike Craig, I see no reason to expand my business beyond what I can handle myself. I'm an accountant, not an office manager. I don't want a bunch of employees to look after. I don't need millions of dollars to try to hide from the government. I'm happy just the way things are."

Jim looked at the remaining bits of fingernails that had been almost chewed out of existence. He took in the meagre surroundings of the office. He wondered if George really believed what he was saying.

"You say Craig didn't listen to your recommendations?"

"That's not exactly what I said. My recommendations were part of his decision-making process. He had other factors to consider."

"This bothered you?"

"Only if I considered his actions were harmful to the company. There can be a number of right choices for any particular subject. My job was to give him the financial side of the various options. Finances were not always the major deciding factor. I may have misled you. He did listen to my recommendations most of the time."

Jim considered this information. He understood what George was saying about various factors involved in the decision-making process. There seemed to be no reason for George to be considered as the killer or even an accomplice. He could, however, be relied on for honest input if Jim had questions about anyone else.

"What do you know about Keith Grant?"

"Keith? He bluffs at poker. Sometimes he wins, sometimes he loses. Drinks in moderation. I've known him for a number of years but we only meet at card games and the occasional game of golf. He shoots around 100 but enjoys himself anyway. Docsn't seem to take things too seriously."

"Do you know what he does for a living?"

"Financial adviser. Does quite well at it as far as I know. Guess he takes his work seriously. He must, he looks after some of Craig's investments and money was something Craig took very seriously."

Jim made a note of that comment in his notebook. "You didn't handle Craig's personal finances?"

"I'm the accountant for Sky Jet Charter Services not a personal financial adviser. Craig kept the two separate. I do my job well; Keith Grant seems to be more than proficient at his."

"Thanks for your time," Jim said. "I may want to talk to you again."

"You have my number," George said.

Jim nodded.

KEITH GRANT SAT at his desk looking out the window at the activity in the harbour. Since the visit from the police sergeant, he hadn't been able to concentrate on his work. He still wanted to believe that Craig's death was from natural causes but now there was this little inkling of doubt. A doubt that gnawed at the back of his mind and prevented him from doing any productive work.

He had looked after Craig's private affairs and knew to the penny how much money he was worth. This information had been sent by courier to the office of the lawyer who was looking after the will late on Monday afternoon. Keith was pleased with the results of his audit. As a financial adviser, he had seen some people prosper and some not do so well. Sometimes this was his fault, sometimes it was the fault of the client. He could only advise. It was up to the client to follow his advice, or not.

Craig was a risk taker and he had taken an aggressive approach to investing. It had paid off in spades. This brief flash of pride disappeared when Keith realized it was now a moot point. Craig would never benefit from all the hard work. Keith didn't pluck companies out of the air. He did extensive research, studied financial reports and talked to people who had firsthand knowledge of the companies he was considering. Often he would visit the location of the business and talk to the people employed there to get their perspective on how things were going.

Most of his clients, Craig included, did not have enough money invested to make this expensive research pay off. However, one client did justify the expense. Himself. His private holdings were extensive enough that a trip across the country to personally investigate a company paid off big time. A few cents a share added up quickly if you owned enough shares. Craig's investments rode the coat tails of this research and he also prospered.

Keith swung his chair around to face the desk again. The organ keyboard passed his vision as he made the swing. What had Mcdonald said? "Time, you're going to have even less of it in the future." That might be the optimistic view. There might not even be a future. That was definitely true in Craig's case.

Keith got up and walked over to the keyboard, flipped it on. He, too, plucked out *Mary Had a Little Lamb*. He laughed at his selection and then with both hands played a few bars of *The Entertainer*. It was recognizable. His lessons had not been for naught. Too much time had passed since he applied himself to this pastime. The sergeant was right. He should take it up again.

His next task was to find out if Craig's premature passing was caused by too much stress in his life or from some outside source. He owed his client, partner, friend that much.

He went back to his desk, picked up the phone and said: "Judy, get me Shane Martin, please."

SKY JET CHARTER Services occupied a small suite on the fifth floor of the same building used by Phillips Accounting. It consisted of an office for Craig, a reception area where his executive assistant worked and a meeting room where he could meet clients and put on presentations as to why they should choose Sky Jet for their flying needs.

The reception area displayed posters of his planes on three of the four walls: both exterior views, with bright blue skies and dazzling white clouds forming the backdrop and interior shots showing dazzling smiles of satisfied customers reclining in royal opulence as the sun shone through the window and reflected off the ice cubes in their amber drinks. Scale models of the planes hung from invisible wires from the ceiling, also painted sky blue with scattered clouds, or sat perched on pedestals for closer examination.

The fourth wall was all glass. On a good day, with curtains open, the natural sky blended in with the artificial one and encouraged people to "slip the surly bonds of Earth ... Put out their hand and touch the face of God" as the poet/pilot John Gillespie Magee had said about the pleasures of flying. The poem hung on a plaque on one wall adjoining the window. It was every pilot's favourite bit of poetry.

Jim hoped to find the secretary at work and not off due to the death of her employer. The company's clients felt regret at Craig's passing but they had schedules of their own to keep, businesses to run. Several had called to make sure their flights were still a go when they heard of Craig's sudden passing. It was business as usual except for Wednesday morning when everyone would attend the funeral, unless of course business had taken them out of town. Craig would not have wanted them to cancel a flight just to see his lifeless body lowered into the ground.

Jim stood staring out the window to the patio below while one of these clients was being reassured on the phone. Christine's smooth voice had just a tinge of sorrow as she discussed the sudden passing of her employer, but, she assured the man on the other end of the line, everything was in place to insure that his flying plans would not be interrupted.

Jim looked down upon the big maple trees, now all but naked of their leaves. A few yellow survivors clung to the branches but most of them were scattered around the patio where intermittent gusts of wind were creating whirling dervishes of yellow, red and brown as the leaves went spinning 10 or 20 feet into the air in a mini funnel before settling back onto the bricks to await the next gust to take them airborne again.

He watched this repeating act of nature while he waited for Christine to finish her call. His first impression differed from that of Tom Dunford. Christine was dressed in a neat, blue business suit with a slight pin stripe over a white blouse buttoned to her neck. She was attractive but she didn't seem to be flaunting it as Tom had suggested. She had red, shoulder-length hair that rippled as she turned her head to look at him.

"Sorry, it won't be much longer," she mouthed to him with one hand over the mouthpiece of the phone. She was repeating the assurances for what seemed like the third time and her face was pinching into a look of impatience.

"Perhaps if I patch you through to the flight centre and you could talk to your pilot," she said. "He can discuss your concerns much better than I." A smile lit up her face. The caller must have agreed with that suggestion. She put the call on hold, dialed a few numbers and explained what was happening to the pilot before connecting the two men. The explanation was polite and displayed no indication of her repeated reassurances. She listened briefly to make sure the men were talking and then broke off her part of the connection.

"I'm sorry to have kept you waiting," she said, "but I've already talked to the police. They were here earlier this morning."

"That's right," Jim said, "I've had a report on what you told them. I just want to go over a couple of things myself, if I may." He flashed a smile before pulling his notebook from his pocket. He flipped it open and looked up at her, waiting for her consent before going on.

"Sure, go ahead."

Jim studied his notes again while he collected his thoughts. If he had found Christine dressed in a short, short skirt and a blouse open to her navel, the questions would have been easy. Tom Dunford led him to believe that was what to expect, a scheming, conniving gold digger. Instead, he was confronted by a professional executive assistant who was managing the office alone under trying circumstances.

"You reported to the constable this morning that you observed Mr. Flint embracing Mrs. Dunford?"

Christine blushed a little before answering. She seemed embarrassed to be spreading stories about her late boss. "Yes. Last Friday."

"And they kissed?"

"Yes."

"How would you describe that kiss?" Jim looked right into her eyes as he asked the question.

"It was a kiss. He hugged her real close and then put his lips on her forehead and gave her a kiss. It was right there by the office door as she was leaving. I know what I saw." Christine returned the stare without backing down an inch.

"On the forehead?" Jim failed to hide his surprise.

"Yes, on the forehead. They were standing right in front of me. They knew I was there and that I was watching. I had no choice. You could call it a discreet kiss in the presence of others."

Jim shook his head and closed his notebook. "How long have you been at Sky Jet?" he asked.

"Five years. I started when they acquired their second plane and became a multi-aircraft company. Craig had tried to run it all by himself up until then but finally realized he needed help with the paper work."

"Did you tell anyone else about this kiss?"

"I most certainly did not." Christine looked affronted by the suggestion. "I'm not the office gossip. There is a degree of confidentiality that is expected to accompany my position in the company." She hesitated before adding: "With Mr. Flint dead, telling the police was not breaking his confidence but helping with the investigation of his murder."

Murder, Jim thought. Not everyone needed confirmation from the experts. Her conclusion could be understood; this was the second time in the same morning that she was being interrogated.

"I'm not suggesting Tom Dunford is your killer," she went on, "but he has got a temper and I saw what I saw. I also heard Craig and Tom arguing last week, Thursday maybe. They often failed to see eye to eye on things. I thought you should know what took place."

Jim said, "You were right to tell us. Information of this nature often leads to the resolution of a case." He paused. "There was a slight flaw this time. Mrs. Dunford and Mr. Flint are brother and sister. Tom is Craig's brother-in-law."

Christine's mouth fell open. "No they're not. Are you sure? Tom and Craig are always at each other. They can never agree on anything. No wonder Tom never got fired."

The conclusion was swift and zeroed right in on the relationship. This explained why Tom wanted to keep it quiet, Jim thought. Nepotism must be how he keeps his job was the logical conclusion in everyone's mind.

"What about yourself?" Jim asked. "How would you describe your relationship with your boss?"

Christine stood a little straighter and involuntarily straightened her skirt. "Strictly professional," she said. "We occasionally shared a meal after working late and both enjoyed similar interests in the arts. We had season tickets at Neptune and often accompanied each other, but that is all it was. I know better than to get involved in office entanglements."

"Craig was good looking, had lots of money. You never thought, what if?"

"Never. Mr. Flint respected my dedication to the job. He even commented on how well I kept my personal life and office life separated. I was his executive assistant and was well paid for doing a good job. I understand the working of Sky Jet better than anyone except Mr. Flint. There was no other relationship. Did

Tom tell you there was? Sure he did. Let me assure you, any impropriety was only in his evil, little mind. He mentally undressed me so often, I have frostbite on my tushy."

Jim tried to detect if there was a note of disappointment in this description of her relationship with Craig. He didn't hear one. Perhaps the problem with Tom was only in Tom's mind as she suggested. He wouldn't be the first man to have difficulty working with a beautiful woman in a position of authority. Jim assumed part of Christine's job would involve passing Craig's wishes on while Craig was flying in other parts of the country or around the world. This could, to someone already resentful of her, seem like she was giving the orders. Tom had been with the company since the beginning. Christine had not arrived on the scene until a couple of years later and spent her time working very closely with the boss. Jim could understand Tom's resentment. He could also understand a single man's head being turned in Christine's presence. A married man might find the working relationship even more difficult to handle. Although the outfit was suited for business, Christine did fill it out in all the right places.

A tinge of red crept into Jim's face as he mentally redressed her. "Was there anyone with whom Mr. Flint was having a serious disagreement—clients, competitors, suppliers?"

Christine shook her head. "No," she said. She hesitated. "Oh, wait. Bob Lively was in here last week. They are in competition over a new contract for overseas shipping. Mr. Flint was telling Bob that the contract was all wrapped up. It was ours. Bob got red in the face and said 'We'll see about that,' before he stomped out the door. Mr. Flint laughed at him as he was leaving. It wasn't very professional.

"They're not really enemies though. In the time I've been here, I've seen them refer excess business to each other. It worked both ways, us to them, them to us. Mr. Flint was just giving him the needle that day. Laying it on quite thick. Our company is bigger than Bob's now and Mr. Flint pointed that out often."

Jim added this to his notes. The references to the shipping contract were adding up. It was time to go see the suppliers, to see how much was at stake and if Sky Jet really was a shoo-in to win the bid.

"Did this courtesy also exist with Rapid Air, the other bidder?"

"No, I don't think so. I don't know much about them. I've never set up a meeting or even a phone call with anyone at that company There doesn't seem to be the same rapport or animosity for that matter. It's like they are not even a player in the game."

Jim paused momentarily. He could think of nothing more to ask this pretty, young lady. He pulled a card from his pocket and passed it to Christine. "Call me, if you think of anything else. I may be in touch again."

He went out to the hallway to wait for the elevator. Christine seemed like a nice enough person to him, serious, dedicated, competent. He wondered what Tom Dunford's problem was. He also wondered if Christine would still have a job with Sky Jet if Tom and his wife became the majority shareholder in the company. Jim could smell a wrongful dismissal case brewing in the wings.

12

"COME ON, MAN," Shane Martin said. "Are we buying into that murder routine? Are you sure you didn't just faint? It was you going down that turned it from a stroke to homicide. I think Craig got himself overly upset, went out into the kitchen and blew a blood vessel or something. Nobody murdered him."

"I know. I know," Keith said. "I wanted to believe that too, but I got a call from George confirming the cops have determined it is murder." He paused, looking for the right words to express his nagging doubt. "There must be something to it. The autopsy results are not conclusive. They said the cause of death is unknown but of suspicious means. You would think that if it was just a straightforward heart attack or stroke or whatever, they would be able to say that without dancing around the issue."

"People die every day, man. There's not always a logical reason. He was in that dangerous age group, mid-40s. He didn't drink enough booze. Studies show a drink a day is good for you. Let's face it, every time we see him, he's either eating red meat or fried foods. His diet doesn't seem to have been heart healthy. You know he didn't handle stress well."

Keith said nothing. There were no arguments to counter the things Shane was saying. The two men had been friends since childhood and frequently had similar discussions. The beauty of their relationship was that they could agree to disagree. Even in disagreement they would still look at the other person's side of an argument. Keith was going to capitalize on this trait.

"According to George, Sergeant Mcdonald is treating it as a full-fledged homicide. I'm sure he'll be looking you up soon. I told him if he suspects one of us, you are the best bet."

There was laughter from the other end of the line. "I bet you did. I'll straighten him out when he gets here. Tell him you're the money man. They always suspect the money man."

"You're right about that. I was his first stop." Keith sounded serious again. "I want you to make some subtle inquiries around the flight line. See what the scuttlebutt is on Craig's sudden passing. See if anyone is taking an undue interest. You worked on his planes so no one is going to question your interest in the subject."

A deep sigh came across the telephone line. "Sure man, whatever you say. Unlike you, I don't have all the time in the world to fritter away. I work for a living you know. Don't you have investigators on your payroll? Why not use them?"

Keith laughed. "Sure you do. I want to keep this personal. Snoop around. See what you find out. I'll make it up to you. I have a road trip coming up. There's a software company in California I want to have a look at. You can come along as a technical expert, paid technical expert."

"I'd better come along. I wouldn't want to see you get tricked by a scam artist like that last guy we visited. Now, he was a piece of work."

"Don't be so hard on him. You have to admit his prospectus was the slickest thing to cross my desk in years. It's just too bad some of that hard work didn't actually go into developing a viable company."

"He had the patter down, too. Everything was going great until I asked a couple of questions about how he planned to power all that equipment and what his plans were to dissipate the heat it would generate. The questions caught him off guard but even then his answers sounded pretty convincing. Too bad they were so far from real life that even Commander Scott from the Starship Enterprise wouldn't be able to implement them."

Keith inflected a Scottish burr into his voice. "Nay, Captain, we'll never be able to make that work in time. We'll need a shipment of dilethium crystals before I can even start to fix it. It will take at least three days, probably four."

Shane joined in the charade. "We don't have that much time, Scottie. You have 45 minutes or the entire planet will be destroyed along with the Enterprise."

"Nay, Captain. I cannot do it in that time but we'll try our best."

Shane laughed. "And of course Scottie always came through but even he would have been foiled on this operation. There was no way in the world that company was ever going to go into production in the proposed premises, at least not without rewiring the entire building."

"Yeah, well, it was good trip, anyway," said Keith. "We've had a lot of those adventures over the years. I just wish you would come on staff with the company. I could make it worth your while."

"No," said Shane. "I like it better this way. Shane's Electrical is doing just fine, thank you. I like you better as a friend than as a boss."

"OK, friend. Nose around the hangars. See what you can find out. We owe it to Craig. We can throw resources at this investigation that the cops can only dream of. Money is no object. If it was murder, I want the bastard who did it caught and punished." Keith sounded as if he was about to break off the conversation when he added: "By the way, the funeral is Wednesday morning. That's the real reason George called. I told him I would pass the message along to you."

"So they've released the body. Doesn't that mean they know what killed him?"

"I guess so. That's why George said it was murder. They must be holding back the cause of death. Call me when you find something."

"You mean if I find something."

"No, I mean when. Keep looking until you do."

JIM LEFT THE offices of Sky Jet Charter just as the lunch hour was approaching. He was in the downtown area anyway so he decided to give his girlfriend, Stella Martin, a call to see if she was available for lunch. She was. They arranged a restaurant to meet at and both set out for the rendezvous.

Over lunch, he explained to Stella about the young lady he had just interviewed and the contrary opinion he had from that of Tom Dunford. Stella explained the dark business suit may have been just Christine's idea of the appropriate dress when your boss has just died and is still not planted in the ground. At this point, any client she met might be a potential new employer. It may be time to look for greener pastures. She obviously wouldn't have much chance for a future with Tom Dunford if what Jim was telling her was true.

This was an interesting assessment of the situation, Jim had to agree. Stella often gave him insights into things he was working on that would never occur to him or at least not occur to him without a lot of extra thinking. He thanked her with a kiss on the lips and they both went their respective ways until after work ended for the day.

Christine would not have known Tom Dunford was a possible successor to the reins of control at Sky Jet. The family relationship was news to her. Whether she was looking for a new sugar daddy to latch on to or just looking to maintain her position at Sky Jet with whomever took over, Stella's theory still held. Christine could be just dressing for success. Her garb was appropriate under the circumstances, just as the descriptions Jim had received from Tom would have been appropriate under those circumstances when Craig was alive and available.

After lunch, Jim checked in at headquarters to see if anything new had broken on the other active files he was working on and a brief but uneventful chat with the head of forensics. Nothing had been left out of his report. The crime scene just didn't add up to a crime scene. It was only a kitchen. No weapons, no strange powders, no mysterious substances of any description. Not even a body.

They had checked out Craig's remains, but by the time they had their turn, the body had been moved outdoors from the potentially hazardous kitchen, handled by firemen, paramedics and a doctor; and as a final insult, rained on. It was then run around the house and back into the living room. They found nothing on it to advance the investigation.

Both the kitchen door and the windows had been locked from the inside and showed no sign of forced entry. They could offer no suggestions as to how the probable contaminant had entered the kitchen or where the means of dispersal had disappeared, unless of course, the poker players were in on it. In that eventuality, there was no real mystery. They were the ones to call 9-1-1 on their own schedule.

Jim admitted he had come to that same conclusion. So far, he hadn't found either evidence or a motive to back up that point of view. He was still looking.

Jim headed out to the facilities of Shane Martin. Unlike the others who had downtown offices, Shane's Electrical was situated outside the city and near the airport. Once again Jim had done his homework.

He knew that the electrical company repaired, serviced and sold electrical items including components used on aircraft. They had been in business for over 10 years. The aircraft part of the endeavour coincided with the start of Sky Jet. The poker boys were keeping it all in one tight little group.

Jim pulled into the parking lot of the strip mall and looked for the sign. A blue and white neon sign indicated Shane's Electrical.

A chime rang as he entered the door and Shane Martin appeared from the workshop area behind the showroom.

"Sergeant Mcdonald, isn't it?" Shane asked without waiting for the policeman to introduce himself again. It had been only three days since their last meeting and the call from Keith had tipped Shane off to expect a visit from the police. This time he was dressed in a white shirt, a blue and gold tie with Captain Kirk on the front and an open, grey smock that went below his knees. A screwdriver and a continuity tester stuck out of the chest pocket. He wore dark wire-rimmed glasses which Jim didn't remember from their last meeting.

It was obvious that Shane was a hands-on kind of entrepreneur. Shane held the curtain back and said: "Perhaps it would be better if we meet back here in my office. There will be fewer interruptions."

Jim looked around the empty store before passing through the entrance. In back there were two more men dressed in grey smocks working at benches cluttered with bits of multicoloured wire, resistors with bands of red, blue and yellow on them and green circuit boards. Both looked him over before returning to their work without even a nod of greeting. Shane opened the door to a small office containing a desk, three chairs and a filing cabinet. On the walls were pictures of planes similar to the ones in Craig's office. Shane indicated a chair to Jim.

"Would you like tea or coffee?" Shane asked. An electric kettle sat on top of the filing cabinet with steam coming out of the spout. A half-dozen blue mugs hung from a rack on the wall with Shane's Electrical written on them. A squat bottle of instant coffee sat beside the kettle. Jim declined.

Shane unplugged the kettle, poured some water over a tea bag, took a similar chair on the same side of the desk as Jim and sat down.

"Any developments?" he asked before Jim could start the interview.

"Nothing definite," Jim found himself explaining again. "We are still waiting for forensics to come back."

"Man, it all happened so fast. One minute he was alive and enjoying his favourite pastime. The next, laid out on the floor, dead. It makes you think, doesn't it?"

"Ah, yeah," Jim said. He had seen so much sudden death that he seldom gave the matter much thought anymore. It took someone to remind him of how quickly things could change, someone who seemed shocked that it could happen, to make Jim realize the fragility of life. He should be more aware than most but instead sometimes he found himself immune to the concept. Death was a routine part of his job. "We never really know from moment to moment what is in store for us."

Shane nodded in agreement. "Right on, man. It makes me wonder why I'm here working so hard and not on some Caribbean island enjoying what's left of my existence on this planet."

Jim reached into his pocket and pulled out his notebook. It was time to get away from this philosophical talk. He found it depressing.

"You worked for Sky Jet Charter Services?" he started.

"No," Shane replied.

Jim was about to go on with his next question when the answer to the previous one registered. "You don't do work for Sky Jet? I thought you looked after the electronics?"

"Sky Jet Leasing is the one I'm contracted to, not Sky Jet Charter. They're two different companies. One's good to work for, the other, well, it would pay the bills but would be hard on your personal psyche."

"You work for Sky Jet Leasing? Who's your boss?" Jim was under the impression this was only a paper corporation. He didn't realize it actually employed people.

"Keith Grant contracts my services. I'm my own boss."

"Contracts your services?"

"Shane's Electrical takes care of all the radios, nav equipment, radars, stuff like that, on the planes. They don't belong to Sky Jet Charter, you know."

"Yeah, I know that but I thought it was a big secret. No one else seems to know this but you. George, the accountant, Tom, the brother-in-law, they don't know this." Jim hesitated. "Or if they do, they're telling me a different story. Do they know?"

His eyes flashed a little fire in Shane's direction. Jim did not like being lied to.

"No, they were telling the truth. This information is on a need-to-know basis. I was there when the deal came together. One of the card games seven or eight years ago, Keith and I had a little too much to drink. We thought it safer to stay at the cottage than to drive home in the wee hours of the morning.

"Craig had breakfast ready for us when we crawled out of bed the next morning. Don't you hate those people who abstain from alcohol? We sat around, ate our bacon and eggs and shot the shit for a while. Craig was always going on, in those days, about starting his own air charter company. He was like a broken record. When the subject came up again that morning, Keith asked him if he was serious about this."

Shane stopped talking and looked like he was lost in thought. Not only had Craig benefited from this conversation but Shane had moved out of his basement workshop into a real workshop with people working for him. He recalled the conversation for Jim almost word for word:

"Are you serious about this charter service or is this all just a bunch of pipe dreams?" Keith asked Craig when Craig started describing what he could do if only he had the seed money.

"I'm friggin' serious," Craig said. "As soon as I get enough put away for a down payment on a jet, I'm in business." He took a sip of his coffee and emphatically nodded his head to indicate this was no bullshit.

"So money is the only holdup?" Keith asked. "If you had the money, you would quit your job and start working for yourself. That would mean no security, no weekly paycheque, no holidays until you were established and maybe not even then."

Craig gave him a dismissive look. "You make it sound like getting hold of money is not a problem. These jets are expensive. The down payment is a big chunk of change. You might think you're well off but this is out of your league."

"You don't know who you're talking to, Craig," I said. "Well off doesn't even begin to describe what he owns."

Keith gave me a scalding look and turned back to Craig. "How much money are we talking about, just to buy the plane?"

Craig thought before answering, not sure if this was a serious conversation or just a couple of hung-over poker players having fun with him. "Eight million would cover the plane I want. You got it with you?"

"Not in cash, but I could write you a cheque."

Craig had his coffee mug on his way to his mouth when the statement was made. He spilled the coffee all over the front of his shirt. "Jesus," he yelled as he jumped up from the table. "Don't bullshit me on this. I'm serious about starting this company. I'm working on ways to raise some capital. You guys will see when I'm a millionaire."

Keith threw a cup towel that was hanging on the back of a chair over to him. "I'm serious too. I could buy the plane and lease it to your company exclusively. It could work out for both of us. Of course, I would want a piece of your action. Leasing fees alone wouldn't justify the risk."

"Get out of here," Craig said. "You don't have that kind of money."

"Funny thing," Shane said to the policeman. "We had been meeting once a month for about seven years by then to play poker and nobody knew much about the others. We had vague ideas about what kind of job each of us went to, but that was it. We all knew Craig was a pilot, George an accountant, I did electrical work and Keith was a financial adviser. My dad used to play with us in those days. He was retired."

"You seemed to know that Keith could swing this airplane deal. He must have been a successful financial adviser."

"Oh yeah, Keith and I were friends long before he had any money. He was just a struggling financial planner working for someone else then. Then one day this kid came in and wanted to know how he could raise some money fast. He had an idea for a company on the Internet. This was before most people even knew what the Internet was. It's hard to realize how recent a phenomenon it is. It was just before the dot.com boom.

"Keith listened to his idea. All the kid needed was some money for some computer equipment to set up his own website and the servers to run them on. They were more expensive in those days than they are now but still not out of Keith's reach. He made him the same offer he would make Craig a few years later. He would provide the equipment for a 30 per cent share in the undertaking. Pay the rent on a small office space for a few months.

"Well, the kid was a computer genius and anxious to get his business in operation. He jumped at the offer. Soon they were both dot.com millionaires. Keith soon lost interest in the company. He likes to feel the substance of his investments, and a few servers and storage disks didn't justify the value placed on the company shares. The value was in the data stored on the computers, the membership lists and stuff. That wasn't solid enough for Keith. He was a hard assets kind of guy. He and the kid sold out before the big bust came. He likes to let his customers think he saw it coming and shrewdly sold his shares while they were at their peak, but he told me it was just dumb luck.

"He came out of it as at least a multimillionaire, maybe even a billionaire, I'm not sure. He never talked much about his money. He bought a flashy car, started his own company, moved to better offices downtown and became his own best customer. Since then he has run the money beyond your imagination but other than the car and office, his lifestyle hasn't changed much. Well, he travels a lot more and works a lot less but he still has the same circle of friends."

"I thought all that dot.com crap was urban legend."

"Not in his case. The kid's family tried to accuse Keith of taking advantage and the boy told them all to get lost. He pointed out they all had the chance to get in on the ground floor but it took a stranger to put up the money he needed. Keith deserved any profits he earned."

"I guess that's true. He could just as easily have taken a bath," Mcdonald said

"He could have, but he's a good judge of people and not just stocks. You sure you don't want a coffee? I'm having some."

Shane got up and plugged the kettle in again. In seconds the already hot water was steaming. He made two cups of instant and sat down again.

"He offered to set me up in business a few times. I was happy doing what I was doing. Electronics has always been a hobby of mine. It was nice to make a living at it. I travelled with him now and then, when he was checking out some new business offering. Then when he started the leasing company, he needed someone to look after the equipment. Each plane he bought included courses at the company headquarters down in the States. This time he wouldn't take no for an answer. I was the one to take the training. I'm not a millionaire yet, but I get by quite well. I'm the exclusive dealer in the area for a lot of the stuff you see out there in my showroom. People who own their own planes generally have money to spend on them. It doesn't take much to convince them they need the latest and greatest gadget to come along."

Shane laughed out loud. "You should have seen the look on Craig's face when Keith pulled out his cheque book and wrote out the cheque right there at the kitchen table. He let Craig arrange the purchase. Craig knew what he needed. We agreed at the time to let everyone think that Craig was the sole owner of the company. We didn't want business getting in the way of a good poker game. At the time everyone thought $20 poorhouse was a big enough stake for the game. It has never changed. As Keith says, 25 cents, 25 thousand dollars, it's all the same to him. The important thing is winning."

Jim shook his head. These figures were beyond his comprehension. He was happy if he had enough to pay his bills each month and take his girlfriend out for a couple of restaurant meals with drinks. Eight-million-dollar airplanes were unthinkable and Keith Grant owned three of them.

"Does Tom Dunford know that Craig doesn't own the planes?" Jim was thinking that some people were in for a surprise at the reading of the will tomorrow.

"No, no one knows except me. Well, George must know that Craig leases them but I don't think he knows from whom. Isn't that what you told me when you came in?"

"That's my understanding. He just knows the name of the holding company. Who around the airport would want to see Craig dead? You must hear the local gossip."

"Dead is a pretty final beef, man. I don't know of anyone who takes the game that seriously. Most of the players get along with each other quite well. Pilots are sort of a fellowship unto themselves."

"Upset clients, girlfriends?"

Shane shook his head. "Craig never had either. He took care of people and they appreciated it. They always came back to him with their business."

"Are you sure it wasn't a stroke? I've seen people who've had strokes and it looked like a stroke to me, man. I hope you've got another source than Dr. Dow. I'm not sure he's even qualified to practice medicine anymore."

"The medical examiner is pretty sure it's murder. She's still looking for the exact cause. He died from respiratory distress from an unknown source. Once we know the source, we'll focus on how it ended up in the kitchen. You were there. Any ideas?"

"None. We had all been in the kitchen about 20 minutes earlier. The outside door was locked. I tried to get it open to ventilate the room. It's a mystery to me." Shane sipped his coffee and appeared to be in deep thought. Finally he shrugged his shoulders. "Can't help you."

"So who takes over the company now?" Jim asked. "You must spend a lot of time on the planes talking with the crew members. Who has the inside track?"

Shane shook his head. "Damned if I know. It might take two people to replace Craig, a pilot to take over his flying and an administrator type to run the company. The two positions don't have to be one person. Tom stands to have a say in who takes over. It may even be him. He's Craig's brother-in-law, you know."

Shane stopped talking. He seemed to be picturing Tom in the role of CEO of Sky Jet Charter. He nodded his head. "He could probably handle it. He has a good understanding of what is going on day to day. But, he's no Craig."

"Tom was alone outside before Craig went into the kitchen for the last time. Did he seem different in any way that night? Preoccupied? Nervous?"

Shane laughed out loud. "You suspect Tom of killing Craig. Man, you are so wrong. Tom wouldn't kill a mosquito if it was biting him. He hasn't got a violent bone in his body. The only things he was killing that night were brain cells. He was drinking whiskey on the rocks and sucking on cancer sticks."

He continued to chuckle. "I worked with these guys, remember. I was on board when they would be bickering about what kinds of towelettes should be in the washroom and where the coasters should be placed on the bar. Petty things. They appeared to be always at each other's throats but in truth they had great respect for what the other did. They loved each other, man. They wouldn't hurt each other."

Jim reached out and put his coffee mug on the desk. An interesting observation from someone who was in a position to see the two men in unguarded moments. He would consider what Shane had to say but murderers were often the least suspected people. "What about his competitors? Could any of them be responsible for this?"

Shane took a slow sip from his cup before answering. "Bob Lively really wanted this fish contract. He's looking to get another plane but can't secure the financing. That's the scuttlebutt around here. This contract would give him the leverage he needs to raise the capital for another jet. Right now he's too big for one plane and too small for two. He hasn't got an unlimited source of financing in his back pocket like Craig."

Shane snorted out another burst of laughter. "Craig kept telling Bob that if he knew how to run a company, he would be able to expand like Sky Jet. He even offered to take over the management of the company for him." Shane looked down smiling into the cup in his hand before going on. "They are supposed to be friends, no, they are friends, but Bob has got a temper.

He may have done something stupid but I'm not suggesting he did. It's just that Craig's teasing can be relentless sometimes.

Clients didn't receive the same treatment. Some may say Craig was shallow, but it was just good business practice to suck up to his regulars. They were the kind of people who expected it. Craig gave them what they wanted."

Jim perked up at this new information. None of the poker players seemed to be panning out as suspects.

To be honest, he was investigating them because he needed someplace to start and they happened to be handy. The $20 they played for wasn't the kind of money trail Jim was looking for. The millions involved in the lobster contract made a more compelling case for murder. It was time to take the investigation to the next level.

Jim had one more thing to do before abandoning the personal life of Craig Flint. He had to find out what was in the will. Craig may not own the planes, but he carried no debt for them either. They were not a liability of Sky Jet. There was going to be large amount of money distributed the next afternoon. Jim wanted to see which way it flowed.

I, CRAIG FLINT, being of sound mind and body, do hereby leave and *bequeath all my worldly goods in the manner prescribed below.*

Everyone in the room leaned in a little closer as the lawyer started to read the blue-covered document in his hand. There were no other sounds in the room, not even the sound of breathing. Everyone was listening for two things: the sound of their name and the list of things that followed it.

Present in the room were Tom Dunford and his wife, Mary, a surprise to no one, Keith Grant, Shane Martin and George Phillips, a surprise to them all. The last three were summoned while attending Craig's funeral that very morning. Craig had stipulated the reading of the will take place on the same day as the funeral. Also present were two other people, a man and a woman, unknown to the others, who looked lost and confused.

The lawyer, William Piers, senior partner of Piers, Robertson and Schofield, paused at this point and surveyed those sitting around the table.

"Please bear with me. This will is a little stranger reading than most, but what would you folks expect? You knew Craig as well as I did. To Dr. Falkner and

Mrs. Johannson, please be patient. You will not be disappointed, I'm sure."

The two people indicated shifted uncomfortably in their seats. They had only a vague idea who Craig Flint had been or how eccentric he had been. They only knew that they were invited to the reading of his will and both assumed that their respective organizations would be in for a bequest. That being the case, they were more than willing to put up with any strangeness.

Dr. Falkner had checked hospital records on Craig's name. He had been a patient on a few occasions but was not a great benefactor when it came to donations. He had been hesitant about giving up an afternoon to attend the reading but when he found out that Craig was reasonably wealthy, he opted to show up to represent the hospital.

Mrs. Johannson had also done a check on Craig before sacrificing her afternoon. Craig was on their list of donors but had not been a major contributor, averaging about $20 a year. The primary recipient of their money was a women's shelter and she had no information to indicate Craig had been an abuser of women or a relative of an abused person. Often people who included the shelter in their wills felt guilt in their final days and contributed heavily to the cause. Others were leaving behind sisters or nieces about whom they were worried and wanted to make sure help would be available if needed. Truth be told, Mrs. Johannson had shown up because she enjoyed sitting in on these readings and observing the heirs at their worst. Any donation would be a bonus.

Mr. Piers reached behind him to a small cart that had been wheeled in. He removed a white, linen cloth with gold flowers embroidered around the edge. Under it sat eight fine-cut crystal shot glasses, three-quarters filled with a golden amber liquid. The lawyer passed a glass to each attendee and kept one for himself.

"This is a single malt whiskey from our own Cape Breton Highlands, Glen Breton Rare," he said. "The bottle was part of the company's first run and has been sitting in my safe for the past five years. Craig invites us all to share in a toast to good times and good friends. Saluté." With that the lawyer threw back his drink. The others looked around the room at each other, surprised by the turn of events.

Keith looked at his watch. "2:05," he said. "One hell of an afternoon coffee break. To Craig." He raised his glass in the air before bringing it to his lips.

"To Craig," the others mumbled and together they drank from their glasses. Some took a little sip just to honour the memory of their host, others followed the lawyer's example and drank down the contents in one swallow. Deep expirations of air could be heard from a couple unfamiliar with the tendency of a single malt to steal your breath away. Tears came to their eyes.

"Good stuff," one of them said in a voice barely above a whisper.

Keith Grant took a sip. "This is too valuable a resource not to properly savour," he said. He took another sip, looked thoughtful for a second. "Incredibly smooth on the palate, with lovely fruity sweetness, gingery spice, rich nutty character and lots of dry peaty smoke and oak on the finish." He set his glass down and looked around the table. "Agreed?" The others looked at him without saying anything. They were unsure whether or not he was being serious in his analysis. "What's next in this little dog and pony show?" he asked.

Piers smiled. At least one of the crowd realized the afternoon was not going to proceed as a usual reading is expected to. He opened a drawer built into the table and withdrew a new deck of playing cards, found the red cellophane strip and peeled it around the box and removed the packaging.

"Gentlemen, when I asked you to attend this function, I requested that you bring $20 in cash." There were nods of agreement from around the table. He was only addressing Keith, Shane and George. The others looked confused but said nothing.

"One final game of poker, $20 poorhouse." The lawyer was reading from a paper in front of him again. "For years, money has never been a factor in our games. Today, we are going to make it a little more interesting. Only four of us have been in it from the beginning. Only those four get to play. I have no further use of the money, but I do love to win. If I win the hand, the money splits between the hospital foundation and the women's shelter. There are representatives from both organizations present to collect. If one of them failed to show, all the money will go to the one who did."

All eyes shifted to the two strangers. This explained their presence. The doctor took another sip of his whiskey. He wasn't sure what was going on but would accept any money coming his way. Heath care always needed any money it could get its hands on regardless of the means. The doctor said nothing but a secret wave of relief passed through him that he had opted to be at the reading and not out playing golf.

"Each of you, Keith, Shane and George, will ante up $20. My ante will be a cheque for one million dollars." Bill Piers held up the cheque for all to see.

A gasp came from the doctor. He drank the rest of his whiskey in a single gulp. Perspiration beaded on his forehead. Beside him the lady from the charity foundation slowly slipped from her chair in a dead faint. As soon as she touched the floor, she came to again, looked around in an embarrassed manner and crawled back into her seat.

"Did you say one million dollars?" she asked. The foundation she represented was a small one. This money was beyond their wildest dreams. It would keep them in operation for a number of years to come. "That would be one-half million each?"

George poured a glass of water from the pitcher on the table and offered it to her. "Five hundred thousand and thirty," he said. She took a big drink of the water and then held the glass to her forehead. "Go on," she said.

The lawyer fought back his look of concern and continued. He knew it was going to be a strange afternoon. "At the time of this writing, I cannot cover this cheque. If Keith Grant has done his job right, and I've lived long enough since writing this will, then I now can. If not, I expect Keith to cover it. He promised I'd get to play in a $1,000,000 poker game before I died."

Keith smiled at the instructions. Even from the grave, Craig was calling the shots. The others looked at him to see if Craig really had that kind of money available to cover the cheque without dissolving his company to get at the assets. Keith reached into his wallet and took out two tens. He threw them into the centre of the table.

"Let's play," he said.

A smile crossed Shane's face. He threw a 20 onto the table. "I'm in." He laughed. "One hand, one million bucks."

George sat there with a serious look on his face. He seemed to be pondering the enormity of the pot. He reached into his pocket and withdrew two 10-dollar bills folded neatly together and extracted one. He placed it on the table and smoothed out the creases, then placed the other one on top and repeated the procedure. "I'll play the hand," he said. His crisp new bills joined the others in the centre of the table along with the cheque covered with a string of zeros.

"Wait a minute. What the hell do you guys think you're doing? We're not going to squander a million dollars on a hand of poker." Tom was red in the face and standing at his spot at the table. "This is ludicrous."

The others turned and stared in the direction of the outburst in shocked silence.

"Let's not count our chickens before they hatch," Keith said breaking the hush that had settled over the table. "It's not your money yet." He laughed. "For now it's still up for grabs. Who deals?"

"I'll file an injunction. I'll contest the will." Tom wasn't giving up that easily.

"Sit down, Mr. Dunford." Piers took command of the situation. "Craig's instructions are very clear. This is part of his wishes and as Mr. Grant pointed out, it's still the estate's money at this point. Believe me, the will will stand up in a court of law."

Tom remained standing, looking from one to the other for support. He focused on George.

"George, you can see how wrong this is. Tell them it's wrong."

George shrugged his shoulders. "As usual," he said, "Craig will get his own way."

"Well then, I'm in too."

Tom pulled his wallet out of his pocket and opened the billfold section. A blush went over his already red face, turning it even deeper scarlet. He turned to his wife. "Put $20 in the pot for me, Mary, and deal yourself in too. We may as well increase our chances of winning."

The lawyer reached out and put his hand on Mary's arm. "Don't bother, dear," he said with fatherly concern. He had been the family lawyer for a good number of years. "Things have to be done as prescribed in this document. Tom, you're not in the game. Please sit down."

Mary gave Tom a scathing look, not because she disagreed with him, but because she knew if William Piers had drawn up this will, it would be worded in such a way as to make it incontestable. She had already fought that battle when her father died and most of his assets went to Craig, despite the fact that Mary had taken care of him in his declining years. She thought she was entitled to a much larger share because of her devotion to her father. Craig blamed her for the man's early death. He accused her of not providing the proper care. The wounds ran deep on both sides.

"Sit down, Tom," she said in voice designed for his ears only.

Tom took one last look around the table before conceding to his dead brother-in-law. He dropped heavily into the chair, his lower lip coming out into a pout. The two outsiders were embarrassed for him but they had a chance to win a half-million dollars for their cause. They were embarrassed but not sympathetic.

"OK," said Shane, "enough of the theatrics. Let's play poker."

The lawyer once again referred to the document in front of him.

"This being my last hand, we shall play it as we finished up every other poker night: five cards, dealt face up, best hand wins. Keith deals." The lawyer shuffled the deck of cards a couple of times and passed it to Keith.

A smile lit Keith's face as the cards came into his hands. "Gentlemen, let's play some big time poker." He divided the deck of cards into two piles and did a riffle shuffle, repeated the move twice more, then holding the deck in one hand he poked the centre cards forward and placed them on top. "As my father used to say, 'a poke for luck.'" He looked around at his fellow players. "Anyone want to cut the cards before I deal?"

"I will," said George and started to reach across the table. He pulled his hand back realizing how the speed with which he took up the offer might look. "It's not that I don't trust you, I just want to change your good luck for my own."

Keith grinned. "Go for it," he said and pushed the cards towards him.

George cut the cards almost to the bottom of the deck. "As my old grandfather used to say, 'A deep cut for deep luck.' We'll make this an ancestral battle."

Shane wiggled his fingers in front of him in the direction of the deck. "Opa, opa, opa," he said. "I might as well get my spell on the cards." There were smiles all round the room except from the Dunfords. They were sure it was their money being frittered away.

Keith slid the deck back in front of him without picking it up again. He took the top card of the deck by both ends causing it to make a snapping noise.

"Ace of spades, the death card. How appropriate." The others exchanged uneasy glances. Mary's face became visibly pale. Keith placed it in front of Shane.

"Spooky, but I'll take it."

Snap. Another card came off the deck. "Jack of clubs, first royalty." He threw the card across the table to land in front of George.

A third card came off the deck. "Seven of diamonds. Too bad, Craig, you're low man." He lay the card in front of the lawyer. "You are representing Craig's interests, I assume."

Piers nodded. "I guess I am." He studied the card. "I hope you can find a mate for that lucky seven though."

Keith removed the top card from the deck and placed it in front of himself. "King of spades. No royal flush for us," he said to Shane.

Keith wet his fingers and removed the next card from the deck. This time he didn't snap it, just slid it off.

"Two of spades, possible straight flush."

Shane smiled as if that was actually a possibility in this game. Of course it was, just highly unlikely.

Keith peeled off a five of diamonds and threw it over to George. "Two cards," he intoned.

He placed a 10 of clubs in front of the lawyer. "Possible straight." Piers remained silent.

Once again Keith wet his fingers. "King of diamonds," he said "A pair." He laid the card on top of the other king with both K's showing. He flashed a smile at his fellow competitors. No one returned it.

"Keep dealing," said Shane. "You haven't won yet."

"No, not yet." Keith flipped over the next card and slid it Shane's way. "Five of hearts, still straightening."

"OK, keep them coming," said Shane.

Keith's gaze shifted to George. "Not much there yet George. Let's see what we can do for you." Keith snapped another card off the deck and tossed it over to George's building pile. "Nine of hearts, sorry, pal."

"OK Craig, if you're here and have any control, now is the time to make your move." He turned up another card. "Three of diamonds." Keith made a show of looking towards the ceiling. "Gotta do better than that, Craig, old man. My two cards still beat your three."

Keith dealt the top card on to his pile. "Six of diamonds. Still a pair."

Keith paused so that everyone could grasp the situation before he continued.

"George's jack," he said as he turned up the jack of hearts and tossed it to Shane, "but you're not out of it yet."

He slid the two of hearts over to George. "No help. You're out of it George, sorry."

George studied his cards. He rearranged them in every possible way he could. He squared them up and spread them out again. Regardless of the rank of his fifth card, his hand could not become a winner. No combination of his cards and any other card in the deck would enable him to beat the pair of kings staring at him from across the table. His shoulders drooped and he slumped into his chair. The million was gone but he had never bet $20 before on one hand of cards. It was gone, too. It was the $20 that hurt the most. That was his own money.

"Make your move, Craig," Keith said. "Let us know you're still fighting." He turned over the next card. "Ooh, king of hearts. You're still a contender."

Mrs. Johannson leaned in closer for a better look. "Can we still win?" she whispered to the doctor. He was weighing the various options as the cards presented themselves.

"If we get another king, we will have a pair of kings-ten to that loud mouth's pair of kings-six. We're not out of it yet." The doctor had taken a dislike to Keith and his incessant chatter. He failed to realize this was a part of the game and a tradition that had been going on for 15 years.

Keith turned over his fourth card. "Four of diamonds. Still winning but no improvement."

There were still smiles at the table but now they were more forced. A million dollars rode on the turn of the next round of cards. Everyone except George still had a chance to win.

"Give me an ace," Shane said. "For a million bucks, lay an ace on me."

Keith grasped both ends of the top card, hesitated and then snapped it. "No luck," he said. "Four of hearts. I could have used that, Shane. You keep taking everyone else's good cards."

Shane studied his hand. "Did we say one-eyed jacks were wild? That gives me a low straight if they are." The others looked at the line of cards stretched out in front of Shane. Sure enough, he had a straight if the jack was wild. In many of the games they played one-eyed jacks, hearts and spades, were wild, but not this afternoon.

"Sorry buddy," said Keith. He sounded as if he might mean it. "Maybe we'll make that a rule the next time one of us dies."

Shane nodded. "Yeah, we will, man, we will."

Keith threw the queen of diamonds to George without comment. His chances had ended with the last card.

"If psychic power is in the room, we will know with this card," he said. "There is one chance in 34 of getting the other king. The odds are in my favour unless Craig intervenes himself." Keith turned up Craig's last card. "Five of clubs." Despite himself, Keith couldn't hold back the big smile that ripped across his face. "I guess the money is mine. You will never know if Craig could cover the cheque or not." He turned over a nine of diamonds onto his own hand. "Pair of kings are the winners. One million and 60 dollars."

Mrs. Johannson slumped back in her chair. "That's it? It's all over. He wins with a lousy pair of kings. One fucking million dollars on a pair of kings. I should have stayed at the office. I sure had enough work to do."

The mouths of all the others, except the doctor, dropped open. Stress can loosen the lips but no one expected anything like this from innocent looking Mrs. Johannson. Shane looked at Keith and winked. No one said anything.

The doctor looked at the cheque still lying on the table. The possibilities had been racing through his mind about what this sudden windfall money could provide, from more efficient sterilizing equipment to even hiring additional staff. He slid back his chair, too upset to risk talking. A half-million dollars could have been put to a lot of good use and here it was just gambled away. He stood.

"Please, doctor," the lawyer said, "sit down. That is not all you were here for. There is a bequest in the will for your hospital. This was just a little bonus that might have come your way. I had little control over Craig's whims but even I wouldn't have been a party to having you come for just this little display. Please, take your seat. Your afternoon is not going to be wasted." His gaze shifted to Mrs. Johannson as he made the last remark but the doctor took it to heart as well. It was as if the lawyer had been able to read his mind.

The doctor blushed a brilliant red. He was displaying the attributes of a bad loser. These other men had known the deceased for more than a decade. They were sharing a last moment with a friend. He, on the other hand, had to look up the name in the hospital registry to see who he was and even then he didn't bother to do any more research other than to find out that Craig possessed some wealth. He was listed as the owner of an airline charter service. The doctor resumed his seat. "Sorry," he said in a low voice. "It was exciting." He forced a smile.

"Not that exciting," said Shane. "The rich get richer. We poor working stiffs go home with $20 less. No beer this weekend." He struggled to look serious but then started laughing. He gave Keith a friendly punch on the shoulder. "Give the people the money. They need it more than you. Put a smile on their faces."

Keith scowled at Shane. He then looked from Mrs. Johannson to the doctor and back to Mrs. Johannson. Neither had any idea who he was. They didn't believe Shane's suggestion had any idea of becoming reality.

He could even sense the doctor's dislike for the way he had teased the others as he dealt the cards.

"What the hell, why not?" he said. There was no reaction from the others at the table. The import of his comments failed to sink into their funk from not splitting the million. Only the lawyer reacted.

"Is that what you want to do?" He was privy to the inner workings of both Sky Jet Charter and Sky Jet Leasing. He had handled the paper work. The move came as no surprise to him.

"Only if you will look after transferring the money from the estate to me and then to them with no additional cost to me. In other words, if you will do it pro bono. Make your contribution, Mr. Legal Eagle. Make the cheques out to them instead of me but still give me the charitable deduction."

Piers smiled. "I can probably make that work but only if they are willing to hang around for a few minutes longer after we dispense with the reading of the will. Let's not forget why we are here."

Mrs. Johannson looked at the doctor, then the lawyer, then to Keith Grant. "Did you just give us the million dollars?" she asked. She had suffered one disappointment already this afternoon. She wanted to be sure of her facts before getting excited about this. "I'm sorry. I must have misheard you." To her, the concept of someone winning a million dollars in one hand of poker was something you read in fiction books. That they would then turn around and give it away 20 seconds later was beyond her comprehension.

"Put it to good use," Keith said. He was no longer smiling. "I don't want to see your executives suddenly living the good life, or driving high-end automobiles. I want to see your clients' lives greatly improved. I'll be watching." The tone of his voice left little doubt as to the seriousness of his statement. He turned to the doctor. "A half-million dollars will just get lost in the black hole of expenses you people have. Please, try to squeeze some good out of it."

He turned to Shane. "I suppose you want your $20 back, as well?"

"No," Shane said. "You can take me out to supper after this show is over. You just won a mill. You can afford it. Bring George along, too. Force him to enjoy his money for a night. Buy the first round of drinks with his crisp new 10-dollar bills." Shane reached out and plucked the cash from the centre of the table. He separated George's bills from the others and stuffed them in Keith's chest pocket. The rest he threw in front of Keith. "I want you to buy me an imported, brown ale with that money. One of the expensive ones from one of these new craft breweries."

The rest of the afternoon went almost according to script. Each of the charities received another million dollars. Mary Dunford, Craig's sister, received most of the remainder of the estate. Along with her bequest came the tag line "To my sister Mary, who always tried to tell me how to run my business, here is your chance." The others weren't sure if it was humour or sarcasm. Mary simply blushed and passed the line off with "Craig was always such a kidder."

There was one principal exception to the estate. The cottage on the lake went to Keith.

Everyone, except Shane, was surprised that Keith Grant was such a benefactor. Shane understood the deep debt of gratitude that Craig owed Keith. Not everyone gets to fulfill their dreams. Craig had. The big surprise was yet to come. Mary and Tom Dunford were going to find out they were partners with Keith Grant in the ownership of Sky Jet Charters. The really big surprise would be that Keith, not they, was the principal owner of all the planes. With ownership of the hard assets came a large say in the running of the company. What is an air charter company without any planes to charter?

After everything was explained, Piers squared up his papers. "Any questions?" he asked.

"Only one," said Shane. "Are we going to divvy up the rest of that Glen Breton Scotch?"

DETECTIVE-SERGEANT JIM Mcdonald got to his feet as the elevator door slid open in the lobby of the law offices where Craig Flint's will had been read. All three men disembarking looked in his direction and then at each other. A look of annoyance passed among them.

"Here we go again," said Keith Grant. He scowled at the approaching police officer. "We've spent the day burying a very good friend and overseeing the divvying up of his estate. Now we just want to have some private time together. Make an appointment with my secretary."

Jim was doubly surprised. First, by this outburst. His opinion had been that none of these men seemed emotionally involved with Craig Flint. All three interviews he had held with them had been in their places of business. Life goes on seemed to be their attitude. And second, none of them had given any indication that they would be invited to the reading of the will. In fact, just the opposite was true. They had indicated they would not be present. More lies?

"Just one quick question," he said. "The will is a public document. I can read it at my leisure." He looked at all three men to make sure they understood they would not be revealing any confidential information with his question. "How about a quick summary?"

Keith Grant stepped up to him. "Two mill to charity, a mill to a poker hand, I get the cottage, the rest goes to his sister. Quick enough?" He pushed past the cop and headed for the door. Shane followed. George gave a quick shrug of his shoulders and joined the other two without adding anything to the description of the will.

Jim tried to digest the statement. "Poker hand?" he said. "Would you care to elaborate on that?"

The three men disappeared through the door leaving Jim standing there with more questions to seek answers to. What was the value of the cottage he referred to? What was the value of the "rest" and which charities got two million dollars? Motives for murder abounded in that five-second explanation. Follow the money.

The elevator doors opened again discharging Mary and Tom Dunford. This was not the place to confront a grieving sister. She may have inherited the "rest," but she didn't look happy. Tom followed his wife from the elevator. There was a slight smile on his face. He seemed to have gotten over his grief.

While he was deciding what to do next, he felt the vibrations of his cellphone. The caller ID indicated Brenda Davis again. The young constable was a digger. Jim took the call.

"Sergeant, Scott asked me to convey some information to you. It seems the mechanics who work on the Sky Jet fleet have picked up some rumours about Craig's death. Two men were in the airport coffee shop discussing the hiring of contract killers last week."

"Hit men?" Jim asked.

"That's what they claim. Both of them agree that is what the discussion was about. They tried to listen in but the others noticed them and changed the topic. This was before anyone was killed so they wrote it off as someone talking about a TV show or something. Now, in the light of what happened to Craig, they're not so sure."

"Do they know who these men were?" Jim had dealt with professional killers before. It was not a direction he wanted to see the case take. A professional would be long gone from this jurisdiction.

"Not exactly, but they've seen them around. They think they either work for one of the other charter companies or one of the outside companies that flies into Halifax now and then. Sometimes those guys bring their own crew. Scott wants me to remind you of the rental car near Craig's cottage." Brenda sounded like she was talking and listening at the same time.

"I was thinking about that, too" Jim said. "Where is Scott?"

"He's driving the car. We're on our way back to town. Do you want to meet somewhere?"

Jim watched as the Dunfords disappeared through the front door and onto the street. He would catch up to them later when he had more details about the will. "Meet me at headquarters," he said. "I'll be there in about 10 minutes. I'll wait for you."

"We'll be there in about 10 minutes as well. See you then."

The phone in Jim's hand went dead. Hiring a professional put everything in a different light. His conclusions about these people having the balls to kill someone would have to be revisited. Hiring a killer didn't take the same kind of nerve as personally carrying out the act. It also explained the difficulty of coming up with a cause of death. How had the medical examiner explained it? Death of unknown origin. That was in keeping with a professional hit.

Who had the resources to hire a professional hit? Three of the four owned their own successful business. No, that was four out of four. The fourth's spouse now owned her own airline.

Jim's thoughts turned from means to method. Not coming up with the exact cause of death didn't make the task of finding the killer impossible. Someone had dispersed a toxin somehow. People were involved. If a professional had been hired, someone had to know how to contact this person. Someone had met him, talked to him. Talking was the key word.

People loved to talk. They loved to share their secrets. The "I know something you don't" factor was at work here. Sooner or later someone always bragged about what they knew. The person bragged to would impose him or herself into the front line and spread the story. The trick for the police was to trace the thread of truth back to the source, not the friend of the friend but the actual source of the story. That process was now underway. Jim could only hope for a break to bring quick results. He went out to his car and headed back to the office.

16

KEITH, SHANE AND George sat in a booth at the Lion's Gate Pub, a modestly named, high-end restaurant across the street from the lawyer's office. Each held a small shot glass in his hands, the contents untouched.

"What shall we drink to?" asked Shane. "Craig's life, his death or to those of us left behind?"

"No, let's drink to dreams and having them fulfilled," said Keith. "Craig was one of the lucky ones to have achieved his. Anything else that would have happened to him would be anticlimactic. Owning his own airline was his lifelong dream." He held up his glass. "To life. To dreams. To having the two come together."

"To dreams," the other two murmured and clicked their glasses together before throwing back the shot of liquid.

Keith caught the waiter's eye and made a circle with his finger over the empty glasses. "Same again," he mouthed.

The waiter was too far away to hear the words but he got the message. Soon he appeared with another round of drinks. This time the three men just sipped the beverages.

"Trust Craig to turn the reading of his will into such a display. I'm surprised Bill Piers went along with it."

Shane laughed. "It was unique, but entertaining."

"Every time I suggested he get a will written, he would scoff at me. Thought he was too young. I guess by not taking it seriously he was laughing in the face of death."

"Death won," George said. "Always does."

"What do you think about this detective that is constantly hanging around?" said Shane. "Do you really think there's anything to this murder angle?"

Keith shook his head. "I don't know. I can think of a few times I wanted to kill Craig myself but I find it hard to believe anyone would actually do it."

George agreed. "Sergeant Mcdonald assured me it was poisoning but I still find that hard to believe. It looked like a stroke to me."

"No, it wasn't a stroke," said Keith. "The medical examiner said his throat closed off and instantly suffocated him. That sounds more like an allergic reaction or perhaps poisoning. It's just so hard to accept that someone you know so well could have been murdered. Besides, we were all there. How could someone poison him without us seeing or hearing something? You can't poison a person over the telephone."

Shane took another sip of his Baileys. "I don't know. Could the sound of the phone have tripped some switch that distributed the drug? It's hard to believe. Not only that, the investigators didn't find anything out of the ordinary. That cop is definitely treating it as a murder, though."

The other two men looked at him. "He's not telling us everything he knows," said Keith. "We seem to be his prime suspects." He looked around the table at the other two men. "I didn't do it."

"Me either," said Shane.

They both looked at George for his declaration of innocence.

"Don't be stupid. Of course, I didn't do it. Why would I?"

The three were silent for a minute, each lost in his own thoughts.

"What about Tom?" George said. "He had a lot to gain from Craig's passing. His wife now owns the company and he's probably in line to take over as chief operating officer. That's quite a move up from cleaning the planes."

"That's strictly serendipity for him," said Keith. "He hasn't got either the brains or the balls to pull something like this off. Whether he takes over the company or not remains to be seen. I was thinking of getting you to take over as caretaker manager until we can come up with a permanent replacement."

"Me?" said George. "What do I know about running an airline?" He paused for a beat. "And what makes you think you have any say in who takes over? It belongs to Mary Dunford now."

"That's right. I'll have to set up an appointment to talk to her right away. Do either of you know her? Is she a sensible person?"

George nodded his head. "I've met her a few times. We went to the same school but she is younger than me. She used to drop into Craig's downtown office on occasion. Usually she was interceding on Tom's behalf after another one of his arguments with Craig. Her reasoning may be blinded by her love for her husband.

"Tom did his best to hide the fact that he and Craig were related. He resented his wife intervening."

Shane studied his drink before looking up at Keith. "I know her as well as you do." He hesitated, thinking. "Not well at all. We met her once before all this happened. Tom brought her to the poker game one night, remember? She wanted to play and Craig went ballistic."

Keith smiled. "Right, I definitely remember that. It was about six years ago. We didn't argue with Craig because we all secretly agreed with him. Women would have ruined the game. Limited the freedom of expression." He laughed. "Craig could be stubborn." He bolted down the rest of his drink." The few times I met her after that were tainted by that encounter."

Shane allowed himself a slight smile as he remembered the discussion after the Dunfords had left. All macho "we don't need women around to have fun" talk. The consensus agreed with Craig's point of view. He became serious again. "She also wanted to work for Sky Jet at the time. Again, Craig put his foot down. Family was family and business was business. His subsequent squabbles with Tom proved that the two shouldn't be mixed, especially with Craig as part of the equation. Now she owns the company. It will be interesting to see how well she runs it."

"Great," said Keith. "I wonder how much the lawyer told them about the company or if they have yet to discover the behind-the-scenes workings."

Shane stuck his tongue in his glass to get at the last drop.

Keith scowled at him. "Show some class, will you? The owners here have standards." Both men laughed.

"Tom may not be a bad choice," Shane said. "He knows the day-to-day operation better than most people. His arguments with Craig weren't over personal things but operational things. He has some good ideas about how to run the company. Often, Craig implemented Tom's suggestions after a suitable period of time had passed. He never gave Tom credit but he did use his ideas."

"That was Craig," said George. "I'd tell him there were better ways to be doing things and he would laugh at me. A month later, some version of my suggestion would be put into place. He claimed he got advice from a number of sources and melded them together to form a new policy. He would thank me for my input but would never give me total credit." George shook his head as if he were thinking of some specific incidences. Then he brightened. "I didn't really care. I have my own company to operate. I'm not interested even if it was offered. I'm willing to bet my $20, that you took, that Mary has no intentions of having anyone run the company but herself."

"Maybe," Keith said. "But no bet. I don't know the woman well enough and I only bet on sure things."

Shane looked from George to Keith. "What about you? Did he steal any of your ideas?"

Keith shook his head. "I never gave him any. It was his company. He could run it any way he liked as long as he made money. On the few occasions I put my two cents worth in, they weren't suggestions. It was understood that I had veto power anytime a lot of cash was involved. After all, it was my money on the line."

George looked surprised. "Your money? What was your money?"

Keith realized what he had said. "I was an investor," he said, "and chairman of the board of directors." He laughed. "It was a small board, me and Craig. Let's just say I had a vested interest in the success of the company and leave it at that."

Blue Bird Enterprises, George thought, but said nothing. That's why Keith got the cottage. He was Craig's source of money and owned the bulk of the leasing company. George had been a long-time family friend. He knew of the animosity between Craig and Mary and why. As petty as it was, refusing to let Mary have the family cottage was so like Craig. Discretion was the backbone of George's line of work. He moved on to another topic.

"Where did the three million dollars come from that went to charity? I didn't realize Craig had that much money lying around."

"It wasn't exactly lying around," said Keith. "Most of the money came from a fund to buy a new two-seater executive jet. Craig thought a small, fast jet would add to the company's image. Right from the start he wanted a machine like that. I disagreed but set up a fund to buy one. It was invested fairly aggressively and was paying off. Possibly wasn't the best time to liquidate it, but, what the hell, he didn't need it anymore."

"So he was going to purchase his own planes instead of leasing them?"

"No, it was a personal dream of his, not a company dream. He just wanted it as a plaything. When he made out his will, I guess he accepted the fact that the dream would die with him and came up with an alternate way to disperse the funds.

"Now the poker game was pure genius. He once told me he'd like to go to Vegas and play in one of those million-dollar poker games. I told him to give me some money to invest every month and I'd see that he made it before he died. Initially, I thought he was joking, but one day he asked me how the fund was coming along. He caught me off-guard, but from that point on I added a hundred a month to one of my more aggressive venture capital funds.

"It drove my accountants crazy. I would invest sums like $250,000,100. 'What's with the extra hundred dollars?' they would ask and I would chuckle and tell them not to worry about it. I would have easily made several million if he had lived for another 25 years, but the fund did well. He died earlier than we planned. He could cover the bequest but just barely. Mary will get a couple hundred thousand in cash out of it. She'll think she's rich, for a while."

Keith looked at George and realized the depth of his statement. George was the accountant for the firm. Three million dollars was a lot of money for him to be unaware of.

"Sky Jet Charter and Sky Jet Leasing were completely separate companies. Nothing illegal was taking place. Your interest was strictly with the charter company. I looked after the leasing company myself. I also did Craig's personal investing and income taxes. Don't worry, everything was declared as it should be."

George forced a small smile. Keith had read his mind.

The maître de came and asked if they were ready to order yet. There was a table available in the dining room. As one, all three men checked their watches. Then they laughed.

"One would think hunger would be the deciding factor and not time," said Shane. "I'm ready to eat."

The others nodded their agreement, downed the rest of their drinks and moved to the dining room. They were led through the plush restaurant to a small alcove with a window looking out on the street. The table was set with fine crystal glasses and a full array of silverware.

"I was thinking of a hamburger," said Shane.

"They serve them here," said Keith. "They start at a little over $20 each."

Shane laughed. George shifted uncomfortably in his chair.

"Relax George. I'm paying. Ask me a business question and then I can write off the meal as an expense."

"No, no. I don't mind paying for myself. I've just never eaten here before. I'm not sure about the food."

Shane laughed. "I bet you haven't. Order the most expensive thing on the menu. It may be your only chance to try it."

"Look who just walked in," said Keith. "I'm willing to bet you're not the only virgin here, George."

The other two followed his gaze. Standing at the doorway waiting to be seated were Tom and Mary Dunford. They were both anxiously looking around at the unfamiliar surroundings. Mary looked like she was in awe of the place. Tom was trying to give the impression that this was old hat to him, just another routine meal. The host was paying little attention to them.

"Should we invite them over?" Keith asked.

"No," said Shane. "I think they are celebrating their new-found fortune. Let's let them enjoy it for a while and then drop over to their table after they've eaten."

Keith signalled for the waiter. "We may as well at least see that they get a good table. Otherwise they're liable to end up by the kitchen door."

The waiter hustled over to where the three were seated. "*Oui, Monsieur* Grant," he said. "You are ready to order?"

"Not quite. Those people waiting at the door are friends of mine. See that they get a good table, perhaps in the sun room. Take them a bottle of Jost '96 Riesling."

The waiter looked over at the entrance. "*Oui, Monsieur.* I shall speak to the maître de." He hurried over to his boss and whispered discreetly in his ear. The maître de looked over at Keith, nodded his acknowledgment and went to seat the Dunfords.

"Don't tell me," said Shane. "You own this place, too."

"A little piece, not the whole thing, maybe 30%."

"So much for discerning owners," said Shane. "The sky's the limit. Let's order."

"Try the hamburger. You'll never have another one like it. We start with the finest beef tenderloin, grind it so it's not too fine and then add just the right amount of fat to give it a taste and consistency to die for. I highly recommend it. It used to be one of Henry Ford's favourites, the son, not the old man. We got the recipe from Lee Iacocca."

All three ordered hamburgers and cold beer. It was too early for a fancy dinner. When the meal was finished the conversation turned back to murder and intrigue.

"Shane, as I said yesterday, you hang around the airport a lot. What have you found out?" asked Keith.

"Nothing yet, but I'm still asking."

"Good. Keep looking. See what you can find out. Talk to the people on the ground out there. George, check out the finances. See if there was something going on we don't know about. Let's give this poor policeman a hand. I'll talk to the other company owners who were bidding on the lobster contract. I'm curious about the tender process anyway. Let's see if anyone is changing their bids or if they are just relying on us not being able to compete."

George took a notebook out of his pocket and made a note to himself. "What if the Dunfords don't keep me on as the accountant?"

"I'm sure they will," said Keith. "They'll be curious to know exactly what they've inherited. You would be the obvious choice to tell them. I'm surprised Craig's lawyer didn't have you lay it all out for them at the reading of the will. I gave him a report on Craig's personal assets."

"He called me on Monday and wanted me to give him a complete financial report of the company for Wednesday. I told him I'd try my best but he wasn't giving me much time. I do have other clients to service as well. The report should be ready by tomorrow. It would have been ready this afternoon but with the funeral and the reading of the will, I ran out of time. With finances, you can't do a half-assed job. The figures have to be right. There can't be any bureaucratic double-talk covering up your lack of research and there can't be any guesses, no matter how good they might be. I'll finish it up tonight when I get away from you guys."

"What's another day or two?" said Shane. "Enjoy yourself tonight."

A shadow loomed over the table. "Thank you for the wine. It was excellent." Tom and Mary stood by the table. Keith signalled the waiter. Two more chairs appeared.

"Glad you enjoyed it. Sit down."

Tom looked at his watch and then at his wife. "We can't. Mary took a Valium along with the wine. I have to get her home. I have a meeting to attend. It's about the business."

About the business, Keith thought. He's slipping into the role of entrepreneur quite quickly.

"Sit down. The business can wait. You've only owned it for a couple of hours. You don't want to be making any hasty decisions until you get up to speed with what all is involved. I was just telling George, here, to meet and bring you up to date on what all you own. He thinks he'll have the report ready for you tomorrow afternoon or Friday at the latest."

Tom hesitated and then sat down. "I had a call from Roberto Masserati on Monday. He owns Rapid Air. In anticipation of Mary becoming owner of Sky Jet, he had a proposal for me. He doesn't think we'll be able to put a competitive bid together in time to meet the deadline on the overseas lobster contract. He's offered to buy one of the jets. We only got it for the new contract anyway so I told him I'd think about it. He wants to meet me tonight."

Shane looked at Keith with a "who's going to tell him what he owns?" look then said to Tom: "I wouldn't be making any commitments until I was sure of exactly what I owned. You want to be checking the terms of the will a little closer."

Tom scowled at him. "The terms were quite straight-forward. Mary got everything except the charity donation and the money from that stupid hand of poker. We're going to look into the validity of that. For some reason Keith got the family cottage. I don't understand that. Craig must have done that just for spite."

"Yeah man, Craig made major decisions out of spite." Shane returned the dirty look. He didn't like to be looked down on as hired help, especially by someone who had only moved up from that level in the last couple of hours. "That's how come he had an airline to leave to you."

"Sorry," Tom said to Keith. "I'm not quite sure what his motives were, but I'll find out tomorrow. We have another meeting with the lawyer in the afternoon. He's going to spell everything out then. Seems all the papers weren't ready for today." He looked at George as he made the last statement.

"Until that meeting, I'd hold off on all decisions," said Keith. "Call Masserati and cancel your appointment with him."

"I can't," said Tom. "He needs an answer right away so he can put his proposal together. I hold all the chips right now. He needs the plane more than I do."

"Cancel the meeting, Tom. You don't own any airplanes." The look on Keith's face should have left no room for argument.

Mary looked up. She had not been paying attention to the conversation. It seemed the weight of her brother's death weighed heavily on her.

"What do you mean?" she asked. "I remember telling Craig he was expanding too fast. He said not to worry; the planes were all paid for."

"Paid for, yes," said Keith. "Did he say who owned them?"

"He did," said Tom. "It was his company. He told me that enough times when we were discussing how things should be done."

"Cancel the meeting," said Keith again. "Wait until you talk to the lawyer. It will save you a lot of embarrassment."

Tom slid back his chair and took Mary by the hand. "The days of you guys telling me what to do are over. I'm my own man now. Let's go, Mary." He turned and headed for the door, his wife in tow.

Shane looked at Keith. "Aren't you going to stop him?"

"No, he can't sell what he doesn't own. Besides, I wonder what kind of price Masserati is offering." He signalled the waiter for another round of drinks.

17

SCOTT BOWEN PULLED his patrol car into the Irving gas station on the way back from the airport. Brenda got out and inserted the department credit card into the slot and started filling the tank. Two rows over, a man of about 30 replaced his nozzle, jumped into his car and sped off. The clerk came running from inside the station.

"Son of a bitch," she said. "That guy didn't pay for his gas."

"Blue Chevy?" asked Scott and pointed to the car speeding off down the street.

"That's the one," she said.

Scott looked over at Brenda. "That's enough. Get in." He flipped on the overhead flashing lights.

Brenda pulled the nozzle from the half-full tank and jumped into the car. "Grab my receipt," she said to the girl. "I'll be back for it."

Scott squealed his tires out of the station and on to the street, the siren howling. Cars pulled over. Scott could see the relieved looks on their faces as he sped by. The speed limit on the street was 50 km/h. The average speed was 70. Everyone was speeding.

He pulled up behind the blue Chevy five blocks from the station. The man pulled into the right-hand lane but kept on driving.

"That's him," said Brenda. She took the microphone and flipped the switch to the outside speaker. "Driver of the blue Chevrolet. Pull over."

The man looked into his rear-view mirror, slowed down and pulled to the side of the road. Brenda swung the computer towards her and ran the licence number for wants and warrants. Scott stopped the car behind the gas thief and got out.

He tapped on the closed window of the Chevy and waited as it powered down. "Licence and registration," he said.

Brenda approached the back of the car and stopped. She held up three fingers.

Scott took the man's papers and walked back to Brenda. "Three what?"

"Fourth time this car has been involved in a gas-and-dash. First time we've caught him. Last three times they didn't get the plate number, just a good description of the car."

Scott smiled and handed her the papers. "Run these while I have a chat with," he glanced down at the licence in Brenda's hand, "Mr. Dexter."

Scott returned to the open window. "Would you step out please, sir?"

Sweat ran down the man's face. "I know what this is about. I forgot to pay for my gas back there." He forced a chuckle. "I was thinking about the list of groceries my wife had given me to pick up and simply forgot. I'll run back and pay them."

"Step out of your car, sir." Scott opened the door.

Reluctantly, the man slid from behind the wheel. Traffic slowed down to view the action and then sped away as Scott swiftly patted the man down.

"Step back to our vehicle, please." Scott indicated the police cruiser and at the same time firmly took hold of the man's right arm.

Once Scott seated the man in the backseat, he looked over at Brenda. "This is the fourth time?"

"At least," she said. "Sometimes they don't get a description of the car."

Scott nodded. "Sir, you're under arrest for theft-under-$5000. We're taking you downtown to be booked. Your car will be towed."

"No. I forgot. It can happen to anyone. I have a lot on my mind. Those other three times are bullshit. It wasn't me."

"Well, sir, it appears to have been your car. So if you weren't driving, it must have been your wife. We'll go talk to her when we finish with you."

A look of horror appeared on the man's face. "No, my wife has her own car. She never drives this one."

"OK, for now you are under arrest. As a measure of good faith, I will take you back to the service station so that you can pay for today's infraction. The rest you can explain to a judge."

Scott climbed behind the wheel, ignoring the man's complaints and pulled a u-turn in traffic.

He turned to Brenda. "Give Sergeant Mcdonald a call. Tell him we are going to be a little late for our meeting." Brenda nodded and reached for her cellphone.

They drove the man back to the gas station where he paid for his gas, apologized but still insisted it was all a mistake. From there, they made the trip to police headquarters.

"You know we can't hold him," the desk sergeant said to Scott out of earshot of the perpetrator.

Scott smiled. "I know but look at him. He's sweating bullets over there in the cage."

It was true. This had become the man's worse nightmare and all over $30 worth of gas. He didn't know he would have to be released. Five minutes in jail on this occasion, bailing his car out of the impound lot and losing an afternoon's work to appear in court would serve as a future deterrent. The system could be made to work.

18

TOM DUNFORD WALKED into the Tim Horton's coffee shop and looked around at the patrons. The smell of freshly brewed coffee tickled Tom's nostrils. A man in the corner looked his way, smiled and waved. Tom eased through the tables and chairs and shook hands with Roberto Masserati who was now standing waiting for him.

Roberto had the carefree dress of a pilot from another era, leather bomber jacket, white open-necked shirt and even a silk scarf visible around his collar. He reached out a hand to Tom.

"Again, I am so sorry to hear about your brother-in-law," Roberto said. "It was all so sudden."

Tom acknowledged the expression of sympathy but said nothing. Both men sat down.

"Allow me to get you a coffee," Roberto said. He started to stand again.

Tom put his hand on Roberto's arm and held him in the chair. "No, that's not necessary. I just finished eating a few minutes ago at the Lion's Gate Pub." He looked to see if Masserati was duly impressed. Masserati showed no recognition of the restaurant.

The two men sat in silence for a few seconds before Roberto asked: "The reading of the will? It went as you expected?"

"More or less. Mary now owns Sky Jet Charter Services."

Roberto nodded his head. "Every cloud has a silver lining. Still, I'm sure that owning the company is little consolation for the loss of a brother."

"Yes, it is a sad time. The funeral was this morning."

Tom was saying all the right words but Roberto didn't notice any real sense of loss on Tom's part. He studied Tom for a moment longer before getting into the reason for the meeting.

"I haven't met your wife. Will she be actively running the company or will that chore pass on to you?"

Tom considered this question but instead of answering, he said: "We've been meeting regularly for a couple of months now. It's about time you met my wife and I, yours. I'm sure they would hit it off. We should go out for a meal sometime, soon." Money was no longer an object of concern. He could dine out as often as he wanted and wherever he wanted. It was time to expand his circle of friends to include other people in his class—other airline owners.

"Uh, yeah, sure," Roberto said. "We'll have to do that." He sipped his coffee. "About the planes. I really have to get my new bid together for the lobster contract. Are you going to risk putting a substandard proposal ahead or can we talk about a sale? If I were to take one of your jets off your hands, it would be a benefit to both companies."

"Yes, the jets. I guess that comes down to how much you're willing to pay. There will be no fire sales just because we lost our former CEO. I'm sure I can grow the business enough to utilize all three of our aircraft."

"No doubt you can, but let me assure you, it costs as much money to have one of those planes sitting on the ground as it does to have it in the air. This is a deal that will benefit both of us. Don't be insulted, but there is a learning curve you are going to have to participate in. Running an airline is not as straightforward as most people think. I would be more than willing to lend you my expertise while you get your feet under you. That's an offer I wish I had had when I first started. It would have saved me a lot of mistakes and thousands of dollars."

"I'm no neophyte. I've been in this business all my working life."

Roberto reached across the table and placed his hand on Tom's arm. "Of course you have. Don't misunderstand. I'm just making an offer as one friend to another. If there is ever anything I can do to help, please don't hesitate to call. I'm not suggesting you can't handle the job of running the company, I'm just offering my experience to make the transition from employee to owner easier for you."

"One friend to another," said Tom. "I like that. I'll keep you in mind if I come up against anything that I can't handle." Tom squared his shoulders and pulled down the cuffs of his shirt. "Now, about the jets. What kind of dollars are we talking about here?"

Roberto reached under the table and brought up a briefcase. He snapped it open and took out a sheaf of papers. "You currently own three planes. One is seven years old, a little long in the tooth. One is four years old. It still has some good hours left on it. One is less than a year old." He looked through the papers in his hand before continuing.

"For now, I just want to have my fleet looking better on paper while the bids are being considered. I would be willing to take the older plane, it's a Beechjet of some sort I believe, off your hands. It's due to be replaced anyway. My records indicate it has a lot of hours on the frame. This will only be a stopgap method for me until I get the contract and then I'll probably have to replace it myself."

Again he riffled through his papers, stopped and studied one with a list of figures on it and looked up at Tom again. "We're friends. I'm not going to take advantage of you. I'll give you almost a million dollars for the seven-year-old plane. Its best flying days are behind it but it will serve my purpose."

Tom's eyes brightened at the sound of the dollar figure. A smile lit up his face. "Why stop at almost a million? Let's make it an even million."

Roberto winced. "I thought these negotiations would be between two friends. I made my best offer right up front." He studied the figures again and then offered the paper to Tom. "You can see how many flying hours the plane has and look at the amount of service time it requires to keep it in the air. Over the past couple of years the latter figure has gone up while the former has gone down. This plane's a money loser but I will be honest, I do need it for my bid."

Tom studied the figures. He wondered where Roberto had obtained this information. These details would not be available to just anyone. He, for example, had never seen them. At the top of the page was the tail number of his jet. The figures had to be accurate and the number of hours of maintenance was quite high compared to the number of hours of flying time. It was time to make a decision about keeping this plane. Still, there was a lingering doubt about how this confidential information had come into Roberto's hands.

"Let me take your proposal, study it and I'll get back to you," Tom said.

Roberto looked disappointed. "I'm sorry," he said. "I misjudged you. I thought you'd be able to make this decision on your own. I guess I should have contacted your wife to start with."

"I can make the decision. I'm just not going to do it right here, right now. If you have a written proposal, give it to me and I will get back to you."

Roberto hesitated and then dug through his briefcase again. This time he pulled out a blue-covered proposal and offered it to Tom. He held on to it for a second after Tom had reached out for it.

"Of course, there would be a broker's fee that goes along with this proposal. That would come in cash to you when the deal is signed, say five percent. Get back to me as soon as possible, tomorrow night at the latest."

With that, Roberto drank down the last dregs of his coffee, got up and walked out the door leaving Tom alone at the table with the offer in his hand, almost a million dollars plus another five-percent, 45 thousand dollars, off the books that would be his alone. He dropped the file onto the table top and clasped his hands together to stop them from shaking.

19

"I DON'T UNDERSTAND. How can we have inherited an airline company and not own any airplanes?"

Tom and Mary Dunford, Keith Grant, George Phillips and Craig's lawyer, William Piers, were meeting in the firm's law offices. Tom had the report prepared by George Phillips in his hands. It outlined the assets of Sky Jet Charter Service and placed an approximate value on the company. He threw the papers down on the table.

"Craig told me on several occasions that he was the owner of Sky Jet Charter. He didn't have to answer to anyone when he made a decision except himself. He held this fact over my head like a goddamn hammer every time we got into an argument. This was always the line he used to close the argument. He answered to no one."

"That's true," the lawyer said. "Craig was the majority shareholder of Sky Jet Charter. He had complete control over the company. Now Mary owns his share of the company, 70%. She is the majority shareholder. Keith owns the minority interest in it. It just happens that Keith also is majority shareholder of the company that has ownership of the jets. Craig owned 30% of that company. Now that's yours. The planes are exclusively available to Sky Jet Charter. They're yours to use but not to sell."

Piers stopped for a breath. "Let me tell you, the sweetheart deal you are getting on the leasing terms verge on being illegal. I expect the Canadian tax people to open an investigation every time I see them. I don't even want to know how Mr. Grant justifies the existence of the company to the tax people but Sky Jet Charter is the big winner. The operation has been running smoothly for seven years."

Keith laughed at the tax implication. "You only have to show an expectation of profit in your business dealings, not an actual profit." Keith looked over at George for verification. "Right, George?"

"Somewhere down the line they expect you to make some actual money, that's right."

Tom was not interested in listening to reasoning. "We own one-third of the company. There are three planes. That means one of the planes belongs to us. I can do anything I want with it." He gave the others in the room a smug smile.

Keith Grant pushed the papers in front of him to the centre of the table and got to his feet. He leaned over the table in Tom's direction. "Your wife owns one wing and the tail section where the SJC logo is displayed on each of three planes. I own the cabin, the other wing and the engines. You, my friend, own nothing. I thought Craig was pigheaded. At least he knew what he was talking about. His main desire was to own a charter company. Be in charge, his own boss. Money was secondary to him. But he ran it successfully and it made money because of his hard work."

"Everyone settle down," Piers said. He turned the thrown papers around to face him and flipped to the last page. He tapped his fingers on the bottom-line figure and looked at Tom. "I don't know why you're so upset. Sky Jet Charter Services is worth a considerable amount of money and thanks to the arrangement between Keith and Craig, your company is debt-free. Craig was more than pleased with the arrangement. It enabled him to expand three times as fast as comparable companies in this field. Take a look at Lively Charters or Rapid Air. They are all competing in the same environment and they are lagging further behind every year."

Piers tried to hide his irritation. This was an all-too-common part of distributing assets from an estate, especially when there was a considerable amount involved. There was always at least one heir who overestimated the value of what he or she should be receiving. In this case, Tom was not even an heir. He was only married to one.

Piers shifted his gaze to Mary. "Right now, Mary, you are the owner of a viable and successful company. It is important for you to realize what is involved and to make sure that the business keeps running as it has in the past. You will eventually put your own stamp on it but for now, my advice is don't rock the boat. Keep things going the way they have in the past, at least until you get a feeling for what is going on at the company.

"Keith and George are here to offer you advice and to help you in any way they can. Use their expertise. It's up to you to pick a new manager but do it wisely."

Tom perked up at that comment. "A manager? We can manage the company just fine ourselves. I know more about the company than these two jokers do. I've never even seen Keith Grant anywhere near the place except as a pampered customer. What the hell does he know about running a business?"

"Are you even listening?" Piers asked. "Keith owns the airplanes. He leases his planes to you. He puts the air in your airline business."

Keith placed his hand on the back of the lawyer's to stop him from talking.

"Listen Tom," he said, "I understand you feel like you've been left out of the loop. No one knew of our arrangement except for myself, Craig and Mr. Piers, who set it up, and Shane Martin who services the planes. Even George didn't know about this until yesterday and he's been the accountant from the beginning of Sky Jet Charter. This was the way Craig wanted things done and as you know, what Craig wanted, Craig got."

Tom involuntarily nodded at that statement. It was more than true; he knew that from personal experience.

"We've had a successful partnership running for seven years. There's no reason for that to change now. I never told Craig how to run the business, I don't intend to tell you. But you must realize I do have a vested interest in the success of the company. If I see something I think is amiss, I will offer my advice and I would hope you would consider if very strongly."

Keith reached his hand across the table. "Let's shake on our new partnership."

Tom stared at the hand but made no move to reach for it. His wife looked at him, shoved him aside and took Keith's hand. "To a successful partnership," she said. "I'm quite sure I can manage this company myself. I look forward to working with you."

Keith smiled. "And I with you. I'm glad that's all straightened out." He looked over at Tom. "Did you have that meeting you told me about last night or did you postpone it?"

Tom glared at him. "I had the meeting."

This was a reminder of one more embarrassment. Now he had to tell his friend, Roberto Masserati, that he couldn't sell him one of the jets, not because he couldn't make a decision, but because he didn't even own it.

"Good," Keith said. "I'd like you to brief me about what went on." This was said in a crisp business-like manner and not with any suggestion of "I told you so." The acrimony of just minutes ago seemed to have been forgotten. "Perhaps we could meet briefly when this session breaks up."

Tom was surprised by the suggestion. This was not the wise-cracking, smart-mouth Keith Grant he knew from the poker games. This one was all business. "Sure," he said, "if you want to."

"I do. I'm curious about the offer. Let's grab a coffee."

SERGEANT MCDONALD WAS back at the airport. He and Scott Bowen were sipping coffee in the cafeteria where the smell of jet fuel and grease competed with the aroma of coffee. Most of the clientele wore either coveralls or one-piece flight suits, blue being the favoured colour. Most had some sort of hearing protection hanging around their necks. Conversation at the tables around them, all of it loud, centred on maintenance techniques and turnaround times. No one paid much attention to the two men dressed in their business suits.

"Sorry, Sergeant, I don't see the men who gave me the information about guns for hire," Scott said. He studied the faces of those around him. The large, round, white-faced clock over the door indicated it was now 25 minutes to 11 and the crowd was starting to make its way to the door. The morning coffee break was over.

"You have talked to most of these people?" Jim swept his hand around the room to indicate just about everybody.

"Everyone I could. When they leave here, they disappear into all sorts of nooks and crannies. I was in uniform yesterday. It gave me access to walk around freely. They don't recognize me dressed like this. Some of the offices were empty. The planes were dispatched and most of the company with them. There are some small operations here, one-and two-man."

"Maybe they were just avoiding you. Who knows what they carry on these jaunts in and out of the country? A uniformed cop could be there to arrest somebody."

Scott winced. That thought had not occurred to him. "Maybe. The hangar where I talked to the mechanics yesterday is empty. That means the men are either off today, or have flown out with their plane to some other location."

"Let's find the field administrator. He might be able to give us a lead as to where to find them. Did you say they worked for Sky Jet Charter?"

"Yes, I did."

"I'll call Christine at the downtown office. She must know the procedure." Just the mention of her name brought back the image of the attractive red-headed secretary. "Maybe I should drop in and talk to her in person."

"Talk to her in person? That's a long way to travel to ask a simple question."

"You wouldn't think so if you had met her." Jim moved his hands in a downward motion describing the curves of a female body. The death had happened almost a week ago and although the investigation was as serious as ever, the solemnity of the event was fading. Finding the solution to the crime was becoming the main factor. The fact that a man had died was merely the triggering action of the exercise.

As they were about to get up and leave, a familiar face entered the cafeteria. By now the staff outnumbered the customers. Shane Martin immediately noticed the two policemen.

"Good morning, Sergeant. What brings you out this way?"

"We just have a few more people to talk to. Perhaps you could help us."

Shane grabbed a chair from a nearby table and hauled it up to where the two cops were sitting. He signalled one of the cafeteria line people to bring him a coffee and sat down.

"This is a cafeteria," the man said. "We don't do table service." Despite his words, hc had a cup of black coffee in his hands and set it down in front of Shane.

"Roger that," Shane said and flipped a toonie at the man. "Keep the change." He then turned to Sergeant Mcdonald. "How can I be of service, man? Anything to get this thing cleaned up."

Jim pulled his chair back a little from the table. Shane was right in his face. "Do you know the mechanics who work on the Sky Jet planes?

"Sure, we work together all the time. You don't suspect them, do you?" Shane let out a deep laugh. "Man, you are barking up the wrong tree with those guys. If they wanted to kill Craig or anyone else, they would clock them on the side of the head with a wrench. There would be no subterfuge designed to imitate a stroke. But, that said, they would have no reason to want to kill the hand that feeds them. Working on Sky Jet planes is a pretty good gig, believe me, I know."

"No, no. They're not suspects. We believe they have some information that may be helpful to us. We just want to talk to them."

"Closing down for even a half day yesterday jammed up our schedule. All the planes are out and depending on where they are going, they usually take a mechanic with them. Some of the places we land don't offer much in the way of support services. It's wise to take it with you if you have a tight schedule. I'll check the logs and see where everyone is."

Shane took a sip of his coffee before going on. "I work on the planes. Is there anything I can do to help?"

Jim thought about his offer. A hired killer was an intriguing idea but he didn't want to crank up the rumour mill without talking to the mechanics personally. Scott was a good cop but Jim followed his own instincts when it came to how much information was released. For the moment he would keep these suspicions under wraps. Just one question about a hired hit would be enough to spread the story through the airport and out into the public domain. Jim wanted to prevent that from happening until he learned more.

"You haven't thought of anything new since we last talked, have you? Haven't picked up any scuttlebutt?" This opening gave Shane a chance to talk about any rumours he might have heard, his own hit man stories. Jim waited, unsure of what kind of answer he wanted to hear. The mechanics may have already talked to others about their suspicions.

"No. I'm still not convinced it was anything other than a routine, middle-aged, premature death. He lived the lifestyle. Rich food, irregular hours, lots of stress, didn't drink enough. Sorry, still can't help." Shane had yet to buy into the homicide scenario.

Jim flipped through the pages of his notebook, going over his notes on the case. He was quiet for a moment, pensive. Finally he laid his book on the table and tapped a page with his finger.

"Let me assure you, your friend was murdered. We know that for a fact. Accidents don't clean up after themselves and he didn't have a stroke. It was murder."

Shane sat back in his seat. Both Keith and George had told him Craig had been murdered. The death lacked the drama that should have accompanied a homicide. Shane had fought the urge to buy in to the story. Murder could mean that one of his friends was a murderer. Now the cop had spelled it out in no uncertain terms. It was time to get on board with reality. He slowly shook his head. "It's so hard to believe."

"True, but now it's time to catch the killer. What can you tell me about Lively Charters? Would you consider them the most likely successor to the lobster contract now that Sky Jet is out of the way?"

"Is Sky Jet out of the running? I hadn't been told."

This answer caught the policeman off guard. Everyone else he had interviewed thought it was a given that Sky Jet would drop out of the competition for now. He had accepted it as a given. Maybe that was an incorrect presumption.

"Bob Lively's business has suffered a little since Sky Jet added the third plane to its fleet," Shane continued. "They were used to getting our sloppy seconds. Craig treated Lively as a subsidiary. He would accept business that we were too busy to handle just in case there was a cancellation. Then he would pass it on to Bob who would jump through hoops to work it into his schedule. He was happy for the business but resented the way Craig passed it on to him."

The sergeant added this information to his notes. Others had told him that Sky Jet often passed business on to Lively. This description of how the business was passed on threw a new light on the relationship. The previous view would suggest cooperation. This view could generate resentment.

Shane waited. When no more questions were forthcoming, he slid back his chair. "I just came in for some pastries for my staff. Meet me at the Sky Jet hangar and I'll tell you who went where and for how long." With that, he went to the counter, filled a small, white box with a few varieties of Danish, some fruit-filled, some cream-filled, and went out the door.

Jim and Scott took one last gulp of their coffee and followed him. A Learjet 60 started letting out a high-pitched whine from its high mounted twin engines as it prepared to head out from the hangar area to the flight line. Heads could be seen in four of the five windows running down the side. Shane slipped on the earphones. Jim and Scott covered their ears with their hands to little avail and picked up the pace towards the Sky Jet hangar. The sleek, needle-shaped plane angled away from them, increasing the noise level. Jim and Scott slipped inside the hangar behind Shane.

Three clipboards were hanging on the wall with a picture of a different plane above each. Shane scanned the top pages.

"Your men have left the country, Sergeant. They are cruising around Europe. Will be for a week. Sorry."

He flipped up a couple of pages.

"I can give you an itinerary if you would like to try and track them down."

Jim thought about the offer and then declined. He would rather talk to them in person. He could gather more information that way.

"I guess I'll have to settle for a return date and time," he said.

Scott looked over Shane's shoulder. Monte Carlo was part of the trip plan.

"Maybe we should take an overseas trip to interview them," he said with a smile.

"Yeah," Jim said. "That would come from your budget."

TOM DUNFORD SAT at a table in the same alcove where he and Keith Grant had exchanged words the night before. He squinted out the window at the traffic moving by on the street. The bright sun streamed in the window when he pulled back the curtains.

People were walking, head down, ignoring all those around them. By reaching out their arms, they could touch at least two other people but they knew absolutely nothing about these strangers and couldn't care less.

Tom had been playing poker off and on with the same people for almost seven years. Craig Flint was his own brother-in-law and employer. And yet, he knew as much about them as the strangers passing in the street. Nothing. Keith Grant was filthy rich. Tom had had no idea of that. He owned what should have been Tom's airplanes. Tom didn't have an inkling of that before today. Craig ran an airline without owning any airplanes. Tom had worked on those planes for seven years and didn't know they weren't Craig's. How could he have been associated with these people as regularly as he was and not know any of this? Was one of these people a murderer? Had they stolen the assets of his company after Craig died? Was the family lawyer involved? Tom was confused.

A waiter brought over two coffees and a tray of cheese and crackers. Tom looked around and saw Keith still talking to the maître de. Did he own this place as well? Nothing surprised Tom anymore. He sipped his coffee and smiled. Now, this was good coffee. He put a small amount of Danish blue cheese on an onion cracker and crunched it in his mouth. Hanging out with Keith Grant did have its advantages. He looked around at the other patrons. Conservative business suits on the men, sedate but fashionable outfits on the women. This was not the Tim Horton's crowd.

Still, he had to remember why he was here. Grant intended to pump him about the meeting that he, Tom, had held with his good friend Roberto Masserati. He had to figure out where his loyalties lie. Were they with his old friend Roberto or his new business partner, Grant? Tom had no time to contemplate this. Grant was on his way to the table.

"Well, Tom," Keith said, "what does Masserati think our planes are worth?"

There was no small talk. Not even "how's the coffee?" Tom was being welcomed into the world where time was money. He had to decide right now whose side he was on.

"Roberto is willing to take the Beechjet 400, that's our oldest plane, off our hands for about a million dollars. He realizes the plane is a money loser but he needs to pad his bid for the lobster contract. He needs an answer right away."

The expression on Keith Grant's face remained unchanged. "A million?" He seemed to think about the figure for a few seconds. "Do you think that's a good offer?"

Last night Tom thought it was a great figure if it could be rounded up a little to the even million. A million in cash would be a great way to start his new life. He and his wife had inherited a viable company but there was little in the way of liquid assets, no really serious hard cash. He tried to read Grant's face. He could seldom read it at the poker games. Here, with this kind of money on the line, it was impossible. Grant was waiting for an answer.

"I told him I would have to think it over."

"My question is 'Do you think it's a good offer?'"

Grant's eyes burrowed into Tom's eyes, seeming to look right into his brain. Tom wanted to look away but knew he shouldn't. He had to come up with an answer, an answer that made sense.

"It is an old plane, the oldest in the fleet. It's past its prime and is costing us money to keep in the air. He showed me the figures on the maintenance costs. If we sold it and replaced it with a new one, we would be saving money in the long run." Tom smiled. He liked the sound of his reply. It showed he belonged at this table with Keith Grant. He was every bit the businessman that Keith was.

Keith said nothing. He picked up his coffee, black, and sipped it without taking his eyes off Tom's face. Tom found the silence unbearable. He felt he should be saying something more to defend his position. But what more could he say? All he knew was what Roberto had told him. He hadn't even checked to see if the figures were accurate.

Finally, Keith put down his coffee. "Have you given any thought to making a new bid on the lobster contract yourself?"

The change in direction caught Tom off guard. He couldn't admit that his only thoughts had been on the million dollars Roberto had offered. A new bid should have been his first priority, even if only to decide it was not feasible. Was it a possibility? He didn't want to guess. Grant had most likely weighed the options and knew the correct answer.

"I have been considering it but have not reached any conclusions yet."

"Time is ticking. We only have a day or so to decide. The new bid has to be submitted by the end of next week. What changes would we have to make in Craig's bid?"

Craig's bid? Tom hadn't even read it.

"I'll get you a copy and we can go over it," Keith said.

Being a big-time businessman seemed to be about how fast you could dance, how well you reacted to the changes in the music.

"How do you know Roberto Masserati?" Another sudden shift in direction.

"Roberto and I have been friends for a little over a year. He filled in for you at the poker game a couple of times. Shane Martin introduced us."

"Shane Martin?" This information caught Grant off guard for the first time since he sat down with Tom. Shane never indicated he knew Masserati well enough to be introducing him to people. When had he missed a poker game? Last March, he remembered. He had been caught in China on a business trip and couldn't get back. Craig was pissed. Thought he should have tried harder. The deal was worth a little over a billion dollars, but Craig could only see that he missed the poker game. Masserati had filled in for him. He didn't know that.

"I was in Shane's electronic shop," Tom was saying. "There was a light array burned out in the cabin of one of the planes and I dropped in to inform Shane as I was passing. Roberto was there looking at some equipment. It was some sort of entertainment games unit, as I recall. Shane introduced us and since we had similar equipment on our jets, Shane sought my opinion of the value it added to the service. He was seeking an endorsement so he could make the sale, I guess. I thought it was a worthwhile addition and said so. Roberto invited me for a coffee to discuss why. Turns out we have a lot in common, both in the business, and we've been meeting off and on ever since. In the last couple of months we've been meeting two or three times a week."

Keith rubbed his chin. "Interesting. Did he know you were related to Craig?"

Tom blushed a little. He had implied to Roberto that his role in the company was a little more than was the actual case and suggested the family involvement gave him a stake in the company. He told none of this to Grant. "It may have come up in our discussions," he said.

"So Roberto knew you were in line to inherit the company? Or at least that Mary was?"

"I don't know. It never came up."

"But he did approach you about selling one of the planes as soon as the news of Craig's death became known?"

Tom thought about this. "Yes, I guess he did. On Monday, in fact."

"Interesting," Keith said. He looked as his watch. "Let's get together later this afternoon and see what kind of a proposal we can put together for the lobster contract." He reached out to shake Tom's hand. This time Tom responded. Keith stood and left, leaving Tom still sitting there.

"What should I tell him about the offer to buy the plane?" Tom called out. Either Keith didn't hear him or ignored the question. At any rate, he didn't look back, leaving Tom to draw his own conclusions. "I guess we're not selling," he said to himself.

22

"THE COPS ARE trying to track down a couple of our mechanics," Shane Martin said to Keith Grant. The two were sitting in Shane's office at the airport. Keith had driven there immediately after talking to Tom. He wanted to bring Shane up to speed on this new information about Roberto and Tom. To Keith, this relationship smacked of conspiracy.

"It seems they gave some information to one of the uniformed guys who were around asking questions yesterday," Shane said. "Now Sergeant Mcdonald wants to talk to them himself. I couldn't get a lead on what it's all about but the mechanics won't be back for a week. Both planes are on an extended jaunt around Europe. Robert St. Louis has chartered them both. He's taking a group of veterans of the Second World War on a tour of some of the old battle sites."

"Our mechanics? Which ones?"

"Harry and Jerome."

"Christ, they've been with us from the beginning. They wouldn't want to hurt Craig. What would they know?"

"That's what I told the sergeant but he wouldn't give up any info. He's one cool dude when it comes to interrogation. He really plays his cards close to his chest."

"Does he or is it just that he doesn't know anything and wants to imply that he does?" Keith took a pastry from Shane's desk and nibbled a bite off one side. "Tom Dunford told me you introduced him to Roberto Masserati."

"Who?"

"Masserati. He owns Rapid Air Jet Delivery Service. Played at one of the poker games."

Shane furrowed his brow as he concentrated on remembering the introduction. "Masserati's a customer but I don't remember hooking the two of them up. When was this supposed to have happened?"

"A year or so ago. You were trying to sell Masserati something and asked Tom for an endorsement. They've been meeting ever since but a lot more often lately."

"Right, the game system for the passenger compartment. Masserati couldn't afford it. He tried to get me to install one as a demonstration item. Claimed he would be able to sell a bunch of them for me. I passed. A short time later he showed up at one of the poker games. I thought it was Craig's idea. He asked too many questions and was never invited back. What's Tom doing mixed up with him?"

"Exactly what I was wondering." Keith took a bigger bite of the pastry and returned it to the box. He took a sip of his coffee, screwed up his face and scowled at Shane. "Instant. I'll have to teach you how to make this the right way so you can serve it to your customers and not be embarrassed."

"You're supposed to drink it while it's hot. I didn't know you were an expert on coffee. Don't tell me you own Tim Hortons."

Keith frowned and shook his head. "I had the chance. Years ago someone asked me to invest in it. I told him you'd never get rich selling coffee and donuts. I guess I don't know everything."

Shane laughed. "I was never under that misapprehension." He got back on topic. "Did Tom meet with Masserati last night?"

"Oh yeah, that meeting took place. Masserati offered him about a million for the Beechjet." Keith made little quote marks with two fingers on each hand to emphasize the words "about a million." "Told him the plane was past its prime and Tom bought the story."

Shane choked back a laugh. "Past its prime? That plane is practically new. We've only had it for seven years. It has another 25 years of easy maintenance left in it. I hope Tom straightened him out."

"I don't think so. Tom was dazzled by the thought of picking up a quick million. He still thought the plane was his last night. Masserati also knew that Tom and Craig were related. Knew or speculated that Tom would be an heir. Do you think he could have had Craig killed in order to pick up an airplane cheap and at the same time improve his own bargaining position on the newly tendered contract?"

Shane didn't answer right away. He got up, walked over to the window and looked out at the field of small, commercial planes. These planes represented the dreams of several men and women who were trying to move up into the big time, a dream that required a lot of investment in both money and hard work. He turned back to Keith.

"Every one of these planes has a story behind it. Craig was one of the lucky ones. He ran into you with your big chequebook. Remember how he was before you set him up. He talked of nothing else. Most of these guys are struggling day to day to keep their dream alive. If it wasn't for their joy found in flying, a lot of them would have thrown in the towel. But they keep on slogging day after day, deferring bills, extending their credit because someday they will come out on top and have a fleet of planes that sets them apart from everyone else. Your question is: how far would they go to reach that dream?"

Outside there were a variety of aircraft. There were two-seater, single-prop planes, larger Cessnas which carried four or eight people, and a selection of sleek-looking jets that could carry from two to 12 to 24 passengers. Written along the sides of the planes, the names of the companies were equally diverse: Adventure Tours, Eagle, Coastal Flying, King George Air, Rapid Air Jet Delivery Service, Lively Charters. On their tails were corresponding logos of birds, crowns or icons that indicated speed. Most were restricted to one plane of each name.

"Craig was a role model of sorts to these guys. He was the success they could someday be. No one knew how he became that success." Shane laughed. "And Craig never let on that it was anything other than his own business adroitness. Would one of them kill him just to advance their own chances of moving on up? My initial answer would be no, it's not in their nature. But, and it's a hesitant but, if there is one among them it would be Masserati. I don't care what the cops say, I still think Craig died of natural causes."

"What about Tom?" Keith hesitated. "Could he be a party to murdering his own brother-in-law? Had Craig fired him once too often? Had Masserati suggested he might be in the market for a plane and Tom came up with a plan to supply him with one?"

Shane looked shocked at the suggestion. "Don't be silly. Tom wouldn't kill a fly if it was biting him on the ass." He returned to his chair and sat down, then pulled it a little closer to Keith. "However, he could easily be duped by someone like Masserati. Let's face it, Tom is a follower and Masserati is a leader. Masserati has only been on the local scene for a couple of years and already he is one of the major players. He and Craig had a lot in common. The same drive, the same determination."

Again Shane got up and approached the window. "Look at all these planes out here. Most of them are one-man, one-plane companies. In less than two years, Masserati made the short list on one of the most lucrative contracts being offered around here. No one thinks he is a serious contender but he is on the list. He could easily have Tom eating out of his hand. If Masserati is involved, Tom could be his unsuspecting pawn."

Keith had heard of Masserati but knew next to nothing about him. He wanted to know more. Also, he wasn't sure he concurred with Shane's assessment of Tom. Money changed people.

"You say two of our planes are in Europe. We've got the third one booked for a trip to California. I want to talk to those mechanics in person. I want to know what they know. What they might have said to the police. Repack your bags buddy boy. We're not going to the land of sunshine after all."

Keith Grant operated on a different budget than Sergeant Jim Mcdonald. Shane didn't even hesitate to wonder who was paying for this. The cost wasn't even a consideration for Keith. The trip was necessary. That was all that mattered.

23

TOM CHECKED HIS appearance in the elevator mirror. Always a natty dresser, he now had upgraded his image to the executive level. The stripes in his new suit were a little finer than before. The lining was real silk. The price tag would cover all of his previous wardrobe. He was a great believer in dressing the part to get the part. In his hand was a thin briefcase made from real leather. Gold initials TJD were prominent in one corner. Inside was Roberto Masserati's proposal. He would call Masserati and tell him that after due consideration he had decided to decline his offer. Craig had created a myth that all the planes belonged to him, and Tom would perpetuate that myth. Keith had agreed.

The elevator was empty on the way up to his fifth-floor offices. Tom had hoped to rub shoulders with some of the other business owners in the building. The address wasn't as fancy as Keith Grant's but it was in a prestigious location. Craig had chosen it when the business was first formed because these were the people he wanted to do business with. It was time to move on up. He would check the availability of space in Grant's waterfront building. He might want to keep an eye on his new partner.

He stepped from the elevator outside the doors of Sky Jet Charter Services, squared his shoulders and opened the door. He was going to have a confrontation with the company secretary. Christine was going to learn who the new boss was and had better show some respect. If not, he would show her the door.

There was no one behind the desk in the reception area and the door to the corner office was open. "What the hell," Tom said. He crossed the room in four long strides hoping to catch Christine in some illicit act, riffling through drawers or something. Instead, as he walked through the door he came to an abrupt halt. There was Mary behind his desk and Christine was leaning over her shoulder pointing out something on a paper in front of them.

Mary looked up at her husband in the doorway. "Tom," she said, "come in and take a chair. I was just looking over this proposal for the lobster contract. I think we still have a shot at it." She paused as she noticed the surprised look on Tom's face. "What's the matter? You look like I startled you."

"No, no. I just didn't expect to see you here. What are you looking at?"

"Where else would I be? I've got a company to run now. If we're going to make a new offer for this contract, we've got to get our asses in gear. There's not much time. Christine was just pointing out some of the features in the proposal that Craig thought were important to emphasize. It was the winning bid the last time. I don't see any reason to make too many changes to it. Close your mouth and sit down, I'll see you in a minute."

Christine smiled. "Good morning, Mr. Dunford. You certainly look nice today. Is that a new suit?"

Tom blushed. "Yes, it's new."

Mary looked up again. "Yes, it is nice. A little fancy to be wearing to clean planes, don't you think?"

Tom was stunned. It had never occurred to him that he would find Mary sitting in his chair. They hadn't discussed who would take over the company but he assumed he was the logical choice. What did Mary know about running a business? True, she did have a business degree with a minor in economics but she had never actually used it. She had always been a stay-at-home mom even after the children were grown and moved on. Most of her time had been dedicated to managing charities.

Tom's eyes shifted from Mary, in his chair, to Christine who was laughing at him behind that big smile. All the contempt he had for her came to the surface.

"Step outside, Christine. I want to talk to my wife." The tone in Tom's voice was much harsher than he had intended.

"Excuse me," Christine said.

"Christine and I are having a meeting." said Mary. "Either sit and wait or go out to the reception area. I'll be with you in a minute."

"Would you like some coffee while you're waiting?" Christine asked. "There's some fresh over on the sideboard." She smiled and indicated the opposite side of the room.

Tom just stood there. He was at a loss for words. He did not intend to fight with his wife in front of Christine or with Christine in front of his wife but this was the time to establish that he was to be the boss. If he lost control now, he would never regain it.

"Cream and two sugars," he said and turned to sit on the chesterfield on the window side of the room.

Mary looked from Tom to Christine. The tension between these two had not just happened in the last couple of minutes. This was a pre-existing battle. She inclined her head towards the coffee pot and Christine walked over and prepared the cup for Tom. She carried it across the room and bent from the waist to place the cup on the low table in front of Tom. She was still wearing a conservative business suit so Tom received no view of exposed flesh but he did get the message. Christine was taunting him.

He blushed, said nothing and took a sip from the cup. "Perfect," he said. He looked over at his wife. "I'll just sit here and wait."

Mary closed the folder in front of her. "We can finish this up later. Could you leave us alone Christine? Tom and I have to discuss a few things."

"No problem," Christine said. She eased the door shut as she left the office.

Mary came from behind the desk and sat beside Tom on the chesterfield. "Mind telling me what that was all about?"

Tom hesitated, not sure whether to get in this discussion or whether to start the one about who would be running the company. "She has disliked me ever since she came here. She was making a play for Craig and I warned him to be cautious. She was nothing but a gold digger." Tom looked towards the door, wondering if Christine was listening on the other side. "Craig laughed at the suggestion and she has had it in for me ever since. She even told the police that you were having an affair with Craig."

"An affair? He's my brother, or at least he was." Mary looked down and tears welled up in the corners of her eyes. Her determination to carry on was faltering.

Tom reached out and put a reassuring arm around her shoulders. "I know and I straightened out the cops. That just shows what a scheming bitch she is. She was undermining my credibility with the police and trying to indicate that I might have been involved in Craig's death."

He took his arm from around Mary and turned her to face him. "I think we should fire her right now."

Mary composed herself and moved away from Tom. "We don't want to do anything hasty. She appears extremely competent to me. She knows more about what is going on in this company than I do. I'm going to need her input, at least for a little while. Then I'll examine our relationship and decide."

Tom shook his head. "That's another thing. What are you doing here? I thought I would be taking over the company. I know more about what is going on than anyone does. I've been here from the beginning."

Mary reached out a hand and placed it on her husband's arm. "I know you have and everyone says you are doing a bang-up job of taking care of the planes. Even Craig used to acknowledge that when he wasn't firing you." Mary smiled, trying to take the edge off what she was saying. "But Bill Piers thinks I should be the one in charge. George Phillips and Keith Grant are both going to be available to help me out. We want to keep you doing what you do best. It's important to maintain our image as the charter company of choice among our discerning clientele. They expect a certain standard and you are the one to make sure they get it."

Tom stood up, knocking the coffee table askew, and stared down at his wife. "Whose words are those? The lawyer's or Keith Grant's? We have to watch out for him. I think he's trying to steal our company from us. He's just trying to get me out of the way."

Mary took his hand and pulled him back down onto the couch. "They're my words. I've been looking for something challenging to do and this is it. Remember my major in university was in business administration. I intend to be the CEO of Sky Jet Charter." Her face hardened a little. "You've been here since the beginning and you didn't even know whose planes you were working on. Don't tell me you know everything that is going on. I'll make you a vice-president but your division is still going to be taking care of the physical appearance of the fleet. As for Keith Grant and George Phillips, I'll keep them around until I'm up to speed on the operation. Once they've served their purpose, I'll dump Phillips and hire my own accountant, a woman. Jane Samson. She's secretary-treasurer of my area council. We work well together."

What area? Tom wondered. *What council?* He didn't know and he wasn't going to ask. To him it was just one more impediment to his rightful position as CEO of the company.

"Grant we're stuck with, for now," Mary continued, "but I'll work at that. Christine, Jane and I may even start regular poker nights. No men allowed."

"Poker games?" Tom was confused.

Mary waved off the question. "You wouldn't understand." She got up and walked back to her desk and sat down. "Is there anything else?" Dismissal was evident in her voice.

Tom remained on the chesterfield, too stunned to even get up. Things had been in a spiral ever since the reading of the will on Wednesday, actually ever since the card game on Saturday. Craig's death had not had the silver lining he had hoped for. Now, he hardly recognized his own wife. This was an entirely different woman from just a week ago.

"Nothing?" Mary asked. "Send Christine back in on your way out."

Tom knew it was time to make his case for leadership, time to press for his position as head of the company, but when Mary used that tone of voice, there was no arguing with her. He slowly got up and walked to the door. He turned. "University was a long time ago, Mary. This is the real world, not some theoretical classroom situation. I'm your best choice for CEO. You could be chairman of the board or something."

Mary did all her talking with her eyes. Tom turned back to the door, composed himself for the trip through the reception area and quietly left.

After his plans to become CEO of Sky Jet Charter were put on hold, Tom decided a phone call to Roberto Masserati was all that was required. He could not bear to meet the man face to face. Already Masserati had chided Tom for not being able to make a decision. Tom was not in the mood for any further rebukes.

As expected, Roberto was disappointed in Tom's decision not sell him the jet. Tom explained Sky Jet was in the process of putting the final touches on its new bid. Roberto attempted to discourage him. The proposed price escalated rapidly and settled at two million before the conversation ended. Tom realized he had been played for a fool. What must Keith Grant have thought of the slightly less than a million-dollar offer? Grant was no doubt having a laugh at Tom's expense as well.

Once Roberto realized the plane wasn't for sale, he then had the gall to tell Tom he was wasting his time making a new offer on the lobster contract. Sky Jet Charter didn't have a chance with Tom at its head. At that point Tom had slammed down the phone and now was just sitting in his office brooding. The jets had all been dispatched to various parts of the globe and there was nothing for him to do but paperwork. Paperwork was the last thing on his mind at the moment.

He picked up the phone and dialed again. This is the phone call he should have made on Monday when Masserati first suggested buying one of the jets. No wonder Keith Grant and Bill Piers suggested to Mary that she try her hand at running the company. If he, Tom, expected to be treated as a serious contender for that role, he had best start acting like he belonged in that world. Dressing for success was not enough. He had to walk the walk as well as talk the talk.

"Johnson Aviation Brokers, Roger speaking."

"Hi, Roger. This is Tom at Sky Jet Charter in Nova Scotia. We've got a seven-year-old Beechjet 400a, little less than 3000 hours on it, 1800 landings or so. It's got all the toys. Top of the line when we bought it. Meticulously maintained. I'm looking for a ballpark figure of what it might bring us if we sold it on the open market."

Through the phone Tom could hear the clatter of the computer keys.

"That's a good little plane. There is lots of demand for them."

"So I've heard." Tom impatiently tapped his fingers on his desk. He knew there was a demand, what he wanted was a price tag.

"You realize someone would have to see the aircraft to give you a locked in value?"

"Of course, of course. Just looking for a ballpark figure for now."

Roger hesitated again. Tom knew he was just making conversation while he calculated a value. "Three mil, four maybe if it's top of the line. Possibly a little more. Sorry, I'd have to see it. These are just values for planes that are that age and with those hours."

Tom collapsed back into his leather chair. "Between three and four million. Thanks." He hung up and pushed the phone across the desk. "Jesus Christ. Four million dollars. Masserati was playing me for a fool."

He slowly rubbed his temples with both hands. Why didn't he know the plane would be worth millions? Surely Craig must have rubbed his nose in the value of his fleet on several occasions. But, when Tom thought back, he could not think of one time when Craig had expressed a dollar value of any of the planes. Why would he? Four million was the price of a used one. What were they worth new? More than Craig could ever have afforded on his own, that was certain. That was why Craig kept his mouth shut about their worth. He wanted to maintain the image that the company was solely his. If Tom knew that they had 30 or 40 million dollars worth of rolling stock, he would know that someone else had to be involved in the equation. Craig was rich but not that rich. He had been duped.

He pushed himself out of his chair and walked over to the small screened window. Outside were 15 or 16 planes of various sizes and ages. Tom had no idea of the true value of any of them. His whole life had been spent working on airplanes, from the big jets at Air Canada down to the seven-passenger Beechcraft he had almost sold.

Why didn't he know these prices? It was his own fault. Because of his jealousy for his brother-in-law, he never talked to the other owners about Craig and his success. If he had, they would have pointed out that there had to be additional funding coming from somewhere other than just the charter business. They, themselves, saw nothing wrong with Craig's success. It was their dream as well to build up a fleet of planes, regardless of who funded it. They all wished they had their own sugar daddy hiding in the woodwork. They let Craig pretend he was doing it on his own. In a way, they were vicariously living the same dream of success. But all of them had to know the business was not that lucrative to cover the cost of three jets in seven years.

Tom was mad at himself for not knowing, at Craig for not telling him, at Roberto Masserati for trying to take advantage of him and at Keith Grant for—What was Keith Grant's sin?

He was following Craig's wishes while Craig was alive, to keep quiet. He tried to talk Tom out of the meeting with Masserati until the lawyer could fill Tom in on all the details of the bequest. Short of laughing in Tom's face when Tom claimed to be considering an offer that was 25% of what it should have been, Keith had done nothing wrong. Tom had best not slam the door between the two of them. Keith could afford to buy the planes. Tom didn't know how but there was no denying the planes' existence. Tom knew he wanted to play on the same side as Keith Grant. At least, he was smart enough to realize that.

24

SERGEANT JIM MCDONALD and Corporal Scott Bowen were still at the airport. They had observed the arrival of Keith Grant at Shane's Electrical and then later the return of Tom Dunford. They had no need to re-interview either of them. Instead, they were putting the finishing touches on a cafeteria lunch while they waited for an appointment with Bob Lively.

The sergeant figured it was time to talk to the owner of Lively Charters in person. Various points of view were being floated about the relationship between the two companies, Lively Charters and Sky Jet Charter Service. Jim wanted to get the view from the other side of the street. Did Bob Lively resent the way Craig treated him? Only Lively could answer that question.

Jim stuffed the last of his chicken pita wrap into his mouth. The flavour of the neat rows of chicken, tomato, green peppers and lettuce had been a pleasant surprise. This place may have catered to the small timers in the airline business but the food was first rate. He dabbed the corners of his mouth with his napkin and looked over at Scott, who was playing with his fries.

"Those things will kill you," Jim said. "You have to learn to eat heart-healthy."

"Nah, the secret is to leave a few on your plate each time. Don't eat the pile they give to you. It's only potato, you know. Potatoes are good for you." Scott had been born in Prince Edward Island where the potato was king. He still promoted them at every opportunity. His family back home was still in the business.

Jim pulled back the sleeve of his suit coat and checked his watch. "Mr. Lively awaits. His plane should have landed a half-hour ago. Let's see what his take is on the whole situation."

Scott threw down the fry he had been toying with and stood up. He buttoned up the unfamiliar suit jacket, brushed a few crumbs from the front and turned towards the door. He stopped dead in his tracks. In the corner of the cafeteria sat the man who had evaded the gas bill the day before. He was dressed in the coveralls of a mechanic, but Scott was sure it was the same man. The mechanic was turned slightly away from Scott and didn't notice him. The suit instead of a uniform made a large difference in the appearance of the policeman as well.

Jim noticed the change in his companion and looked in the direction of his gaze. There were no apparent felons in the line of sight. He raised his eyebrows questioningly. Scott shook off the inquiry and started for the door. Outside, he turned to Jim.

"That's him. That's the son of a bitch that kept me late for yesterday's meeting; the son of bitch that ripped off the gas station for 30 bucks. I never thought I'd see him out here. He wasn't here yesterday."

Jim leaned back and took another look through the door window. "It takes all kinds," he said. "He must be making good money as an airplane mechanic." He shook his head wondering what motivated people to petty theft. Thirty dollars worth of gas hardly seemed worth the chance. Over the years he had seen a lot of unexplained foolishness on the part of people. He had given up trying to reason it out.

He looked back at Scott. "There are probably a lot of people we haven't talked to yet. The charter business doesn't seem to be a routine Monday to Friday, nine to five."

Scott nodded. "Around here that seems to be the exception. We'll have to make another pass through during the off hours."

With that they proceeded across the tarmac to the offices of Lively Charters. The sign hung over a man door on one of the smaller hangars. The building was made of metal that had aged to a dull finish that didn't even reflect the sunlight anymore. Jim tried the door. It was locked.

He moved over and looked in the window. Inside was a small office furnished with a war surplus desk, two filing cabinets and a desktop computer exhibiting the flying windows screen saver. Someone had been there recently or the screen would have been blank. All the new computers were energy efficient and went to sleep when not used for a while.

Scott looked into the window on the big hangar doors. No planes sat inside. While he was looking, a small door opened and a middle-aged woman stepped through. The bathroom, Scott realized. He tapped on the window, startling the lady inside. She recovered, checked to make sure her skirt was adjusted and signalled for Scott to go to the other door. She unlocked it and invited them in.

"You must be the police," she said. "I tried to call you but they said you were out. I figured you must be on your way here. I told Bob that you wanted to talk to him but he had another flight booked that I didn't know about. He was picking up a client in Moncton and had to get there right away. He was already cutting it close. He apologizes and said call back and make another appointment with him. Sorry."

The policemen exchanged glances. The appointment had been made with the secretary slash office manager slash wife. She was to inform Bob of the interview when he landed. Another appointment in Moncton. No one knew about it but Bob. Very strange. If one was paranoid, one could feel Bob was avoiding them

Jim forced a smile. "When do you expect him back?"

The woman shook her head. "He didn't say. He was pumping fuel at the time and had to concentrate on that. Then he took off. I'll call you when he gets back. Can I tell him what it's all about?"

This was the second time that question was asked. Again, Jim declined to answer. "Just an ongoing investigation," he said. He turned to Scott. "Let's head back to the city.".

25

"COME ON, GUYS, if you have to wave with just one finger, make it the forefinger and sort of wave it in a friendly 'we're number one' motion."

Shane Martin circulated around the perimeter of the cafeteria with his Sony hand-held video camera. Each person present smiled, frowned, hammed it up or sat stoically through their three-second command performance.

"I've got two hours of video here to reduce to a three minute promotion on using private flying services. You'll be well compensated if you make the final cut. Let's see those pearly whites and look like you're enjoying yourselves unless you don't need any new business."

The pseudo-commercial was Keith Grant's idea. "Everyone thinks they're an actor underneath whatever else they do. They just need the chance to get their first big break. Grab a video camera from your store and film everybody at the flight centre. We'll fly over to Europe, find Jerome and Harry and see what they told the cops. If they've identified someone here as being involved in Craig's death, they can point out to us who it was."

The two men had been brainstorming ever since Shane had told the police that the mechanics were out of reach. What information could Harry and Jerome have that would be of interest? The only conclusion they could come up with was that the mechanics had identified someone else. To believe they were involved in Craig's death was unthinkable. A phone call to Europe confirmed their theory.

Outside the Learjet 60 sat warming up on the runway.

Keith Grant poked his head through the cafeteria door. "Ready to roll," he said.

Shane turned, acknowledged him and returned to his filming. "Did anyone miss their audition? This could be your big break out of here."

A variety of comments answered his question.

"Right, Spielberg. We'll check out the Academy Awards for best documentary."

"Are you sure you filmed my best side?"

"Check with my agent before releasing anything."

And finally. "Wait, you didn't get this late-night shot of the moon." Shane swung the camera over to capture the exposed buttocks of a pilot standing on a chair. The room filled with laughter.

"Stop that. Stop. This is a cafeteria. Food is served here." A burly white-clad chef emerged from the kitchen. "Get your clothes on or get out."

Shane caught the outraged man on camera and then backed out the door. The smile disappeared from his face as soon as the door swung shut.

"That's everyone here today and last night. I filmed everyone at least once. If our guys think some other person is involved, we should have that person on video."

Keith Grant slapped him on the back. "Good work. The plane's on the tarmac and ready to go. Your bag is stowed and a cold drink of whiskey has your name on it in the main cabin. The ice cubes are just starting to work up a sweat."

The pilots were going through the final flight check as the two men boarded the plane. Keith poked his head into the cockpit. "Good morning, Captain. Are you up to a change in plans?"

The pilot turned to face his passenger. Recognition changed the forming scowl to a spreading smile. "Mr. Grant. What do you have in mind?" Keith Grant was a frequent client of Sky Jet Charter, possibly one of its best. All the pilots knew him and were familiar with his propensity for changing his destination at the last minute. It was easy to do if the $1500 per hour cost was of no interest to you. Although Keith expected the first-class service the company was famous for, he didn't expect to be pampered. He made no outrageous requests of the crew. They enjoyed flying with him.

Keith passed a file forward into the cabin. "I was thinking Europe would be nice this time of year. Here's a flight plan, weather charts and navigation instructions. The tower has a copy already. Let's set a northeast heading of 52.2 degrees and head for Gander."

The pilot looked over at his co-pilot. "Gander? Is that a problem?"

"Not with me. It's about 450 nautical miles. We have lots of fuel to go that far. Should be there in a little over an hour. We were scheduled to be gone for three days anyway. What difference does it make where we spend the time?"

"Good," Keith said. "From there a hop to Reykjavik and then on to Ghent in Belgium."

"Belgium? That's where the rest of the fleet is scheduled to be. We can have a bit of a reunion." The captain entered the new information into the Collins FCC-850A autopilot computers. "We should be in

Ghent by midnight our time, that would be about four in the morning over there."

"Great," said Keith. "I'll arrange a breakfast meeting with Harry and Jerome." He started to leave, then turned back: "One more thing, Captain. Can we keep this change of plans on a need-to-know basis?" He wasn't quite sure whom to trust yet. He wanted to believe in Tom's innocence, but time would tell.

Keith and Shane settled into facing navy blue leather seats. The plane had flown in late the previous night and was immediately prepared for today's trip. It was serendipity that Keith had the plane booked for another flight. He and Shane had planned to check out an investment opportunity. For now, that would be put on hold. This assignment was more important.

"No problem with the change in plans?" Shane asked as Keith settled in and buckled up his seatbelt.

"You know Sky Jet. They go out of their way to keep their customers happy. This time it's a long distance out of their way." The original destination had been California with the first stop in Boston. The new route was in the opposite direction. "We'll be there in time for breakfast local time. What's in Ghent anyway that would take two of our planes there?"

"Robert St. Louis is leading a party of vets on a tour of the war theatres where they saw action during the war. One last fling for old-times-sake, I guess. They're ending the tour in Monte Carlo."

"Oh, that Robert St. Louis. I guess he can afford it."

"You know him?"

"We served on a few boards together. He was as disinterested in most of them as I was. Nice old guy though. Everyone referred to him as The Colonel. That's why I didn't recognize the name. He seldom uses it. So he really was in the army?"

"Yeah, has the Canada Medal. One of the first to receive it back in 1943."

Keith looked surprised at this information. "I've drunk with him on a few occasions; he's never even mentioned the war." He studied his drink for a few seconds. "A genuine hero, who'd have thought? Anyway, we'll set up a meeting with Harry and Jerome, show them the video and hopefully learn something useful."

With that both men fell silent, lost in their own thoughts of what the mechanics might know. In what seemed a very short time, they started losing altitude as they approached the end of the first leg of their flight and their first refuelling stop.

At Reykjavik, the four men grabbed some supper while the plane was being serviced and then flew on to Belgium.

"I hope you gentlemen brought raincoats," said the captain over the intercom. "Ghent radar is showing heavy rain. We can reroute to France if you want. Paris is our alternate landing site."

Keith got up from his seat and walked up to the cockpit. "All this money for a plane and it can't land in a little rain?"

"We can land. It might just take a couple of passes to be sure of where the ground really is. I'm game if you are." The captain flashed a challenging smile at the image in the doorway of his office. "You might want to fasten your seatbelt, just in case."

Sheets of rain swept off the cabin windows making visibility near zero. "I don't see anything," Shane said. He had his hands at the side of his face to cut down on the interior lighting. His nose was pressed against the glass. "Are you sure you don't want to go to Paris? Look, there's the runway. I just caught a glimpse of it." His words were drowned out by the roar of the engines as they powered up again and the plane regained height.

"No problem, gentlemen" the intercom cracked. "We know where the ground is now. We'll probably set down on the next pass."

Neither man said anything for a couple of minutes while the plane circled. They could feel it losing altitude and speed for the third time. Shane was no longer looking out the window. He was content to sit and wait. There was a slight bump and a screech of rubber and then the deceleration as the jets reversed pitch. The cabin lights brightened.

"We are on the ground in Ghent. Temperature outside is 18 degrees C and it is raining a bit. On behalf of the captain, crew and Sky Jet Charter, I hope you enjoyed your flight and will consider flying with us again." The intercom went silent and then laughter could be heard coming from the front of the plane. The laughter had a quality of relief as much as hilarity to it. The men in the front of the plane had been holding their breath in the same way as those in the back. The pilot walked into the passenger compartment.

"Next time we're going to Paris," he said.

26

STRAWBERRIES OOZED FROM the ends of the small rolled-up pancake and onto the plate as Keith Grant sliced another piece off and transported it to his mouth.

"These crepes are the best I've ever had," he said before his tongue flicked out to catch the red juice escaping from the corner of his mouth. "My compliments to the chef. I'm surprised he's working at a cafeteria."

Colonel St. Louis dabbed at a bit of cream stuck to his mustache and laughed. "Chef Marcel is making a special guest appearance here this morning. He is the head chef at the Excelsior Hotel in Brussels. But when he heard that the men who liberated his hometown were visiting in Ghent, he insisted that he come and prepare a meal for them. He was only a child when the Canadians rescued his people but he has never forgotten them. His only regret is that he only gets to serve breakfast. Unfortunately, we will be flying on this afternoon."

The Colonel slid back his chair and looked around the room once more. "I've got to make sure the buses are ready. Will you still be here when we get back this afternoon?"

Keith shook his head. "Probably not. We have some discussions with your mechanics and then we'll see where that takes us. Enjoy the rest of your trip and—" Emotion filled Keith's face. A tear formed at the corner of one eye. "–thanks for everything you guys did for us. We might not express it often enough but we are truly grateful for the sacrifices you made." He stood and shook the old man's hand. An awkward silence filled the room as all eyes turned on the two standing men.

"Yeah," Shane said. "All of you, thanks." His gaze swept the entire room. The old soldiers smiled and nodded their heads in unison. "You're welcome," one of them said. "You're welcome."

With that the two interlopers excused themselves and went out to the flight line in search of the Sky Jet planes. Harry and Jerome were overseeing the servicing of the plane that had brought Keith and Shane across the ocean. They wanted to make sure it would survive the return trip. Their own planes were just making a short hop into the Netherlands. They were fuelled and ready to go.

"I don't know what we told the cops that would bring you all the way over here," Jerome said. "Did you tell them something, Harry?"

Harry shook his head. "Well, we mentioned those two guys talking about the hit man but we made it clear they might have been talking about a TV show. They weren't serious. They were sort of kidding around."

They boarded the small jet where Shane already had the video set up and ready to roll.

Shane searched Keith's face for some sort of reaction. "A professional hit?" He had overheard the outside conversation.

Lines of worry could be seen around Keith's eyes. His brow furrowed. There was no trace of a smile. "What guys are we talking about?" he asked.

"Just a couple of guys," Harry said. "I see them around sometimes but I've never talked to them. I think they pick up work from whoever is willing to hire them. Sort of contract labourers. Clean the planes, load and unload cargo, lug stuff around, that sort of stuff. They've never approached us. Tom might know them. It's more his field that they work in."

Shane looked at Keith and raised his eyebrows in a questioning look. Keith picked up the remote control for the VCR and pushed the on button. "What exactly did they say to each other?"

Harry leaned forward to get a better look at the built-in TV. "They were sitting against the wall so we could only hear what one of them was saying. We weren't paying any attention until they started making shooting noises."

"Yeah," Jerome said. "The guy said something like 'he flies into town and then pop, pop, pop. It's all over and you never see or hear from him again.' The other guy said something, they both laughed and the first guy says 'Just remember to pay him off or you'll be next.' They found this funny and then the guy with his back to the wall saw us listening. The smile disappeared from his face and he asked the other guy if he wanted another doughnut or something and dropped his voice so we couldn't hear anymore. That was the end of it."

Jerome looked from Keith to Shane and then back to Keith. He shrugged. "Hardly worth a trip across the pond to hear that. Wait, back up the video. That's him."

DETECTIVE SERGEANT JIM Mcdonald submerged the red and white shrimp into the creamy dipping sauce before popping it into his mouth. He dropped the piece of tail shell on to the pile at the side of his plate and reached for another.

"These suckers are addictive," he said. He counted the pile of tails. "That's five of them I've eaten since I said no to your generous offer to have some lunch."

The man across the table laughed. "We all have to eat and these shrimp are like peanuts. It's hard to just eat one." Marcel Deveaux peeled another shell from the small crustacean, dipped it in sauce and ate it. "My company banks on the ability of these little creatures to hook people on their irresistible flavour." He brought his fingers together at his mouth and made a kissing sound. "Ah, the taste. Magnificent. Unbeatable."

Marcel was CEO of Worldwide Seafoods. His company had requested the tenders for shipping Nova Scotia lobsters to the overseas markets in France. Jim's request for an interview had turned into a luncheon date. This was the only time Marcel could spare from his hectic schedule. Although Jim had declined the offer of food, he found his hands had taken on a life of their own and kept reaching for the delicate shrimp displayed on the circular tray in front of him.

The food was exquisite. The information was sparse.

"The tender process is still open," Marcel explained. "I can't really get into a discussion of any of the companies involved."

"I'm not asking who is going to win the contract," Jim said. Then he paused. "Well, actually I guess I am. That person could be either a murderer or the next victim."

Marcel's hand stopped on its way to placing the next morsel of shrimp in his mouth. He returned it to his plate instead and stared into Jim's intense eyes. "I think you might be overstating your case, Sergeant. I hear Craig Flint died from natural causes. He had a stroke."

"No, he didn't. The cause of his death is still being determined but it was definitely not a stroke. You have been misinformed. He was murdered."

Marcel smiled at the policeman like a kindergarten teacher might smile at one of her young charges. "Asthma attack. Respiratory distress. All natural causes. Nothing was found at the so-called crime scene to suggest otherwise. There is no evidence of a violent death. My company has millions of dollars on the line here. Believe me, we have checked this out."

Jim was taken aback by this information. It had never occurred to him that others would be investigating this event on their own. "Checked it out? How?"

"My people talked to the paramedics. They've seen the autopsy and crime-scene reports." Marcel hesitated. "It seems it is only you two who think there was a murder. Well, you two and some washed-up doctor who is trying to protect his reputation. We've talked to him as well. He is not very credible."

Jim looked at Scott Bowen, who had been quiet up to this point. Scott understood Jim's predicament. The crime scene was clean. The autopsy was inconclusive, but it was a homicide. The seafood company's investigators may have seen the autopsy reports but they didn't have a private tête-à-tête with the medical examiner. A medical examiner who was reluctant to even share her views with her friends on the force. She would not offer any unproven theories to strange investigators from some commercial concern. Jim understood these conversations were to be kept confidential. He could not quote her as a source. The fact was that the cops had information the general public was not privy to. He knew he was right.

"Everything you say is true," Jim said, "but sometimes you just have to go with your gut. There is more reason to believe it was a homicide than it was natural causes. We are still putting the case together. Have you decided who is going to win this tender yet and is it different from your first decision?"

Marcel shook his head. "Under the circumstances I opted to reopen the tendering process. It was highly irregular to do so but I thought it to be in everyone's best interest. The three leading companies still have until the end of the week to make their new bids. I can't really discuss the matter in any more detail until after the tender is awarded. If one were to jump to conclusions, the obvious one would be that the previous winner had experienced a change in its structure," he shrugged his shoulders and raised his hands, palms up, in front of his chest, "like an unexpected death of one of its principals, however it came about, changing the playing field."

"Who is handling the contract in the meantime? This change in closing date must affect some other airline, the one currently doing the deliveries. Someone must be pissed off about losing this business."

"Up to now, it has been an in-house thing. We used our own plane but it has passed its prime and is no longer economically viable. It was a corporate decision to contract out the service rather than replace the plane. Down-size, I guess is the current buzz word." Marcel looked from one cop to the other. "Any more questions?" he asked in a voice that didn't really invite any.

They really had learned nothing but neither could think of anything relevant.

Marcel took the white linen napkin from his lap, wiped his hands, dabbed at the corners of his mouth and stood up. "Gentlemen, I have an empire to run. Please excuse me."

The two cops stood also. It was obvious the meeting had come to a quick conclusion. Marcel made a sweeping gesture across the table with his hand.

"Enjoy the rest of the shrimp. There is no reason for them to go to waste."

"No," Jim said. "We must be on our way." Even as his mouth was forming the negative words, his hand was reaching out to capture another of the tasty delights. This was without a doubt the best seafood he had tasted in a long time.

Marcel vacated the room, leaving the two policemen alone with the plate of food. Each reached for another bite.

"Next time we arrange a meeting," Scott said as he rolled the shrimp in the dish of sauce, "order the lobster."

Jim smiled, as his hand made one last trip from the tray to the sauce to his mouth. Gone.

"What do you make of his conclusions?" Scott asked. "Do you think his investigators could be right?" For the first time, Scott was experiencing doubt about his own conclusions. "The medical examiner has still not pinned down an exact cause of death and I've been back to the cottage and scoured that place from top to bottom. Nothing that I could find held or released any kind of poison."

Jim shook his head. "One of two things happened at that cottage. Craig upped and died all by himself of some strange unknown disease or this is the work of someone who really knows what they are doing. This has all the earmarks of the perfect crime." He paused and looked at Scott. "We both know there is no such thing. Let's find the killer."

28

"**H**ARRY, HAVE YOU tried the Nova Scotia lobsters that are shipped over here yet? They cost four times as much over here. They must be four times as good."

The four men were standing on the tarmac outside the jet. Keith insisted his pilots lay over and get some sleep before flying back to Canada. He was trying to fill in the time while he waited.

Harry laughed. "I can't afford them when I'm home, mate. We've been waiting for you to treat us over here. The prices are a wee bit out of our league. Plus we're only here for a week and the reservation list is about three months long."

"Three months? Are you serious?"

"Oh yeah, quite serious. There's a whole ceremony involved. Cocktails are served at the airport while they await the arrival of the shipment. The plane lands, people pick out their choice crustacean which is quickly couriered to the restaurant while the cocktail hour continues here. Then a fleet of limos take the patrons to the hotel downtown where the lobster is already cooked, the butter is melted, the wine is chilled. It's all inclusive and I'd have to take a mortgage out on my house to afford it."

"Decadent," Shane said. "We'll have our next staff party here. Keith, you're paying." He slapped his friend on the back. "I'll book the flight."

"Do that," Keith said. The look on his face was more thoughtful than joking. "This sounds like someone is turning a pretty penny and showmanship seems to be the main ingredient after the cost of importing the food. Showmanship can be bought for a song. Worst-case scenario, we end up with an elaborate meal and the government helps pay for the trip. That's not a bad downside."

Harry and Jerome exchanged looks. They had been kidding. Even though they regularly travelled with the wealthy, the ease with which money was spent always boggled their mind.

"We could do this back home," Keith said. "Instead of meeting a plane, the initial party could start on the docks waiting for the fishermen to bring their catch ashore. From the boat to the pot in less than five minutes. We'd build the restaurant right on the wharf."

"Why not?" Shane said. "We could fly people in from all over the continent."

Keith nodded. "I know a charter service that is going to have some air time available. They've had a big contract cancelled. I'll get some marketing people looking into this as soon as we get home."

Jerome shook his head. "You're not serious, are you? Just like that you're going to start a new business?"

Keith looked surprised. "It's a great idea. Don't you agree? I'll prepare a business plan first. Do some feasibility studies. But I think, properly promoted, it will make money. We don't have to pay to ship in the lobsters. You say these people have a three-month waiting list. All we're adding is a flight to picturesque

Atlantic Canada to go with the best seafood in the world fresh from the ocean. That's not a hard sell."

"Sky Jet isn't going to go after the lobster contract?" Shane asked. "I thought they were."

Keith turned his attention to Shane and slowly shook his head. "Mary's preparing a bid but I don't think Worldwide Seafood is going to give it serious consideration. They have too much at stake to let an amateur handle their product. It seems timing is everything at this end. Bob Lively pretty well has the deal sewn up. I talked to Marcel about it last night. He didn't completely let the cat out of the bag. We'll have to wait until next Monday for that but don't plan on any free lobster suppers."

Keith looked back at Jerome. "The guy in the video. He didn't work for Lively Charters did he?" Then he shook his head. "No, Bob wouldn't do anything underhanded, especially not murder."

"They were freelancers," Jerome said. "Worked for anyone who would pay them a day's wages. Lively may have been one of their contacts."

Shane walked over to where Keith was standing. He spoke in a low voice. "Three guaranteed hops across the pond a week. Man, you could soon pay for another airplane. I like Bob a lot, but everyone has their weak moments. Craig did ride his ass something fierce.Do you think Bob had someone take Craig out of the picture?"

Keith looked into Shane's serious stare. "That's the problem with weak moments. They are irretrievable if you do something stupid. Real life seldom gives you a do-over."

29

ONCE AGAIN TOM Dunford found himself in a coffee shop. Once again he shared the table with Roberto Masserati, the owner of Rapid Air. Heavy, dark clouds covered the sky. Tom had added a London Fog overcoat to his new wardrobe. He lay it across the back of his chair.

"Tom, my friend, you must sell me one of your planes. Lively Charters is going to get the lobster contract, not you, not me. Without the contract, you will be in over your head with your new jet. With another plane, I could clinch the deal. We both win."

Everyone, Tom, Mary, Bill Piers, agreed it was best to keep Keith Grant as a silent partner. That way, the Dunfords would be taken seriously as the people running Sky Jet Charter. No one would second guess their decisions or try to go around them and deal directly with Keith Grant. More than any of them, Keith Grant thought it was a good idea. He had no desire to be involved in the day-to-day operation of an airline. He wasn't a day-to-day person. He preferred the big picture. Others could look after the mundane details. Mary seemed to catch on fast. He had faith in her ability to fill her brother's administrative shoes. In time she would refine her customer relation skills.

Tom declined to mention he had no planes to sell. He sought revenge.

"Roberto, you underestimate my abilities. Three planes are just a start. I will take Sky Jet to heights Craig could only dream of." In his own mind, Tom believed this. The trick was to convince Mary to let him take over the controls.

Roberto reached a calloused hand across the table and firmly gripped Tom's. Tom looked down at his chewed-up fingernails and folded his fingers under and out of sight. An ugly habit, he thought. He would have to control it.

"No offence, my friend," Roberto said, "but you have to learn to fly before you can soar. Those things will all happen in time. For now, you must be practical. Help me and I will help you." Roberto's dark eyes found and held Tom's. "I accepted losing the contract to your brother-in-law. He, too, was a businessman. But, don't you see, fate has stepped in. The contract can be mine. I won't lose to that old fool, Bob Lively. Sell me one of your planes. Name a price."

Momentarily Tom was transfixed by the stare. Then he yanked his hand back. "You don't want me to sell you a plane. You want me to give it to you. Your last offer was a fraction of the value of the plane. You're a crook." He pushed back his chair, knocking it askew, and leaned across the table, his face inches from that of Roberto.

"I'm not the dummy you think I am, my friend. We haven't lost the contract yet. Perhaps fate has awarded it to me."

Roberto grabbed him by the upper arm and squeezed, hard, drawing him even closer.

"You, my friend, are a joke. I will wait for Sky Jet to go belly up and then pick off the bargains. You will be pleading with me to purchase your planes for half of what I offered."

He released the arm and pushed at the same time. Tom stumbled back, struggling to retain his balance. The other patrons in the shop had all stopped talking and focused their attention on the tableau before them. Tom caught himself, stood up straight and gave the sleeves of his suit a tug. His new overcoat lay like a mat on the floor. A dusty outline of his footprint could be faintly seen. There was no dignified way to retrieve it. He bent over, picked it up and slipped into it before looking back at Masserati.

He spoke in a low, tightly controlled voice. "Go fuck yourself," he paused, "friend."

Tom turned on his heel and mustering as much composure as was possible, headed for the door, staring straight ahead. He exited the shop without looking back. Outside he kicked at a plastic garbage can beside the door. How could he have been taken in by this shyster? For a year he had posed as a friend and now the truth was out. He just wanted to use him.

He hustled across the sidewalk and opened the door of a dark green Mercedes 380SX. A temporary permit was taped to the side window. Tom had 90 days to establish himself as the rightful man in charge at Sky Jet Charter. That was when the first payment on this baby came due.

It was time to straighten Mary out. Time to make her realize they were co-owners of the company. Time to remind her that matrimonial rights made him an equal owner.

She had to stop playing games in the corporate world and get back to looking after their house. Better still, it was time to move on up into a bigger and better house. Then Mary would stay home to look after all the decorating. She could do what she did best and he could do what he did best. Run Sky Jet Charter.

He would start looking for a new place today. Keith Grant and Shane Martin lived in the same upper middle-class neighbourhood. It was nice, but he could do better than that. In fact, he wasn't sure why they lived there. They could both do better than that. He would swing by the office, pick up Mary and establish himself in the lifestyle that befitted an owner of an airline company, even if was only a three-plane charter business.

He checked the sky and decided the rain would hold off for a while longer. Now to find a real-estate broker that he could trust.

30

ROBERT CROSLEY HUNG up the phone. This morning's USA Today had carried a message for him, an offer of more business. He had been paid for his last job and was in no hurry to work again. Still, he had recognized the number in the ad and had placed the call.

The caller wanted someone whacked. Nothing strange there. They wanted it done right away. That happened often enough to be considered ordinary. The death couldn't generate any suspicion. Now there was the challenge with a premature death. Those things took time to set up even for an expert in the business. And in this case, Crosley was several hundred kilometres away in another part of the country with no ambition to go back east. Winter was coming. Southern destinations beckoned.

His immediate thoughts suggested he decline the job. No one dictated terms to Robert Crosley. All he needed was a name and an indication of how accidental the death had to appear. From there it was his baby. He decided the time, the place, the method. After all, his freedom was on the line. Maybe even his own life, depending on the judicial system of the country where the hit took place. He had one irrevocable rule: it was his way or no way.

The caller pleaded for Crosley to reconsider. They shared a history. Crosley had serviced this client before, recently. Sometimes repeat business was good, a compatible relationship already existed, and sometimes it was less desirable. Murder as a means of solving problems soon starts waving red flags at the local constabulary. He had some concerns about this client's mental state. Collateral damage didn't seem to be a concern, not always a good thing from an investigative point of view. On the other hand, sometimes it simply muddied the waters. From 3000 kilometres away, he could maintain some distance from the crime and let the chips fall where they may.

He convinced the client to give him two or three days while he tried a long-distance solution. If that failed, he might fly in and take care of business, no promises.

"Please, get it done by next Monday," the client said. "That's all I ask."

"No promises," Crosley repeated. "You're not paying me enough to get careless. To me, it's more important to do it right than it is to do it fast. You can get a sloppy job from someone local for a lot less than you're paying me."

The conversation finished with that understanding. Now Crosley would engage Canada Post to become a co-conspirator with him. They claimed 90 per cent next-day delivery for first-class mail. He had a plan. He would test the system.

31

THE RETURN FLIGHT from Europe proved uneventful. Clouds covered Nova Scotia. Moisture smeared across the side windows as the plane broke through the clouds to the clear air below. Here, a typical fall day greeted them. Overcast, but dry. The jet landed safely and rolled up beside the plane of Bob Lively. A coveralled worker stood in the doorway of the cargo hold. He looked up as the sleek jet taxied in beside him. He lifted his right arm in a slight wave to the pilots.

Shane Martin glanced out the window as he gathered his few belongings in preparation to disembark. "That's him," he said. "That's him. There's the man from the video."

He grabbed Keith Grant's sleeve, almost pulling him off balance, to make sure he was paying attention. Keith was. He took in the carrier name embossed on the side of the jet.

"I don't believe it."

"Lively Charters? That's hard to believe, man."

Shane leaned closer to the window for a better look, looking back as the other plane disappeared from view. "Is this an omen?"

Keith moved across the narrow aisle for a better look through the cabin window. "The first person we see as soon as we land is our man. Where's the challenge in this?"

"The challenge is believing Bob is involved, man. I know we discussed it but—"

The jet continued rolling along the tarmac towards the hangar of Sky Jet Charter. The man disappeared from view. Keith and Shane sat in silence. On the flight back from Europe they had discussed what they would do when they arrived home. The first task would be to locate the man in question. Check that off the list. The search proved easier than either expected.

From there the discussion wavered back and forth between confronting the man themselves or just finding out who he was and passing the information along to Sergeant Mcdonald. They decided to play it by ear. Now, as Sherlock Holmes used to say: "The game is afoot." The time for the final decision was thrust upon them.

"Let's just strike up a friendly conversation," Keith said. "Then, we'll slowly bring it around to hiring hit men. See what he knows."

"I don't know about that, man. We don't want to muddy the waters for the cops."

Keith stared intently at his friend. Despite his outward appearances, Shane was the more conservative of the two. He served as the anchor of reason to Keith's exuberance.

"No bright light in the face. No grilling. Just a few innocent questions."

Shane slowly shook his head.

"If he's involved, there are no innocent questions, man. He doesn't know you from Adam but he may be able to tie me to Craig. Most people think I'm part of his crew. We don't want to spook him."

Keith unfastened his seatbelt and stood up.

"You're right. Let's not screw this up. If someone had Craig killed, it wasn't this joker. Let's find who's behind it."

He patted his pockets looking for something he knew wasn't there. "Did you keep any of those cards the cop kept passing out? Mine are back at the office."

"Mine too. Who ever thought we'd need them? It still stretches my imagination to believe someone murdered Craig."

They disembarked from the plane. The clouds were now sprinkling some rain on the airport. They hailed a cab to drive them to Shane's Electrical. By the time they arrived, the rain was bouncing off the sidewalk. They pulled their jackets over their heads and ducked inside the store.

"Good thing we landed when we did. We might have had to divert to Paris," Shane said.

Keith shook the water from his coat. "Next time," he said.

Shane took a stack of business cards from his drawer and riffled through them.

"Here it is. Detective-Sergeant James Mcdonald, Major Crimes." He passed the card to Keith. Keith picked up the phone.

After he hung up, he looked back at Shane with a look of grim determination. "We've done our civic duty. Now, let's find this professional killer ourselves. We'll find out who hired him and kill two birds at once."

Shane was stunned. "Are you out of your ever-loving mind? What do we know about finding a professional killer?"

Keith shrugged. "Can't be too difficult. He's in business. He deals with the public. How do people who want to hire him find him? There's got to be a way."

"You check the yellow pages. I'll try the classifieds," Shane said. His voice dripped sarcasm. "Do we look under 'a' for assassin or 'h' for hit man? Or is it under 'n' for not in my fucking lifetime?"

Keith ignored the comments. "Let's think this through. Craig had no mob connections. He wasn't running drugs or anything else illegal. He wasn't dating some mobster's girlfriend or wife. Whoever had him killed would not be part of the underworld." He was silent for several seconds. "It has to have something to do with his business. Someone here at the airport has to know how to get in touch with a hired killer. You have to find that person. Keep out of the cops' way, but find him."

"Me? Why me?"

"Because everyone here knows you. I can't come around here asking questions. Who's going to confide in me? Some stranger in a suit. It has to be you. We'll start with that clown on Lively's plane. As soon as the cops finish with him, strike up a conversation. See what he knows. After that, your best bet will be to talk to the flight crews. They get around. They are the ones most likely to know someone who knows someone who knows someone who can find you a hit man. Be casual but do it fast."

"And just what happens when or if I find out about this hit man? What do I do with the information?"

"Why, we hire him." Keith gave his shoulders a nonchalant shrug as if that was the most logical conclusion in the world.

"Hire him? Hire him to do what, man?"

"What hit men do. To kill Craig's killer."

"You mean commit suicide? If we find the right person, he will be the one who killed Craig."

"Only technically. The real killer will be the guy who paid him to do it. That's the person we're after. We want to know who and why."

Shane shook his head. This whole conversation had taken on a surreal tone. "You're out of your ever-loving mind. We can't hire a professional hit. That's murder. That's insane."

Keith seemed to contemplate that statement for a moment. "Maybe you're right. You just find him for now and then we'll see where that leads us. I don't know how these things work, but if all it takes is money, that's no object. Whatever it takes. We owe Craig that much."

Shane looked away. He didn't like the turn this conversation had taken. He recognized the look on Keith's face. When he had that look, there was no stopping him. Electronics, Shane knew. Finances, Keith knew. When it came to murder, they were both virgins and they were about to greet a ship of sailors returning from a year on the high seas. He looked back at Keith. "Let's be really careful about this, man. Really, really careful."

SERGEANT MCDONALD STARED at his phone with a baffled look. The call from Craig Flint's friends came completely out of the blue. The information rattled him. They had gone to Europe to seek the information he needed.

Sergeant Mcdonald thought Craig's friends were all in denial about murder being a possibility. Final results from toxicology shed nothing new on the cause of death. An unknown substance induced metabolic asphyxiation. This was not a natural occurrence. To someone in Jim's occupation, homicide jumped out as the most likely alternative.

If a professional killer committed the act, he may have had a special synthetic drug designed to baffle police testing labs. If that were the case, and he overused it as a final solution, the drug would eventually end up in police data bases.

Before signing off on a hired gun, Jim had wanted to personally discuss with the mechanics what they thought they had heard in the cafeteria. That was not possible. They were still hobnobbing around Europe on an extended charter. He did not have the resources for an overnighter to chase them around the continent. Keith Grant did.

The announcement of the winning bid for the new lobster shipping contract was imminent. Realistically, he had to admit that the perpetrators of this crime could escape detection. He must act to prevent the murderers from being rewarded with huge sums of money. Now, it appeared, he had an unlimited source of funds on his side. This could swing the pendulum of fate in his favour. With this source of funds came the responsibility of keeping a couple of amateurs safe. He had to get them to back off and let him do his job. At the same time, he wanted to keep the resources offered available. It was better if he controlled their direction rather than letting them run off on their own. His investigation into the psyche of Keith Grant had not gone deep enough if he thought that was a possibility.

He pushed the button on the phone to get a fresh dial tone and called Scott Bowen. Together they would interview the airport worker. Despite the dreariness of the weather, things were looking up.

The surprise experienced by Keith Grant and Shane Martin at stumbling across the object of their intended search before their plane even finished taxiing was a mere blip compared to the bomb dropped on Scott Bowen.

"Over in the corner." Shane Martin pointed to the man from the video. Shane and the two policemen stood inside the doorway of the airport lunch room. Shane had tasked himself to keep an eye on the man until the police arrived. He was now passing him off. Outside the rain was letting up. "He's your boy."

"Holy shit," said Bowen. He turned to face Jim. "That's the asshole I arrested the other night for the gas-and-dash at the self-serve station." He looked at Shane. "Are you certain that's him?"

"Yeah, man, I'm certain."

Bowen rubbed his hands together. "This is going to be fun."

Jim reached out and shook Shane's hand. "Thanks for the help. We'll take it from here."

Shane recognized a dismissal when he heard it. "Yeah, OK." He turned, pulled his jacket close around him and walked out the door, leaving the cops to do their thing.

They sensed the disappointment in his voice. Shane wanted to watch but this was a murder investigation. There was no room for civilian sightseers.

Jim would have been shocked to find Shane had more on his mind than satisfying his morbid curiosity. Shane had begun the journey of tracking down the assassin himself. His crack at the subject would come after the police had warmed him up.

The two policemen snaked their way between the plastic tables and chairs, mostly empty. The majority of the patrons of the cafeteria had regular hours and had returned to their places of work. The object of their concern was a self-employed contract worker. He had finished working on the Lively Charter plane. He was waiting for everyone to get back to their offices before he went looking for another assignment.

Scott Bowen tapped him on the shoulder. Both cops displayed their badges. The man's first reaction was surprise. Then he recognized Scott.

"What do you want?"

No small talk, no introductions. Scott Bowen smiled at the stricken man backed into the cafeteria corner. He turned to Jim Mcdonald.

"I told you he would be cooperative, Sergeant. Just an innocent man misunderstood by the justice system."

Pat Dexter looked from one cop to the other. He had nightmares from his humiliating public arrest for driving off without paying from the local Irving station.

Now here was the same policeman at his place of work. This was harassment.

"I don't know what you want but my lawyer told me the theft under $5000 charge on a gas drive-a-way was a crock of shit. He said the judge won't give you the time of day. I just have to explain that I inadvertently forgot to pay the clerk. It happens all the time. People have other things on their minds."

Scott pulled out a chair from the small table and sat down. His back was to the rest of the cafeteria so no one but Dexter could hear what he had to say. Jim drew up a chair on the other side of the table.

"Your lawyer told you that, did he?" Scott asked. "Your lawyer has an inside track on how the judge's day will be going when you appear in front of him. Your lawyer knows that the judge's wife gave him the best sex ever the night before and then got up in the morning and prepared him a full, nutritious and satisfying breakfast. Traffic was light allowing him time for a leisurely coffee before court. That would work in your favour. Your lawyer knows that's going to happen? Right?"

Scott looked back over his shoulder to make sure no one else was paying any attention to the conversation taking place in the corner of the room. Satisfied, he turned back to Dexter and continued in the same low, menacing voice.

"Of course, if the judge was up until two in the morning waiting for his teenage daughter to come home from her date, only to see her driven up by some black-haired Goth with rings and bangles dangling from every part of his body. Then said daughter informed her daddy she would live her own life, date whomever she pleased and he had no control over her any more. Then he tossed and turned unable to get to sleep because he sees these pieces of shit like the boyfriend everyday in court and he knows what they want from his little girl."

Scott took another look around and leaned even closer to Dexter. "He finally falls asleep at 4:30 in the morning, oversleeps, skips breakfast. Then he arrives at the courthouse to find some asshole in his parking spot before walking into court and the first person he sees is you. Your lawyer knows for a fact that if that happens, he will go easy on you. He won't have to prove that he has control over someone. If not his daughter, his life, then you."

Again Scott paused in his narrative and looked around the room once more.

"Your lawyer knows that." Scott grunted out a half laugh, half snort. "Ask your lawyer if he ever came up before an irrational judge."

Scott looked over at Jim. "Ever seen a judge having a bad day, Sergeant?" He looked back at the shaken Dexter. "You could take that chance if you want to or you could answer some simple questions for the Sergeant and myself and maybe the whole theft case will simply go away."

Dexter knew how his own life was going, the arrest, the apology, explaining to his wife why he needed a lawyer. He could accept the fact that the judge could be having similar problems of his own. He believed the tale spun by the policeman could be a true depiction of events in the courtroom. Dexter had that kind of bad luck. Why should it change when he got to court? Besides, what information could these cops want from him? He wasn't a criminal.

"What kind of simple questions? Go away, how?" He looked at Scott and remembered the righteous indignation in the man's face on the day of his arrest. "You're going to go into court and say it didn't happen? I'm not that stupid. You're not going to do that."

"Easier," Scott said. "You cooperate with us and on the day of your court appearance, I don't show up at all. I have another engagement. I'm out of town. I forget. The judge asks the bailiff to check to see if I'm waiting out in the hall. I'm nowhere to be seen. The judge dismisses the case. If he's mad at anybody, it's me, not you. You walk out the door a free man. No record. No fines. No jail time. Happens all the time."

Scott studied the man in the corner. He could almost see the wheels turning in his brain.

"Or I show up and paint you as the most despicable person I've ever had the displeasure to arrest. I tell how you refused to pull over until we practically had to force you off the road. How you wouldn't cooperate on the roadside, shot off your mouth. It won't be pretty. You decide."

Silence hung briefly in the air.

"What do you want to know?"

MARY DUNFORD LOOKED up as Tom walked into her office. He removed his overcoat and hung it on a rack in the corner of the room. An ear-to-ear smile lit up his face. Mary smiled back and pushed away the papers she was studying. She arched her back and stretched her arms, both stiff from the long period of concentration on the figures before her.

"What's up?"

Tom fanned out three colour brochures in front of him.

"It's decision time."

He approached the desk and laid the three brochures out in a tableau in front of Mary.

"Which of these will be our new house?"

"What?" The smile disappeared from Mary's face. She glanced at the glossy brochures. These would not be cheap houses. Houses in her price range came off an ink-jet printer not high-gloss printing presses. "Don't you have work to do? No wonder Craig wanted to fire you all the time. I thought he was being a jerk."

Tom was stunned by this reaction. He had spent a full day with a real-estate agent selecting houses he knew Mary would like. These brochures represented the best choices.

"Which of these will be our new house?" This time, his voice carried a harder edge.

"Tom, I'm busy. I don't have time for idle dreaming."

Outside the rain started beating on the fifth storey window. The room darkened noticeably. Tom's mood darkened to match it.

"The agent told me these places will be snapped up fast. If we want to grab one of them, we have to act now."

Mary was silent for a moment, staring into her husband's eyes. The sparkle had returned to them. Winning her over would require more effort than just flashing the brochures. Tom's gaze returned to the desk.

"I like this one the best." He tapped the pamphlet in the middle. "It's got two guest rooms and four baths. Lots of room for the kids to visit." He looked back up at his wife. "But the choice is yours. You'll be the one running it."

"Tom, I have work to do. Please let me get back to it."

Tom slammed his fist down on the desk. His emotions were on a roller coaster.

"Dammit woman," he said. "It's time to stop playing games. You've had your fun but now is the time to get back to reality. You know nothing about running a successful business. You're a housewife."

Mary's eyes turned to two simmering coals. She rose from her desk and leaned towards her husband. "Craig used to say the same thing when I encouraged him to hire me as his office manager. Well, he never let me work with him but I did learn one thing from him. You're fired," she said. "And this time there is no one to run interference for you." She picked up the packet of papers she had been working on and waved them in Tom's face. "Go home. Home to the house we can barely afford."

Tom became instantly subdued. "I don't understand," he said. "We own an airline. Craig always had lots of money. Why don't we?"

Mary softened, a little. "If you had been in here checking out the business instead of out looking at overpriced houses, you would know. Craig lived on his salary as a pilot. Neither of us can fly. He ran the company close to break even. That's why he was able to be so competitive. The rest of his money came from the leasing side and investments Keith Grant made for him. Those, the idiot gave away to charity, remember. Three million dollars. A misguided attempt to buy his way into heaven."

She threw the papers on to the desk.

"I've inherited the job as CEO from a predecessor who didn't draw a salary."

She slumped back into her chair.

Tom looked stunned. "Didn't draw a salary? Craig always had money in his pockets."

Mary shook the papers in front of her. "Of course he did. Aren't you listening? Do you know what we pay those pilots? A hell of a lot more than you ever brought home. And somehow Keith Grant made all of it tax free. Craig's paper losses from the leasing company wiped out the taxes from his pilot's salary. Grant says he can do the same thing for me."

Tom's eyes lit up at that suggestion.

Mary glared at him. "First of all, I need a goddamn salary to pay taxes on."

Tom drew a chair up in front of the desk. He swept the housing brochures aside. "We never ran this place on a shoestring. Everything was always first class. There must be money in the budget somewhere to pay your salary, or mine, if you let me take over and run the place."

"Give it up, Tom. Be happy to do what it is you do best. If everything is first class, then that's your doing." She laughed. "I guess it runs in the family and I've inherited this trait from my brother. You've been fired and rehired already." Then she turned serious again. "But let's get one thing straight. I now run this company. This is what I do. So get rid of the June Cleaver image. That person no longer exists."

She walked around the desk and gave him a hug. "We'll do this together. This is what I've always wanted to do. I am the one with the business administration degree. George Phillips is coming up in a few minutes to go over the books with me. Stick around so you understand what is really going on."

Right on cue, the intercom lit up. "George Phillips is here," Christine said.

"Send him in."

George knocked and then entered the room followed by Christine. Under his arm, he carried two blue binders with the SJC logo on them. Mary indicated the more informal setting to her left. She and Tom sat on the blue leather chesterfield. George pulled the matching armchair closer to the coffee table between them. Christine placed cups and saucers on the table and retrieved the coffee pot.

"Should I take notes?" she asked.

"No," Mary said. "We'll keep this friendly for now. I'll call you if I need you."

Christine got the message and returned to her desk.

"Let's start with the good news," Mary said. "Am I going to get paid for my work?"

George looked confused for a second and then laughed.

"When you own the company, you're last on the list. You get what's left over." He flipped open the first binder. "The good news is there's lots left over. Let me explain how Craig got it instead of the tax man."

The meeting went on for another two hours.

34

SCOTT BOWEN AND Jim Mcdonald aimed their car back towards the city. Although they convinced the gas-stealing Pat Dexter to cooperate, he didn't have a lot to offer. Yes, he remembered joking about somebody hiring a hit man but now he wasn't sure what triggered the conversations. For sure, he had nothing to do with an actual hit, he said. It was just some conversation they had overheard. He wasn't even sure where. Yes, he had worked for Bob Lively. Yes, he had worked for Roberto Masserati and yes, he had even worked for Craig Flint. Like a janitor for any big company, most people didn't even notice when he was in the room. They talked freely in his presence and in most cases he simply ignored what conversation was taking place as he went about his duties. He honestly didn't remember who had said what.

"Well, Scott, what do you think?" Jim said after five minutes of driving in silence. "Can we believe anything this guy tells us?"

Scott did not answer right away. He concentrated on the flow of traffic in front of him, all of it ten kilometres an hour above the speed limit. "I think he and his buddy got caught up in the idea of a professional hit," Scott said after several seconds. "I think they are confused with the television version of it where only politicians and bad people get whacked."

Jim laughed. "Isn't that a redundancy?"

Scott ignored the comment. "One thing is certain. They did hear something. Someone, somewhere on this air strip was talking about hiring a pro."

Now Jim got serious. "We know for a fact that Dexter worked for Lively Charters. The poker buddies saw him on that plane. Lively appears to have the most to gain from Craig's death."

"Do we know for sure that Lively is getting the contract now?"

"Not positively, but everyone I've talked to think it's a done deal."

"He's also worked for Sky Jet. Remembers Tom Dunford. Who else did he say he's worked for?"

"Most of them out there at one time or another. Once our little gas thief gets home and checks his records, we'll know what companies he worked for that week. If he stoops to stealing gas, we can only speculate on how accurately he kept independent records of his wages. What the tax man doesn't know—" He looked over at Jim who easily finished the thought for himself. "If Lively is on the list in the proper time frame, I think a visit is in order."

Jim glanced up into the sky as a small plane flew directly above them on the way to the airport. "The trouble with these small charters," he said, "is they can get out of our jurisdiction at the drop of a hat. Today was the second time we just missed Lively. We'll have to get Shane Martin to tell us when his plane is at the airport and then give him an unannounced visit."

"In the meantime, we could check his phone records. He must have contacted the hit man somehow."

Jim shook his head. "Way ahead of you. He has calls from all over North America and Europe. He's either calling customers trying to drum up business or calling to confirm contracts or just calling home to chat with his wife. If we start tracking all the calls, someone will tip him off. We don't want him disappearing completely."

"You know, if he has all this business already, he's going to need another plane to take on the new contract. Otherwise, he'll be putting all his eggs in one basket. We should check the leasing companies and see what arrangements he might have made."

"Eureka." Jim gave his partner a light tap on the shoulder. "If Lively needs extra capacity then Sky Jet is going to have too much capacity. Let's check with them to see if some sort of agreement has been reached between the two companies. We know they've cooperated with each other in the past. Why not now?"

"Oh wow, the irony of that situation. Lively has Craig killed so he can get the contract instead of Sky Jet and then uses Sky Jet planes to fulfill his obligation." Scott shook his head. "What a weird turn of events that would be."

"We should check to see if there was some sort of pre-existing arrangement between the two companies. Maybe Craig was an unknown party to his own death. Swing towards their offices."

Scott parked the car in the lot behind the building housing the Sky Jet offices and the two policemen made their way inside. George Phillips stepped off the elevator as they were about to get on.

"Anything new on Craig's death?" George asked.

"Still working on it," Jim said. "Have you thought of anything helpful?"

George shook his head. "Sorry, nothing." He turned and headed for his office.

The two policemen boarded the elevator and pushed five.

"Craig had great taste in secretaries," Jim said as they exited the elevator. "I wonder if Christine survived the transition. She and Tom were not the best of buds."

"Craig never showed much interest in women," Scott said. "Flying and making money were his main concerns, along with playing poker once in a while."

By now the two men had reached the office door.

"Tell me that again after you meet Christine," Jim said. He opened the door. Christine looked up from her desk as the two men entered. A visible change came over her at the sight of the policemen.

"Why, Sergeant," she said, "I hoped you'd be back again. Do you have any news?"

Jim showed some surprise at the reception. He definitely remembered Christine but didn't think he had made that much of an impression on her. He noticed a new brass sign on her desk: "Office Manager."

"Nothing yet," he said in answer to her question. "You seem to be moving up in the company. I thought there might be a possibility that you would no longer be with them."

Christine laughed. "You mean Tom? We get along just great." She reached out and turned the sign towards herself. "Words are funny things," she said. "When I was a secretary, everyone resented me telling them what to do. I was only passing on Craig's wishes but that didn't matter. Now I'm the office manager. I do the same things as I did before except when I say jump, people ask 'How high?'

"I no longer go in to take a letter from Mary. I go in and have meetings with her, then I handle the correspondence arising from the meeting. It's weird."

"Sounds like a promotion to me," Jim said. "It looks good on you. Is Mary in?"

"Do you have an appointment?" Christine said and then laughed again. She pushed a button on the intercom and waited. "Sergeant Mcdonald is here to see you," she said when Mary responded to her signal. She made a waving motion with her hand. "Go right in."

Mary came around her desk to greet the two policemen. "Do you have any news?" she asked. The eagerness on her face added to the intensity of her voice. Jim hesitated for a couple of seconds. He found himself so caught up in the investigation that he failed to remember Mary was Craig's sister and not just the new owner of Sky Jet Charter Services. Her interests in solving this case were personal, not professional.

"No," he said. "I'm sorry to bother you but I have a few questions that we hope will help move the investigation along."

Mary hesitated, giving the policeman a questioning look. "Anything that will help," she said and gestured towards the chesterfield for the two men to sit. She sat in a facing chair. Tom took the seat behind the desk. Jim thought he was trying it on for size. He looked back at Mary.

"You have a bid in on the lobster contract with Worldwide?" he asked.

"Yes. We simply updated Craig's bid. It was a winner the last time, no reason why it shouldn't win again."

The two men exchanged glances. Word on the street suggested she was not being realistic. Speculation led in the direction of Bob Lively.

"May I ask if you have a contingency plan if someone else wins?"

Mary hesitated before answering.

"Christine and I have knocked around a few suggestions. You always need a Plan B."

Jim couldn't hide his surprise. "Christine?"

"Yes. She's the office manager now. Let's face it. She knows more about the company than I do. She pretty much ran it when Craig was out gallivanting around the world. Why waste the talent?"

Neither man could find any argument with that statement. Scott stole a look in the direction of Tom. He appeared to be fighting back the urge to say something. His silence prevailed.

"Have you been approached by Bob Lively with any of his plans? I understand he thinks things are going his way this time."

Again Mary hesitated. Jim realized he was delving into the inner workings of the business. However, these questions were important to where the case would lead him. "Did Lively have any arrangements with Craig as to what the two of them would do if Lively Charters got the contract?"

Mary laughed out loud. "Craig? Lose the contract? That much I did know about the business. He never even considered that a possibility. My brother could be an arrogant little twit. To be perfectly honest, I thought he already had the deal wrapped up. He talked as if it were a done deal. When I took over, I was shocked to find out it was still up for grabs."

Jim gave Scott a disappointed look. So much for that theory. If Mary was right, there were no pre-existing agreements from either side.

"We weren't quite so presumptuous," Mary continued. "Christine pointed out that there was a great deal of cooperation between the two companies in the past. We believe Lively will need some additional flying power, especially in the short term. We are prepared to work out a deal with him if he wins."

"Does Lively know this?" Jim asked. If he and Scott had come to the conclusion that cooperation would be beneficial to the two companies, it would be an easy leap of faith to think that Bob Lively reached that same determination. Whoever took over Sky Jet would be an easy target under the circumstances. They had to keep their new plane in the air to make it pay.

"We haven't officially discussed it yet. We have to appear to believe that our bid can win. Otherwise, why bother making it? It's still the same company as it was when Craig ran it. Our bid is viable. I still expect to win."

"Do you know Bob Lively?" Scott asked entering the conversation for the first time.

"I met him at the funeral. Christine has had some dealings with him. Sharing business is not a new concept. He and Craig did quite a bit of it." She looked over at Tom. "What's your read on how Craig got along with Bob?"

Tom shrugged his shoulders. "Bob is a pilot. Craig got along with all the other pilots. They did share business from time to time. Usually Bob took over some of our extra business."

"So," Scott said, "you think he will be open to the idea of sub-leasing your planes?"

"Not only open, I think he will expect it. In the past everything was quite informal. We did our best to keep all the planes as occupied as possible. Craig and Bob went way back together. They were rivals at one level but pragmatic businessmen at another. If he lands this bid, he may want something a little more official. This could be his chance to really move his company ahead. He should add another plane to his fleet within a year of signing the deal. In the meantime, one of our planes could end up working under his logo." He gave his shoulders a shrug. "That's all academic. We already have all the flying power we need. We should still win the contract."

Mary gave her husband a surprised look. This was the first real expression of faith he had exhibited in his wife's entrepreneurial abilities.

"But the bottom line," Jim said, "is that you think Lively will expect some sort of cooperation if he does land the deal?"

Tom nodded. "Why not? Everyone would benefit."

Again the two cops exchanged knowing looks.

"Why?" asked Mary. "You don't think he has anything to do with Craig's death?" She laughed at the thought. "Christine says they were good friends. I find it hard to believe it would be anyone in the flying fraternity. They are just one big good-old-boys club out there. Anyone without wings on his chest is an outsider. Those with are part of the clique." Her voice carried a little resentment as she made the last statement.

"That appears to be true," Jim said, "but we have to follow all the leads. It's almost as important to eliminate suspects as it is to find the right one."

Jim flipped through a few pages of his notebook before looking up at Mary again. "What about Rapid Air's Roberto Masserati? Have you given him the same consideration?"

Mary shook her head. "According to Christine, Craig didn't trust Masserati. She doesn't know of any reason. It's just the impression she had. But if he were to win, I guess I'd be open to discussions." She again looked over at her husband. "He's a friend of yours, isn't he, dear?"

"He is not," Tom said, his voice louder than he intended. "We'll be having no dealings with him."

Mary looked surprised. "I misunderstood. I thought you had lunch with him on a regular basis." She turned back to Jim. "We'll deal with that if it happens. I get the impression he's not a real contender."

Jim's gaze went from one to the other. Something was amiss. He waited for further discussion but none came. "Thanks for your help," he said. He looked at his partner. "Do you have any further questions, Scott?"

Scott got to his feet and reached out a big hand towards Mary.

"Thank you ma'am. We'll let you know as soon as we find anything out. Craig was a good friend of mine too, as you know."

"Thanks," Mary said. She remembered having a crush on Scott in school. He was two years ahead of her and didn't know she existed. Still, she had had her dreams. That was before Tom came on the scene. Even now, Scott didn't remember her. She looked over at her husband.

"Anything to add, dear?" she asked.

Tom shook his head. He was thinking of Masserati's offer to buy the plane. He wondered if Lively had approached Mary with an offer of his own.

"**H**IRE A PROFESSIONAL hit man? Are you serious?"

Shane picked up his three new cards to replace those discarded from his hand. Cigar smoke hung in layers at the back of the hangar, filtering the light from high overhead fluorescents. Barrels of hydraulic fluid formed a wall to cut off the view from the front of the hangar. A tool rack formed the other wall. Shane kicked over a beer bottle, one of several cluttering up the cement floor around the table. It rolled in a half circle, coming to rest at the feet of the burly mechanic who had asked the question. His fellow players were all either electronics people like himself or mechanics. They all worked on planes. They all travelled extensively.

"No, no, man," Shane said. "I don't want to bump someone off. I'm just curious how these guys get their clientele. Let's face it, they can't run an ad on TV or in the paper. Don't you ever wonder about stuff like that?"

"See your buck and raise a buck," a second mechanic in red overalls sitting to Shane's right said. Two loonies clanked down on the metal table. "I think it's a word-of-mouth business. If having people killed is in your company's mission statement, you travel in the circles that know how to reach those people."

Shane threw a toonie on to the table. "Call," he said. "But what if you're not a mobster? What if some guy is stalking your wife? The cops aren't doing anything and you want to get rid of him once and for all?"

"Ah ha. You're not married. You're afraid someone has a hit out on you." Everyone laughed. "Raise three dollars." A five-dollar bill floated into the centre of the table.

"Fold." Cards were tossed to the side of the table and another beer hissed open.

"Five to me and I raise it five."

Shane recoiled a little. The price of poker was a little more than he was used to. There was no upper limit on how much he could lose. Keith, my man, he thought, you will be getting a bill for this little adventure. I hope it's worth it.

Shane had hung around the Sky Jet hangar keeping an eye on the cafeteria until he saw the two policemen leave. He then hustled over and sat at the table next to Pat Dexter. "Those two suits looked like cops if ever anyone did," he had said to Dexter.

Dexter then proceeded to give Shane an earful on what was wrong with the justice system in this country: crooked cops, corrupt judges and thieving lawyers. He blamed the police for everything from his inability to get and hold a permanent job to the huge influx of reality shows on television. Scott Bowen was the principal target of his abuse.

Shane patiently endured this outpouring of hate, in hopes of finding something out about professional hit men. In the end, it was all for naught. Shane learned even less than the police had discovered. After valiantly struggling for more than 10 minutes to keep Dexter on topic, Shane gave up and went back to work. Now he was trying his luck at this poker game.

"I've heard you can reach these guys by running an ad in one of the national newspaper's classified section. You have to know the proper wording sequence. You leave your number and the killer calls you."

"Wanted: Professional Killer. Call Joe at 555-7512. That won't attract too much attention. We all know the cops can't read."

Everyone around the table smiled but the speaker. "No, there's a coded message. I don't know the code. I talked to a guy in Montreal on one of my stopovers who claimed to be on the inside. The people he ferried around were not your usual upstanding businessmen. His clients frequently talked about taking people out. I believe him."

"What's his name?" Shane asked. He realized he sounded a little too anxious. He tried to cover up. "This sounds more like an urban legend. You know, a friend of a guy who knows a guy."

"Well, it's not. He's head mechanic for Royal Charters, out of P.E.T. airport in Montreal. No friend of, he is the guy. Call him." There was no humour in the statement. No one likes to be called a liar, even in jest.

"OK, fellows. Settle down. What's the bet to me?"

"Eight bucks. More to raise." The betting round had circled the table and was starting another circuit.

"Up another five. Thirteen to you, Shane."

Shane looked at the stack of loonies and toonies in front of him. The buy-in for this game was a hundred dollars. Twice he had visited his wallet since his initial investment. He had barely enough left on the table to cover the bet. He studied his cards for a minute. A third jack had joined his opening pair. Too good to fold, not good enough for another trip into his pocket.

"Call." He slid all of his coins except one into the pot.

"Too rich for me. Fold."

"Call. Whatdoyagot?"

"Three kings and two of them are married." Red overalls laid a full house of all picture cards on the table. "My pot?" He looked around the table for any dissenters before pulling in the pile of money. He added the bills to a stash sticking out from the edge of an ash tray and started stacking the coins.

Shane picked up his last toonie. "Bus fare," he said. "See you guys later."

"You're welcome to come back anytime," red overalls said. "We like your style." The others laughed and anted up for the next hand.

Shane pocketed the toonie and went out of the hangar and back to his store. Once inside, he grabbed the phone and dialed Keith Grant's number. "Got the information already," he said. "Only cost you three hundred bucks."

"Already. It was that easy?"

"Yeah man. Scary, isn't it? Supposed to be a mechanic in Montreal. I've done business with the company, installed some equipment on site. We have a passing acquaintance if it's the man I think it is."

"It's only ten o'clock there. Call him."

"Call him and what? Tell him I'm looking to make a hit?"

Silence dominated the line for a few seconds. "Is he one of the good guys or one of the bad guys? How come he knows what he knows?"

"He's one of the good guys. His clientele can be on the shady side. Russian mob. Bulgarians. Canadians looking to get rich quick. Politicians. I'm sure he's just an observer, but over the odd cup of coffee and three hours of instruction on a piece of new equipment, it's hard to be certain."

"OK, OK." Keith's mind shifted into overdrive. "Tomorrow morning, we fly to Montreal. We'll make an assessment and craft a story accordingly. He's a good guy, we tell him the truth. He's shady, we tell him we want to make a hit. Is there a plane available or do we have to go commercial?"

"Commercial? Do you ever fly commercial, man?"

"This time I will. We don't know who down here might have hired this hit man. Our movements must be on the QT. We don't want to tip anyone off."

Shane stood, walked over to the window and looked out.

"I can see the SJC logo on the tail of one of the jets on the flight line. I'll see if it's booked for the morning. Ordinarily, I'd give Craig a call. Who is it now? Mary?"

"No, don't phone Mary. I'm still not clear on Tom's involvement in this. He seems awfully anxious to be selling off the rolling stock."

"Come on, Tom's clean," Shane said. He hesitated for a second or two before adding, "I'll call Christine. She's newly promoted. Let's introduce her to the burdens of upper management."

Keith laughed. "Right, midnight phone calls go with her new position."

As it turned out, the Sky Jet plane was booked, putting the two men on an Air Canada flight to Montreal. Keith stretched out and sipped his champagne and orange juice breakfast.

"Two first-class seats at short notice would make a down payment on a new plane," Shane said. He spread some cream cheese on his heated bagel.

Keith set down his juice glass and ignored the comment. He had other things on his mind. "If we have to place a classified ad in the newspaper, we have to meet their deadline. We need the information this morning. Your man is going to meet us at the airport, right?"

"Yeah, when I called him last night, he remembered me. Says the entertainment unit we put on his plane is working like a charm. It's more than paid for itself in customer satisfaction. Gives the thugs something to do on the long flights overseas besides hassle the crew. Let's them play shoot-em-up games"

"Did you mention why we wanted to see him?"

"Awkward, but I did. Surprisingly there is no problem, except he will only give me the information face to face. Wants to make sure it's me he's talking to and not the law. He doesn't care why I want to know this but insists that nothing ever comes back on him."

Keith spread some jam on his toast and took a bite.

"I can promise him that. I want the same thing myself. We're getting into a world where being anonymous is a virtue."

"You've got that right, man. Anonymity and paranoia seem to go hand in hand. He declined my offer of money for the information and insists that he choose the place of our meeting before any discussions take place. I'm willing to bet it will be near some high-pitched jet engine howling at full RPMs. One other thing, you're not invited to the meeting. No witnesses to what he tells me."

"I'm hurt. But who cares, as long as he tells you."

36

ROBERT CROSLEY TOSSED his copy of the *USA Today* onto the chair beside his. He leaned back and rubbed his eyes, staring out at the early morning sun. His hotel room faced east and a couple of palm trees offered a degree of shade to his balcony. Below, Fort Lauderdale's early morning traffic increased in volume.

Ads in the personals sections of America's national newspaper alerted him to new job opportunities. Today, he had looked from force of habit. In his mind, this was to be the first morning of his vacation. He had flown in late last night.

This ad troubled him. The area code was 902. He hardly ever did business in that part of the world and now he found himself reading the third message in less than two months. The first two had been from the same client. This was a different number. More repeat business or a friend of the first getting in on an easy way to solve problems? His instincts told him it was too small an area for this much activity.

He poured coffee from the carafe delivered to his room along with a selection of fruit on a tray. Slowly he sipped the brew, contemplating his next line of action. He could ignore the ad. He was on holiday.

White sandy beaches. A swim-up bar in the pool. Smiling, happy people doing nothing. He scheduled these furloughs on a regular basis to keep himself from getting stuck in a killing rut, to allow himself to forget man's inhumanity to man.

He picked up the paper and reread the ad. Some schmuck expected to hear from him. The number looked like a cellphone. The potential client would keep it charged and within reach at all times. Crosley would call him and respectfully decline the offer of employment. His wrist watch read 7:13. That would be 8:13 in 902 land. He slipped a cellphone out of his shirt pocket and dialed the number from the ad.

It took three rings before a male voice answered. OK, here we go, Crosley thought. Let the dance begin. "You placed an ad in USA Today seeking some highly specialized services?"

"I did, but before we start, let me point one thing out. I'm sure there is some sort of protocol that goes with this kind of thing. I'm a rank amateur so you might have to either direct me or forgive any glaring errors in procedure."

Keith got up from his desk chair and walked to the office window. A freak October snowstorm had eliminated his view of the harbour a mere 30 feet away. When he arrived at the office shortly after six a.m. there were already two inches on the ground. Since then, the storm had increased in both wind intensity and volume of snow. This had the makings of a long winter.

Crosley laughed at the amateur designation Grant had assigned himself. "Rest assured, the expertise is all at my end. I discourage people at your end from using my services enough to become experts. I like to think of myself as the solution of last resort."

Now it was Keith Grant's turn to laugh. "You provide counselling and mediation as well?"

"No mediation. I do like to point out that my solution is irrevocable. There are no do-overs so you'd better be sure of what you're asking. How can I help you?"

"I'm not seeking counselling but I would like to meet you face to face to discuss a business arrangement."

"Not going to happen. This is as close as you're ever going to get to meeting me. Actually, I'm on vacation. I'll have to turn down your offer of employment. Sorry."

"Wait. Don't hang up. This is going to be financially beneficial to you. Money is not an object. But I don't hire a pig in a poke. Before I hand over any payment to you, I want to meet you."

Crosley started to hang up. He had already declined the offer. He had fulfilled his obligation by responding to the ad. Responding to the offer carried no obligations of any sort. It was time to get back to relaxing.

"Please, hear me out." The voice from the phone pleaded for his attention.

"As I said, mate, a face to face is not going to happen. Things are done my way or no way. Right now I'm not looking for any new business, sorry."

"We need to establish a little faith here. I understand your reluctance. I'm going to give you my name, address, website, social security number, anything you want. Check me out. See that I am who I say I am, that I can deliver what I promise and then call me back. See that I have as much to lose as you do. We'll set a fee just for meeting. No commitment beyond that on either side. You distrust me, you walk away. Same for me. You get paid a substantial stipend regardless."

Neither man said anything for several seconds. "Substantial. Interesting word, but rather vague."

Standing in his office looking out into the snowstorm, Keith Grant allowed himself a smile. "Let your imagination run wild."

Silence stretched out over the phone lines for several seconds. "OK, I'm intrigued," Crosley said. "Give me your info and we'll see what happens. No promises."

"Keith Grant," Keith said. He provided the rest of the information Crosley requested. He had crossed the line. He was now dealing with a potential murderer. No matter what fancy name the killer chose to use for his profession, his business was murder. Grant looked at the phone. I hope I know what I'm doing, he thought as the reality of his actions settled over him like the mounds of snow building up outside. He took one last look at the jammed traffic on the street below and returned to his desk.

37

DETECTIVE SERGEANT JIM Mcdonald also stood looking out his office window at the snow. He had been there since 7:30 a.m. He had driven through five inches of snow to get there. By now, less than an hour later, he surmised there was at least eight inches down. The meteorologist on the radio had called it a fast-developing nor-easter, a weather-bomb. Everyone had been caught off guard. Jim was glad he was not on traffic duty. The streets would be chaos. Already, rush-hour traffic was making that term seem a gross contradiction. No one was rushing anywhere. The sounds of howling tires came from various directions as commuters were caught still driving on summer treads. It was a good day for catching up on paper work.

The phone on his desk came to life. He turned his back on the raging blizzard and answered the phone.

"Good news, Jim." He recognized Scott Bowen's voice. "I've managed to score a super four-wheel drive vehicle."

Jim was silent for a few seconds. "Couldn't the traffic division make better use of it on a day like this?"

Scott laughed. "Not this one. Remember Roger Johnson, the Big Boss so-called?"

"The drug kingpin? I personally witnessed his arrest."

"That's the one. We have his grey, Ford Explorer. It was seized as part of his proceeds of crime. It hasn't been auctioned off yet, so the department uses it when we don't need lights and sirens. I thought we could catch a few people we've been trying to interview at home. There will be no planes flying in or out today."

"Bob Lively? Good idea."

"I'll come by and pick you up in about 15 minutes, maybe 20. I'll have to stick to the back streets. The main roads are a zoo."

"Good luck with that. The streets are jammed around here."

An hour later, the two men spun their way along Henry Street running parallel to Robie Street. The residents of this street mostly worked at nearby Dalhousie University. Those that bothered going to work had walked. The rest had left their cars safely in their garages. The Explorer broke the trail, heading for the South End. One street over, on Robie, motorists sat fuming in a solid line of unmoving cars.

Scott swung off Henry and onto the street where Bob Lively lived. Before leaving, Jim had dialed Lively's residence and got a male voice answering the phone. Good, Jim thought and hung up. Now they pulled into his unplowed driveway. No tracks sullied the clean, white snow. Lively would be home.

Jim pulled his blue, nylon parka close to his face and trudged through what was by now 10 inches of snow. He tried the doorbell, waited five seconds and knocked heavily on the door. Scott, following his superior's tracks, came up behind him. He, too, wore the department-issued blue parka with RCMP insignia on the shoulders. He peered around Jim and tried to see through the curtained sidelight window.

"Should I go around back in case he makes a run for it?"

Jim shook his head. "They probably can't believe there is anyone really at their door. Or if there is, they may be afraid to open it. Only a fool would be out in this weather and who wants to open the door to a fool?" He knocked again.

The curtain beside the door moved aside and a face appeared. The eyes widened and then the face turned back into the house. No doubt announcing the fools at the door were policemen. The door opened a few inches and a hand beckoned them to enter. Both men squeezed through the small opening and stomped the snow from their boots. They recognized Mrs. Lively from their earlier meeting at the airport office.

Jim smiled. "We thought your husband might be home this morning. Can we speak to him?"

Mrs. Lively looked at the policemen, looked down the hallway towards the kitchen and then back at the policemen. "It must be important to be out in this weather. Bob, it's the police. They want to talk to you, dear."

Bob Lively came from the kitchen, a cup of coffee in one hand, the morning paper in the other. He was in his stocking feet, had a cardigan sweater over a buttoned-up shirt and dark casual slacks. "It must be damn important. Get your coats off and come in. There's no need to talk in the porch."

Jim noted that Bob Lively appeared older than he thought he would be. His research had pegged Lively's age at 47 but Jim doubted that anyone would refuse him a senior's discount. He slipped his coat off and hung it on a hook. He put his overshoes on the rubber boot tray and followed Bob Lively down the hall. Before he reached the living room, Mrs. Lively showed up with a pot of coffee and two mugs.

"You probably want to warm your innards a bit. What do you take in your coffee?"

Jim looked over at Scott Bowen. They had only been teamed up for a week this time around, but they knew each other's habits. "Both black," he said. Scott nodded his agreement.

The three men sat down in the overstuffed, floral-patterned chairs. Various framed pictures of airplanes were scattered around the wall. Jim noted that one of them showed a younger Lively in an air force flight suit, helmet under his arm, standing in front of a Voodoo fighter jet. He had a full head of jet black hair in the picture but even then, worry lines were forming around his eyes.

"How good do you think your chances are of landing the Worldwide Seafood contract?"

"What? The Worldwide Seafood contract? They're damn good. What business is that of yours? Are you with the commercial branch?"

"No, major crimes. Robbery and homicide."

Lively's eyes grew wider. "Why are you asking about Worldwide Seafood? Has someone been murdered there? Who? Is Marcel all right?"

Jim held his hands up in a placating manner. "Everyone at Worldwide is fine. We're investigating the murder of Craig Flint."

Lively looked even more shocked. "Flint had a stroke or something. He wasn't murdered. I went to his funeral. Too much stress in his life."

The cops exchanged glances. Lively was putting on an impressive display of innocence.

"We believe otherwise," Jim said. "We believe he was poisoned."

A loud gasp came from the doorway to the living room. "Craig was poisoned? I don't believe it." Mrs.

Lively had just returned to the room with a plate of muffins. Steam could be seen rising from them. Melted butter ran down the sides.

"If that's true, and I find it hard to believe, what do you want from me?" Lively was recovering from his shock at the news. "Craig and I were good friends as well as business associates. I sure as hell wouldn't have anything to do with his death."

"No, no. Of course not," Jim said. "We thought you might be able to point us in the direction of anyone Craig might have been having problems with. What's the gossip around the airport?"

"The gossip around the airport is that he died from a stroke. I've told you that. It's not even gossip. His sister, Mary, told me at the funeral that it was a stroke. Surely to God, she must know how her brother died."

Jim took a deep breath and let it out slowly. "Believe me when I tell you that Craig Flint did not die of a stroke. It was not natural causes. He was murdered. Corporal Bowen and myself are heading up the investigation. We are seeking your help. Now, is there anyone you know of who would gain from his death?"

Enlightenment dawned on Lively's face. He made the link between the two questions, one about the Worldwide contract and one about who stood to gain. He jumped to his feet. "Now just a goddamn minute. You're accusing me of killing Craig to get this lobster contract. That's absurd. You're out of your fucking mind." He looked at his wife, who still stood in the doorway, for backup. "Mother, tell them how stupid that suggestion is."

"Now, now. Settle down, dear. I'm sure that's not what they meant." She walked into the room and offered a muffin to Jim. "That's not what you meant, is it?"

Jim waved the muffins away. "It's early in the investigation. We're just trying to figure out who the players are." He looked at Lively again. "You did have a lot to gain with the contract being reopened. The general consensus was that Sky Jet had it wrapped up."

"I didn't have enough to gain to murder anyone. I would pick up more than enough extra business if Sky Jet won the contract to keep me busy. Craig's planes could only be in one place at a time. If he was flying lobsters to Europe, I'd be flying his excess passengers. We've always worked together. Besides, I still had a crack at winning the contract. The winner had never been officially announced. Marcel was well known for throwing out red herrings. He liked to keep everyone on their toes."

Jim made a notation in his notebook. Lively leaned forward to see what was written but Jim flipped the book shut.

"What will happen to Sky Jet if you win the contract?"

"Nothing. They've got lots of business to keep them going. All this contract does for any of us is give us guaranteed business. It's a negotiating point if we want to finance another plane. Craig already had his new plane. Somewhere in the woodwork, he has some deep-pocketed backers. If his sister keeps operating the company the same way Craig did, she'll have no problem keeping it busy. I'll be throwing business her way for a while when I land the contract. It takes time to buy a new plane and I have to keep my existing clientele happy. Sky Jet will survive."

Jim hesitated before asking his next question. "One more time, is there anyone else who benefits from Craig's death?"

Again, Lively seethed at the implication. "His dumb-ass brother-in-law Tom Dunford and his wife just became a hell of a lot richer. Otherwise, his death is just a blip on the radar of life. Most other people won't notice one way or the other. At most, they'll notice the absence of sarcastic comments. Nobody will miss him."

Both cops studied Lively a little closer. "Why do you call Tom Dunford a dumb ass?" Scott asked first. "Wasn't he competent at his job?"

"Not according to the stories Craig told. I don't really know the man myself but Craig called him a dumb ass. He would know."

"Now, now, dear," Mrs. Lively cut in. "You pilots think anyone who doesn't actually fly the plane is a dumb ass. Tom worked hard for Sky Jet. He maintained the high level of service the clients expected."

Lively gave his wife a look that would peel paint off the wall. "All I can go on is what Craig told me. He said the man was incompetent most of the time. Let's leave it at that for Christ's sake."

Jim watched the expression on the wife's face change from anger to frustration to acquiescence. Under different circumstances, she would not have backed down. In front of guests, she accepted defeat, for now. "Are you sure you boys won't have a muffin? They're warm. I made them myself." She extended the tray again.

Jim reached out. It was time to soothe ruffled feathers. "Sure, I'll have one."

Scott smiled and reached across his partner. "Me too." He hadn't wanted to refuse them the first time around. He was only following his partner's lead to make the setting one of serious business.

"Take two," Mrs. Lively said. She made no offer to her husband.

38

ONCE AGAIN, KEITH Grant found himself flying commercial. This time alone. His instructions from Robert Crosley had arrived in an email message shortly before lunch. Fly to Miami International Airport. Keith had barely made the Air Canada flight to Toronto that put him on this Airbus 319A with more than 120 other people winging their way to the warmer climate of Florida. By noon, the traffic in Halifax had cleared up and no new cars were venturing out in the snow. Several passengers had failed to show for their flights and Keith was able to grab a seat on the first plane out. Florida was looking good compared to what he had left behind.

The hour and a half layover in Toronto gave him a chance to think about what he was doing. Was this the stupidest decision he had ever made? He hoped not. He tossed some story ideas around in his mind before deciding honesty was the best policy when dealing with someone who might not hesitate to kill you if he found your tale unbelievable. Keith's intentions were not to hire him but to purchase some information. Money would not be a factor. Keith was prepared to pay. The airfare on this leg of the trip alone was approaching $2000 with taxes and fees. The cost of persuading a professional hit man to violate his own so-called code of ethics on client confidentiality would require considerably more. Keith had dumped several million dollars into an account which could be easily transferred offshore when the deal was made. He would negotiate from a position of strength, dazzling the man with zeros. Failure was not an option. Finding Craig's killer had become an obsession.

He looked down at the blue waters of the Atlantic. Years of flying had attuned him to variations in a plane's behaviour. The change of pitch in the sound of the engine indicated they were making their approach to land. He gave his seatbelt a reassuring tug and waited for touchdown. It had been over seven hours since he departed from Halifax. He was eager to get on with the job.

The plane safely landed and Keith made his way to customs. He had brought no luggage with him so he was first in line to clear through. The agent looked at the floor beside him and then up into Keith's eyes.

"No luggage?"

Keith shook his head. "I'm here on business. Once it's completed, I'm on the first plane back to Canada."

"No carry-on luggage either?"

"Just this." Keith threw his passport on the counter between the two men. The agent flipped through page after page of stamps from all over the world.

"You get around," he said. He stamped the passport with a flourish and passed the book back to Keith. "Enjoy your stay, no matter how brief." His eyes turned to the next person in line.

A sign bearing his name caught his attention as he stepped into the arrivals area.

"I'm Keith Grant," he said.

The sign-carrying man smiled. He passed Keith a white envelope and stood waiting. Keith recognized the stance. The man expected a tip. He slipped a five-dollar bill from his clip of American money and passed it to him. The man nodded briefly and melted into the crowd.

Keith found a quiet spot away from everyone else. He tore one end from the envelope and gave it a shake. An airline ticket and a note fell into his hand. Delta Airlines, leaving at 7:40 from Concourse H. Keith checked his watch. It was 7:32. He had eight minutes to reach the flight. He looked for a sign to see which concourse he was on. A large letter G covered one wall.

Thank goodness for that, he thought. It's right next door. He glanced at the note: "Turn off your phone," it read. He fished his phone from his pocket, turned it off and hustled down the corridor to Concourse H. Quickly he presented his ticket in exchange for a boarding pass.

The attendant looked at his ticket, looked at the clock and then at Keith. "You'd better hurry, sir. The plane has already been boarded." She reached for a red phone on the counter with one hand and pointed to the gate with the other. "Down there," she said. "I'll make sure someone is at security and have them hold the ramp for you."

Keith took off in the direction indicated. He had to give the killer credit. This guaranteed Keith would meet him alone. He stepped onto the plane and the big door swung shut behind him. He was the last to arrive. He made his way to the back of the plane. The flight attendants were already in the aisle waiting to go through their pre-flight. Keith sat down, fastened his belt and the plane started to taxi away to prepare for takeoff.

His ticket had him booked through to Atlanta with stops in Tampa, Jacksonville and Charleston. He was on the milk run. He looked around at his fellow passengers trying to pick out a hitman. No one paid any attention to him. They were all lost in their own little worlds. Keith pulled the in-flight magazine from the rack and started flipping through the pages. All he could do was go with the flow until the hired gun was ready to meet him.

The plane took off, hardly reached altitude when it started its descent for Tampa. They were scheduled for a 10-minute stop. No one was to leave the plane except departing passengers. New ones were waiting to take their places. Keith continued to read the magazine.

"Excuse me, sir. Are you Keith Grant?" A blue-clad flight attendant was leaning over to talk quietly with him.

"Yes," he said. "Is there a problem?"

"No, sir. No problem. We've had a call from your office asking you to meet a client here in Tampa. They will have a local person waiting to meet you."

Again, Keith fought off the look of surprise. The resourcefulness of this killer was beyond anything Keith had expected. "OK," he said and reached down to undo his seatbelt.

"You'll have to hurry, sir. We'll be taking off in less than a minute."

Keith made his way up the aisle and through the door to the jetway. Again the door slammed shut behind him. Again no one had any chance to follow him. The mechanic in Montreal had told Shane this man was one of the best in the business. Keith realized that wasn't an idle boast. He headed into the arrival lounge curious to see what the next leg in this little adventure had to offer.

A uniformed chauffeur held a sign in the air with "Keith Grant" prominently displayed. Keith identified himself and was led outside to a black stretch limo. The driver stopped by the back door and hesitated before opening it.

"Excuse me sir," he said, "I know this is unorthodox, but I wonder if you could pay before we take the trip downtown. You are from outside the country and the fare is $250. I accept all major credit cards."

Keith was taken aback. Paying up front for a limo was foreign to him. He took three bills from his wallet and handed them to the man. "I'm sorry, I don't tip for service until I see how good the service is," he said. "Do you know where you are taking me?"

"Of course, sir, Largo. We needed your destination before we could set the fare." He opened the door and Keith slipped into the luxurious interior. "Help yourself to the bar, sir. It's included in the price. With traffic, the trip may take about 30 minutes unless of course, there's an accident on the bridge and then, who knows?"

"Where's the girl? For $500 an hour, I must get more than a taxi ride."

The chauffeur smiled. "You'd think so, sir. But you don't." He pushed the door shut with a solid thunk.

39

"TELL ME, MRS. Lively, have you heard any unusual gossip around the airport?" Jim was putting a small dab of strawberry jam on his muffin. He looked up at the woman and smiled. "You spend more time there on the ground than your husband does. How do you fill your day when he's out travelling around the country and beyond?"

"Are you stereotyping me, Sergeant? I'm a woman. I must be involved in the local gossip."

"Not at all. I asked your husband the same question. I'm just wondering if you heard any references as to how someone might get rid of some obstacle in their path. You seem to know Tom Dunford quite well. You must spend time with the ground crews."

Scott cleared his throat and coughed into his hand. Jim looked over at his partner. He was coming dangerously close to suggesting a professional hit man but he needed to move this case along. Someone must have heard something.

"I'm sorry, Sergeant. There was no talk of murder around the hangar of Lively Charters. My husband made that quite clear. If you've ever talked to Tom Dunford, you must know he is not capable of murder.

Now if you'll excuse me, I have dishes to do." She took the empty muffin plate and started for the kitchen, stopped and looked back at her husband. "Where's that dishwashing cube that came in the mail? I may as well try it and see if it lives up to its claims."

"Dishwashing cube? I don't know, Mother. Probably with all the other goddamn junk mail on the corner of the shelf." He looked back at Sergeant Mcdonald. "Women. They believe everything written on glossy paper with fancy pictures. This one is new and improved. Until this morning, we were perfectly happy with the old one."

Jim smiled. He thought of his own cleaning cupboard. Most of the items came in the yellow containers of the no-name brand. Most did an adequate job, at least for a bachelor. Stella would probably change all that if their relationship became something more permanent.

"Look Sergeant, I'm shocked to find you believe Craig was murdered. If you are right, you're barking up the wrong tree looking among the air crews. I don't know what other things he was involved in, but that's where you want to be looking. As I said earlier, someone was providing funding behind the scenes to keep his company in the forefront of the local charter business. Maybe that's where you should concentrate. I've carried a lot of different people on my plane over the years and if there's one thing I've learned, it's as the Bible says: 'The love of money is the root of all evil.' Maybe Craig thought landing this contract would set him free from his backers. Maybe they didn't want to liberate him."

Jim nodded his head as he listened. He knew the source of Craig's money and that person sat less than 10 feet away while Craig was dying. That explanation would answer a lot of perplexing questions: who administered the killing agent, how it was administered and where it and all the containers disappeared to. Grant claimed no advance knowledge of the contents of Craig's will, but what was one more lie in a string of lies designed to cover up a murder? He mentally kicked himself for not searching the poker players the night of the death.

Scott looked at him as if reading his mind. Keith Grant was not the killer. Jim could see that message in Scott's dark eyes. He agreed, but still, it would answer a lot of questions if Grant were. Grant did pick up a piece of prime real estate in the deal. If one was following the money trail, that ownership could represent at least a small part of the path. The location alone made it worth several hundred thousand dollars, the spectacular cottage was an added bonus. On the other hand, the value of the place was a relative item. To Keith Grant, it was pocket change.

Tom Dunford did not fall into that category. He, too, was present when Craig took his final breath. In fact, no one could account for his exact whereabouts. Although he did not come up as an owner, he was sharing the matrimonial bed with the winner in that field. His life had to have dramatically improved. Jim was a long way from crossing him off the list of suspects despite the glowing character references he generated from just about everyone Jim interviewed.

"That's always an option. We are investigating that angle as well. Do you know any of the money men Craig was involved with?"

Bob Lively shook his head in the negative. "He always liked to present the illusion that the company was entirely his own. He never discussed even the existence of partners, but, hell, I know what's involved in this business. If he was doing it on his own, he was heavily in debt. I couldn't find any bankers to back me to that degree. Wherever the money came from, it must have come with some serious strings attached. Those strings sometimes get wrapped around your neck and snuff the life from you."

"Yeah, sometimes that happens." Jim gave Scott a questioning glance to see if he had any questions for Lively. Scott gave a little shake of his head. "Thanks for your time," Jim said. He snapped his notebook shut and stood. "If you think of anything else, give me a call." A business card had materialized in his hand and he gave it to Lively.

Lively looked at the card as if it were something repulsive. "Count on it. I'll be racking my brain for a reason to call." Sarcasm dripped from his voice. He tossed the card onto the coffee table and picked up the empty cups. "If you can see yourselves out, I have a dishwasher cycle to catch."

The two policemen made their way down the hall to the front porch. Sunshine broke through the windows beside the door. The storm had abated. The final snowfall count was slightly less than 12 inches. It would be a record for this day in October. It had served one good purpose. Bob Lively had stopped ducking them. The interview had not turned up anything really useful but it had removed him as a serious suspect. That in itself was a worthwhile accomplishment. They were whittling away at who might have had Craig killed. Roberto Masserati was the next one in their sights although he seemed less likely to gain from Craig's demise. Everyone told them that. Now it was time to go right to the source to see if they agreed.

Masserati lived outside the city in a community near the airport. Even with the four-wheel drive, it might be a challenge to get to his house. By now the main roads were being kept clear but none of the side streets had seen the benefit of a snowplow. Jim knelt and pulled on his boots. Scott stood back to wait his turn in the small porch

"Roberto Masserati is next," Jim said as he straightened up and moved aside while Scott dressed his feet. They pulled on their heavy outer coats and opened the door. Jim looked down the hallway. Neither of the Livelys were in sight. "Thanks for your time," he called out as he closed the door behind him. There was no response. He hadn't been added to anyone's Christmas card list in this household.

40

KEITH LOOKED OUT the limo window at the blue waters of Old Tampa Bay. They had been on the Howard Frankland Bridge for about four minutes and there was still no end in sight. He tried to think about what he knew about Largo. It wasn't much. It sat between Clearwater and St. Pete's.

The bridge finally came to an end and they swung onto Ulmberton Road. Traffic was a little heavier here but not enough to impede their progress. From Ulmberton they took a left onto Seminole Blvd. and then right onto 8th Ave. SW. The neighbourhood was becoming decidedly blue collar and the limo was getting lots of stares from the people in the street. There would be no doubt when he stepped from the car at the end of the trip that he was not some local coming home for supper.

Exactly 31 minutes after leaving the airport, the limo pulled up next to Francesca's Internet Cafe. Keith had passed on the free bar and looked out the window at the restaurant. "Italian," he said. "I can live with that." He took another twenty from his wallet and passed it to the chauffeur as he opened the back door. "Do you recommend any of the house specialties?"

"I'm sure they are all good, sir, but I have never eaten here before. This place was your choice, not mine."

"Of course," Keith said. He went inside and looked around. The smell of good food cooking tickled his nostrils with just the right touch of garlic and oregano in the air. The tables were a little more than half filled. The dinner hour was winding down.

Along the back wall were a bank of computers with the rates for using them posted. Most were occupied. The hostess, like all the patrons, watched the stretch limo pull away.

"You must be Keith Grant," she said. "Your computer is ready."

Despite his surprise, Keith followed her to the back of the restaurant where she seated him at a terminal with Skype already running. The screen contained an image of an empty chair. He put on the earphones and waited.

"Mr. Grant, welcome to Florida," a voice said.

Keith looked down the line to see if anyone else had his image on their screen. They didn't.

"Thank you," he said. "When do we meet?'

"We are meeting right now."

"I could have done this from my office in Halifax," Keith said. "The deal called for a face-to-face."

"No, Mr. Grant, your deal called for a face-to-face. I explicitly told you that would not happen. Nothing has changed. Are we going to discuss business or should I order your limo?"

Keith contemplated both choices. What he wanted was the name of the person who had ordered the hit on Craig. Did it matter if he met the assassin? This might actually be the safer choice.

"Why the runaround if you didn't plan to meet?"

"Mr. Grant, I have checked you out."

Keith Grant had surprised Crosley with his appearance. He had expected someone older based on what his client had achieved, starting from nothing and becoming one of the richest men in North America. This had been accomplished by investing and that method usually etched a few worry lines into the face as one built up a cash reserve. Grant's net worth did not suggest a conservative strategy.

At first, the story seemed too extravagant to be true. He suspected this was manufactured to attract his attention. However, when he dug deeper, the sources all verified the existence of Keith Grant over the past number of years. Many of the officers of the companies Grant was involved with had met the man in person. Crosley moved down the corporate food chain to the factory floor in his inquires. Some of these people also remembered briefly meeting Grant before their factory's ownership changed hands or at least underwent a major overhaul. If he was a plant, he was a damn good plant, deep roots and in for the long haul.

"I've checked your story and I'm impressed with your accomplishments. I won't tell you how to conduct your business; in return, don't tell me how to run mine. I have a lot more on the line than mere money."

Keith sat passively, staring at the image of the empty chair. He reached into his pocket and withdrew a piece of paper. He held it up to the computer's camera.

"The agreement called for $100,000 to meet. I'm not sure this qualifies as a meeting." He placed the cheque on the table. "What do you think?"

"I think this is as good as it gets. Put the cheque back in your pocket and I'll call your limo. One-hundred-thousand doesn't buy my freedom." After a brief pause, the voice continued. "But you've come a long way to make me an offer. As Dr. Frasier Crane used to say 'I'm listening.'"

Keith picked up the cheque and tapped it on the table. He would only have one chance to pick this killer's brain. In fact, getting this close exceeded his expectations. He leaned back in the chair. "Let's talk business."

"As I said, I'm listening."

"You've checked my CV." Keith continued. "You now understand that when I said money wouldn't be a factor in our discussion, I wasn't blowing smoke up your kilt?"

A slight chuckle could be heard in his earphones. "Money is not my only driving force."

"Right, you expect me to believe you're out to save the world by killing off bad people one person at a time. You're free if I can justify my reason for hiring you? Don't blow smoke up my kilt either, mate."

The chuckle became a laugh. "Free? That word doesn't exist in my vocabulary. I do have guidelines though. I don't make hits on politicians. The general population deserves to live under the clowns they elect. Besides, the police get fanatical about tracking down political assassins. You're messing with their extended family."

Grant nodded his understanding. "OK, no politicians. Like I said, you're not out to make the world a better place."

Another laugh. "Who is the person of interest?"

"Person of interest?" Keith looked confused then realized this conversation would be one of oblique references. "There is no person of interest. I merely want to buy some information about one of your former clients."

All signs of merriment left the voice in Keith's ears. "That's not going to happen, my friend. Selling information is not my line of business."

Keith stared intently at the camera. "Maybe it's time to look for a more lucrative line of work. This one job could put you on easy street for the rest of your life. Investment counselling comes at no additional charge."

"Confidentiality is my bread and butter," said the disembodied voice. "No amount of money will make me change my mind. Word gets out that I'm telling tales out of school and a lot of people around the world will start getting nervous. I know how they deal with things that make them nervous. Sorry, no deal."

Keith reached into his pocket once more and pulled out another piece of paper. He held it up to the camera. "One, two, three, four, five, six zeros," Keith said, pointing to each one as he counted. "What each of us does for a living is irrelevant. The question before us is simple. Do I want the information you possess more than you feel the need to keep it confidential? This is a cashier's cheque. You can cash it anywhere. No questions asked."

Keith though he detected a slight gasp. "A million dollars. You think money is the solution to every problem."

"I think it goes a long way in your line of work. It's what makes you get up in the morning."

"You're saying I'll do anything if the price is right? That I have no obligation to my former clients?"

Keith laughed. "You're a sociopath. You feel no obligation to anyone but yourself."

"That's harsh." Keith could hear the anger in the voice. "I could be in the next room you know."

"Good. Let's meet." Keith realized he was holding his breath. Had he crossed the line? He looked around. No one showed any interest in this corner of the room.

After a long pause, Crosley responded. "Maybe some slight sociopathic tendencies. We're never going to meet." The anger was gone.

Keith relaxed and held up the cheque again. "A million dollars, free and clear."

"I'm not saying yes," Crosley said, "but what would you expect for that kind of money?"

"Someone killed my partner. You, I expect. I want to know who hired you."

"You want me to confess to murder? A million bucks would buy a lot of cigarettes, but those prison walls would take most of the fun away from being a millionaire."

"You're still talking, so you do have a price. Name it. Putting you in jail means nothing to me. I want the person who hired you. You've never been caught to date. Having money should make staying free easier, not harder. You'll never have to kill again." Keith paused. His eyes lost all trace of humour. "Unless you kill for pleasure and not for profit."

"Death is overrated. It's strictly business with me. People all say they want to go to heaven. I just speed them along on their journey. Who knows, they may be thanking me."

Grant snorted. "I doubt too many of your victims qualify for celestial accommodations."

Crosley's voice took on the light air again. "Maybe not. What if I said my price was five million?"

Grant's face remained impassive. "I'd say for that price I need to know what you're offering."

Another period of silence. Keith thought he had caught Crosley off–guard with his tentative acceptance of the offer.

"What would you expect for that price?"

"A conviction. You would have to supply enough evidence to put the person away for life."

"I can't do that. That kind of evidence would go both ways. Part of my job is to make sure there is no paper trail back to me. Conversely, that means there is no paper trail going the other way. The best I could do is supply you a name and a time when they contacted me."

Grant held up the cashier's cheque. "One million buys that kind of information. If you want more, you have to supply more."

"What if I told you this person hired me to make another hit? The two deaths may help make a case against them."

"Another hit? Who? When?"

More silence. Was this a bluff, Keith wondered.

"Two more answers should be worth two more million."

Keith suppressed his smile. They were negotiating. The playing field of expertise had tilted in his favour.

MARY SAT ON the blue, leather chesterfield in the reception room of Sky Jet Charter's downtown office. Her hands were tightly wrapped around a mug of hazelnut flavoured coffee. Outside the storm was abating but it had left a generous dollop of snow on the roofs of the buildings around her. Gusts of wind picked up clouds of the rooftop snow and filtered it down on the people on the streets below. Down there, it appeared the storm still raged. From Mary's perspective, she could see the sun breaking through the clouds.

"How many flights were cancelled this morning?" she asked Christine, who likewise clung to a steaming mug of aromatic, brown brew.

"None of ours. We still have two planes in Europe and the third got away at six this morning before the full force of the storm hit. The commercial lines were only delayed for a couple of hours but a lot of the planes going to New England are still grounded because of closures at the other end. Getting from the city to the airport proved to be the biggest challenge around here. Tom said most of the charters are still on the ground. Anybody not there by 8 o'clock didn't get there until after noon." She sipped her coffee. "Rescheduling will be a nightmare."

Mary smiled. "This would be a good time to have a couple of extra planes sitting around to take up the slack. When are our planes back?"

"The European planes will be over there for another four or five days. The home plane is due back at supper time. We could turn it around in about an hour and have it in the air again. There's nothing else scheduled for it for two days."

"Tom's at the airport. Get him working on that. Have him start with Bob Lively. If Lively expects our cooperation on the lobster contract, he should be prepared to throw some business our way now."

Mary looked at her watch. "What time are these new clients supposed to be here?"

Christine consulted a pad in her lap. "Right about now, but—" she glanced at the street below, "—traffic is still creeping down there."

Mary set down her mug and got to her feet. "Call Tom. I'll be in my office when they get here." She started for the door but stopped and turned around. "Do you have a cellphone number for the new people? Call and see if they want us to send a four-wheel drive to pick them up. They will probably say no but you can't beat it as a PR move." She flashed Christine a smile and disappeared through the door to her private office.

Good idea, boss, Christine thought. Now you're thinking like your brother. Christine went out to the reception area and hit the speed-dial button to connect her to the airport office.

"Sky Jet Charter Services." Tom's voice had a smooth melodic quality to it. Christine smiled in spite of her dislike for the man producing the sound. Clients would find the voice inviting.

"Hi, Tom, Christine here. Mary would like you to see if you can pick up any business for a night flight. She figures the other companies should be backed up by the storm. Start with Bob Lively." She tried to keep her voice professional. She could hear a deep breath at the other end of the line.

"You think I'm just sitting around here doing nothing. I have my own work to do. I can't just jump up at the drop of a hat and go on a wild goose chase for customers."

"Mary thinks there may be some opportunities out there. You're on site and can assess the situation first hand." She spoke slowly knowing full well she sounded patronizing. "I'll tell her you're too busy and I'll do it blindly by phone."

"No. Wait. Bob's plane is still out there. I can see it through the window. I'll talk to him." He walked over to the window. "I don't think he's here. There are no tracks leading to the hangar and the door is not shovelled out yet. Let me get back to you."

Tom hung up, grabbed his coat from the hook and made his way through the snow to the hangar housing Lively Charters. He knew Christine was only passing on instructions from Mary but still resented having her order him around. He was a vice-president of the company now. He deserved more respect.

The sun reflected off the office windows, restricting his view. He put his hands up to his eyes and peered in. His gaze was met by a total lack of activity. The place was empty. He turned and started back for his own office when the door of the cafeteria popped open. Two mechanics in blue coveralls came out.

"Any sign of Bob?" one of them called out.

Tom faced the speaker. "He doesn't seem to have gotten in yet. Maybe he has no flights scheduled. I sure wouldn't want to come out here for nothing on a day like this."

"We're supposed to get his plane ready for an afternoon flight. Supposed to have been this morning but the client postponed till the weather cleared up. Not like Bob to be late. He's one of the most reliable people I know."

Tom looked back at the hangar. If he could capture this business, he could score some brownie points with Mary. "Who's the client?"

"Sorry, we just fuel the plane, make sure all the flaps arc flapping, all thc wheels are turning. His missus takes care of the bookings and she's not here either."

Tom hid his disappointment. It would not be good to be caught trying to poach customers. He looked around the parking lot to see if anyone appeared to be waiting for Bob to arrive. His own plane wasn't due back for a few more hours so Bob would have to be a complete no-show for Sky Jet to capture the business. Still, if he could reassure the passenger that a flight would be available, either through Lively Charters or through his own company, this could go a long way in securing future business.

"He could just be tied up on the 102 Highway. I'll give him a call, see what's happening."

The mechanic who asked the first question shook his head. "I've tried both his home number and his cell. No luck. The co-pilot is over at Meteorology checking the weather. The storm appears to be over." He shrugged. "Can't go without Bob though. He is the captain."

Right, thought Tom. The high and mighty pilot/captain. Can't operate a business without them. Craig had made that point often enough. "If the client shows up, send him over to our office. We'll entertain him until Bob arrives." Tom smiled and headed back to the warmth of his own office. He would check the other charters and see if they had any extra business to throw his way. Mary's idea was sound. He had to admit that.

She was fitting into the executive chair at Sky Jet more quickly and more efficiently than he would have ever anticipated from his stay-at-home wife. Craig was a fool for not capitalizing on her abilities when she offered them to him. She had the education, she just needed the opportunity to prove herself. Starting out as president of the company gave her that chance.

42

THE INFORMATION RATTLED Keith Grant to his core. Someone else was about to die. Could he stop this madness or was it too late?

"Is the person dead yet?" His hands clutched the edge of the table as he leaned towards the computer. Crosley had sounded as calm as if the statement had been to order mineral water instead of tap water, not to end someone's life.

"I'm not sure but it is a definite possibility."

"Not sure? What do you mean, not sure?"

Crosley's voice in his ears took on an edge. "Keep your voice down. You're in a public place." Keith looked at the other patrons. No one seemed to be paying any attention to him.

He gave himself an internal shake. He had inserted himself into this world of violence uninvited. He had better learn to live here quickly.

"Like I said at the outset, I'm new at this. Do I care who this new victim is? Should I be worried? Is it me?"

All he knew for sure was that Craig was dead, had been murdered. He still did not know why or who had arranged it. He and Craig were business partners. It was not a great leap to believe he could be next if, for whatever gruesome reason, someone had decided to kill the owners of Sky Jet Charter. And now here he was talking to Craig's killer and on his own dime. The killer had not even had to come north to find him. Crosley may have been in over his head negotiating with Keith, but Keith now realized he too was in over his head. What idiocy had possessed him to do this?

Crosley laughed out loud. "That would be ironic, but alas, it's not the case."

Grant was shocked at how easily Crosley dismissed the death of another human being. A tremor came into his voice. "I can't calmly sit here chatting with you when someone may be dying back home. Who is it?"

Crosley sighed. "People are dying all over the world, my friend. Focus on why you're here. I only mentioned it because it might or might not tie into the death of Craig Flint. It might justify the money you're about to pay me. It will definitely raise the price. Regardless, it is out of your hands."

When Crosley talked about people dying, there was a detachment, an indifference, that sent chills through Keith. Despite the Florida heat, his body had turned cold.

He realized the conversation had taken a shift. The discussion now centred on how much, not if. Keith tried to find some pleasure in the success of his mission. It eluded him.

Crosley outlined his terms for giving up the information Grant sought. Money first, then the information. Four million dollars.

Grant patted a couple of his pockets before pulling out another envelope. He opened it and as before, held the cheque up to the camera.

"Four million, payable to the bearer. That will be you."

"How high were you prepared to go?" Crosley asked, obviously surprised a cheque for that amount had been pre-prepared.

"Four million," Keith said. "You tapped me out at my top figure. Let's have the name."

"Not so fast. Put the cheque back in the envelope and give it to the waiter. Tell him there's a courier waiting outside."

Keith followed the instruction and watched $4 million waltz out the door. "Done," he said.

"They say everyone has a price." Crosley sounded reserved. "I believed that and wondered what mine would be. Now I know." He became businesslike again. "Does the name Dunford mean anything to you?"

"Tom?"

"Who?"

43

A S SOON AS Keith Grant exited Francesca's Internet Cafe he sought out a pay phone. He spotted one across the parking lot and sped over to it. He had a $100 Visa cash-card in his wallet and plugged it into the phone and dialed Sergeant Jim Mcdonald's cellphone.

He listened to the ringing of the phone and pondered what he would say. His first thought had been to alert the police to the danger to Bob Lively. From there, he had no plan.

He whipped a handkerchief from his pocket and put it over the mouthpiece. Anonymity might be in order while he planned what to do next. The person who hired Crosley posed no immediate threat to anyone else. At least, Keith hoped that was the case.

"Sergeant Mcdonald," he heard in his hear.

"A professional killer is after Bob Lively. Find him; save him."

Keith hung up. He stood there with the phone in one hand, his handkerchief in the other, staring at the passing traffic. Could he do anything more? He thought not.

Crosley refused to give him any details. They had argued for a few minutes before Keith realized he was wasting time. He had to alert Mcdonald. The method didn't matter.

He looked around the parking lot for his limo. Getting back to Canada would be his own problem. Crosley had cut the ties. The next commercial flight would leave in the morning. Keith couldn't wait that long. He flipped open the phone book to charter services and placed a call.

Shane Martin sat sprawled out in the arrival lounge of Stanfield International Airport. He wiped the sleep from his eyes. The clock above the door for arriving passengers from outside the country read 4:32 a.m. An overseas flight was expected in another half hour and a few greeters shared the area with Shane. Keith Grant would not be on that plane. He had called Shane the night before telling him to be there between four and five. He had chartered a Learjet 60 and would be back in Halifax as soon as possible.

But what was so important? Shane knew Keith was meeting with the alleged hit man; knew he was seeking the name of the client; knew the intention was to inform Sergeant Mcdonald of the newly acquired name. Why was he flying home so abruptly? Could an extra half day make that much difference? Had he informed Sergeant Mcdonald of the contractor's name? That was the plan. Find out the name, turn it over to the cops. It was a good plan. If he hadn't done that, then this new plan made no sense.

The door popped open and Keith stepped through.

"Have you heard anything about Bob Lively?" Keith asked as soon as the two men were alone.

Shane gave him a confused look. "What about Bob Lively? He didn't hire the killer did he? My God, I don't believe that. You'd better recheck your information."

Grant shook his head. "I'll take that to mean you haven't heard anything." He looked around to see if anyone was in earshot. "Let's get out of here. You're not going to believe any of this. Swing by the hangars."

The two men headed for the parking lot and Shane's car. They could talk privately there and Keith was not going to say anything of substance until he was sure they were alone. Spending a few short hours with the ultra security conscious killer had imbued Keith with a little paranoia of his own.

They swung through the charter flight line. Most buildings were locked up tight. A few planes were being serviced for an early morning departure. Bob Lively's place stood in complete darkness, snow still piled against the office door.

Shane slowed down as he drove by. "I remember Tom telling me that he arranged for one of Bob's clients to fly out on one of our planes last night. Said Bob failed to show up."

"Tom? That shows initiative. Maybe I was wrong about him."

"No man, it was Mary's idea. Tom was in the cafeteria complaining about it. Seems Christine passed the word on to him. He has a real hate on for her."

Keith shook his head. "Man has no taste in women. No red-blooded Canadian male would have a hate on for Christine."

"Unless you think you should be CEO of the company and the secretary is giving you orders." Both men laughed then turned serious again. "Listen man, it's hard to believe Bob Lively is involved in this. I've been dealing with him ever since my company moved out here. He can be crude at times, but he's no killer."

Keith gave him a wry smile.

Shane could no longer hold back his curiosity. "Come on, man, what did the sergeant say when you told him?"

Keith continued to stare out the windshield at the long beams of white light cutting through the blackness. Without turning, he simply said: "Haven't officially called him yet."

Shane had seen these actions before. They occurred when Keith knew without any doubt what he should be doing, the proper procedure, but still hadn't bought into the idea of following it. He took his own eyes from the road ahead and stared at his friend. "And why not, might I ask? That was the plan, man. Remember the plan."

Keith remained silent for a couple of more kilometres. "The plan took a new turn. Bob Lively may have also been murdered. I'm not sure." He turned to meet his friend's gaze. "I called the police before I called you. It may be good that you've heard nothing."

"Murder Bob Lively? Someone is trying to win this contract by killing off all the competition?"

Keith looked out the side window into the darkness flashing by them. "I don't really understand what is going on. I've asked this before, but how well do you know Mary Dunford?"

"Mary?" The car swerved slightly as Shane digested that unexpected question. "What has Mary got to do with any of this? Is someone trying to kill her as well?"

Keith faced his friend again. "How well do you know her?" The question demanded an answer.

Shane paused and studied the silhouette of the man sitting beside him in the darkness. Again, the car lost speed. "You're not trying to tell me that Mary had her brother killed. I don't believe that. You've been sold a bill of goods, man. You should have let me go down there with you. Did this thug intimidate you, make you lose your sense of reasoning?"

Keith met his friend's stare. "My senses were working fine." His voice lowered. "Name me someone else who had as much to gain from Craig's death as Mary. She doesn't run Sky Jet like a grieving sister. She slid into that corporate chair as if it was her destiny. Most people thought Tom would take over, you included, but he never even had a shot at it. If anything, he has less say in the company now than when Craig was at the helm." Keith fell silent again.

Shane looked down at the speedometer. The speed had dropped off to 70 km/h. His foot pushed the pedal towards the floorboards and the car surged ahead until the reading was 120 km/h. He looked back at Keith. "What now, man? You think it's Mary. You've got to call Sergeant Mcdonald."

Keith shook his head. "The original plan was so black and white. Find the name. Inform the cops. Stand back and watch the fireworks." He looked out the side window into the darkness again. "Now there are other considerations."

"Other considerations?" Shane sounded shocked. "What other considerations?"

"Our businesses. Sky Jet Charter, Sky Jet Leasing. Even Shane's Electrical has a small stake in all of this. What's best for us in the long run?"

Shane jammed on the brakes and pulled the car over to the shoulder of the road. "One of our friends was murdered and you're looking at the business effects." Shane was practically shouting in the small space in the car's interior. "There are no other considerations, man. If you're right, and I'm not saying I believe you, the woman is a killer."

Keith sat calmly in his seat. "Craig's dead. Nothing changes that. Mary, by herself, is no real threat to anyone. We have to take our time and figure out what is best for everybody. People with families work for these companies, so let's not act in haste. We've got to remember the big picture. I'm no lawyer but I'm not sure you can murder someone and then inherit all their worldly goods."

Shane shook his head. "Probably not."

So what happens to the estate in the meantime? Does everything get tied up by the courts? All the assets? The jets?"

Again, Shane shook his head.

"I'm not taking any chances. We have to get control of those companies. Not just control, ownership." He looked at Shane for confirmation. Shane was still digesting the idea that Mary had arranged the death of her brother. Keith continued: "At the very least, we have to get total command over the planes. Once we have them, we can slip the charter company out from underneath the Sky Jet name if we have to."

"You've given this a lot of thought."

"Nothing else to do all the way back." Keith shrugged. "Once we're in charge of everything, then we call Sergeant Mcdonald, not before. He can tie up anything he wants after that."

"I imagine you have a plan."

Keith looked over at Shane and smiled. "Get this bucket of bolts back on the road. Do you know where Bob Lively lives? I want to see if there's any action at his house."

44

DARK POUCHES SAGGED under Jim Mcdonald's eyes. He had received the anonymous tip regarding Bob Lively shortly after 10 p.m. His call to Lively's house triggered the answering machine. The same thing happened with the business number at the airport. A quick call to Scott Bowman produced the 4-wheel drive vehicle and the two men headed back to Lively's home on Harvard Street. A patrol car parked in front of the house held two officers whose foot prints displayed a return trip to the backdoor. Their own tracks to the front door had filled with snow and no other new ones had been created.

The street itself had one narrow path down the centre where a plow had made one pass earlier in the day. An additional six inches of snow had fallen since then.

The two patrol men had greeted them with the news that two bodies were waiting for them on the kitchen floor. The responding policemen had broken through the back door, discovered both bodies had reached room temperature, and then exited the scene to wait for the experts. The medical examiner and forensic team had both been notified, but neither had arrived yet. The storm had put everything on a different time schedule, one in which speed took a back seat to safety.

Jim and Scott had waded through the snow and into the house.

The bodies of Bob Lively and his wife were sprawled on the kitchen floor. One chair lay on its side and three coffee mugs were on the floor. Otherwise there were no signs of violence. Jim recognized the mugs as the ones he and Scott had used that morning. These people could have been dead before the two policemen had even left the premises. It was a disconcerting thought.

Jim tried to re-create the morning visit, especially the departure. Lively had taken the dishes to the kitchen while he and Scott exited to the small porch. They had called out a goodbye to the Livelys and received no answer. The two had attributed it to the unsatisfactory conclusion to the interview. Bob Lively resented any implication that he was involved in Craig's death. Rightly so, it now appeared.

Now, all these hours later the complete investigation team had taken over the south-end residence. Techs, in white overalls, snapped pictures, scraped up samples, dusted for fingerprints, in a quiet methodical manner. The medical examiner could give no apparent cause of death. The best he could do was put the time at sixteen to eighteen hours earlier, sometime in the morning.

"I don't believe in coincidence," Jim said to his partner. "There are too many similarities between Craig Flint's death and the death of these two. The poker playing buddies were sitting in the next room and heard nothing. We quite probably were standing in the hallway of this house when it occurred. Both men appeared to be shoo-in winners of the Worldwide Seafood contract, a deal that was worth millions to their respective companies, I might add." Here he hesitated and looked at the prostrate bodies before him. "My non-medical guess would say they both had a stroke, simultaneously, just like Craig appeared to."

"We know what killed him," Scott said. "Somewhere in this kitchen is some kind of lethal airborne poison." He looked around. "Yet the first cops on the scene exhibited no breathing difficulties. Whatever had been here was gone long before they arrived."

"That jibes with the half-life theory of Dr. Melnick," Jim said. "Whatever it is appears and dissipates quickly." He looked around the kitchen. "A fucking locked-room mystery."

Scott was surprised at the outburst. "Those puzzles always have a solution, Jim. Just flip to the back of your notebook for the answer." He flashed a smile, breaking the tension.

Jim returned the smile but his was more forced. He turned to the head crime scene technician. "Make sure you document everything that's in here. Lots of pictures. Lots and lots of pictures. Nothing is too trivial."

"What about Masserati?" Scott asked. "Is he a suspect or the next victim? He may want to think about withdrawing his offer on the Worldwide contract. The winning bid seems to be a ticket to heaven."

"Or hell," Jim added.

The two men had interviewed Masserati the previous afternoon. It had not gone well. Masserati was instantly defensive from the very first question. He accused the police of profiling him because of his Italian background. The policemen had to struggle throughout the interview to keep Masserati on topic and off the subject of his human rights. When they asked him about his attempts to buy one of Sky Jet's planes from Tom Dunford, he insisted it was a straight business deal.

"This is not profiling," Jim had said. "But now that you've planted the seed, we'll definitely be doing a deep background check on you. If you have any skeletons in your closet, now is the time to tell us about them."

On that note, the interview ended.

The death of Craig Flint formed one link in a chain leading toward the Worldwide Seafood contract. The chain had doubled in length with the additional death of Bob Lively and the damn thing was only three links long to begin with. Masserati would be in for another visit. This time at police headquarters, probably with his lawyer present.

"Despite his lack of cooperation, I didn't really suspect him when we left this afternoon," Jim said. "Now we have to wonder if all that bluster was just a cover-up to throw us off."

"I think he lives in a dream world," Scott said. "His secret alter ego might wish he had mob connections, but I don't make him as a wise guy. He's a pilot. I think he spends too much time with his head in the clouds. He had nothing good to say about Craig. Called him a 'big feeling snob.' Others shared that view, I'm sure. He did suggest Bob Lively could be capable of murder." He glanced down at the floor. "We can disregard that proposition. It's pretty safe to say Masserati didn't get along with his fellow competitors."

"Maybe so, but from everything I've heard, he's a pretty shrewd businessman. He did make the final cut for this contract and from what I gather, every charter company out there was in on the initial bid. Let's not underestimate him."

He took one last look at the two bodies, shook his head and said: "Let's go home and grab a little nap. That's all we have time for now. I'll see you in the office at eight."

Scott looked at his watch. "Maybe I'll crash on a couch down at headquarters. By the time I drive home, it will be time to come back in."

Jim nodded. "And you said the life of a detective was too boring for you. No patrolman ever had this much fun."

Both men walked out into the cool night breeze.

45

KEITH GRANT AND Shane Martin were parked in the corner of a church parking lot one-half block away from the home of Bob Lively.

"Doesn't look good for Bob. The forensic van doesn't set up shop if you're still alive and kicking. You know Bob would be doing the latter if the former were true."

Several police cars, vans and obviously unmarked cars filled the street in front of the Lively home. Keith had insisted they park back here out of sight, yet still able to keep an eye on events. He was trying to tie Craig Flint's death to Bob Lively's.

This was as good a place as any to ponder the motives of the person who had hired the killer. Unlike the two detectives, his deductions didn't lead to Roberto Masserati. He needed no deductive reasoning. He knew who paid Robert Crosley. In Keith's eyes that person became the real killer. Crosley was merely a weapon.

"I don't understand why Bob Lively had to be killed. It doesn't make any sense."

Shane studied his friend in the darkness of the secluded car. "Same reason as Craig, I would think. Bob stood in the way of something the murderer wanted."

"The Worldwide Seafood contract? Craig had that in the bag if he hadn't died. Bob seemed to be a shoo-in as well but the timing is all wrong. Did the assassin jump the gun, so to speak, and kill Craig prematurely? A week later would have made a lot of difference.

"If Craig's death is unrelated to the seafood contract, killing Bob muddies the water. It makes the two seem connected. Is Sergeant Mcdonald now heading down the wrong path? Bob's death might just be a red herring."

A look of understanding spread across Shane's face. He gave Keith a light punch on the shoulder. "Of course, that makes sense. Now it's more important than ever to tell the sergeant what you know."

Keith shook his head. "Not yet. There's still too much at stake. A couple of days won't make any difference. The worst thing that can happen is Roberto Masserati is given a hard time by the cops. Remember he tried to steal one of our jets from Tom. Offered him a quarter of its true value."

He took one more glance up the street at the activity or lack of same. No one had come or gone since they had arrived. "Let's get out of here. Take me to my office."

46

CHRISTINE AND MARY exited the elevator on the fifth floor of their office building. It was not yet eight o'clock. Both were excited to hear the final announcement of the Worldwide contract. This was the day and Mary believed her bid had a valid chance at success. She had made one major change from Craig's proposal. She had offered exclusive use of one of the jets to Worldwide Seafood. It would be available whenever and for whatever they wanted.

This was offering Marcel the advantage of his own personal plane without the complications of ownership. Mary was appealing to his male ego. She would paint the plane like a giant phallus if that would clinch the deal. There were no standby fees. Payment was per use and availability was guaranteed unless the plane was delivering lobsters. Marcel controlled that.

This clause had been added to the bid without Keith Grant's knowledge. He might have pushed Craig around, she wasn't sure about that, but he wasn't going to push her around. He only owned 30% of the company. That gave him a say but not a veto. Her 70% share made her the final arbiter in all decisions. He would have to learn to live with that.

He could bluster and threaten to withdraw the use of his planes but that wouldn't happen. He and Craig had signed a 10-year deal at the sweetheart rates that allowed Sky Jet Charter to grow so fast. It still had three years to run. Mary had gone over the contract with a fine-toothed comb. It was ironclad. Grant was locked in.

George Phillips said getting in bed with Worldwide was a bad deal for Sky Jet Charter; they would be gobbled up whole by the larger company. Mary disagreed. To her it was a passport into Worldwide's executive offices. If she had walked in off the street, they might have offered her a low-level secretarial job at best. Coming in as CEO of one of the companies they did business with on a daily basis would help her jump the queue to upper management, upper management of a Fortune 500 company. In three years, Keith Grant could charge her whatever he wanted for his services. For now, she controlled him.

Christine picked up a fax from the machine's tray. It had come in an hour ago and was from Keith Grant requesting a meeting as soon as possible. This morning would be best, he said. She passed it over to Mary. Mary read it, checked her watch and said: "What's he want? Call him. I'm available right now."

Christine had picked up a second page. "He wants Tom present, as well."

Mary took that page. "Tom? Why would he want him here? They don't even like each other."

Again Mary looked at her watch. "I wonder if Tom has left the house yet. Call him on his cellphone and get him in here. This is the day we win the Worldwide contract. He should be here anyway to help celebrate. He is a vice-president." Her voice held a hint of derision. She laughed. "I'm sorry that was in poor taste. He just takes the title a little too seriously."

She threw the fax on Christine's desk. "Call Grant. See if you can find out why he wants this meeting. If he won't tell you, suggest I might have a full day scheduled. We'll at least see how important it is to him."

Keith personally answered the phone on the first ring. He had no problem discussing the reason for the meeting. He had an offer for Mary that would be mutually beneficial to everyone. He could be there in less than half an hour.

"Let me get this straight. You want to swap your 30% of Sky Jet Charter for my 30% of Sky Jet Leasing." Mary stared across her desk at Keith Grant. She, Keith and Tom were in her office. For this meeting she did not offer the informal setting of the chesterfield and easy chairs. She sat behind her desk, the other two had the lesser position, side by side, in front of her.

Keith shifted uncomfortably in his seat. What he was about to say was suggested by Shane Martin. It wasn't entirely untrue but it was a stretch of the truth. "This charter business has never really fit into my overall corporate planning strategy. I more or less got into it as a gesture of friendship to Craig. I thought he could fly me around whenever I needed to make a quick trip and the rest of the time he could play at being a business owner." He looked down at his hands as if in deep thought before continuing.

"I underestimated your brother. He grabbed the bit in his teeth and ran like a wild horse on the open prairie. The sky was the limit, literally. The next thing I knew we had purchased a second plane and he was a leading contender in the local charter business. I never tried to rein him in and the company flourished. The success of the company was due more to Craig's passion than any other factor. It was a fun trip but, as

I said, it didn't really fit into my overall scheme of things. It was a distraction."

"And now that Craig's dead, you don't think I can run the company as successfully as he did and you're going to lose money." There was an edge to Mary's voice.

Keith laughed. "Not at all. The company never made a profit for me. We plowed everything we made back into the business. Neither one of us needed to make a living from the company profits. You must have discovered that Craig didn't even receive a salary. I have great faith in you. In the short time you've been here, you've impressed me. I just think this is a good time for me to make a break from the company. It's yours to run as you see fit."

The hardness disappeared from Mary's face and she smiled. Everyone likes to hear a little flattery. "So now you want a straight swap of the shares of the two companies?"

"My shares of Sky Jet Charter and some cash to sweeten the deal. The leasing company is worth more than the charter company."

"How much cash?" Tom asked. Mary scowled at him.

Keith smiled inwardly but on the exterior maintained a businesslike expression. "I don't know how much you know about the leasing end of the business but the two companies are fundamentally different. The leasing company's value is in hard assets; the charter company's value is in how it is perceived by the public, their customer list. People want to do business with them, make them their first choice for flying.

"One is easy to value, the price of the planes, the other is more empirical, the price of good will.

"Craig and I had a great deal of discussion about this when we set up the companies. We worked out the tax implications. Then we brought in the accountants to make it happen."

Keith paused. He looked deep in thought. "Let me try to put this in layman's terms."

Mary listened to the explanation, asked a few pointed questions. It became apparent that Keith's understanding went far beyond that of a layman. Also what became obvious to Mary was this deal was much too complex for Craig to fully understand. Had Keith taken advantage of her brother? She didn't think so. Would he give her the same courtesy?

Tom had been looking from one to the other as this discussion took place. His eyes had glazed over listening to the financial mumbo-jumbo. He had one question on his mind. "How much money? How sweet are you going to make this deal?"

Mary glared at her husband. She was afraid he would jump at any offer Keith made. This was no time to get careless. She may as well come out of this with as much as she could get.

"Like you and Craig, I would like to think we are still friends," she said. The corners of her mouth raised into a smile, her teeth sparkled white, but her eyes still remained hard and shrewd. "Give us a figure and Tom and I will talk about it in private and get back to you." She willed her husband to keep his mouth shut.

Keith picked up his briefcase and opened it on his lap. He closed his hand around a sheaf of papers but didn't bring them out. "I too would like to do this as friends. I have here my final, what I think is fair, offer. This would be non-negotiable, take it or leave it." He lifted the papers from the case and put them on the table, keeping his hand on top of them. "I also have in this case another offer. It is lower than the first, drudges up every penny I spent out of pocket in the last seven years. Splits hairs wherever possible. If you want to play the offer, counter-offer, counter-counter-offer game, I can give you that instead."

Mary knew she was being played by a pro. If she took the first stack of papers, she would be tied in. If she took the second, negotiations could drag on for a long time. She knew that once the Worldwide contract winner was announced and if that winner was Sky Jet Charter, the company would become more valuable. That included Keith Grant's 30%. His offer of a swap would reflect this increased value of his interest and she could expect to get less of a cash settlement. She might possibly not get any cash at all. He didn't know she had sweetened the deal after he had signed off on the company's bid. Conventional thinking gave the contract to Bob Lively. Mary knew that would never happen.

She had heard that Grant sometimes made snap decisions like this, acted on some impulse. She also knew that most of the time his research was considered in the extreme. He and Shane Martin flew all over the continent, actually the world, checking companies before he invested a cent in them. Rumours claimed he had an investigative team on staff that worked for him full-time behind the scenes. This move could be designed to put extra pressure on her if he knew she had already lost the seafood contract. Get her to sign off now before the value of his share went even lower.

She looked at Tom. This was what she had wanted to avoid, discussing the offer with Tom in front of Keith. She settled back in her chair and the smile became more genuine. She appreciated gamesmanship when she saw it. She looked from the papers on the table to the papers still in the briefcase.

"We're friends. Let me have the offer under your hand, but," and she held up her hand to stop him from passing them right away, "I still reserve the right to counter offer if I disagree with your assessment of the two companies."

Keith nodded. "You can always disagree." He slid the papers across the desk. "But," he continued, "this is a non-negotiable offer. The worst case scenario is we remain both friends *and* partners."

Mary picked up the papers. "I think you're bluffing."

He slid back his chair and stood up. "I never bluff. Ask Tom." He started to turn for the door.

"Wait," Mary said. "Answer one question for me. If Sky Jet Leasing ran at a loss and Sky Jet Charter rolled all its profits back into the operation, how did Craig become a millionaire? Where did the money come from that he gave away in his will?"

Keith sat down again. He looked from Mary to Tom and back to Mary before answering. "Craig had built up a bit of a nest egg before we started the company. He was trying to reach this dream on his own for years. That's what owning this company was to Craig: a dream." Again he paused and looked at Tom before continuing. "He also came into a considerable sum of money a few years ago. As you know, I was his financial adviser. We invested those moneys quite aggressively for a couple of years and—" Keith shrugged, "—I guess you could say we were lucky. I don't, mind you. I call it hard work and smart thinking." He laughed.

"You made almost three million dollars in that short time?" Tom asked. He looked over at Mary. "We need a financial adviser."

Before Mary could object to this suggestion, Keith nipped it in the bud. "Sorry, Tom, but I'm not taking on any new clients at the moment." He studied Mary intently for a moment before continuing. "I believe you already have someone helping you out. How's she working out for you?" He smiled.

"We're doing better than the market," she said, "but obviously not as well as Craig did." She maintained a stoic look, not giving in to Keith's jibe.

"Now that we have a lot of money, maybe we should look for someone else," Tom said, unaware of the conflict between Keith and Mary.

Keith's attention turned back to Tom. "As I said, I'm not taking on new clients at this time, but I could recommend someone if you're not happy with your current adviser."

Mary gave Tom an icy stare. "I'm not dissatisfied."

Tom looked devastated at the rejection. "Don't bother. We can find someone without any help from you if we want to."

"I'm sure you can," Keith said. He looked back at Mary. She smiled at Keith who returned it with a slight nod. "Let me know what you decide," he said. Without shaking hands, he got up again and started towards the office door when it suddenly flew open.

In the doorway stood Christine. Her face was as pale as her ivory blouse. Her eyes glistened. One fist covered her cherry-coloured lips. The other contained a sheet of paper from the fax machine. "I'm sorry to interrupt," she said, "but you've got to hear this."

She held up the paper and read: "It is with deep regret that Worldwide Seafood announces an additional postponement in the awarding of its tender to ship seafood products overseas. This decision was prompted by the sudden and unexpected death of one of our principal bidders, Robert Lively of Lively Charters. Our deepest sympathy is extended to the family of Mr. Lively. Further details of the rescheduling of the announcement of the winning bid will be advertised in the near future. Sincerely Marcel Deveaux, President and CEO of Worldwide Seafoods."

Silence followed her announcement. Tom was the first to react. "Bob is dead? I don't believe it. He looked as healthy as a horse the other day when I talked to him. What happened?" He realized Christine didn't know any more than what she had read on the fax. He redirected his attention to Mary. "We have to find out what happened to Bob. Your life could be at risk."

Keith turned to study Mary's reaction. Tom was the only one in the room who seemed genuinely shocked. Mary caught his gaze and brought a hand to her mouth. "Poor Bob." She looked at Tom. "Why would I be at risk?"

Keith answered instead. "Two deaths. Two apparent winning bidders. I wonder how he died." His eyes searched Mary's for some sign of advance knowledge of the death.

"I never thought of that," she said. "Surely that's just coincidence. Nobody would be killing off prospective winners. That would mean that Roberto Masserati is doing the killing. He's the only one left. The whole idea is absurd." She was an actress as well as a businesswoman.

"Masserati," Tom said, buying into his wife's reasoning. "Of course it's him. I never trusted the bastard. I hear he has mob connections. Mary, you've got to be careful."

"Don't be foolish," Mary said. She turned to Keith. "You don't look too surprised."

Keith shrugged his shoulders. "I don't even know the guy. His death means as little to me as any of the hundreds of others who died yesterday. I am concerned about the Worldwide contract though. It may be up for grabs again although—" He reached out for the fax still in Christine's hand. "—it only says the announcement of the winner has been delayed, not the whole bidding process. Lively may not have been the winning bid. This delay may only be out of respect for the family." He passed the paper on to Mary.

"Interesting," she said. "I should phone Marcel."

Now Keith was surprised. "Marcel? You know him personally?"

"We had lunch together a couple of days ago. He wanted to go over a couple of things in my bid. He's a nice guy. Do you know him?" She had a smug look on her face.

"Yes, quite well. I lunch with him often. We belong to a couple of the same clubs." The smugness disappeared from Mary's face. She was a rookie player trying to crack the big leagues. Keith was already there playing in a starring role.

"Look, about your offer to swap shares. If we have to come up with another offer, things are going to get hectic around here for the next few days. I'll accept your offer now."

"You haven't even read it. I wasn't trying to pressure you into a hasty decision."

"Hey, we're friends. I trust you and besides the deal is non-negotiable. Right?"

"On both counts, but you should have Bob Piers look it over just the same. I don't want to be accused of taking advantage of you."

Tom picked up the papers and flipped through them. Both Keith and Mary knew what he was looking for and could tell when he came to the cash part of the offer. A, he stopped reading and B, his eyes turned to saucers. "It looks like a good deal to me," he said. "I don't think we have to involve a lawyer."

Keith smiled. The offer was generous. This was money well invested. He knew Tom would be swayed by the size of the offer, that's why he requested his presence. He had never expected Mary to capitulate so quickly. Briefly, he wondered about her motive. Then he didn't care. Sky Jet Leasing was now his free and clear. He could safely tell Sergeant Mcdonald everything he knew about the two deaths, accept for how he found out. The sergeant might not be too open-minded about his buying this kind of information and then keeping the seller's name secret. Part of the deal with Crosley was not to involve him in any way. As he pointed out so eloquently, Keith's only knowledge of Crosley's involvement was Crosley's own confession. This would never be made to the police. As an unnecessary afterthought, he had added: "And God help anyone who turns me in." Keith Grant received that message loud and clear.

He had nothing concrete to offer to the police except the name of the person who had purchased the contract for the killings. Once on the right track, it would be up to them to catch this person. All Keith was doing at the moment was generating as much distance as possible between himself and the murderer, as he now thought of her. Step one was complete.

47

RIGHT NOW, JIM Mcdonald would not care a damn how this case was solved. He and Scott Bowen had spent the last hour and half talking to Roberto Masserati at police headquarters. The whole experience put a bad taste in Jim's mouth. These pilots seemed to think they were a special breed, a notch above everyone else. Self-importance seemed to be one of the qualities required for entrance into their midst.

Craig Flint's sister had called Craig "an arrogant little twit" and that was after Craig's death. Most people forgot all your bad characteristics at that point and only spoke well of you. Bob Lively's haughtiness may have cost him his life. He may have known nothing about Craig's death but he went out of his way to be uncooperative. If he had been more forthcoming, things might have turned out differently. And now, Roberto Masserati appeared to have both of the two deceased beat for his insubordinate attitude.

"Mr. Masserati, for the hundredth time, I'm not accusing you of murder, not yet. All I'm saying is that if you're not involved in the deaths of these two men, then you may be next on the list. It appears to be bidders of the Worldwide Seafood contract that are meeting these untimely deaths. You're the only short-listed bidder left. Two of your friends and fellow businessmen are dead."

"Don't confuse the two. We are in the same business but we were never friends. They treated me the same way you do." Masserati looked at his lawyer. "The only reason you are talking to me is because my skin is a little darker, my hair is blacker and the women go crazy when I walk into a room. You think I'm a hot-blooded Italian who kills people who get in my way."

The lawyer, also of Italian descent, dressed in a tailor-made grey suit, white shirt and striped club tie shook his head. "Roberto, we know you're innocent but you may be in danger. Just answer the man's question."

Thank God, Jim thought, some good advice. "Please, dismiss that idea from your mind. Right now, we are talking to you because you are a charter pilot and owner, no other reason." He stood up and placed both hands on the table in front of him and leaned forward. "And if you don't start cooperating with us, you are going to die."

Masserati sat back in his chair. "You're threatening me." He turned to his lawyer. "He threatened me. You heard him."

"No threat, Mr. Masserati. I'm simply stating a fact that is crystal-clear to everyone in this room except you. There can only be one of two reasons it's not obvious to you. One, you're stupid." He paused to let that remark sink in. Masserati's face showed red even through his dark complexion. He sputtered but no real words came out. "Or two, you are involved in the deaths of Craig Flint and Bob Lively. Which is it?" The policeman's voice took on a menacing tone with the question. He continued: "I don't really believe you're stupid."

Jim gathered up a few papers from the interview table. "Get out of here," he said with a wave of his arm. "The corporal and I have police work to do." He and Scott walked out the door, leaving the two men still sitting at the desk.

"That was fun," Scott said once they were out in the hallway. "What do we do now?"

"Put a tap on his phone. Monitor his bank accounts. Keep a very close watch on him. If he's guilty, he'll make a mistake."

"Does he win the lobster contract by default? Attrition seems a strange way to do business."

"I doubt it but let's arrange a meeting with Marcel Deveaux. Put our cards on the table. See what happens next."

"Smart thinking, boss. Let's make it a luncheon meeting."

SCOTT MANEUVOURED THEIR unmarked police car into the head-office parking lot of Worldwide Seafoods. Immediately, Jim pointed to a British racing green sports car parked near the executive offices. "That car belongs to one of the poker players," he said. "I remember it from the first night at the cottage."

Scott looked in the direction indicated. "Keith Grant," he said. "Nice set of wheels. Bought it at the Barret-Jackson Auto Auction in Arizona about four years ago."

"Aren't you a fountain of information." Jim said with a little surprise in his voice.

Scott blushed. "He let me take it out for a little spin along the 103. Handles like a high-priced call girl. Responds to your every request with gusto."

Jim checked his watch. "Our meeting is scheduled for five minutes from now. I wonder what Grant is doing here."

"Cashing in on the free food," Scott said. "That's why I'm here." He pulled in beside Keith's car and parked. "Well maybe I have some questions about the latest contract winner, too. Grant could be here for the same reason. Word of Bob Lively's death is on the street by now. You don't have to be a genius to tie Lively's passing with Craig's."

"Damn civilians. I hope he's not involving himself in the case. Flying over to Europe and getting us some information from the flight crew is one thing. That doesn't give him licence to become part of the investigation team." Jim pushed open the car door and stepped out. He glanced in the sports car's window at the rich leather and wood-grain interior before heading towards the office door.

Keith Grant and Marcel Deveaux stepped out onto the top step. Marcel reached out and shook Keith's hand and slapped him on the back. Bonhomie among the upper crust, Jim thought. They separated and turned towards the steps. Keith was the first to notice the two policemen.

"Sergeant, what a surprise." He came down the four steps to street level. "I was wondering if you and Corporal Bowen play poker. We're having an informal get-together at the cottage tonight as a tribute to Craig. We thought it would be good to have you two along. George was going to call Scott to set it up. He's in charge of getting the food. We want to have enough steaks for everyone."

Jim was surprised by the invitation. "I don't think so," he said, "but thanks anyway."

Keith's face took on a more serious demeanour. "We were going to throw around some ideas about Craig's death, and now Bob Lively's. Everything would be off the record, but it would be worth your time to be there."

"Thanks, but no thanks. We have our own ideas about how the case is going." He started for the steps, went up two and then looked back. "For the record, nothing is ever off the record."

"Supper is being served at six. It would be a big mistake not to be there. We're serving steak and roasted potatoes. Don't worry about the money. We only play for fun. We'll be using poker chips." Keith got into his car and drove away before the sergeant could reiterate his refusal.

Jim looked at Scott who was smiling at him. "We're not going. These men are still suspects. We can't be taking favours from them."

"You know they're digging into this. They told us about Pat Dexter. It didn't lead to much, but we know someone out there was talking about professional killers and then there was the anonymous tip."

"Yeah, the anonymous tip. We don't want to be encouraging them. It's not ethical."

"We could interview them again. Like tonight at six p.m. at the cottage."

"Nothing is off the record. Remember 'You have the right to remain silent. If you give up that right anything you say can be used against you in a court of law.' We can't be rewriting our Charter of Rights and Freedoms."

Now it was Scott's turn to be serious. "Grant knows that. You telling him to stay away from the investigation is not going to make him stop. We should find out what he doesn't want to be silent about. This is about more than poker. What should I tell George when he calls?"

Jim gave his partner a frustrated look. "Tell him we're thinking about it. Don't make any definite commitments. I'll have to run this by the inspector."

During this exchange Marcel Deveaux stood silently at the top of the steps, listening. When he realized the conversation had ended, he spoke up. "Barbarians, the whole works of them. They should be serving fresh Atlantic seafood, not dead cow."

"Fresh fish was Craig's last meal," Scott said. "They served the best haddock in the world at their get-togethers." His eyes became misty at the sudden remembrance. "Those were good times." The other two men remained silent for a few seconds.

"Come inside," Marcel finally said after an appropriate time had elapsed. "I'm just about to have my lunch. Join me." He swung the door open and allowed the policemen to pass before following them in. "Down the hall to my office."

As soon as the door opened, Scott's nostrils were assaulted by the savoury aroma of a fish chowder. He looked back at Jim and winked before disappearing through the door. Jim shook his head and said in a low voice: "We're not supposed to be doing this."

By then Marcel had caught up. "Gentlemen, if you had given me more notice, I'd have prepared something special for you. This chowder is a new product we are test marketing. If you could do me the favour of giving your honest opinion, I would be grateful. It is still being fine-tuned so any recommendations would be helpful."

"The police are always willing to lend a helping hand," Scott said. He looked at Jim. "This is like a public service. A better product will benefit everyone." He accepted the white glass bowl with gold trim around the rim that Marcel was offering him.

"We do have to eat," Jim said as he accepted his proffered bowl. The dish was heavy and Jim wondered how much they cost for a setting of eight.

Steam rose from the basket of browned dinner rolls as Marcel unwrapped the white linen from the top. "These are quite hot," he said. "Be careful."

"Right from the oven," Scott said. "Did you bake them yourself?"

Marcel laughed. "Right from across the street." He indicated a small bakery through the window. "They supply our cafeteria every day at lunch time. These rolls arrived just before you did. Keith Grant highly recommends them, as do I."

Jim became serious. "This may be an inappropriate question but what was Keith Grant doing here?"

Marcel maintained his cheerful attitude. "The same as you, Sergeant. Enjoying my rolls and asking about the delivery tender that was supposed to be announced today." He raised his eyebrows. "Am I wrong? That is why you wanted to see me."

Jim set down his bowl without filling it with the chowder. "That's exactly why we are here. The last time we met, you doubted if Craig Flint was murdered. Do you have the same doubts about Bob Lively?"

Marcel's face darkened. "Have some chowder, Sergeant. Enjoy."

Jim ignored the instruction. "Who knew that Bob Lively would be awarded this contract? How secure is your operation?"

"The winning bidder is known only to myself and two members of my staff. We go over all the information, investigate the companies involved and make a decision. This decision is discussed with nobody until the official announcement is made. Until that time, others can only speculate as to who the final winner will be. The speculation is not always correct." His eyes bored into those of the policeman.

"Are you saying Bob Lively wasn't the winning bidder?"

"I'm saying only three people, three close-mouthed people, knew the winning company."

Jim looked over at Scott for backup on their theory. Scott swallowed a mouthful of chowder and gestured with his spoon. "You do agree that most people in the business believed the contract would go to Bob Lively?"

"Speculation is for fools. All I can tell you is the process has been put on indefinite hold." Again he indicated the bowl on the table. "Please, Sergeant, have some lunch. I will be offended if you don't eat."

"Indefinite hold? What does that mean?" Jim picked up the bowl and ladled a small amount of chowder into it. He wanted to keep Marcel talking until he found out everything he wanted to know.

"Keith Grant convinced me it would be better to delay everything until you have a chance to finish your work. He thinks you are on the verge of a breakthrough in the case. He has offered me the use of a jet plane to deliver the product to Europe in the meantime. I only have to pick up the actual operating costs."

"So you awarded the contract to Sky Jet Charter?" Scott had a spoonful of chowder almost to his mouth but stopped to ask that question. "You do know that Keith Grant is a part owner of that company?"

"I'm not sure that is still true but it doesn't matter. This is not a Sky Jet plane. Mr. Grant has offered me the use of a private acquisition. He said he can have the plane modified for cargo and ready to fly this week. I have accepted his proposal.

"You see, in Europe they pay a premium for freshness. If I offer them a product for their table today that was still in the ocean yesterday, they pay accordingly. It may be a fad but I'm going to cash in on it as long as possible. That is why I wanted a jet to do the deliveries. My old plane couldn't maintain the pace. Mr. Grant's will. When you crack the case, as they say," he smiled at the expression, "I will wrap up the tendering process. Until then, I don't want anybody else to die."

Marcel filled a bowl of chowder for himself and took a mouthful. "Exquisite," he said. "Grant wants to meet with you tonight and brainstorm the case. Perhaps you should meet with him. He has resources you may not be aware of."

Jim studied the contents of his own bowl. Lots of white fish, some potato, he definitely recognized large red chunks of lobster claws. He looked back at Marcel. Perhaps he was right. Keeping Keith Grant from being involved in the investigation did not seem to be in the cards. It would be senseless not to cash in on any information he uncovered.

"Meeting him can't hurt, I guess. Are you going to tell me who had the winning bid?"

"No, Sergeant, I'm not. Have some more chowder and another roll while they're still hot."

49

AT 5:15, THE two policemen were part of the supper-hour traffic exiting the city on Highway 103. A solid string of rolling metal connected by the glow of white lights in front to red lights in the rear stretched as far as the eye could see in both directions. Both men were lost in their own thoughts when the chirp of a cellphone broke the silence.

"Mine," Scott said. He fished the small silver instrument from his pocket and flipped it over to the sergeant. "I've always wanted a secretary to screen my calls."

Jim looked at the display. "Unknown name. Unknown number," he said to Scott and then pushed the appropriate button to answer the call. "Corporal Scott Bowen's office." Scott shot him a scathing look.

There was a pause before Jim said "This is Sergeant Mcdonald. You can talk to me."

Another pause.

Jim held the phone out to Scott. "Pat Dexter. He wants to talk to you."

Scott glanced in his rear-view mirror, snapped on the signal light and coasted to a stop on the wide shoulder of the road. He took the phone. "Mr. Dexter, did you remember who you heard talking about professional killers?"

Pause.

"Yes, I remember our deal. You give me some information and I won't be in court tomorrow." Scott fished a wire from the glove department and plugged one end into the phone and the other end into the car radio. Pat Dexter's voice came over the car speakers.

"I was working on Bob Lively's plane about a month or so ago when one of the Sky Jet planes pulled onto the tarmac beside us. Four women got out. It must have been a champagne flight because all of them were tipsy I believe is the polite expression for drunken, rich broads. They were laughing and giggling like teenagers. They had lots and lots of shopping bags and boxes."

"Did you know any of them?" Scott interrupted.

"I wish. A couple of them were real beauties. Skirts up to their ass. Blouses wide open showing lots of cleavage. Jiggling all over the place. Looked like they would flop out of their tops at any minute. Well, they had my full attention. That's when I heard it."

"Heard what?"

"Like I said, they were all drunk. They were talking about all the stuff they bought, the different shops and boutiques, comparing notes. That's when one of them said, and I swear to God this is the truth, 'You have to love Montreal. You can get anything there from the flimsiest lingerie to your own private, professional assassin.' Then another one said: 'Whatever will you do with an assassin? Who do you want to have killed?' And then they all laughed as though that was the funniest joke they had ever heard."

"You just suddenly remembered this? You're not making it up to save your ass in court tomorrow?"

"You can't make this stuff up, Corporal. Who would believe you? I was scared and confused the other day. I wasn't thinking straight."

Both Scott and Jim were writing furiously in their notebooks. "So who did you tell about this?"

"The assassins? Nobody. I was telling my friend, Mark, about the sexy women the next day in the cafeteria. We don't see too many women like that out there. The clients are usually conservatively dressed businessmen or hunters and fishermen. This was a treat. Then I noticed the two men at the next table listening to what I was saying. I clammed up. You're not supposed to talk about any of the clients. Especially drunk ones. Confidentially is part of the service they pay for. I could be blacklisted for talking about them."

"You never mentioned the professional killers as part of the story?"

"I might have, but just in passing. It was the women I was describing. They were something else. When I was going over my records to see who I worked for that week, I came across Bob Lively's name. Then I remembered the Sky Jet plane landing beside us and the women getting off. Their hangars are side-by-side." Dexter paused for a few seconds. "He's dead too, you know. Bob Lively."

"Yeah. We know. Thanks for your help and don't worry. I won't be in court to testify against you tomorrow. But God help me, if I hear about you pulling another gas and dash stunt, I'll track you down and throw you in jail myself." Scott broke off the connection and turned to Jim. "Like I have time to spend in court on a charge that will be treated like a joke. What do you think of his story?"

"I'll call Christine in the morning and find out who chartered that flight. We'll take it from there. Society women throw a new wrinkle into the case. You sure we can trust this guy?"

"I don't know. He's pretty scared about going to court." Scott watched for a break in the traffic and pulled back onto the highway. "I wonder if Craig was the pilot on that trip. Maybe he overheard something he shouldn't and there's another body someplace out there."

"That wouldn't explain Bob Lively's death."

The two men finished the trip to the cottage in silence. Both were trying to work this new piece of information into what they already knew. Both were prepared to dismiss it as irrelevant and unrelated. Three vehicles were already parked in the cottage yard. Scott glanced at the dashboard clock: 5:45 p.m. They were early. It appeared they weren't included in the initial part of the night's discussions.

George could be seen standing over a smoking barbecue just outside the kitchen door. They could hear the sizzle of the steaks as he flipped them for the first time and the hot grill seared itself into the raw meat.

George waved the tongs at them. "Glad you made it. The steaks will be ready in a few minutes. The potatoes are in the oven. Your timing is perfect."

They eased by him and entered the kitchen where Keith Grant was tearing up spinach and dropping it into a salad bowl. He acknowledged their arrival. "The bar is set up in the other room. Help yourselves."

In the combined living-dining room, the big oak table was set with five place settings on a white linen cloth. Two bottles of red wine were set near each end. The corks were removed allowing the wine to breathe. Shane Martin was arranging the silverware in neat alignment with the plates. The domestic ambiance denied the real reason for the gathering: to get to the bottom of Craig Flint's murder.

Shane pointed to the bar. "Grab a drink and have a seat. The meal's almost ready to serve." He indicated a couple of reclining chairs near the large picture window overlooking the lake.

Jim gazed around and took in the exposed wood interior, the lithographs of downtown Halifax from the early part of the 20th century hanging on the walls and the general feeling that this was a place for a man to relax. There was no sign of a woman's touch. Not having a body on the floor improved the ambiance.

Spoiling the whole feeling of tranquillity were two flip charts on tripods against one wall. The top page of each was blank. The underlying pages were thick and curled as if they had been used, flipped back and then forward again. The presentation might be a little more formal than originally stated. Jim poured himself two fingers of Canadian Club and passed a pitcher of water over it. A little splashed out. Scott took a beer from a bucket of ice. Once started, this meeting would not be interrupted by trips to the kitchen.

Jim walked over to the flip chart and looked under the blank sheet.

"Suspects in the murder of Craig Flint" read the heading.

Before Jim could turn to the next page, Keith Grant came into the room with the finished bowl of salad. "Feel free to look through our thoughts," he said, "but it might make more sense if you allow us to present it in an orderly fashion. We've been working on it for a couple of hours this afternoon."

George showed up with a tray of steaks. "Hope everyone likes them medium rare. That's the only way I cook 'em." He looked over at the sergeant standing by the flip chart. "Let's eat first. Discussion of murder while eating supper leads to indigestion. Let's relax and enjoy the steaks." He placed the tray at the open end of the table.

"I'll get the potatoes," Keith said. He vanished into the kitchen. The others sat around the table.

Reminiscences of previous poker games filled the gaps between the silences created by eating good food and drinking fine wine. Scott had sat in for many of the meals. He easily fit in and freely took part in the discussions. Jim was envious of the obvious camaraderie among the men. Although Craig was the frequent topic of discussion, no mention was made of his murder.

The meal ended with the traditional raiding of the liquor cabinet for exotic after-dinner drinks. Cointreau, Baileys, mint-flavoured green drinks, throat-burning clear liquids were all available to be sampled. Many were. Then the mood changed. Dirty dishes disappeared into the kitchen. Linen tablecloths landed in the laundry hamper on top of a couple of towels. Cards and poker chips appeared from nowhere, but remained in their respective boxes.

"Before we start the actual game," Keith said, "perhaps we should have a look at those charts. It will give us some fodder for discussion." George and Shane nodded their agreement. Scott and Jim realized poker was never a priority for this meeting. Five yellow, legal pads and pens came from a side table and were distributed to the men.

Keith flipped back the first page, revealing the heading the sergeant had seen previously.

"Suspects in the murder of Craig Flint."

He looked at the sergeant. "We've taken the liberty of putting together a list of names. I'm sure you've considered some if not all of them. Feel free to add any of your own."

"Let's have a look," Jim said. He held up both hands, palms facing Keith, "But let me be clear about one thing. Scott and I have no intention of involving you people in our investigation. We will not be adding to your lists. We will listen to any suggestions you might like to make." He looked at Scott for confirmation.

"Flip the page," Scott said. He took a sip of his beer.

Keith flipped the page.

Keith Grant
Shane Martin
George Phillips
Tom Dunford

"Obvious suspects," Keith said. "We were all here when the murder took place."

He flipped another page.

Scott Bowen
Brenda Davis

"What the hell," Scott said. "We're not suspects."

"You were the last outsiders in the kitchen on the night of the death, man" Shane said. "You were out there alone after that domestic violence call came in. You've been involved with Craig since childhood. Who knows what animosities lurk out there? We tried to make our list as complete as possible."

"But Brenda and I, that is foolishness."

"We'll drop your names from the list if you'll drop ours," Keith said. Neither cop replied to the offer. "Fine, your names stay. By the way, during our discussions today, we realized you two were the last ones in the kitchen. Was the kitchen door locked when you left?"

Scott set down his beer and thought for a moment. "Yes. It automatically unlocked when I turned the inside knob, I pushed the button on the knob back in when I went out. The door locked behind me. I remember testing it when it closed. It was locked."

Keith nodded. "That's what we thought." He flipped another page.

Bob Lively
Roberto Masserati

"We've tried to divide the names by connection to the case," George explained. "Friends, business associates, happened to be on the scene." He looked at Scott with the last category. "Guess we can rule out Bob Lively."

Keith flipped to the next page.

Mary Dunford
Tom Dunford
Keith Grant

"Beneficiaries from the will," George said. "Some names appear in multiple categories."

Keith flipped again.

Others

"This is where you can supply some thoughts," Keith said. "Or not. It's up to you."

"Not right now," Jim said. "Let's eliminate some of the obvious names." He consulted the yellow pad in front of him. All the suggestions were listed. He was taking this exercise seriously. "I don't think Brenda Davis even knew Craig. Had never met him before the fatal night."

"OK," Keith said and flipped back a couple of pages. He drew a red line through the name of the police constable.

"And me," Scott said. "I didn't do it."

Keith changed markers from the red one to a blue. "Let's make red definite nos and blue probable nos. He drew a blue line through Scott's name. He flipped back to the first page of names. "The three of us agree that none of us are involved. Can I blue line our names?" He looked at the sergeant.

"Light blue lines. Our investigation to date has turned up no reason for suspicion but that doesn't mean we've stopped looking." The others weren't sure if he was serious or joking.

Keith took a cyan maker from the package and made light blue marks through the top three names.

"With good reason. We didn't do it." Tom Dunford remained untouched.

"We don't suspect Tom, but he did have a lot to gain," Keith said, "and he was here when it happened. Do you have any idea how the poison or whatever was administered? Where it came from and where it disappeared to?"

"That's the big mystery," Scott said. "We have to figure it out before we take someone to court or the case hasn't got much chance of success."

Jim gave his partner a keep quiet look.

"Bob Lively is looking innocent," Jim said. "He was a prime suspect, but ..." His voice trailed off.

Keith turned to the page of business associates and put a red line through Lively's name.

"I guess Roberto Masserati stays," he said. He looked at the policemen for confirmation. Neither responded.

Keith stepped over to the second flip chart and turned back the blank page. The heading indicated Roberto Masserati. Reasons for suspicion followed the name.

Second chance at winning seafood delivery contract
Tried to purchase Sky Jet plane cheap
Disliked Craig

"Anything else you might want to share with us?" Keith asked, looking at Jim.

The sergeant shook his head. "It's your show."

Keith nodded and turned back to the list of reasons. He added:

Third chance at winning seafood delivery contract.

"If he's not the killer, man, he'd better be hiring some protection," Shane said.

No one else had anything to add. Keith left the flip chart open and returned to the first one. He turned to the heirs page and put a cyan line through his name. "The cottage is nice but not worth killing someone for." He made a gesture to include the whole room.

"I don't know, man," Shane said. "You had better be careful. This may just be the final reason I need." A much needed laugh went around the room.

"Did you know what was in the will?" Jim asked.

"No. I was as surprised as everyone else. As his financial adviser, I encouraged him to keep his will up to date. I made recommendations about what should be in it." He shrugged. "I never saw it while he was alive."

"Did he follow your recommendations?"

Before Keith could answer, Scott laughed out loud. "You don't know Craig, Sergeant. He never followed anyone's recommendations."

"You got that right, man," Shane said. "It was one weird document."

Jim ignored the others and continued looking at Keith. "Only on the basics," Keith said. "The frills were all Craig. Even Bill Piers couldn't talk him out of them."

"Bill Piers?" Jim raised his eyebrows.

"William Piers. Craig's lawyer. The family lawyer. Sky Jet's lawyer. Graduated from Dal at the same time as Craig's father. They were on the same rowing team or something like that. Has been the family's lawyer ever since he passed the bar."

"Right." Jim noted the name on the pad in front of him.

Keith tapped the sheet of paper on the tripod. "Mary Dunford had the most to gain from Craig's death. Not as much as she would have thought but still she was the big winner." He looked at Shane.

"She's every bit as ambitious as Craig," Shane said. "Already we've had a few discussions on ways to improve the aircraft to attract more clients. If she had a period of mourning, it was not during business hours."

"She knew what was in the will," George said. "She knew she was the sole heir to the estate." The seemingly spontaneous comments were well orchestrated. Keith wanted to make the policemen see Mary as a leading suspect without giving away what he knew about the assassin.

"How do you know she knew what was in the will?" Jim asked.

George blushed. "Craig told me things in confidence. I would act as a sounding board when he wanted to get things off his chest. He knew he could depend on me to keep things to myself."

"He told you what was in the will?"

"Not exactly. He wanted a clause to make sure that Tom never took control of the company. Their arguments were real in the sense that Craig didn't trust Tom's judgment." George squirmed and looked around the room. It was apparent that even with Craig dead, he felt wrong in breaking the confidence they shared. "Bill Piers argued against it. Claimed it would leave the will open to all sorts of litigation. Finally he refused to do it."

George looked down at the table. "He told Craig if he tried to control his sister from the grave, it would create his own special kind of hell. It couldn't be done. His advice was to tell Mary she would inherit the company and exact a promise from her not to put Tom in as CEO. Then he would just have to trust her judgment. It appears she listened to him."

Keith rubbed his chin in a thoughtful manner. "I agree with Craig's opinion of Tom. Shane disagrees.

There must have been more to make Craig go to such extremes."

"I don't think Tom knew about the will," Shane said. "We should look at the other things in the will. I don't think Mary knew about them. Why did you get this place, for example?"

"I've wondered about that," Keith said. "I think there are two reasons. As a thank you for financing his dreams. To us Sky Jet Charter was just a company. To Craig it was a dream fulfilled."

"And the other?" Jim asked.

"To keep it out of Mary's hands. There was an animosity there I never understood. No matter how hard I tried, I couldn't get Craig to talk about it."

"I've dropped in here often while patrolling the area," Scott said. "I don't ever recall seeing Mary here. I don't think she was too interested in the place."

"When Craig's father died a few years ago, both Mary and Craig came into a considerable chunk of change, mostly from an insurance policy." Keith walked over and joined the others at the table. "I invested Craig's for him. He suggested I take care of Mary's as well. She turned me down cold. She went out on her own and hired some woman investor. I knew her in the business. She'd never lose your money, but she'd never make you rich."

"Your point being?" Shane asked. Keith had gone off script. This was a new area of discussion.

"Tom never mentioned the money." Keith looked around at the others. "We all know Tom liked to be a little ostentatious. He tried to give the impression he was more than he was. Look at the suits he's wearing now. They're more expensive than anything I own."

"Nobody ever accused you of being a fashion plate, man."

"No, but if Tom knew Mary had come into a lot of money, we would have heard about it. We didn't. Tom didn't know. He didn't even know about Mary's financial adviser this morning when I met with them."

Jim perked up at this bit of information. "You're saying she has secret accounts?" He got up and went over to the flip chart and opened it to a new page and wrote:

Mary Dunford
Knew about inheritance
Had secret source of money

"I'm a firm believer of following the money. What else do we know about her? Do you know who actually handled her investments? I would like to talk to them."

"Yes," Keith said. "Bradshaw Investment Services. Margaret Bradshaw specializes in female clients. The two of them were a good fit. Call my office in the morning and I'll give you the details."

"Flip the page of the other chart to see what else we had," Shane said. Jim complied. He was surprised to see Mary's name on the sheet under Roberto Masserati's page. She was an initial suspect because of the inheritance but Jim had since moved her down the list. He studied the thoughts of the poker players.

Mary Dunford
Knew about inheritance
Marriage possibly in trouble
Felt controlled by Craig
Really wanted to play a senior role in Sky Jet Charter

"How badly did she want to work for Sky Jet?" Jim asked.

"She approached Craig several times," George said. "He kept putting her off and not always in a tactful way."

"Yet, he left the company to her," Scott said. "It doesn't make sense."

"It does if you don't really plan on dying," Keith said. "Craig thought he would live forever. Putting her in the will was a way to placate her. Give her some hope for the future." He paused for a couple of seconds and looked thoughtful. "I hate to say this, but it could have all been a cruel joke if he outlived his sister."

"Telling her about her inheritance may have been a bad mistake, man," Shane said. He slowly shook his head from side to side as if contemplating wanting something bad enough to kill your own brother to get it.

Jim lifted this sheet to see what other names were listed in more detail. There were none.

"You only have two serious suspects?" he asked.

"No one else stood to benefit from Craig's death," Keith said. "The other strange thing in the will, besides me getting this place, were the donations to charity. Why did he choose the ones he did? Craig was not philanthropic by nature."

"The hospital was obvious," Shane said, looking at Keith. "He thinks they saved his life while you were trying to kill him." He laughed.

The sergeant did not. "What is that supposed to mean?"

"That money Craig inherited from his father's death. Keith invested it for him, aggressively. Craig developed so many stomach disorders, he literally thought he was dying."

"He made a ton of money. You could have been in on it too. I made you the offer."

"No thanks. I like to wash my meals down with wine, maybe beer, definitely not Pepto-Bismol. I've never missed a meal because of worry."

Keith looked at the sergeant who was still waiting for a better explanation. "Craig wanted to make money in a hurry to buy his own planes. That can be done, but there are risks. Craig followed the daily fluctuations of the market religiously. When values went up he was all smiles. When they went down he developed pains in his chest, stomach, back, head, legs, you name it. Something in his basket of investments was always going down. Stress was killing him.

"I tried to convince him to leave the worrying up to me and just look at the big picture. I don't know if he believed me or not. At the time, he was unaware of my personal investments.

"After he spent a month in the hospital, I realized he was averse to this level of risk. I cashed him out. Returned him a 100% profit to reinvest in a moderate manner and track on his own. Stocks that gradually increased in value. His aches and pains went away. He credited the doctors and the hospital instead of me.

"He allowed me to take the remainder of his profit to invest as I saw fit. At the end of each year, I gave him a bottom-line figure without ever telling him what he was invested in. I promised him five million dollars before he turned 50.

"That accounts for the bequest to the hospital," Jim said. "I still don't understand the women's shelter. Half-a-million dollars is a lot of money."

"Craig knew about Mary's secret accounts," George said. "He suspected things were not going well between Tom and his sister. I think he was wrong but being wrong never stopped Craig in his thinking. He may have been guaranteeing a soft landing if things went bad in the marriage, a place where Mary could seek emergency shelter with people who knew how to handle those kinds of situations."

"Why not just give her the money?" Scott asked. "That would be the simplest thing to do." He looked around the table for agreement.

"Not if Tom blew it," Keith said. "Anyone seen the car he's driving? Even Shane, who's never missed a meal, couldn't afford one like it. For that matter neither could Tom until this morning."

Jim let out an exasperated sigh. "What happened this morning?"

50

THE CLOCK IN the lobby of the building housing Sky Jet Charter Services registered 8:00 p.m. as Mary, Tom and Christine tumbled in from the street. All were laughing and carrying on. They had just come from a downtown restaurant where they had enjoyed a five-course meal starting with lobster cocktails, followed by vichyssoise, vegetable salad, pork chop supreme and rounded out with baked Alaska. The restaurant did not belong to Keith Grant, even partially. Tom made sure of that.

They had spent the day working on a new mission plan for Sky Jet Charter. Mary and Christine had great ambitions for the newly minted company, newly minted without Keith Grant that is. Tom had sat and watched the two women while in his mind, he spent, re-spent and spent again the money Keith Grant had paid for their share of Sky Jet Leasing.

Mary insisted they stop at the office before continuing their celebrations. She wanted to see if Marcel Deveaux had faxed an update on the awarding of the new contract. Christine argued he would probably wait until after Bob Lively's funeral. Tom wanted to know what difference it made. They no longer needed the contract in his estimation. He was ready for retirement. Not Mary.

"Damn," she said when the fax tray yielded only junk mail advertising money-saving office products. "We should have phoned him this afternoon before we went out. Are you sure there were no messages from him?"

"Nothing. We were both here all day. No faxes, no emails, no phone calls." Christine dropped the unsolicited flyer into the recycling bin.

"Come on Mary," Tom said. "We no longer need to beg Worldwide Seafood for business. We should be planning a vacation. The Caribbean or Hawaii would be nice. Someplace warm and exotic. We have all the money we need now."

Mary slapped Tom across the face, leaving a welt on his pale skin.

"This was never about money," she said. "My brother did not die so we could go cavorting around beaches filled with scantily clad women. We have to take this company and make it bigger and better than even Craig dreamed of. Any money we made this morning will go back into the business."

Tom stood shocked, his mouth open, his eyes wide. Mary had never struck him before, not even in fun. Christine brought a hand to her mouth but said nothing. Mary glared from one to the other then seemed to realize what had just transpired. She reached out for Tom's hand.

"I'm sorry, Tom," she said. "Just when I thought I was recovering from the shock of Craig's death, Bob Lively's passing brought it all back to me, only intensified." She brought the hand to her lips and kissed the knuckles. "But we're still not going to waste this money and we're not going to stop competing for business. I'll call Marcel in the morning. See what his thoughts are. It will show initiative. He still has to award this contract to someone."

Tom closed his other hand over Mary's. "It was you I was thinking of, my love. The strain of Craig's death, now Bob Lively's. You should, we should, get away for a while. Just forget about airplanes and business and contracts for a week or so. Then, when we come back, everything will seem better for you."

Again, Mary's eyes flashed fire. She shook her hand free. "We are not going anywhere. We have a contract to secure with Worldwide Seafoods. You two go home. I'm going into my office and look over our proposal. We might have to submit it again and I want to be ready."

Christine looked from Mary to Tom and back to Mary. "I can stay and help if you want. I have nothing else planned for the night. I thought of a couple of things to add to the bid that might improve our chances."

The two women disappeared into Mary's office leaving Tom standing in the reception area alone. He debated joining them before heading to the bar across the street. He could now afford the premium stuff, Johnny Walker Black instead of Red.

SERGEANT MCDONALD LOOKED at the three men sitting at the table with him and Corporal Scott Bowen. "What happened this morning?" he repeated.

"A simple business deal." Keith looked at George. George hadn't been told this part of the plan. Shane, of course, helped draft the transaction. "I swapped my shares of Sky Jet Charter for Mary's shares of Sky Jet Leasing. We are no longer partners, silent or otherwise."

"A straight swap?" George asked.

Jim looked at George then back at Keith. "A straight swap?" He repeated George's question.

Keith laughed out loud. "It will be fun to get you at the poker table. You're a natural born bluffer. Why do you ask?"

A smile spread across Jim's face. "Because the accountant asked with concern in his voice. It must be a legitimate question."

"No, it wasn't a straight swap. Money changed hands as well. I sweetened the deal."

"Why now? When did you find out about Bob Lively's death?"

"If Mary is involved, I didn't want my assets tied up in litigation over the will or seized as proceeds of crime. Can she inherit if she had Craig killed?"

"That's a question for the courts. I'm sure you've sought legal advice and didn't get a satisfactory answer."

Keith stole a glance at Shane. They hadn't consulted any legal source. There was no time for that, considering what they knew. They just created distance between themselves and the murderer as fast as they could. The second part of the sergeant's question went unanswered. That would be too hard to explain.

"What kind of car is Tom driving?" George asked. His own was a five-year-old sedan.

"A Mercedes 380SX," Keith said. "A mid-life crisis car if ever there was one."

Shane whistled. "Getting into your league. You sound jealous."

"Only because I paid for it."

Jim took his notebook from his pocket and made note of this purchase. "Why are we giving Tom a pass as a suspect?"

"Because he hasn't got the brains to do it," Keith said.

"Because murder is not in his psyche, man." Shane gave Keith a dirty look. "He contributed more to that company than he got credit for. I worked with both him and Craig. You are underestimating him."

Keith shook his head. "No, I'm not."

"Anything besides gut feelings?" Jim pursued the question.

"He was here when Craig died," Shane said. "It really shook him. He's not that good an actor. He was as shocked as the rest of us."

"Mary hasn't given him any position of increased authority at Sky Jet," Keith said. "She doesn't trust him to do more than service the planes. She's sure as hell not going to trust him to be in on a murder plan. Shane's right about that. Tom could never handle having someone killed."

"There's something I don't understand," Scott said. "I find Mary killing her brother a stretch but why would Mary kill Bob Lively?"

"A good question," Jim said. He looked at Keith who seemed to be the chief spokesman for the investigative poker group.

"Who's your chief suspect right now?" Keith countered.

"We're considering a number of people at the moment," Jim said in an evasive manner.

Keith slammed his hand down on the table, causing everyone in the room but Jim to jump. "Cut the bullshit. You think Robert Masserati did it." Keith's voice was loud and challenging. As quickly as his emotions flared, he settled down again. "I don't blame you. It makes sense."

"He's a suspect," Jim conceded.

"Off the record, Sky Jet was going to get this contract. Not Lively." Keith looked from eye to eye for someone to challenge him. "Whether Mary knew this or not is open to discussion. Most people assumed Bob Lively was the apparent front runner. Now he's dead."

"So why do you suspect Mary? If she had the contract anyway, why kill Lively?

"Because now Masserati glows like a huge blimp on everyone's radar. Sky Jet has already been hit. Craig's dead. Who would suspect someone there? Mary's home free whether Masserati ever gets charged or not. He'll always be everybody's first choice as the man who hired the killer."

Jim came back to the table and sat down. He appeared to study the names on the sheet of paper in front of him "That's a big leap. Mary has motive and means, I agree. But killing her own brother?" He slowly shook his head from side to side. "I don't buy it on what we have." He looked Keith straight in the eye. "Do you have information you're not revealing?"

Keith met the stare without answering the question. He did, but couldn't divulge it and still keep his promise to Crosley. Crosley was not a man to be crossed. The silence stretched into nearly a minute.

"Don't be an idiot," Jim said. "You're in over your head. Tell me what you know." The room seemed to close in to focus on these two men.

Suddenly and loudly, Shane Martin pushed back his chair and stood. "I don't know about you guys, but I need another drink." He looked around the table. "Are we going to play poker tonight or just sit around and talk? Where's the poker cloth?"

"Right here," George said, evident relief in his voice. He produced a green, felt table cloth from the sideboard and spread it over the table, forcing the others to grab their yellow pads, pens and drinks and move them.

Keith picked up the deck of cards. "Dealer's choice. First jack deals. The ante is two reds. Bets are limited to five reds at a time. Maximum of three bumps. Any questions?"

"Yes," Jim said. "What aren't you telling me? Understand me, friend. This is not a game."

Keith stopped shuffling the cards. "Have you ever had a hunch you just can't shake, Sergeant? This is a collective hunch. We've all been working with the new management team at Sky Jet Charter and something is not right. We all agree. Mary does not act like a grieving sister. She acts as if she is fulfilling her destiny."

Shane came back to the table with his refreshed drink. "We started with the hunch. When we looked closer, things started falling into place. You said she has the motive and the means. She also has the inclination. Once she found out about the inheritance, she was like Prince Charles waiting for his shot at being king. Only she couldn't wait. She expedited matters. All the Flints were ambitious. Craig fell victim to an even more ambitious family member than he."

"Where's the concrete proof?" Scott asked. "Everything you say is only speculation. I've known Mary since she was a kid. She's always been strong willed, but a killer? I can't believe it. And another thing. On the Friday before Craig died, Mary was in his office arguing for Tom's job back. Why would she bother if she knew the company would be hers in two or three days? It doesn't make sense."

Keith looked at the Mountie. "You only assume she was trying to get Tom's job back. As you know, he already had been rehired. Perhaps Mary was just there saying goodbye to Craig. Strange as this sounds, considering what we are proposing, she did love her brother."

Jim studied Keith's face as if considering this proposal. These men had an agenda. He would have to let it play out if he wanted to learn everything they knew.

He shrugged, reached out and took the cards from Keith. "First jack deals?" He started flipping cards over in front of each player. The second one was a jack. He slid the deck over to Shane. "Your deal." As an afterthought, he asked: "Any of you guys know about four women taking a shopping trip to Montreal about a month or so ago? They were on a Sky Jet Charter."

Keith and Shane shook their heads.

"I do," George said. "It was a birthday present from Craig to his sister. A shopping weekend in Montreal. He provided the plane, meals and accommodations for Mary and three of her friends."

"I do remember that, man," Shane said. "He provided the booze too. According to the pilot, they put away a barrel of it."

"So, Craig wasn't the pilot?"

"No, man. Jack Northrup. He drew the short straw. I guess a couple of the women put on a real show on the plane. Modelled all their new purchases. Used the main cabin as a changing room. Man, he had to lock himself in the cockpit to keep from being voluntarily raped. It was a wild party." Shane gave the cards a riffle shuffle. "Low Chicago." He looked at the two cops. "Do you know how to play?"

"Refresh my mind," Jim said. "It's been a while. I thought we'd be playing Texas Hold'em."

"No," Keith said. "We like to play games that keep people at the table, not ones that eliminate them. Most of our games are split the pot. Two winners."

"I see," said Jim. He was coming to realize that poker was just an excuse for these guys to get together. Camaraderie was the main feature, not winning money. It was one more reason to eliminate them as suspects.

"Seven-card stud," Shane explained. "Two down, four up with a betting interval after each up card and last card down. Low spade in the hole takes half the pot." He looked around to see if everyone understood. There were no questions. He dealt the down cards and the first up card.

"You're looking at a professional hit in these murders. Right, man?"

"Everything's on the table at this point." The sergeant checked his two down cards.

Shane looked around the table at George and Keith before continuing. They were back on script. "I was playing poker at the airport the other night with a bunch of mechanics. Just for fun. No real money involved." He laughed. "Wouldn't want the vice squad raiding the place."

"We're in major crimes," Scott said. He knew this was just the preamble. He threw two chips into the pot. "My king is high. I open for two."

George added two but said nothing.

"Raise you two," Jim said. "The same mechanics who overheard the story about the professional hit men?"

Shane looked at Keith who added four chips. "No, they're still in Europe. Should be back anytime now. But the subject of professional hits did come up. It became the buzz of the airport once word got out that Craig was murdered." He threw in four chips and dealt another round of cards. "Pair of sevens bet, man."

"Let's make it five," Keith said. "Get the pikers out." He tossed a blue chip into the pot.

"So what did these men have to say?" Jim asked. The pace of this discussion was too slow for him. He wanted information, now.

"One of them, don't remember who, said often you can reach these killers by running a classified ad in some of the major newspapers, USA Today or something like that."

Scott scoffed. "Killer wanted. Call 555 –"

Shane pointed a finger at Scott. "That's exactly what someone there said, man. You weren't listening in to our conversation were you?" He added a blue chip to the growing pile in the centre of the table.

"How does it work, then?" Jim asked. He was familiar with the concept.

The game came to a halt as all eyes turned to Shane.

"You have to be referred, so to speak. Someone who is familiar with the procedure gives you the exact wording. The killer sees the ad and knows you are being recommended by whoever gave you the info and he calls you, man. From there, I guess you set up the hit."

"And he gave you the wording of the ad?" Jim asked.

"No, man. He just knew how it's supposed to work. He didn't know anyone who actually did it."

"Oh, so now we're into urban legends," Scott said. "Happened to a friend of a friend."

Keith looked from the skeptical face of Scott Bowen to the intrigued face of Jim Mcdonald. "Finding someone local in contact with *USA Today* in the States could be a lead. There are no offices for the American paper in the city. It would have to be done by phone and with a credit card. You folks can do stuff like that, can't you?"

The question seemed so innocent. Jim knew that Keith knew these things could be done. He still felt like he was being manipulated. He leaned back in his chair and crossed his hands in his lap. "My father once told me something about poker." He looked around the table at the others. "He said there's always a mark, a patsy. If you don't see one, you'd better check the chair you're sitting in. Why don't you guys cut the act and simply tell me what you know? I can act on ideas other than my own."

Keith laughed out loud. "We're just a bunch of guys sitting around brainstorming. I've always been amazed at things that come out in these types of sessions. Can you people trace phone calls and credit card use or is that another TV myth?"

Jim held up his hands in surrender. He would play it their way. "That might work for Mary Dunford but Roberto Masserati is in the United States on a regular basis. He would not necessarily leave a trail."

"Mary was in Montreal," Scott said. He realized there might be some merit in this line of discussion. "She could have paid cash up there."

"Unless he or she was careless," George said. "The deaths were meant to look like strokes or something. No one expected a police investigation into Craig's death. Bob Lively was a ticking time bomb for a heart attack or stroke. He was always stressed about something."

"Except you don't often see simultaneous strokes," Jim said. "His wife died with him."

"What?" Keith said.

"Oh, no," Shane said. "She was such a nice woman, man. Everyone at the airport caller her Mother. You could always stop into her office and have some homemade cookies. Jesus, man, what happened to them?"

"It's been all over the radio. Don't you listen to the news? I would guess they inhaled something, the same as Craig. An autopsy will confirm that, one way or the other. In the meantime we're going over their kitchen with a fine-toothed comb. When Craig died, we didn't know what we were looking for until later. This time, it's different. We at least know the class of the killing agent."

"Both are dead. The killer was either careless or indiscriminate." Keith shuddered to think that he had been dealing with this man the night before. "When did they die?"

"We were there yesterday morning. Left around nine. They may have been dead before we left. If not, shortly thereafter."

"During the storm. That must have kept them from going to the airport. Tom picked up one of their flights." Keith paused and then added as an afterthought: "I was still in my office. Stayed there until noon."

Shane looked at Keith as if reading his mind. "They lay there dead all day. Scary, man, they could have ended up there for days."

"Our tip came from a pay phone in Florida. Know anyone who's been there lately?" Jim looked at Keith when he asked the question. "You say you were in the office at the time of the deaths?"

"There till noon. Then I flew down to Florida to check out an investment."

"The tip came in around 10 o'clock. Where were you at that time?"

"Ten? I'd have been in the air flying home. A private charter. Got in around four."

Jim's gaze moved down the table to Shane. "You?"

"Watching Blue Bloods on TV. Gotta love that Commissioner Frank Regan. Gets results."

"Alone?"

"Afraid so. Hadn't been plowed out yet."

George didn't wait to be asked. "I was still at the office. Security in the building can verify that. No sense leaving until the streets were cleared."

Keith turned serious. "Phone calls are the way to catch whoever hired the killer. They leave a trail. Within a day or so of contacting the newspapers with the ad, the professional would contact the person back here to set up the hit. The call could come from anywhere. Could you isolate that call from her records?"

"Perhaps, but I doubt if the professional would use a traceable phone. In Masserati's case, he has calls from all over North America. It's the nature of his business. We've already looked into them."

"But Mary was a housewife up until Craig's death," George said. "Any unusual calls should stand out. Or if you know her home phone and cell numbers, the newspapers could check their databases to see if she used those numbers in an ad. She would have to have used a number where she was sure she could be reached."

Any interest in the card game had ceased. All five men grappled with the problem of tying Mary to the killer. George's ideas held merit.

"With a specific number to search for, that is a possibility," Jim said. "Let me get on that right away." He looked at Scott. "Had enough of a break from the case? Let's get back to work."

Scott groaned. This was the part of detective work he hated. Jim would have him spending the rest of the night delving into Mary's phone records looking for a connection to the killer. He drank the last of his beer. "You'd better drive," he said.

52

"**D**AMMIT, DAMMIT, DAMMIT." Mary slammed down the phone in frustration. "Marcel says the overseas contract is indefinitely postponed pending the police investigation into Bob Lively's death. The cops think there's a connection between the two."

Christine nodded in agreement. "First Craig, then Bob. There seems to be a link. Our new bid is a sure-fire winner. Maybe it is best to wait. I'd hate to see you be next." She smiled at her boss and watched as Mary's features softened.

"But these guys are as slow as honey flowing uphill. It's going on two weeks since Craig died and they aren't any closer now than that first night. What if the killer is too smart for them? The contract will never be awarded."

"These are the Mounties. They always get their man. We have to be patient."

"Patience be damned. This delay is costing us hundreds of dollars a day. That contract was mine. Marcel as much as told me so last week over lunch."

Christine leaned forward in a conspiratorial manner. "Then, I guess the only thing to do is give the cops a hand. I'm willing to give that Sergeant

Mcdonald all the help he needs. Keith Grant is rumoured to be involved in the case."

Mary's head snapped up. "What? Involved in what way?"

Christine leaned back in her chair, surprised by Mary's reaction. "He flew to Europe to talk to Harry and Jerome. The rumour says they overheard someone talking about professional hit men. Keith Grant went over to find out who, then passed the information on to the investigators."

"Jesus, can't that man mind his own business? What did he find out?"

Christine shrugged her shoulders. "Rumours don't go into that much detail. Mostly people were talking about the expense of the trip. Grant has offered the police any help they need." She hesitated before going on. "Keith and Craig were close friends. They often went out to lunch together. If money can solve a crime, this one will be solved quickly."

Mary slumped back in her chair. She thought she had severed her ties with Keith Grant. Was it the other way around? Grant was distancing himself from her. She thought back over their conversations of the last couple of weeks. Until Craig's death, she knew nothing about Keith Grant. He had been present at her abortive attempt to join their poker game and watched her embarrassment at her brother's rejection.

Only Tom had come to her defence and it immediately became apparent to her that no one cared what Tom thought. The other three men—Keith Grant, Shane Martin and George Phillips—allowed Craig to walk all over her without raising a single objection. All three had connections to Sky Jet Charter, her company. One of her early goals was to end any relationships they had with the company. Grant had been first, Phillips was next and Martin appeared to be untouchable. His association was indirectly through the leasing company.

When it came to business, Grant and Phillips had different personas. Both seemed to go out of their way to try to help her get established in her new role. Both were efficient in what they did. Now she wondered if that were true. Were they really poking around trying to see if she had a link to her brother's death? That made no sense. Why would anyone suspect her? Roberto Masserati was the obvious link. Surely the police had figured that out.

Christine was still talking. "Only yesterday, Keith Grant, the two detectives and Marcel Deveaux were seen talking outside Worldwide Seafood. I have a secretary friend there who thinks Sergeant Mcdonald is a dream boat, too. She was torn between the sergeant's good looks and Keith Grant's flashy car. She can be so superficial."

"Grant was at Worldwide Seafood? What is that son of a bitch up to?" Mary hammered her fist on her desk. "Tom warned me not to trust him. Damn it, was Tom right? The cops were there, too? I wonder what he's paying them. Goddamn men all stick together." She grabbed the phone and hit redial.

Christine recoiled from this new outburst. "I'd calm down before I called anyone," she said in a low voice intended not to offend but with hope the advice would be taken. "Some of these CEO types are egomaniacs. They don't take criticism well." Christine hesitated and studied Mary. This was not the same upbeat Mary who had taken over the company two weeks earlier.

Mary glared daggers at Christine. She replaced the receiver. "You're right. See if you can set up a luncheon meeting with Marcel. I want to find out what his intentions are."

"Sorry, I didn't mean to offend you. I'd like to think we're friends and not just employee-employer."

"Me too. I apologize for that outburst."

"Your brother used to get upset like that when things didn't go his way." Again Christine appeared reluctant to go on. Then she continued. "At times like this, Shane Martin would punch him on the shoulder and say 'Relax man. You're not the centre of the universe. The world doesn't revolve around you. Those people may not even be talking about you.' Craig would laugh and say 'Maybe not, but who else would they be talking about, you?' and the situation would be diffused."

Now it was Mary's turn to laugh. "Please, don't tell me I behave like my brother. Anything but that."

The smile faded. "Still, I've got to know what Grant is up to. How well do you know his executive-assistant?"

"Judy? Only as a phone-a-friend. We've often talked to arrange those luncheon meetings, but never met face-to-face. Keith was Craig's personal financial adviser or something."

"See if you can find what Grant's up to. We've got to be prepared for any tactic he may employ."

Christine looked down for a second and then faced her employer. "I'll try, but that is the kind of information I'd never give out to anyone. Judy and Keith go back a long way. She worked for him before he started his own company. She's more loyal than a wife."

Again Mary's voice took on an edge. "Try anyway. I've got to know."

53

KEITH GRANT POKED the last errant bite of apple fritter into his mouth and reached out for a paper napkin to wipe the excess sugar from his fingers. He took a sip of black coffee.

"I thought we might have heard back from Sergeant Mcdonald by now. It's been two days."

Shane looked up from a circuit board to which he was applying a touch of solder. A small blue and yellow suction device whisked away the excess material and he examined the joint. The two men were in the workshop of Shane's airport office. "That should tell you something. We're not part of the investigation team. He never promised to include us in his findings. In fact, as I recall, he told us to stay out of it."

Keith threw the paper towel in a high arc and bounced it off the edge of a nearby garbage can. "Still we did all the leg work. We handed him the killer's name on a silver platter. He should tell us something just to keep us interested. I thought our presentation was pretty good." He eased his tilted back chair down on to all four legs, retrieved the tissue and slam dunked it into the garbage can.

Shane snapped the circuit board back into the chassis of an electrical device. "Don't you have any work to do, man?"

"I am working. One thousand, two thousand, three thousand." He held up a finger with each number. "There, three thousand more dollars to hide from the tax people and counting."

The phone on the bench rang and Shane reached over and picked it up. "Shane's electrical." His voice had a friendly ring to it. He passed the phone over to Keith.

"It's Judy. Get back to real work."

Keith took the phone. "Judy?"

His face took on an annoyed look. "He says it's important but won't tell you who he is?" He listened some more. "Do I remember Francisco's?"

A light went on in Keith's eyes. He looked at Shane. "Can I take this call in your office?"

"Sure, man. Anything to get you out of my hair. I do have real work to do."

Keith hustled across the floor and into the office. He snatched up the phone. "Keith Grant."

"You know who this is?"

"Yes."

"Our mutual acquaintance is trying to contact me again. This morning's paper."

"What? Again?"

"I'm retired, but I thought you might like to know."

"Are you going to call her?"

"No man. I'm out of the business. I don't need to work anymore. Remember."

Keith sat down behind the desk. His mind was racing. "This could be the break we need. Nothing you told us before can help convict her. If we could tape her talking to you, that would be conspiracy to commit murder. Just talk to her."

"Not me, pal. No tapes. No contact."

"If you could let me know when you're going to call her, we can tap her phone at this end."

There was a long period of silence on the line. Keith spoke first.

"I can make it worth your while."

"Oh, man. That hurts. I don't need your money. I'm rich now. Greed is one of the seven deadly sins, you know." Laughter could be heard coming across the phone lines.

"Just talk to her. Let her ask you to do it. Then turn her down. That may be all we need."

"Never stick in court. You need her to make the first payment. That's conspiracy."

Keith drummed his fingers on the table. He could not let this chance get away. "We at least have to know who the victim is. I have an idea and the bastard might deserve to die but we need verification. At least do that much for us."

"Three killings is a bit much. I tried to dissuade her the last time. Maybe it is time to stop her. Murder seems to be becoming part of her mission statement."

Keith pumped a fist in the air but kept his voice neutral. "What number did she give you? Is it a cellphone or a land line?"

"Damned if I know." Crosley held up the newspaper and read the number.

"Great, that's a cellphone. We won't even need a warrant. When are you going to call?"

The two men finalized the details to set the trap before severing the connection.

Keith looked out through the office window into the work area. Smoke curled up from a point in front of Shane. Best not to disturb him. Keith opened the top desk drawer and removed the stack of business cards. Randomness seemed to best describe their filing order. He shuffled through them until he came across the one for Sergeant James Mcdonald, Major Crimes. His finger hesitated before he pushed the first button on the phone. It was time to come clean and tell the cops about his source of information. There was no time to waste in convoluted explanations. Capturing Mary Dunford was all that counted now and only truth would make that happen. He punched in the numbers.

A strange conversation followed. It was a game of who could surprise whom the most.

Sergeant Mcdonald was already aware of the ad. The call to *USA Today* confirmed that Mary Dunford's cellphone had been used to book not two but three ads. One of these ran in the current edition. "We are already monitoring her phone," the Sergeant informed Keith.

"Good," Keith said. "This is when the call will come in." He gave Jim an exact time. "Let me explain how the initial payment for the hit will be received. An account must be set up in the name of the police department at a local bank. Mary will deposit money directly into that account. Everything needed for a conspiracy conviction will be in place. The media can be told Mary had solicited a hit from an undercover operative."

The sergeant listened intently, holding back the urge to ask how this all came about. "That would cover the conspiracy but not the first three murders. We don't sanction undercovers to follow through on their hits."

"I know," Keith said, "but one 25-year sentence is equal to four 25-year sentences when they are served concurrently. It doesn't make a hill of beans worth of difference."

"The cases would still be open in our files," Jim said. "It matters to us."

"Put a Post-it note on the outside of the file saying killer currently in jail. Beat a confession out of her. Who cares?" Keith's contempt for the justice system showed in his voice. "What about Masserati? Are you going to tip him off that his life is in danger?"

"Not yet. That would be presumptive. We will wait until we hear the actual call before deciding how much information will be distributed. He will be told before it goes to trial."

"I'd like to be there when it all goes down. I feel I have a vested interest." Keith crossed his fingers waiting for the answer from the policeman.

"Not going to happen. The best I can offer you is to let you listen in as we monitor the phone call. Never hurts to have an independent witness."

Keith smiled into the phone. That was more of a concession than he expected considering the circumstances. He had withheld some crucial information. He knew the sergeant would address that at a later date. "Where will I meet you?"

Five men sat in the white van outside the offices of Sky Jet Charter—Jim Mcdonald, Scott Bowen, Keith Grant and two police technicians. The logo of a local cable TV company was emblazoned on the sides of the van. This gave justification to all the antennae and the small dish prominent on the roof. An earlier phone call verified Mary's presence in the building.

A digital clock above some of the recording equipment indicated two minutes to the expected time of contact.

"We have to talk when this is over," Jim said to Keith. "You don't realize how much of a risk to your life you took. You might think there are sharks in the business world but in the field of murder-for-hire, you're dealing with ruthless predators."

Keith nodded and hung his head. In retrospect his actions had been rash. Before he could answer, a gentle buzz indicated Mary's cellphone was ringing. The van became as silent as a funeral home in the wee hours of the morning. No one even seemed to be breathing.

"Yes," Mary's voice filled the van. A light came on over a digital recording device indicating it was picking up the voice. A small tape machine spun into action as a backup.

"You ran an ad in *USA Today*. I'm interested."

"Yes, yes." Mary's voice reverberated with excitement. "I need your services right away."

Jim shifted in his seat. "They've got to be more explicit than that. Any talking in code or innuendo will never stand up in court."

"My contact realizes that," Keith said. "He has to follow his usual script at the beginning or Mary might become suspicious."

"Is this going to be like the last two times?" Crosley's baritone voice over-rode the conversation between Keith and Jim. "Natural causes not to arouse suspicion."

"Buddy, you failed on both counts with the last two deaths. The cops are all over them like rain on a windshield." Mary had abandoned any pretense of discretionary language. She continued. "This time, I don't give a shit. The more the prick suffers the better as far as I'm concerned. Just make sure that at the end of it, he's dead."

Under ordinary circumstances, Crosley would have broken off the connection before that sentence had finished. That was the old Crosley. The new Crosley smiled inwardly. Keep talking, bitch, he thought, it's your funeral. Aloud he said: "We can offer that service. What's the name of the target?"

"Keith fucking Grant." The words were accented with venom.

"Could you spell that middle name?" Crosley said. Having sold out his obligation to his client, he may as well play it for all it was worth. The anger would make good listening when the tape was played in court.

An audible gasp sounded in the police van. Keith Grant's face drained of colour. Jim reached out to support him as he teetered in his seat. "My God, why would she want to kill me?"

"Make it happen as soon as possible," Mary was saying. "I'll make it worth your while. I've come into some extra money." A hag-like cackle filled the van.

Keith tried to compose himself. "She's even paying for it with my money."

One of the technicians looked back over his shoulder and started to smile. "Isn't karma a bitch?"

The look on Sergeant Mcdonald's face told him this was no laughing matter. The man focused his attention back on the panel in front of him.

The recording of the conversation continued. Both cops were scribbling down the details of when the money drop was to take place. Keith Grant fell silent again, lost in his own thoughts.

When the connection was broken, Jim put a consoling hand on Keith's arm. "It could have been much worse. The killer could have been on her side instead of ours."

Keith forced a smile. "I don't know what I did to her. I thought I treated her fairly in all our dealings." Then he realized where he was sitting. "Well up to now, but she doesn't know about any of this."

"We're going to follow her and pick her up when she makes the drop," Jim said. "The techies will take you back to headquarters. Stay there out of sight until the arrest is made. We don't want anything screwing this up."

There was no argument from Keith. The police station seemed like a fine place to hang out.

The two cops slipped out the front door on the side away from the building and walked around the corner to their waiting car. From there, they had a good view of the front door of the office building. Jim radioed his dispatcher and had two cars sent to the drop site. The cars would be close enough to move in when needed but far enough away not to be suspicious. Now there was nothing to do but wait.

Five minutes later, a woman with a ball cap, leather biker jacket and sunglasses hurried from the building. She turned away from the two men and hustled down the sidewalk.

"Is that her?" Scott asked.

54

MARY STEPPED FROM the elevator with a determined look on her face. She checked the lobby, pulled her black ball cap down over her eyes and headed for the door. She paused on the sidewalk, gave a cursory glance up the street and then headed in the direction of the bank.

A number of thoughts fought for position in her mind. Uppermost was what did Keith Grant know about her activities? Suddenly suggesting the swap of shares in their two companies seemed completely out of character for him, even though she quickly grabbed onto the opportunity. Now she was having second thoughts. In the past couple of weeks she had discovered he was rich beyond imagination. Her instincts told her he had not become that way by being a nice guy. That was not the way the world worked. He would have looked for opportunities and then struck like a hawk to a hen. Did he think she was his next take-over? Not for long.

Another thing bothered her. What did Keith Grant and the head of Worldwide Seafoods have to discuss as reported by Christine? Was this the old boys club ganging up on her? It looked that way.

Marcel had all but agreed the lobster contract was hers. Granted, she had to sweeten the deal with unlimited use of one of Sky Jet's planes to make that happen. But why had the death of Bob Lively stopped the presentation of the contract and why was there no resolution in sight?

Goddamn men, they screwed up everything.

That damn fool, Bob Lively, suggesting that she lease him one of her planes until he made the arrangements to purchase a new one was the final straw. He simply wrote off her chances of succeeding in landing the contract because she was a woman. To him, that conclusion was obvious. He seemed so confident of his own success that Mary couldn't take a chance. Losing this contract would ruin all her plans. She had expended too many of her emotional assets to let this deal fall apart now. To hell with him. He got what he deserved for his chauvinistic attitude.

Her brother had been worse. All he had to do was give her a chance to prove she could handle executive responsibility at Sky Jet Charter. It would have worked out for both of them. She was the one with the university education; he was a damn pilot, a sky jockey. Together they could have made Sky Jet Charter soar. Instead he dismissed her without even the benefit of discussion. Women have no place in the charter business. End of story. Then he hires Christine instead of her. He believed Christine was *just* a secretary but in fact she was the one running the company.

Mary felt bad about having Craig killed but it was the only way for her to get her career moving before life had passed her by completely. Discussing his will with her might not have been in his own best interest, especially when he had the gall to tell her what to do with the money after he was dead. Don't give any to my husband. This from a man who had never been married.

Mary pulled the leather jacket a little tighter around her. Leather jackets were not her style. This was the perfect disguise. She risked a quick look around and continued her analysis of what she was about to do.

Keith Grant held the crown for arrogance. He gave her lip service. He offered her help to get established. He said all the right things. All the while he was planning on pulling the rug from beneath her feet. He would pay next, pay the ultimate price that all the money in the world could not save him from.

She heard a car slowly approaching from the rear. She kept her eyes steadfastly on the road ahead. She would sneak a glance when she reached the red light at the next intersection. For now, she didn't want to raise any suspicions. The time to put her final action into play had arrived. Keith Grant could join Craig and Bob Lively in hell and together they could try to figure out where they had all gone wrong.

The car behind her stopped. Without looking back, she proceeded through the intersection and walked into the bank to make the initial payment of what she hoped would be the final hit.

55

JIM SHOOK HIS head. "I'm not sure." He looked back at the building. "Let's do a drive by. She knows you better than me. Keep your eyes straight ahead."

The car cruised slowly to where the woman was walking. The light at the approaching intersection turned red. This would be dicey if it was Mary and she looked around. This was not the time to be identified. Scott pulled into the curb behind her.

"It's her," he said. "I'm sure of it."

Jim looked from his partner to the back of the woman, to his partner. "We haven't seen her face."

"I've known her since she was a kid. Thought about dating her once or twice. It's her."

"OK. I'm going to follow on foot. Stay back until she reaches the bank. Move up when she goes inside. We'll grab her as she leaves." Jim reached for the door handle.

Scott grabbed his partner's arm. "One more thing, Jim. Let me be the one to arrest her. It might go down better."

Jim hesitated. "Maybe." He slipped from the car as the light turned green.

The bank in question was located in a strip mall near the downtown train station. The doors opened on to the parking lot. Jim spotted the two patrol cars, one at each end parked snugly beside SUVs. Neither was conspicuous.

Mary stopped at the door, took a cursory look around the area and marched inside. Jim peered through the plate glass windows forming the front of the bank. He watched as Mary transferred money from her account to that of the killer. Scott pulled up and parked in front of the building. He stepped from the vehicle and walked around to the sidewalk, crossing his arms and trying to look casual.

Mary finished her business and exited the bank in a hurry. She didn't even notice Scott until she almost bumped into him. Then it was too late.

Scott placed a hand on her shoulder. "I'm sorry Mary," he said, "but you're under arrest for—"

Mary shook her arm free. "Not you, Scott. Tell me you're not in on it, too. Why are all you men out to get me?"

As Scott reached out to grab her again, he noticed the small canister that appeared from nowhere in her hand. His eyes became hot as fire as the spray swept across his face. He coughed as the burning followed his gasping breath into his throat and nostrils. He floundered for a second, just long enough for Mary to break free and start running across the parking lot.

Jim reacted immediately. He signalled the two waiting cars to jump into action before taking the four quick steps to his partner. The car from the opposite direction to Mary's travel pulled up beside the two detectives and screeched to a stop. Brenda Davis threw a bottle of spring water through the open window to Jim.

"You're getting soft. The uniformed Scott Bowen would never let that happen." Brenda Davis laughed and wheeled across the lot after the fleeing Mary Dunford. The other car had already cut off her progress. Brenda stopped behind her, jumped from the car and started to reach for her gun.

"No guns," Jim said softly. That was a decision for the member on the spot, not his. It was her life at stake.

Brenda did not withdraw her pistol. Instead, with her fingers lightly on the grip, she ran up behind Mary. Mary had the can of pepper spray aimed at the other patrolman who stayed safely behind his open door. The window was covered with the fine mist.

"Stay back," Mary shouted in the direction of the car. "This stuff can hurt you bad." She kept moving back and forth trying to get a better angle of attack on the policeman.

"Settle down, ma'am," the officer said. "Just put the can on the ground and no one will get hurt." His voice was loud enough to cover any noise Brenda might make on her approach.

Mary looked to her left and then her right trying to figure out an escape route that would allow her to elude the cop in front of her. She would have to run in a direction that he couldn't follow with his car. She brought back the now empty can to throw at the car.

Brenda reached over Mary's shoulder with one hand grabbing the arm with the spray can. Her other arm snaked around Mary's neck and then she let her own weight take her to the ground.

Mary tried to twist free and then let her body go limp. It was over.

Jim poured water into his partner's eyes. "Stop rubbing," he said. "Paramedics are on the way. Just relax."

Scott dropped his hand and then brought it up to his eyes again. "That's easy for you to say. I'm on fire here." He squinted across the parking lot at the two police cars. "They've got her?"

"They've got her. You were her last victim. Good thing, too. She's a psychopath."

56

KEITH GRANT JUMPED up from his seat in the lobby as the two detectives walked through the door. He looked over their shoulder to see who was following.

"What happened? Did she get away?" His voice exhibited genuine concern.

Jim looked at him, confused, then realized the reason for the question. "No, we got her. They've taken her to a holding cell for now. She's raving like a lunatic. We're going to let her calm down before we interview her."

Keith noticed the red, tear-streaked eyes of Scott Bowen. He shot him a questioning look.

"Pepper spray," Scott said. "I let friendship impair my judgment." He wiped away some of the water trickling down his face. "That won't happen again."

"I still think you should have let the paramedics take you to the hospital," Jim said. "You can't be too careful with that stuff."

Scott held up a container of eye drops and squeezed two drops into each eye. He soaked up the excess with a tissue. "This is the treatment. I've taken victims in before. I don't need someone in a white coat to administer this. Besides, I want to be in on the questioning. I want Mary to see what she has done. I want her to tell me why she murdered her brother."

The three men took the elevator to the second floor, exited into the area occupied by the detective division and headed towards Jim's pseudo office framed by the two blue, shoulder-high room dividers.

As they entered the closed-off area, Jim spied a 9x12 brown, mailing envelope in the centre of his desk. A yellow post-it note replaced the usual stamp. Jim's name was scrawled in big, black letters across the front. He recognized the writing. This had to be a forensics report.

"This is fast," Jim said. He read the note in the corner of the envelope.

"Thought you should see this while we complete our work, VT."

VT was Victor Tanner. His job was to analyze data collected at crime scenes.

Jim pulled two 8x10 photos and a single sheet of paper from the envelope. The others crowded in to see what he had. The pictures were similar. One contained an advertising envelope sitting on a garbage can in Craig Flint's kitchen. The other a similar envelope on a garbage can in Bob Lively's kitchen.

"What's the note say?" Scott said. His eyes were still too teary to do a detailed study of the photos.

Jim read the letter.

Sergeant Mcdonald,

This is a good news, bad news situation.

The accompanying ad flyers in these envelopes say they contained a dishwasher soap sample. The receiver was to use it within 24 hours, report their satisfaction or lack of same to a website and get a five-dollar discount coupon on their next purchase.

The soap was cello-packed and the remnants are soap. The cube was one of those white blue combinations that dissolve at different rates and stretch over the entire wash cycle.

We believe (the good news) but can't prove (that's the bad news) that each side contained a different chemical that when mixed with its opposite produced the dual-component drug talked about by the pathologist. The new, lethal drug was circulated through the vent in the front of the machine and carried by the steam into the kitchen. Anyone nearby died instantly. If you came in a moment or two later, you died more slowly. After 10 minutes, no effect.

The initial mixing took place in the washer. Both machines were set to do two wash cycles, and two rinse cycles of extremely hot water. This effectively either dissolved or washed away any traces of evidence.

That being the case, you may wonder how we reached this conclusion.

Look at the envelopes. One has third-class printed on the envelope stamp. The envelope is in pristine condition. We don't believe it ever went through the mail. It was probably hand-delivered to the Flint mail box to be used on a specific date.

Notice the other. Real first-class stamps cover the printed stamp. Now, something for you to work on. The postmark on the real stamps is Winnipeg, Manitoba. The return address for the company is in Newmarket, Ontario. The envelope indicates it did go through the mail.

All theory and conjecture, but best we can do with what we have. Good luck.—VT

Jim sat down behind his desk and reread the letter to himself. Keith studied the two pictures.

"That would explain the phone call," Keith said. "It was designed to get Craig into the kitchen at the exact moment when the drug was released."

"Exactly," Scott said. "The killer was in the rental car in the parking lot. From there, he could see into the kitchen. He could guess when the dishwasher was started by the activity."

Scott picked up the case file from Jim's desk and started to quickly riffle through the various reports. He stopped, wiped his eyes with the tissue and held up a sheet of paper. "Mary had a call from Winnipeg after the second ad was placed and before the Livelys were killed." He passed the paper to Jim. "It's on there. I just can't read it at the moment."

Jim scanned the sheet and used a yellow highlighter to designate one of the calls. "That's good enough for me but still circumstantial. As Victor said, he is only making an educated guess about the soap cubes."

The initial excitement diminished. "Still," said Keith, "we've got the airtight conspiracy case. Throw this other stuff at her when you question her and maybe she'll be a good girl and confess."

"I don't know," Scott said. "You didn't see her when we arrested her. A good lawyer will be going for insanity."

"Maybe for trying to have me killed." Keith smiled, trying to lighten the mood. No one else took him up on it. "She was sane when she planned Craig's death. That was simple greed. You will have to push for a confession while she's in this distraught state."

Jim picked up the pictures. "He's right, Scott. Let's dazzle her with our evidence." He gave his partner a sardonic grin. "Keep those tears flowing. We'll work on her sympathy."

57

KEITH GRANT, SHANE Martin and George Phillips absorbed the heat from the large stone fireplace at the cottage. Outside the temperature had dropped to near freezing. The crackling wood and flickering flames had a relaxing effect on the three men.

"So she confessed?" George asked. "I really thought she was innocent. She could have taken Sky Jet Charter to new heights. Her entrepreneurial skills were phenomenal. She was a natural."

Shane sipped from a shooter glass of Baileys. "Too bad Craig didn't give her a chance. This could have all played out so much better."

Keith shook his head. "Could never happen. They were like the dual-component mixture that killed Craig. They would have come together in a spectacular combination with a very short half-life. Both were too competitive to work together. They would have destroyed each other, the company or both." He paused for a contemplative moment. "Not would have, did."

Shane took the Baileys bottle and topped up his drink. "This is the life. The sergeant must have ripped you a new one when he found out you were conversing with the assassin."

Keith gathered a handful of peanuts from the dish on his armrest before looking at Shane. "Upset doesn't quite cut it." He popped some nuts into his mouth. "But I pointed out that if you hadn't figured out how to contact the killer, the police would be investigating four deaths instead of three and chasing down the wrong suspect. I expressed some concern about the fourth death being mine."

"Wait a freaking minute." Shane's chair rocked forward into the sitting position. "I didn't contact the killer; you did."

"We made use of your underworld connections. I served only as the paymaster." Keith laughed. "Anyway, we're off the hook. He's agreed not to pursue the matter. These professionals are hard to find when they're active. Now that Crosley has retired, the sergeant doesn't think it's financially feasible to waste his resources trying to track him. Besides, I never really met the man. That said, all his intel has been forwarded to the FBI. Who knows what they'll do with it?"

Shane adjusted the foot rest of his recliner as he lay back. "Are we going to play poker here tonight?"

"Nah," Keith said, "that was Craig's thing. We'll have to think up our own excuse for escaping out here. Something different. Maybe chess or Scrabble."

A twinkle came into Shane's eyes. "I know," he said. "Let's play crokinole."

"Crokinole?" Keith said. "You mean that game where you flick the checkers with your finger and try to knock everyone else's off the board? I haven't played that since I was a kid."

George laughed. "What would Craig think if he knew poker night had degenerated into playing kids' games?"

"That makes it perfect," Keith said. "It doesn't matter what Craig thinks anymore." He raised his glass. "To Craig. We're finally free from his control."

"Yeah, finally," Shane said. He paused with a thoughtful look on his face and then continued: "I know you're not a 'what if' kind of guy but did you ever wonder how different things might have been if we had let Mary play poker with us that night so many years ago?"

Keith slowly turned towards Shane and set his glass on the armrest. "You think Mary killed her brother because he wouldn't let her play poker with us?" He gave a short bark of a laugh. "I think it goes a little deeper than that. Several hundred thousand dollars deeper."

"Don't be too sure," said a voice from the kitchen. The three men looked in that direction as Christine's head popped through the kitchen door. "Mary once asked me if I knew how to play poker. She said she wanted to organize a poker night." She paused and looked from one man to the next, making sure she had all their attention. "She said it would be for women only. No men need apply. And she wasn't joking when she said it."

Silence dominated the room for a few seconds. Then Keith shook his head. "No. Mary wasn't that shallow. Killing Craig was strictly a power play. She was after the company."

"Probably," Shane said, "but, man, she was really pissed off that night. I remember how she grabbed Tom by the arm and dragged him out of here, his feet barely touching the floor. It's a wonder he was ever allowed to come back and play."

Again, silence saturated the air while they all summoned their remembrances of that evening. "She was pissed," George said in a dismissive manner, "but not enough to do murder." He wanted to forget the whole subject. He focused his attention on Christine. "Are we going to eat tonight? What's the hold-up on those pizzas?"

Christine feigned an affronted look. "Just because I'm a woman, don't think I'm going to be out here cooking for you guys."

"Are you a woman? We hadn't noticed," Keith said. "We think you're cooking tonight because you're the rookie in the group. We all take our turns."

"Reheating pizza in the oven isn't cooking," George said. "I'll show you what real cooking is. It's a man thing."

"And your next time we expect lobsters, girl." Shane said. "Your company's main line of business is shipping lobsters overseas. You've got to promote your own product." He looked around at the others. "Right, guys?" Heads nodded all around.

Christine looked wistful. "My company. Pinch me, I must be dreaming."

The three men exchanged glances before Keith spoke up. "I'd be careful where I made that request. You'll have no shortage of takers."

Christine blushed. "Still, it's hard to believe I own a company."

"That was Craig for you, man," Shane said. "A codicil to cover the eventuality that Mary couldn't inherit was the kind of planning he was noted for. He covered all his bases, dotted all his Is, crossed all his Ts."

"And never talked in clichés. He's rolling over in his grave now listening to you talk about him." Keith became serious and turned to Christine. "I'm willing to bet he never told you this, but on several occasions he expressed to me how much easier running the company became after you came on board. He truly appreciated your work. He thought of you as someone special."

Christine's face and neck took on a reddish hue. She looked down. "I thought he was someone special too," she said in a quiet voice.

Keith nodded. "Unfortunately it wasn't in his nature to mention it. He was already married," Keith paused, "to his work. When he added that codicil, I doubt he ever considered the reason Mary wouldn't be able to inherit was because she had had him killed. He believed Tom was the threat. Now if we could only get your cash back from him. To clear out with the money that fast, you would think he did know Mary was the killer."

"Mary called him just before she went out that last time," Christine said. "She wasn't herself. She must have either tipped him off or he figured out something was amiss. Then, when he got the phone call about her arrest—" Her voice trailed off.

"I told you guys, you underestimated him, man. We'll never see him or the money again. He's long gone."

"Don't be too sure. I've got a friend—"

Shane's eyes burned into Keith's. "Don't go there, man. Don't even joke about it."

ABOUT THE AUTHOR

Art Burton lives in rural Nova Scotia in a place called Latties Brook with his wife, Flame and rescue dog, Hobo Charley.

Before taking up the solitary task of writing, he was a printer with the Halifax Herald newspaper.

This is his fifth novel. The others were:

For Hire, Messenger of God

Caught in the Line of Fire

Concealed From Sight

The Bag of Money

He was also the author of two books of short stories about the Hobos who trudged through the East Hants area of Nova Scotia during the Great Depression of the 1930s.

Hobos I Have Known

More Hobo Stories

For more information on these books, go to his website: artburton.ca

www.ingramcontent.com/pod-product-compliance
Lightning Source LLC
Chambersburg PA
CBHW031944260626
47157CB00017B/2316